So F*cking Special: 1996

Raye Murphy

RupertBossier

Copyright © 2024 by Raye Murphy

Book Cover by: *"May I name her Marguerite..." lit services for the modern author and publisher*

First RupertBossier Edition Published 2024

rupertbossier.com

ISBN: 978-1-964011-01-1 (pbk)

ISBN: 978-1-964011-00-4 (ebook)

ISBN: 978-1-964011-02-8 (audio)

This book is dedicated to a childhood best friend, the greatest female lead I knew. Here's to you, fighting for the slab of concrete on the playground, jumping off the top of the barn, swimming like fish, and green front doors~

Trigger Warning: Bullying, mature language, sexual situations, mentions of eating disorder, sexual assault, drug and alcohol use.

NOTE: *So F*cking Special: 1996*, Book One of the YA to New Adult 90's Series is a Young Adult read that is age appropriate to the genre with above trigger warnings applied. Books two and three of the series, *So F*cking Special: 1998* and *So F*cking Special: 2002*, are New Adult reads for 18 + readers.

1996
SO F*CKING SPECIAL
RAYE MURPHY

IF IT MAKES YOU HAPPY Sheryl Crow

NIGHTSWIMMING *R.E.M.*

LOSER *Beck*

FOLLOW YOU DOWN *Gin Blossoms*

CRASH INTO ME *Dave Matthews Band*

GLYCERINE *Bush*

SMELLS LIKE TEEN SPIRIT *Nirvana*

BIG ME *Foo Fighters*

FADE INTO YOU *Mazzy Star*

GOOD *Better Than Ezra*

FOOLISH GAMES *Jewel*

STRANGE CURRENCIES *R.E.M.*

HEAD OVER FEET *Alanis Morissette*

HEY JEALOUSY *Gin Blossoms*

HIGH AND DRY *Radiohead*

BLACK *Pearl Jam*

I'LL STAND BY YOU *Pretenders*

CREEP *Radiohead*

bonus tracks/featured

I GOT 5 ON IT *Luniz, Michael Marshall*

HOW DEEP IS YOUR LOVE *Bee Gees*

Prologue

"July!" I'm practically screaming at the woman.

"Sir, I'm asking for her name, not the birthdate just yet-"

"That IS her name!" I shout again at the airline agent over the phone. Out of character for someone seeking help as much as I need it this moment.

"Sir. I must have the passenger's full name first, middle, and last as it is listed in the ticket purchase before I can track the bag."

"Yes. And I've told you, the luggage tag has my name on it. It is currently in my possession. You sent it to me." I grit my teeth, trying not to yell again.

"Full name of the passenger please. Just give me the name of who flew, and we will start again."

"July Elizabeth Edwards." I don't recognize my own voice; the entirety of her name leaks from my mouth. I say it like it means something to me, and I want it to mean something to the irritating woman on the phone. I need her to get it right. The truth, if I step back from this situation, is that it's amazing I remember or even know her middle name. I guess I must have known it all my life... Just like I've always known her, even if I have no idea where she is or who she is now. That part gives me an odd hollow feeling in my gut. The uncertainty of not knowing where she is or if she's safe. Does she even need saving? Maybe she simply needs her luggage, and the only thing dramatic about the situation is me getting it to her.

I should also consider if she does need saving, does she want to be saved by me? The uncertainty of where we stand or who we are to each other...former classmates? Old friends? Two people who shared a once-in-a-lifetime connection they chose to ignore until they became strangers? Good God, maybe I should just hang up before I tell the airline we were two ships passing in the night, and although I don't expect anything from her, I just want to make sure she's okay, and that she got her suitcase, which used to be mine.

Just in case that part doesn't make me sound like a complete lunatic, wait until I try and explain how someone I haven't seen in two years who lives in New York, was flying to LA with luggage from Pure Pines, Texas with my name and old address on the tags. *That's not insane, right?*

The insanity is that the airline sent the luggage to me. How could they follow a handwritten luggage tag above the barcode or whatever sticker that should match the boarding pass of the person who flew? I thought they were more than strict about that stuff after 9/11. Now, I'm the one who sounds crazy. However, the true insanity here by definition of the word, is in fact on my part... *Why the hell is it bothering me?*

"Sir, give me one more moment. I'm going to place you on another brief hold."

Yes please... play more patronizing background music. I do need to calm down. She is obviously okay. She probably called to check on the luggage, and after being defeated by the system a few times, gave up, and just re-bought whatever she needs wherever she is. But I know that can't be all there is to it. I know because I know *her*. I'm also the fool who opened the damn thing to see what's inside. I know wherever she is right now, she needs it.

Still, if she is in trouble or needs help, she would call her family. This is nuts. I'm going ape shit over a suitcase I threw out years ago. The idea that it landed in her possession by happenstance and then was mailed back to me with her possessions in it... well, it doesn't *have* to mean anything; it's most likely just an inconvenience for both parties. A sane person would ask himself why he needs to be a hero to someone who obviously doesn't need saving. We're adults now. Adults who have gone our separate ways. Adults lose luggage all the time. It isn't a sign in whatever way my mind is trying to insist. It's a suitcase.

Prologue

The nurse wakes me with trepidation. She's a middle-aged woman with a bright, round face.

"Yes, that's me."

"I didn't want to disturb you, but under the circumstances, I thought this important."

"Is there something wrong? Has the doctor been back with x-rays, and I missed them?"

"Oh, no, doll. Not yet. You lay back and relax. You're in good hands with Dr. Zarrabi. He'll be making his rounds here shortly." Her Brooklyn accent is thick. You don't hear one like that often. It's a tough contrast to her kind bedside manner, which you just don't get on the East Coast. "I just came onto my shift, and we got a call for ya regarding the luggage you've been trying to trace."

"Do they have it? Did they find it... If it's here, I have to have it right away!" *Why can't I get out of this bed?*

"Miss Edwards, please lay back and relax. I can't have you getting too excited just yet, not until we have your results. But any information is good information over lost luggage, am I right? The first step anyway. They tracked your luggage to have been mailed to Texas the day after it wasn't claimed in LaGuardia airport."

"So it never made it to Los Angeles?"

"Apparently not, just like you didn't."

"Wait. It can't have been mailed to Texas; I've checked both my Texas home address as well as my current Manhattan address. No suitcase has been delivered to either address."

"I wrote it down for you." I watch her slowly retrieve a yellow sticky note from the front pocket of her worn-out scrubs. She takes a moment, and squints to read her own handwriting. I want to leap out of this hospital bed to read it myself. I can't waste another second on this ordeal. I need my suitcase. *I have to get to work! I need to be in LA... three days ago!*

"So the Texas address looks like a Houston address. 2028 University Lane, Apt. 6 Rice University, Houston, Texas. It's a campus address, does that ring a bell?"

"Wait, what?" She's really nice, and I hope my eyes popping out of my face, along with the intensity I hear in my voice isn't making her feel like I'm directing it at her, but... *what the hell did she just say?* My heartbeat accelerates. It beats out of my chest, and a fucking monitor next to me beeps to give me away.

She moves closer to my bed by my side. She presses her hand on my arm firmly. "Hon, listen to me now. You have *got* to stay calm. Now I know what this means to ya, I can't say I know why, but my colleagues wrote multiple notes. Heck, you're famous at the nurses' station and in the lounge. They knew you needed this here ah' suitcase before ya even remembered to tell em' your name. I think they want to know what's in that damn bag a' yours more than you want to find it. Look, you been through hell in a handbasket the last two days, and if you don't stay calm for me, where or what's in that suitcase isn't gonna matter much to ya or anybody else, capeesh?"

"Yeah."

She returns to the yellow Post-it note I haven't taken my eyes off. "So this Texas address... you're from Texas? What part?"

"Uh... you wouldn't know it. It's small." The alert on my IV me goes off.

"Ah, just a sec, hon, I gotta change your drip." She tosses my yellow sticky note, the only thing that matters at this point, back into her scrubs' pocket. I can't help growing more agitated.

"It's just Palominos and a football field." I rub my eyes trying to focus, but the new dose of the IV must be kicking in.

"What'd you say, hon..."

I watch my nurse through a hazy fog as she becomes two nurses. One is trimmer, in maroon scrubs.

"What the hell's a Palomino?" A new husky voice chimes in. She sounds sarcastic.

"I just changed her drip. I think she's in and out."

"Did you give her the luggage info?"

"We almost got it figured out. I'm gonna wait her out ten minutes and see if she comes to."

"Well hurry up! We're dying to know."

Yeah, you won't get it lady, it's like no borough you've ever known. Images of water towers, small churches, and two-lane highways lined with pine trees threaten my vision. The nurses are drowned out by the sound of a marching band and a cheering crowd. I'm floating through my hometown, seeing what I want to tell the lady with the off-putting accent. I want to tell her things she won't understand, like just how small of a town Pure Pines is in East Texas. The kind with a football field, a few churches, and one privately owned burger joint that feeds the masses on game day. I want her to know there are two things different about this town that probably should come as a warning for anybody passing through it. One, it isn't our town. It is our grandparents' town and their grandparents' before that. And two, it isn't even a town at all. It's an unincorporated community tucked behind a massive curtain of pine trees so tall they hide a multitude of sins. In the beginning, they named it Pure Pines, and that was the start of the elitism.

Every fall, with the first hint of football and hot chocolate weather, yellow school buses from the outskirts of the surrounding towns within a fifty-mile radius pull into our little burger joint to eat. They are there on Friday night for football of course, and select other days of the week for girls' volleyball, and any other sport or academic match our little 3A school competes in.

To say that everyone knows everybody is a gross understatement, but I have come to know it as a mass overstatement. We didn't really know each other at all. No more than we knew the people getting off those buses. You had the Spring Hill Panthers, White Oak Roughnecks, Pine Tree Pirates, Waskom Wild Cats, Bullard Bulldogs, Elysian Fields Lions, West Rusk Raiders, and then there was us, The Pure Pines Palominos. Even our school mascot is a blonde. A palomino is a genetic color in horses that have a gold coat and a white mane and tail. And if that doesn't clear things up for the nurse in the maroon-ish scrubs, she should know that the powers that be like pretty things. Unattainable things.

It makes sense they'd choose a mascot that reflects the image they saw of themselves: Purebred. However, they missed the irony. Horse breeders actually have to cross two different kinds of horses, a chestnut with a cremello, to guarantee membership in the palomino society. Talk about sarcasm; the old saying used about someone who was different than everybody else, "a horse of a different color," was quite appropriate here and could have been coined in Pure Pines.

My stomach feels queasy. *Did I miss my flight?* I look around. I don't know where I put my purse or my luggage. *Wait! How am I going to get out of here?* I try to sit up and pull itching tape off my hand.

"Miss Edwards, are you awake? Can you hear me? Here, let's just fix the tape a little smoother. That must have been itching like crazy." My friend with the accent is putting fresh tape on the back of my hand where my IV is poking through.

"Did you tell her about the horse?" I say the first thing that pops into my head.

"What?"

"I meant, what about the luggage, my note. You said you wrote it down."

"Okay, Okay. Take it easy. You've been out like a light for the past fifteen minutes. It's the drugs I gave you. Better now?"

"Yes, fine. But the address?"

She cuts her eyes at me with a half-cocked smile, pulls the sticky note from her pocket, and picks up where she left off. "This Rice University address... the address belongs or belonged to one, Adrian Reed."

I can't feel my face.

"Recognize it? Cause get this... the bag was apparently forwarded to Adrian individual's current residence, when they found the university address was an old one. Still a Houston, Texas address, but ah'... Miss Edwards... you still will me?"

I have no explanation to give her for why my enthusiasm deflates into pure shock. The heart monitor makes a different kind of alarming sound. Steady, spaced-out beats replace my frantic, erratic energy, and I can only stare up at this woman, completely dumbfounded. She has soft, light brown eyes and crow's feet to match her bright, quick smile dancing around them. I zero in on those, and I'm not sure if I'm breathing anymore.

"July? Are you with me?" She squeezes my hand, and I am finally able to blink back at her. "Who is Adrian Reed?"

If this were a TV movie, the heart monitor would make a flat-lining sound right now. Instead, I lay back, defeated, honoring the nurse's original request to relax. My eyes search her, landing on her name tag. *Renna.* So curious, this RN named Renna. I should be honored that my luggage debacle is more entertaining than the other patients admitted from the ER. She tilts her head and smiles a dubious smile, waiting patiently for me to answer.

"Well, Renna. Who is Adrian Reed? That 's a very good question..." One I've been asking myself since I was sixteen.

"ROUND HERE"

Counting Crows

October, 1996

When I heard the door to the principal's office start to open, I figured I should look attentive. This wasn't entirely my battle. I was only there showing moral support for my two best friends turned drill teammates, as it were. Physical and moral support given the get-up I was wearing to match them. I was encouraged out of my seat in the waiting room when the office door appeared to be opening, and the three of us stood up to be escorted in.

The principal's door closed shut abruptly as if someone changed their mind, then it swung back open wildly, followed by a dramatic exit from the varsity football coach. His face was red, and it was obvious there had been a disagreement in there. Adrian Reed walked out after Coach Craig, and I had never seen a look like that on his face. He brought his estranged expression to the ground as he started past us. Principal Sabella closed the door neatly behind him, nodding at his surrounding staff with a polite "nothing to see here" smile to save face. He approached us while following behind the other two. "I'll be right with you ladies. Just give us a moment."

Adrian cut his eyes at me as they walked by us. They were steel blue, and I couldn't help but feel the concern behind them as he approached and looked up at me. He wasn't choked up. He was mad. Before I could look away from the intensity of his face, Coach Craig spun around from exiting the main office and walked back toward Adrian.

Adrian stepped backward and turned to face him, putting his back in front of me. He had nowhere else to go. The crazed football coach lunged closer and stuck his finger in Adrian's face. Adrian stood less than two inches in front of me. He was practically covering my whole body. If you had randomly approached the scene, it would have looked like he was pro-tecting me from Coach Craig, which obviously wasn't the case. However, I wasn't sure what the case was.

I had never seen a teacher, or a coach for that matter, accost a student like that. Certainly not in front of other students, the principal, and his administrative staff.

"Let me tell you something, boy!"

My God, the coach had Adrian pinned, and Adrian had me pinned behind him. I kept trying to step or slide back out of the way, but there was a chair against the wall behind me. Nothing would budge, and the three bodies beside me, including the principal, all stood in a cramped but appropriate distance to the left of me. I had nowhere to go, either. There was a plant next to the chair behind me, separating me slightly from the other two girls and Principal Sabella, and I hoped it was covering the momentary bind I was in. Adrian was backed up so close to me that I could feel the heat off Coach Craig's red face, and if he had spit on Adrian when he shouted, it likely would have landed on my cheek.

"You just made the biggest damn mistake of your life." The coach stepped even closer.

I felt unexpected warmth on my left leg through my ridiculously thick flesh-colored dance tights. It was Adrian's hand. *What was Adrian's hand doing on my thigh in the middle of a fight with a coach in the principal's office?* I was sure it was an accident, and he was trying to brace himself not to fall backward onto me while the coach was aggressively yelling in his face. The kind of mistake you make of accidentally brushing against someone, and they shift or move right away, no apology necessary...except I couldn't shift or move. I felt an electric charge shoot up my leg when the hand on it squeezed where it touched.

Adrian's fingertips slowly spread apart and squeezed the side of my thigh gently but firmly, and his back leaned even closer to me as in our bodies were touching. If someone saw *that* part out of context or through the office window, it would have looked inappropriate. *What was happening? Was he holding onto me for moral support?*

"This isn't over, son; I'm telling you that right now!"

"Jerry! Now, that's enough." Principal Sabella stepped in, trying to stretch his neck past the group of us girls to get closer to the situation.

"I'll call his damn daddy! We're not done here." Coach Craig stood in Adrian's face a moment, looked back at the principal, then swiftly turned to exit, pushing the main office door open wide in front of him. The door swung back so powerfully that a swoosh of air blew across Adrian's face and mine. I watched the back of his dark hair blow just above me. I assumed my pulse was racing due to the excitement of the traumatic situation.

I took a deep breath to slow my heart from jumping out of my chest, but then I smelled him, oddly for what felt like the first time. Only, it was a smell I recognized. I knew him and had been around him my entire existence at Pure Pines, but somehow it was heightened. Sandal-woodsy, a bit sweet like maple syrup at breakfast, and then a hint of something dark and expensive from cologne he must have put on earlier that morning. I could smell his hair and skin. *Okay. Why was his hand still on my thigh, and could I move now?*

Principal Sabella made his way through everyone to Adrian. "Are you alright, son?"

I felt the fingertips release me and slide down from where they squeezed me tightly before they completely left my thigh. A pair of eyes to the left of me watched with scrutiny. If what just happened looked as odd as it felt, it did not go unnoticed.

"Yeah." Adrian finally answered the principal. "I've got to get to class."

"I'm sorry Adrian, I don't think either one of us expected that reaction. Well...Why don't you come by my office before you go home today, and we'll check in over this, yeah?"

"Thanks."

Adrian took a half step forward, and I finally exhaled. I felt like I hadn't since this bizarre madness ensued. He turned to me, his face still close ... too close above mine. He looked down at me.

I could hear Sabella addressing our little group beside me on the other side of the large plant, yet my eyes were transfixed on Adrian's. I don't know if I was waiting for an explanation for his altercation with Coach Craig, one for practically groping my leg, or if I was waiting to see if he was okay. All of the above were brand-new territories for me when it came to Adrian Reed.

He was still less than two inches from me. His hand landed on the side of my waist, and he looked at me for an additional moment. He gulped as if he was coming back from being out of it.

"I'm-um. Sorry." He said it slowly and in a low, quiet voice. Something happened when he said that to me. It was like a million butterflies were released in my stomach, and where his hand rested between my ribs and waistline, all I could feel was... heat.

I saw Lynn looking over. I turned to look at her, and her face went from mine to his hand on my waist. Then she watched as it peeled off me, and Adrian turned to exit the office.

"Come on in, ladies." The principal motioned us in as if nothing had happened with Coach Craig. Lynn's eyes were still wide on mine. She tilted her head and gave me an incredibly inquiring look. Surely, it was meant to suggest she was just as confused by that moment as I was. However, she seemed shocked at me, as if I had something to do with what had just transpired.

As I followed suit into the office, I kept replaying the events in my head, overanalyzing how it happened, why he touched me like that, and moreover... The part that was even more unpredictable: *Why did it make me feel like that? And why did I feel so caught?* I didn't do anything. Maybe that was it... I mean, I didn't move away. Should I have gotten out of the way, even if it meant pushing Adrian into Coach Craig? Somehow, it felt like he needed me there. *Uh oh.* There it is. Since when did Adrian Reed ever need me for anything? Since when would I give two shits if he did?

What if he just needed a warm body because Coach Craig was pretty fucking scary? He could have simply wanted the assist, or maybe he mis-gauged where everyone was standing and thought I was Lynn standing behind him. He's her best guy friend. That would make sense. *Uhhhh, Lynn. The look on her face...*as if I hadn't told her something or...

Okay, this was getting crazy. I just needed to calm down and retrace my steps. What was the moment before? How did this even become *a moment?* All I know is a little over half an hour before, I was getting ready for the pep rally.

***

45 minutes earlier:

I was opening my locker door when my Biology II book fell to the bottom as I reached for my make-up bag. I guessed that book was going to stay there this week as well. I'd have to skip something and make it to the lab the following week, or I could forget about getting an "A."

It was 1996, the Fall of my junior year in high school. There were no smartphones. The beginning stages of cell phones had just been surfacing via more portable, cordless versions of the 1980s car phone and the internet as we know it today... it was an unimaginable concept called dialup, that hadn't become a household necessity yet. There was no social media, no Facebook, Instagram, Twitter, or TikTok, and I wouldn't get an email address until my freshman year of college.

If you walked the halls of high school with me, you were Generation X, born to parents who were "baby boomers." Their parents, the ones our town belonged to, were part of "the greatest generation" that survived the Depression era. Generation X was the first to be labeled instead of named. We were a letter that usually omits something, crosses it out, or is used in place of an existing signature. A sex chromosome that stood alone and determined nothing. *Weird.*

It was the '90s; what wasn't weird about it? No one was "woke," and they avoided diversity like the plague. I'd heard my whole life that humans have one thing in common with chickens: When chickens come across another chicken that's different from the rest, they peck it to death. There was definitely a pecking order in the halls of Pure Pines High School. It was one that the student body, faculty, and entire community existed by. Welcome to the coop.

I heard familiar voices approaching behind me, and I almost turned around out of habit and smiled. Instead, I quickly remembered when I saw the flash of sky blue, maroon, and white uniforms coming my way that I wasn't one of them anymore.

I remember reading *The Lottery once,* that short story about a creepy quaint town that had an event every year where they drew a number and stoned someone to death. I thought about Pure Pines when I read it, metaphorically, of course. There was no actual ceremony, no number drawn each year, but there was a whole lot of pomp and circumstance, plenty of stones thrown, and somebody's number was always up. That day, Devin Scott had picked mine.

"Hey, July! Haven't seen you come out for a break in a while; where've you been?

Licking my wounds in solitary so you wouldn't have the satisfaction of clawing deeper into them. Okay, that was harsh. These were my friends, or used to be. I turned toward them. Suddenly, Devin Scott, Brooke Pender, Dane Fraser, and Hanna Lewis were surrounding my locker in their brand-new Varsity fly skirts. It was almost the way they used to daily the year before.

There were a few things I must have missed that factored into whether you were popular or not. Funny, I always thought it was just me, that I wasn't good enough or thin enough or pretty enough, or I didn't know how to pick out the right clothes. It was more than that, though. As I mentioned before, it started with our grandparents, possibly even their parents. It mattered who they were, who knew them, and what they did or did not have to offer Pure Pines.

Then, your parents, it mattered who they were when they roamed the halls of Pure Pines High. My parents were divorced, and my dad was just not in the picture. I never knew back then that mattered. I heard the expression "broken home" all the time but somehow never associated it with myself. I didn't know others were applying it to me. It was just me and my mom in our house, three houses down from my grandparents' house. Other than my cousins and a few close friends, I thought I was the only one who knew my dad wasn't present. My grandad more than made up for it. I never noticed the guy was missing or there again; I really didn't think it mattered.

In today's world, people grow up wanting to matter, wanting to get noticed or seen. In Pure Pines, everyone mattered. What you did, what you said, who you did it with, and who you said it to mattered. You couldn't be invisible if you tried. Sometimes, that was truly unfortunate.

Don't let the Friday night lights and pom poms fool you; they mattered all right and were expected, but at Pure Pines, our generation had even more on our plate. Academics.

Something happened in grade school with an overly ambitious female principal who wouldn't accept less than the best. We were the top elementary school in the state before we ever brought report cards home to mommy and daddy with smiley faces for good behavior. She set the precedent with our class, and it stuck. It would follow and shape us until we left the institution and anywhere we went after.

My junior year had been an odd year already. My sophomore year had been pretty great, still reaping the benefits of being a Junior Varsity Cheerleader, but when I didn't make varsity for junior year, it changed everything. I knew it would. I just didn't know how much. This year already felt so intense and had so many layers of added pressure.

We hadn't even begun to talk about the prep for senior year, but already, I was maxed out on AP classes and bonus assignments, and the counselor was grilling us all about scholarships.

I guess it did make sense that this would be the year of reckoning. I could have handled that academically, but all the other bull shit on top of it... It seemed like all my extracurriculars were proving conflictual. If I wasn't late for one, I had missed a practice entirely for another. If AP English was a breeze, Biology 2 was in a foreign language, and my lab was during debate team.

Everything was chaos, not to mention my friends. *I'm sorry; how did my not making varsity cheerleader affect you?* At least that's what it felt like I needed to write across my shirt for those who cared, and why did they? Did they just want to stick it to me? *As in, it doesn't suck enough that you went for something and failed.*

Instead, we need to hold you accountable for that failure. If I had just not tried out and left the cheerleading squad by default, the optics would have fared far better. Pure Pines was great about pushing you, insisting you try and strive for everything possible, but they had no use for you if you failed at it. Failure was not any part of the curriculum.

All of that, and I hated the way Devin Scott said my name. She elongated and broke up the two syllables in July as if every time she said it, she was making fun of it.

Again, this was the 90s. We didn't have gender-fluid or unisex names to represent human beings. They were directed toward masculine or feminine. So, when parents named a girl a masculine name, like Devin, or a boy a feminine name, like Tracy or Ashley, it was unique and deemed hot, and they were automatically popular. It was a phenomenon, and Devin Scott reaped the benefits of it as the most popular girl in our class. She was also a Scott. Regarding those founders of Pure Pines, if you were a Scott, a Childress, or a Bishop, you had it made. She was bossy and self-assured, but she wasn't altogether a horrible human being, at least not when we were kids.

She did get her rocks off by screwing with people, and I couldn't help but think by the way she said my name, she found it humorous. It was as if she was always on the verge of making me look stupid for sport. With the whole gender-switching name thing, you'd think that a somewhat unusual name like July would fall in that category. Not a chance. Oh, there had been a few Summers or Autumns, and of course, April was a common name. I even met a lovely older woman named May once, but July? Let's just say I was never praised for its uniqueness; I was only more often asked *why*.

July was the middle of the summer, the middle marker of the year, and the most dreaded part of the season in our neck of the woods. July in East Texas was hot. I'll say that again: stick to your car seat and burn your hand on the dash or steering wheel; it is hot and humid like no other time or place on earth. Regardless of central air and surrounding lakes offering reprieve, and regardless of looking forward to the fourth and firework shows, its flaws were inevitable.

I could almost imagine my name for someone with light features or even a dirty blonde with green eyes, maybe one of those damn Palomino horses, but I had dark brown hair and brown eyes, winter coloring. It was simply my mom's favorite month, and she thought it might brighten up the Edwards part...left over from her divorce eighteen months after I was born. Thus, I was named July Elizabeth Edwards.

It never bothered me as a child. I liked the way it rolled off my cousins' tongues when they called me across a field or demanded I give them back their new Transformer because we were about to play Hot Wheels or Legos. Their little accents, when we were kids, made it sound like an important name.

Confidence is fickle and, most often, a fleeting attribute. From junior high onward, I had never introduced myself without feeling stupid, gimmicky, or as if I needed to apologize for my name.

"So, I guess we'll see you out there, Ju-ly, huh?"

*I guess so, Devin unless we are going to two different pep rallies, or there is an additional school gym I'm unaware of where they send the lepers and the people who don't get to wear fly skirts. What a C*nt-a-Saurus rex!*

"Yeah. See you out there." I gave them a half smile and turned back to my locker. I hadn't yet changed into my new uniform for the Drill Team. We had never had a drill team before. Our uniforms had supposedly been delivered to the band hall early that morning, and today would be the debut of our first routine and the uniforms. I'm sure that is what they were lurking about to see. Boy, were they in for a surprise?

Two double doors slammed from the same direction they came from, followed by two senior varsity cheerleaders headed down the hall toward me. *Jebus.* I didn't know this was the witching hour. I left homeroom early to get my curling iron plugged in; I wasn't trying to hit every branch on my way down. Talk about a day of reckoning. Seniors Savanna Baker and Sarah Weems were headed my way. Savanna kept walking as if she couldn't be bothered, but Sarah ducked into my locker with me, throwing her arm around my neck she gave me a pretend "noogie."

"We miss you SO much this year! And, as the only senior who can't tumble, it sucks not to have someone to clap on the sidelines with while they're doing Olympic-level gymnastics down the track. Bunch a' FRE-AKS!"

I loved her for her candor. Sarah was a great cheerleader and a lot of fun, but she was old school and didn't tumble either. She was one of the few who scraped through without being able to do a flip-flop. They had so many returning seniors who had been on the squad throughout high school; it would have been crazy if some didn't make it just because almost all the juniors and new sophomores could tumble extraordinarily well. It was abnormal to have so many who were that skilled at gymnastics.

"Will we see you at the Tomlin Twins' party?"

"It's not until next weekend, right?"

"Yeah, and... you're still going right?"

"Did, Savanna cheat on Drew with Jessie Hines and lie about it?" I suddenly had my confidence back.

"Um, I'm not going to make it to basketball season without you!" She squeezed me into a side hug before running off. "Oh, hey wait-"

She pulled me back into her and walked me down the hall with her a bit.

"Don't forget to knock em' dead out there today. It's really great what you guys are doing with a dance line. Especially you...give us bitches a run for our money."

And she was off. Sarah was funny, sweet, ridiculously thin, and brave. She was one of the most popular senior girls for her wit and the ability to not care what anyone thought of her. I did admire that she was an anomaly at Pure Pines, but it must be said that it's easy to be when you are a varsity cheerleader who's been in the in-crowd your entire existence. It's not too far-fetched to exercise your confidence when people fall at your feet, regardless. Even so, it was sweet that she knew this was an awkward day for me. She was a senior. She had nothing to lose. God, it was already October, and this still felt like the first day back dealing with this crap.

The thing was, I was never supposed to have been a cheerleader in the first place. Come on, it was Texas in the '90s; everybody with a pulse wanted to wear a cheerleading uniform. I had been the fluke at the end of eighth grade. I was the chunky girl that everyone teased a little too much because I took it better than the girls who were actually large enough to call fat. That would have just been too cruel, even for the in-crowd. There were only a few spots for freshmen coming in, and if you were one of the lucky eighth graders who made it, you would walk the halls as a JV Cheerleader your freshman year...with automatic status.

I never even thought of it that way. I just showed up because it was the only opportunity to go into high school with something on your plate, other than band, which I was already in. I remember a teacher looking me over and suggesting I wait and try out for mascot the following year when that position became available. My mother and I heard that and raised it one. Short and chunky of an eighth grader, I may have been, but unbeknown to the rest of my grade eight class, and apparently, that teacher, my bonafide stage mother had me in every dance class imaginable since I could walk. Truth be told, she hoped it would "lean me out," but let's not ruin a positive thing with what we now know of as body shaming.

My mom took one look at me and said, "Daughter, do you think you can make cheerleader this year, or would you like to refrain from tryouts and wait for mascot?" Knowing me so well, she couldn't hide the smirk on her face as she waited for me to respond in front of the woman. "I'm not really interested in being a mascot." My mom smiled again and pointed to the line for me to sign in. Less than three hours later, my name had been announced as one of Pure Pine's next JV cheerleaders.

I wish I could say that nothing changed for me, but the truth is, it changed immediately. The remaining weeks of my eighth-grade year were met with shock, scrutiny, and a seat at the popular table I had not anticipated. My mom and I spent the summer working on weight, as in dieting and trying to figure out cute, slimming outfits to put me in for my first cheer practices that would be throwing me to the wolves before my first day of high school.

That, and we prayed for a growth spurt. I wasn't that bad, just short still, with Mary Lou Retton thighs. She was an Olympic champion gymnast when I was a kid who carried all her extra weight and muscle in her thighs.

The hardest part about that year was negotiating friendships. Friends are things that shouldn't have to be negotiated; they should just be there. But what about when I couldn't be there because I was eating lunch with the in-crowd. What about those real friends, the ones who never called me chubby or cared what I wore to school? They just liked to laugh with me, talk about all the things we didn't understand about sex, and teach each other about all the different kinds of music we liked. I missed them the most. Those friends weren't necessarily a collective "them" or all in one group. There were several of them dispersed throughout my high school, forming different relationships, talking about music, and laughing about the unknowns of sex with new friends. I knew it was part of it all. Part of growing in general, but I never thought leaving someone out or excluding myself from them would be the result. It felt lousy and made me feel false as a person.

The truth was, there was nothing you could really do or say to fix it. If you tried to be a hero and sit with your old friends, you would almost insult them with your presence. In terms of Pure Pine's pecking order, it wasn't that I had climbed up the ladder above anyone. I was just in a different position to be pecked.

Because of that cheerleading uniform, I always had a seat at the popular table both freshman and sophomore year, but there was a constant reminder that I hadn't been one of them from the start. I was never really allowed to fit in entirely. I was kept at bay to do their bidding until I scored points if you will. For example, if I stumbled into a great outfit and an elite upperclassman noticed, or I established a friendship with one in a random class, that gave me clout and helped make up for me lagging behind them and still being in the band. Had one of the elites in my own class or their upperclassmen asked me out...as long as it wasn't someone they had their eyes on, that would have upped my ante times two.

As it were, if no one picked you out, they would be keen to source you out. The powers that be would try to put you with someone they thought appropriate to your status. It was sort of their own incestuous match-making thing. The sad part was, as in most small schools, everyone had been friends or involved with each other in some way back in grade school. It's not like they forgot about hanging out with that person or eating snow cones from a Snoopy shaved ice maker with them on their back porch.

Unfortunately, the American stereotypes of high school behavior suggest that whether you had a growth spurt before the next year, if you just happened to naturally be good at a sport or not, or if your older brother was popular, or your mom was on faculty, or you could afford name brands AND they looked good on you, all dictate who people say you are and how they treat you. They dictate if they want to be friends with you or not and who you should be friends with. Again, they made up their own rules at Pure Pines. Even though they were unwritten, somehow, we all knew them and, much worse, abided by them.

During my first two years of high school, I never asked why I wasn't invited to any of those bitches' houses to spend the night apart from a cheer squad thing, and I never invited them to mine either, not that they would come. I went to cheer functions with them and group parties and pretended to know what they were talking about when they discussed the latest time they hung out. A time I, of course, was not privy to.

That's the way they wanted it. It was as if they dared me to ask, but if I did, it would have ruined it. If they could just continue to dangle the carrot, then they had the power to give it to me or throw me a bone when they wanted to. I wasn't their only patsy, and I was probably ranked a bit higher in order than some, although I hate to admit that.

It was an eye-opening experience and one that was shifting and happening all over again now that I had not made varsity cheerleader. My status, position, and who I was in my junior year were changing. *So ridiculous.* Now, everyone who felt I disappeared on them freshman year suddenly thought they had dibs to snub me. I didn't blame them even though they were wrong. It wasn't me doing it. It was our system, but we were all pawns in it, so it may have been fair.

By your sophomore year at Pure Pines, real choices had to be made. If you were excelling in girls' athletics… volleyball, basketball, track, then band just got in the way. Athletics and band were the two major competing activities. Cheerleading was like student council; if you got picked or chosen…if you made it, then it didn't matter what you did or what classes it caused you to miss; you just got to do it by rite of passage. Special allowances were made.

Band fit more of the academic trajectory that was expected of all of us, while a "dump class" or lazy route was Art class, It was not that art was lazy; I just don't think the powers that be found it profitable or stimulating enough scholarship-wise to encourage it. Most people had their minds made up for them when they excelled in a sport; others, teetering between the two, usually decided what would help them out socially. If you couldn't cut it taking the scraps from the in-crowd in athletics, then you may need the band, nerds and all, to have any sort of social life in high school.

Luckily, there were enough cool people in the band and a few popular upperclassmen to keep it relevant. Although most of the in-crowd in my class had left band behind the year before, I was lucky I stayed in. I don't think they liked very much that I did. It kept me away from some of their events and out of their watchful eye, twenty-four-seven, but it also gave me access to a separate tier of the in-crowd. The hot upperclassmen, grunge-phase musicians who used band as their instrument outlet and had the cheerleaders salivating over them.

Also, Reagan Beckett, a childhood bestie and arch-enemy who I went way back with. She was my debate partner, and she had stayed in band as well. She was popular in a different way than the cheerleaders, but in a way that had clout all the same. Then there was Lynn Stokes, who I was privileged to have landed in her court. Thank God, she actually liked being in band and didn't want to leave.

Lynn was popular with everyone and was that long-term friend who floats in and out of your life and various friend groups because she was always wanted somewhere else. Depending on whose class she was in or what major activity took over her schedule at the time determined if you got to be around her. Her older sister had been a majorette and part of the band culture back when it *was* what the elite kids did. She had a follow-in-big-sister's-footsteps-agenda whether she liked it or not.

I was lucky to have stumbled into place with both Reagan and Lynn officially by my junior year. Reagan and I decided a long time ago that even though life had put us in competitive situations, we would be the people who kept our friends close, but the two of us as enemies closer. Our friendship drove our mothers crazy. They were enemies by default, but we didn't care. We understood each other better than anyone else did, and there was no one else we trusted in each other's court.

Reagan did have status of her own. She was a bombshell blonde, but not in the cheerleader, homecoming queen kind of way. She was genuinely pretty. A classic, sophisticated beauty with freakishly pale skin that could magically tan evenly on a dime as if it had a touch of olive in it. She was book smart, had perfect attendance, was president of the student council, and was in line for salutatorian. Her uncle was on the school board, which ticked an additional box, and she drew her popularity and influence through the upperclassmen elite, for example, the Tomlin Twins.

Two black-haired beauties with pale white porcelain skin and blue-blue eyes. They were unique-looking alone, then add the identical twin thing, and Wendy and Whitney Tomlin ruled their senior class.

Since their freshman year, they had been notorious for having the party of the century. It was invite only. An example of status, as it were, was that Lynn, Reagan, and I were invited this year before the "in-crowd" of our junior class. Lynn and I had been in dance with the twins outside of school off and on our entire lives, and Reagan had been on the student council, honor society, and in Globe Scholars with them before the rest of us were inducted. That, my friends, is called GPA, or an attempt at a high one. I really didn't have room to talk; my grades weren't that high, but I took every AP class I could. I was in gifted and talented and took every elective known to man, including being on the golf team.

Forgive me if I didn't have time to study for a quiz or two. I say that glibly as the in-crowd had also made their own rules about that. The few of them that only had an A/B average in regular classes got by without being questioned. I think there was even an honor roll for that. Try taking college-level math, science, and English while attempting every elective you possibly could in hopes of landing a scholarship for something. Anything to get out of Pure Pines, away from that damn water tower with the painted blonde horse on it, and the graffiti of our predecessors.

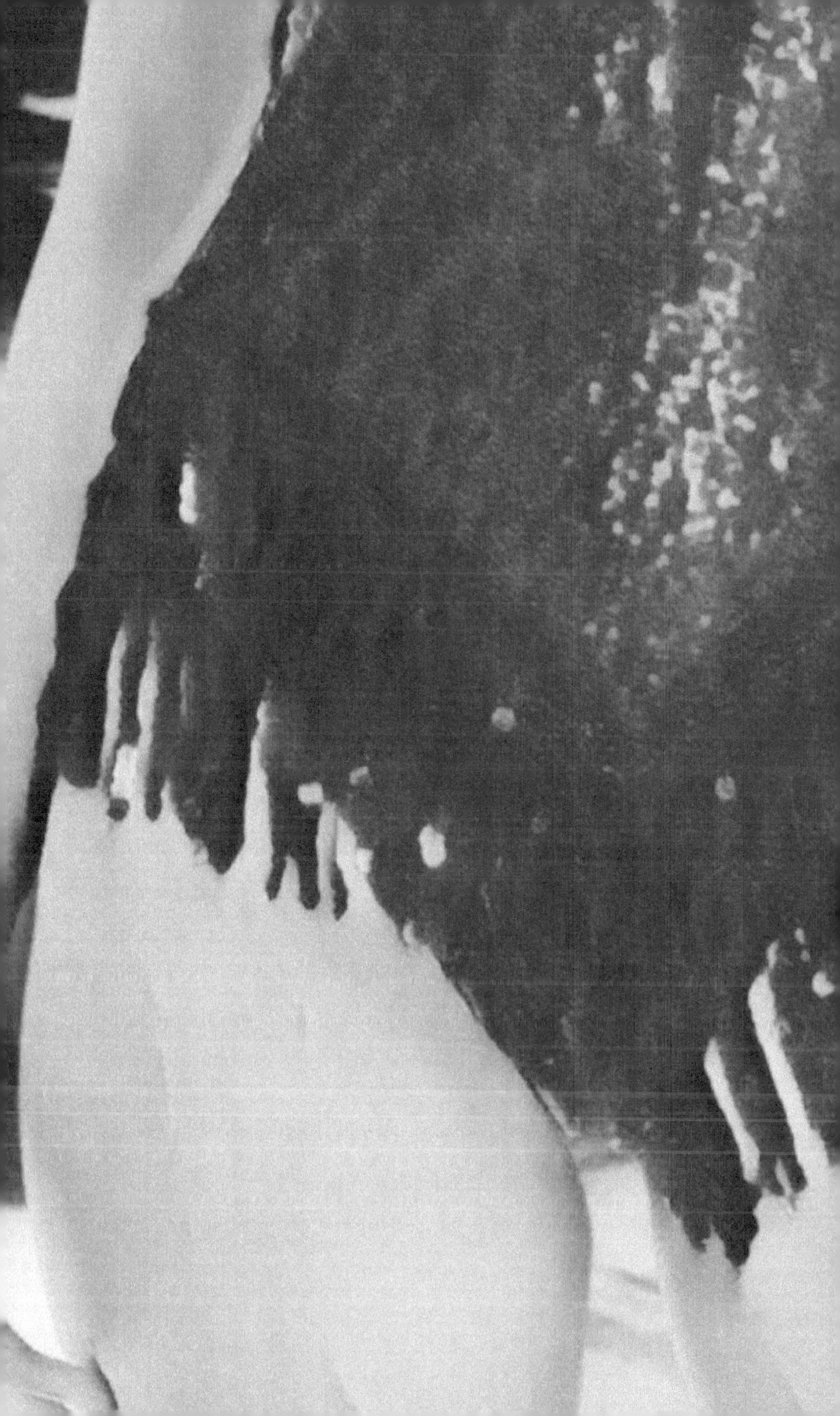

"T. A. K. E. TAKE US ALL THE WAY! WE SAID, T. A. K. E. TAKE US ALL THE WAY. GO. BIG. BLUE!" The varsity cheerleading squad called from one end of the gym. The student body cheered as they made their way out onto the floor in a contagion of chants. "ARE THE BUCKEYES GOING TO WIN TONIGHT, HE-LL NO!" The crowd roared again, and the band shouted on cue from their section in the stands, "SAY WHAT?"

"ARE THE BUCKEYES GOING TO WIN TONIGHT, WE SAID HE-LL NO!" The cheerleaders repeated and cued a drum roll. A chubby senior with glasses on snare drum stepped out and did the honors. "PURE PINE. PALOMINOS...ARE HERE TO STRUT THEIR STUFF. WHATCH-OUT...BUCKEYES." The first six cheerleaders did a backflip from where they stood. "WE'RE BACK AND TOUGH!" *Jesus.*

The band began playing our fight song, and I ran out from the open double doors with the varsity football team for what I hoped to be the last time. I had to wonder if I was going to miss this. They didn't give pep rallies for the track team in the spring, not even if you made it to state, but they gave actual scholarships for it. The odds of getting one around here in football, no matter how fast I was... Let's just say they were stacked against bodies the size of these ass holes next to me that would land on me tonight while I pretended to want to be our team's wide receiver.

It wasn't enough that I negotiated out of running back to hope-fully less of an eleven-car pileup. It's too bad I wasn't all thumbs and could actually catch. I just...I was fast, and I wanted to stay that way for track. The idea that someone *might not let me?* This was absurd to me. "Son, you have to play the game," my grandfather would say. *Which one, Pops? The literal or proverbial game, and for how long?*

They didn't even notice me during my freshman year. I was stuck on JV with most of the guys in my class while they pushed a select few forward to varsity. It would be different if I had been selected immediately and they had always counted on me. It wasn't until last year when my time destroyed everyone at the district track meet by well under the number of seconds anyone could have beaten me with at state. I didn't get to go to state because of debate team, but if I had, the coaches knew we would have won. My freshman year time alone nearly got the team there.

This was all a bunch of BS. I wasn't about to lose my lunch and ticket to my legacy school just because they finally noticed me here and suddenly couldn't make it without me. Make one of these other fuckers spend their summer running their fat asses off like I do. I looked around at the idiots beside me, the ones I called my buddies and those who were truly idiots. Look, I loved the comradery and all the glory that came with it. I loved football even, but I also knew at a certain point, you've got to decide where you're going to thrive and where the real opportunity is. I would be damned if mine was going to be an injury that laid me out just past the twenty-five-yard line in the middle of the season.

I'd already had issues with my knee, which the coach insisted on *handling* for me. That's not how I work. You do it right, or you don't do it at all. He had already lost my trust. We'd made it to the beginning of October. If I could just skate through to the end of the season. It wasn't that far away; at least my stepmom kept reminding me of that.

I wasn't a quitter; I just knew I wanted something else already, and it was okay with me that these guys didn't. Maybe they didn't have other options waiting for them. Maybe football was their opportunity. I had other options. Track was mine. It is what I wanted, and I was exceptional at it. I hated to be held back on anything I'd set my mind to. It was a massive pet peeve of mine. It would be different if I just liked it better, but this was a calculated decision.

I weighed the odds, and this was my opportunity. I didn't need to continue trying my hand at every sport Pure Pines offered to be mediocre at each of them at the end of the day. It was junior year. I needed to streamline and focus on perfecting what could get me noticed and into where I wanted to go.

As I looked up at Coach Craig, cheering with the crowd and slapping some of the guys around in excitement, I understood what he wanted from me, and if I'm honest, I would miss not delivering it. I just kept thinking about what my dad told me. He told me to trust my gut and not let the extras get in the way. Those weren't meant to be my milestones, just distractions. "If you come to a fork in the road, take it." That's what he'd say. He believed that the ability to move forward is what truly made someone stand out above the rest. I knew he was right; telling Coach Craig was just part of it.

Sometimes, I hated this place. If you blinked, you'd miss it and speed right past it down the interstate. However, if you took the wrong turn down a dirt road, a street or two past the high school, behind one of the churches, you'd find miles of all kinds of different houses built by the people who called it home. Pure Pines was in between two small towns north and south of it and two small cities, thirty miles to the east and west.

Those two larger towns had shopping malls and big chain restaurants. The smaller two beside us offered grocery stores, mom-and-pop type food places, and other small business destinations for errand running. They also had the only police and sheriff's departments near us. Imagine growing up in a town so *pure* it didn't need law enforcement. Looking back, I think that's how they kept us all in line. We didn't realize we were walking the tightrope without a net.

Don't get me wrong, I loved that they pushed us. Survival of the fittest was key to life, and it's exactly what you got at Pure Pines.

This town was about control. It had to have stemmed from how this unincorporated little community was founded, or I should say, by whom.

We heard once in our local history class that Pure Pines had the opportunity to incorporate and become a town. However, the vote was swayed to staying as is. In theory, I suppose the people in charge weren't willing to have someone in charge of them.

Pure Pines was stunningly good at compartmentalizing its functions and differentiating between its inhabitants. Regardless, it was often difficult to distinguish the haves from the have-nots. Like anything, what's truly valuable is in the eye of the beholder.

When I think about all the random students who transferred or moved here from Prairie, a much larger school in the town over from us, or any of the surrounding schools within a hundred-mile radius, for that matter, they never could hack it. If they were straight "A" students in honors classes, they struggled to make the A/B honor roll in our regular classes. A lot of them who decided to hang in our AP classes went from "A's" at their former school to straight "C's." It wasn't anything to brag about; it was just the truth of our school and what they wanted for us.

It had been that way from the beginning. None of us could be sure if it was one group of faculty members or perhaps our elementary school principal who made our class the state champs on the required standard testing that we all nailed. She just didn't let failure be an option. I looked out at the student body, all the different kids cheering from all walks of life. It was strange how Pure Pines' true cruelty was that they had given them ALL the same opportunity. They had maliciously, almost set us all up to thrive. Which was an impossibility; however, cruel as it was for those who fell through the cracks, you have to think it was also somewhat championing to have people who expected that of you. I don't even think we knew what poor was in elementary school.

Our reading groups had been divided into groups one, two, and three; if you weren't in the top group, you knew it, and everyone else did. The number two group was middle/mediocre, and the third group was last. The third group was how we learned what less fortunate was. At Pure Pines, it was initially about merit, academic achievement, and skill.

Great, I was about to drop something expected of me. This also went against my own core values. *Damn it.* Why was this such a hard decision to make? I didn't like being on the fence about anything. Especially when I wasn't on the fence and I knew what I wanted.

The drum roll started again, and I watched the varsity cheerleaders chanting before us. Half expectant and disappointed, I didn't see one I had always looked for, just for fun or good luck. Habit, I suppose. The entire semester, I had forgotten she wasn't on the squad anymore. Wonder why she didn't make it this year? Reagan said something about twirling with her and Lynn, but they hadn't done that this year. There was no baton twirler or majorette line like there used to be, either. Who knows. I needed to get my head straight and focus on quitting football. Besides, debate was coming up. She was on the debate team with me. I'd see her then. Or, I could ask her what happened then, I mean. *Okay, Adrian, stop looking at the cheerleaders; not exactly a pro on the list of quitting football.*

RINCIPAL
OFFICE

"POSSUM KINGDOM"

Toadies

The varsity cheerleaders began to disperse to the side as a drum roll announced their last bit before our entrance.

"Okay, ducks, it's show time." My best friend looked back at me with a wink, her blonde curls rolled up to her shoulders. Her blue eyes dazzled under the white suede hat tied tightly under her chin, and her red lipstick parted into a smile when I shot her the finger. The freshman girls on the line froze in fear as she, a captain of our newly formed drill team, walked toward me. She was expressionless and no doubt mustering up quite a show in retaliation.

She stood directly behind me, pulled one of my dark brown curls like a child until she bent my ear toward her and spoke firmly into it where the group could hear.

"These new uniforms are too short, they are far too tight, and yes, our asses are going to show. We look like a bunch of bitchy, hillbilly, call-girl sluts in very nice "Annie Oakly" hats. The Lycra tops are going to roll up to our ribs the first time we raise our arms above our waists, and just standing here, I can already see your left ass cheek where your trunks have ridden up. Now remember, you wanted to be a part of this, or rather, your mother is making you. I'm a captain, and I chose these new uniforms for us. You are my best friend... So are you..."

Reagan grabbed a junior officer and fellow captain from the front row who was pretending not to know us. It was my other best friend, Lynn Stokes, and the three of us were in what you would call a major uniform debacle. Our drill team Pep rally uniforms had not come in at the start of football season. They arrived that morning. Reagan had picked these out of some wayward dance catalog because they were a shiny, lighter royal blue color she thought would make us stand out. She certainly called that one.

They would get us banned from performing at the pep rally if Principal Sabella was there. When we put the spandex skirts on, we all realized the sides of the skirts dipped up to showcase the sides of the top of each of our thighs. That was just a bonus compared to the rest of the shit show. The good news was our monogrammed names on our upper right chest just above our boob on most of us had, in fact, been spelled correctly. That's a win you seldom get.

"You two are going to strut out onto the middle of that gym floor with me with your hats held high, while these other little shits struggle to keep their dignity or duck for cover. We are going to kick higher than you've ever kicked, smile bigger, and when you land in your final jump split, you will forgive me, knowing this will not be the most embarrassing moment of our junior year."

Reagan pinched my butt cheek and pushed me to the front of the line. She locked arms with Lynn and physically raised a smile on her face with her fingers as they stepped into their own line of drill team officers.

"Tits up!"

A whistle blew from the band's end of the gym, and we knew our drum major was counting them off to start our music.

Lynn stopped in her tracks before allowing the officers to take the last step onto the gym floor. "I'd just like to say, I'm almost a foot taller than the rest of you," she looked back at me, then at Reagan, "The exposure is far greater on my end. I'd like you both to think about that while we're doing the star kick to each corner of the gym in what our peers and teachers will basically perceive as bikini bottoms with a ruffle on me."

The band began the intro to the 1969 hit "The Spinning Wheel." I had to smile as I strutted out shortly after my two best friends; after all, the song's first verse, had there been lyrics, is, "What goes up...must come down," then there's something about riding a painted pony... You couldn't help but laugh, especially when the varsity cheerleaders' jaws dropped in unison.

I didn't know teenagers could whistle as loud as the ones in our student body crowd did. Everyone was cheering and yelling so loudly that I couldn't even hear the cowbell on my favorite part of the song. The whole thing was beyond absurd. It was so not Pure Pines. Instead, it felt more like a Parker Posey moment in the indie movie *Party Girl*. Maybe they thought it was a prank. I suppose I would have if I were watching from the stands.

Just when I thought we had to be over halfway through it, that I could close my eyes the rest of the way until it was over...*too late*. We turned the corner to start the succession of star kicks that would eventually end in the jump splits, and there they were...the huddle of varsity cheerleaders fixated on the circus in front of them. Hey, the crowd loved it, and if they were going to stare, I should probably make it worthwhile. I couldn't help myself. As I high kicked their direction, I plastered the biggest fake, over-obnoxious, cheerleading-spirit smile I could achieve. I winked as we fell into the splits, ending the routine.

It must have been one hell of a kick routine. We got a standing ovation. We were supposed to march back into the stands to the drumbeat, but with all the chaos and a few unhinged faculty members, Reagan and Lynn led us back to the double doors we came from. The football team opposite us sat on their thrones on the gym floor. With all the entertainment perceivably for them, they were naturally on their feet whistling and cheering for us as if they were at a strip club.

The underclassmen on the drill team looked like they'd just gone skinny dipping for the first time and loved it. Their eyes were wide as they tried to catch their breath while still peeking out the double doors at the crowd.

"Why don't you all go ahead and get changed for class?" Lynn recommended. "I know we normally stay in..." She cleared her throat. "In uniform for the entire pep rally, but under the circumstances, you should probably get changed."

"Good idea." Reagan chimed in. "We'll let Mr. McClendon and the drum major know we dismissed you all early." Reagan nodded at Lynn. Seconds later, there was a hand on her shoulder.

"Ladies, would you mind making your way toward Principal Sabella's office as soon as the pep rally dismisses, um...before you change into your regular clothes."

Great. She wanted the evidence.

Mrs. Bishop, the office administrative assistant, did not wait for our response. "I can let Mr. McClendon know we've requested your presence, although in his defense he did appear to be as shocked as the rest of us when he turned from conducting the band to see what all the excitement was about. No doubt you ladies certainly made an impression. We'll see you in ten." And she was off.

"You're coming with us," Reagan said before I could open my mouth.

"I'm not an officer."

"There are no senior officers. We are the three juniors who started this line, and we're in it together. She tapped you on the back too."

"She was reaching passed me to get Lynn's attention."

Lynn had walked a few feet away to open the door for the rest of the girls to go get changed.

"May I remind you, you chose to back down and not try out for officer. Some misguided scruples about being fair to others because you were already in so many electives when the truth is, you wanted to punish yourself for not making varsity cheerleader. You didn't want people to perceive you as a showoff.

"Trust me, we all showed something today." I looked over and saw Lynn was headed back toward us from ushering the others off. She'd say I didn't have to go.

Reagan stepped in front of me. "Just remember for life, that's the difference between you and I. I still would have competed against you to be feature twirler, or Lynn for drum major. This just pissed my mom off way more than if either of you had ended up beating me in twirling."

"I hate you." I smiled endearingly at my best friend.

"Do you? Or do you admire my keen ability to see the truth?"

Lynn made an about-face between us and hooked her arms to ours. "Come on, ladies, and I use that term loosely, given our current attire. Let's go take our first beating of the year."

"It won't be our last time in the office together." I smiled triumphantly and walked with them. Although I had nothing to do with the uniform debacle and had advised against ordering them...it felt good to be included, especially when they didn't have to. Reagan was right. In a way, she had taken one for the team and done this for me and Lynn as well, if you got right down to it.

It was a funny thing that sort of trickled into our laps. The rapidly changing times got the three of us into this pickle. The thing about East Texas back in the day is that it was, in fact, as pretentious and competitive as it sounded, but it was also about skill. Baby Boomers were determined their children would have, do, and be everything they couldn't and weren't. It was a lot of pressure to put on Generation X, hence enough teen angst to create the grunge phase. Somehow, not caring seemed like the most impactful way to rebel, even though it would have been complete treason at Pure Pines. The skill part was somewhat due to not having Xbox or Game Boys when we were little. We had barely just gotten Nintendo.

Thus, you had to put your kids in something to get them out of your hair. Most girls took dance and twirling or gymnastics. By the late 90s baton twirling, the really tiny attractive girl with a bun and diamond leotard who looks like she's freezing as she tosses multiple silver batons like daggers, spins around three to seven times, and catches one in her mouth, one between her legs and the other in her hand as she tosses another and bows to the crowd while leading the Christmas parade...had kind of played out. I guess no one wanted to practice that hard for anything anymore. Maybe it became more freakish as there was only one spot.

In contrast, cheerleading had multiple spots available and was becoming more and more of a competitive sport. Enter the popularity of gymnastics. At last year's tryouts, well over half the girls competing could do a standing back flip, if not a round-off back handspring. I tapped out at the cartwheel.

Meanwhile, the feature twirler was fading into most schools, barely having a majorette line that was becoming more and more mediocre and less skilled. When I cheered, Lynn and Reagan twirled on the last majorette line available to Pure Pines. It was a dying art. By the time they got to try out their sophomore year, anyone else who could twirl had just graduated. There weren't enough girls who could twirl a baton to make a majorette line. It nearly killed our mothers. In their day, cheerleaders were just a glorified pep squad that barely moved and did well to hold up pom poms.

The twirlers were the elite who had to stretch, dance, and bust their noses open, trying to catch a "three-turn." Thus, one band director, three mothers, a school board decision, me, who did not make cheerleader due to my lack of tumbling skills, and three best friends later...we had the first Pure Pines High Stepping Drill Team.

Lynn and I had danced our entire lives. She was an excellent twirler as well. Her sister was a head majorette and taught her everything she knew. Reagan and I had been twirling together since we were four. I guess I did that instead of gymnastics. Either way, you had two roles available, a feature twirler that Pure Pines had already done away with, as there was no one good enough to try out the last five years before us, and drum major. It was already unfair to set Lynn and Reagan up for those odds. Then I came along, rejected by the cheerleading squad, and my mom pushed me forward with a baton in hand.

Two unequal positions for three girls talented enough for the feature twirler spot. With all baton-twirling upperclassmen having graduated and no one left but the three of us to duke it out, Lynn and Reagan looked around at our competing schools. They were newly fanatical about the surrounding college drill teams. We didn't live far from America's very first drill team... *The Rangerettes.*

Most of the surrounding high schools already had kick and dance lines mirroring them. Reagan proposed that the popularity of drill teams via the skill of high kicking, dance, and falling into the jump splits while wearing white boots and a hat could be one more thing for Pure Pines to excel in. Our mothers let go of their twirl-or-die mentalities and brought in Mrs. Tandy, a retired dancer from Dallas who apparently privately choreographed tryout routines for *America's Sweethearts*, the Dallas Cowboys Cheerleaders. A woman who would require at least three years of dance for anyone who tried out, a weigh-in, and both the left and right leg splits. The school board had to fight her on the weigh-in, or at least ask her not to say it out loud. Thank God.

It wasn't the fairest solution in terms of giving more girls an opportunity. Still, it gave nineteen skilled dancers in our high school a chance, more than any majorette line of twelve or varsity cheer squad of nine had ever done. Beyond that, it was more than generous of Lynn and Reagan to do for me. *That* is why I refrained from officer tryouts. I thought that should be theirs.

I followed my two captains dressed like shiny blue Smurf-Barbies into the office. I tried not to laugh out loud every time one of us had to tug at Lycra riding up and exposing a butt cheek. All I could think at that point was, God bless Mrs. Tandy and her old-school flesh color dance tights. We all called them ice skater-pantyhose, but they were as thick as a tarp, if a tarp could be made of flesh-colored spandex, and the only saving grace to our uniform debut.

Lynn hated them because they were not easily available for women of color. There were basically only "light, "toast," and "tan" to choose from. That was odd if you thought about it. Why wouldn't all human skin tones be available solely because they existed? Surely the 1980s FAME craze had demanded a pair of flesh color tights for black women and an array of beautiful skin tones? *Hello...Irene Cara and Debbie Allen.* There had been incredibly successful dancers of color for decades. It was really fucked up when things didn't make sense even beyond Pure Pines.

Not that Lynn needed flesh-colored tights anyway. She was tall and lean and had the most gorgeous skin and legs imaginable. Her skin was the perfect combination of onyx and mahogany or midnight combined with honey. Not an ounce of cellulite. Her looks of intelligence and gregarious wit were completed by two dimples on her cheeks you could not hide if you tried. She was famous for them, and they belonged in an ad for face wash, lipstick, or some luxury item that demanded a smile one could not resist. Lynn had face, body, and smarts.

I hadn't thought much about being friends with two people so attractive until I stood beside them in the office across from what appeared to be Principal Sabella...Coach Craig...and...*Adrian Reed*? His football jersey was folded and sitting on the desk. I couldn't help but wonder if he had gotten in trouble or suspended, but no way would that happen to him. I wanted to tug Reagan and Lynn and have them look, but I realized as I turned to Lynn they were already making crazy kiss faces and exploiting our shit show of a uniform at him, trying to make him laugh between Coach Craig's pacing and Principal Sabella's office window. We would no doubt be in there next. It's too bad we couldn't fold our uniforms and leave them on his desk, too.

I was then reminded what I, too, had on, and additionally, that the top of Lynn's Rockette-length leg was practically up to my waist. I had not yet gotten that growth spurt Mom and I hoped for. I immediately plopped down in a chair behind me. At the same time, Mrs. Bishop addressed Reagan and Lynn, letting them know Sabella would be available shortly.

I peeked back up at the window just in time for Coach Craig to pace in the opposite direction, leaving Adrian's gaze directly on mine. He stared at me for a moment through the window until a crooked little smile encroached his face. *"What is that?"* He mouthed with animated brows pinched together, waving his hand across his body, motioning the area of my outfit as much as he could without being seen by the two men pacing about him. I smiled back, and my middle finger rose for the second time that day.

I watched as Principal Sabella lowered the blinds on it. Not really; he was closing the blinds as he realized people were trailing into the office area while Coach Craig looked increasingly upset in whatever dispute they were all having. I dropped my finger when I was in the clear from him.

That was the last time things were normal between Adrian and me. Well, as normal as they could be at Pure Pines.

The Smashing Pumpkins

I didn't go to the game that night. Not in uniform, as Coach Craig insisted, and not to sit in the stands to show support.

We lost. Our winning streak since the start of the season was broken by the first loss. I was never going to live that one down. Wouldn't putting that on me give me far too much credit and power? I would think even Coach Craig would want to avoid that as much as any of the players with any self-pride in their own ability. I took it as Murphey's Law.

That, or the team Bullard promised to be this year with zero losses of their own, simply meant it wasn't hype, and the best team won. I couldn't consider the obvious fact that if I had just played one more game, I might have given them a victory tonight. Sure, and I could have also ended up benched with an injury that would take me out of track.

I couldn't think like that. It wasn't how the fork in the road worked. A decision had been made, and I made it. I didn't tell my dad how poorly Coach Craig had reacted, even with his threat to call my dad. He knew nothing of my father and that we didn't play those bull shit games. My dad set me up for the kind of success he wanted for me, but he always left decisions like that to me.

It was rare and the opposite of what he grew up with. My grandfather was far more pretentious than this town and had his hand in everything my dad did. I was too grateful for my dad's respect and how he treated me to tell him how hard the coach made it for me. All because he was a Neanderthal, and Principal Sabella was not much better, although he feigned neutrality. He was obviously still hoping I'd change my mind and play.

I had the weekend to give Coach Craig to cool off. It would have sucked to see him the very next day in athletics. It was late Sunday night. I had an entire weekend with family stuff, and it wasn't until I noticed the headlights from Lynn's dad's car pulling up their drive next door that I realized I hadn't talked to Lynn all weekend. She lived next door, and I could always see whether she was home from my bedroom window.

I felt terrible. I know she called to check on me multiple times. Reagan had even called once or twice, so it must have been an intense display in that office for them to be so concerned. What an idiot that guy. Some fucking coach. Lynn knew I was going to quit before last week's game. She was the first person I told after my dad. Still, it was weird that we hadn't talked about what went down with Coach Craig since the last time I saw Reagan and her was when they stood there in those ridiculous outfits, watching the scene. *Oh. Yeah... those outfits. Shit. Jesus!*

Was I so self-absorbed with no longer being a part of football that I forgot that happened? *What did happen exactly? Nothing, right?* She didn't even notice, probably. I hit the lights and turned off the late-night TV. The reruns of *Cheers* always allowed me to clock how late it was. I had it muted in the background while I caught up on homework, like most nights.

I tried to replay that moment in the office as I hit the sack. I went over and over what happened while the coach thought he was ripping me a new one. She was just standing behind me. In the line of fire, I guess... then I saw her face in my mind from when I turned toward her just after. As I remembered where my hand was on her waist and how close I stood above her... I had an unexpected physical reaction to the replay. *No way!* It couldn't have been as significant as all that.

I'm sure I was just trying to make sure she didn't get trampled by the fire-breathing coach.

July?

And it was July's face in that ridiculously tight, shiny blue uniform that I saw all night as I tossed and turned into Monday morning. *Whatever.* I'm sure I was subconsciously looking for any distraction to keep my mind off the team, the coach, and the shit talk I would get from quitting them.

***

As I headed down the hallway after first period, I saw Reagan, Lynn, and July walking toward me. July peeled off into a classroom without making eye contact. I don't think she noticed me, but Reagan and Lynn picked up the pace to run smack into me.

"Oh, my God! Oh, my God! What the entire fuck! What happened in there?" Reagan was almost too excited, demanding an answer. Lynn stood beside me with less enthusiasm but a curious expression.

"Look. We do everything they ask of us, when it's humanly impossible sometimes. If they truly want us to get the memo about excelling, if that's what all this is for... our futures, then I'm responding the way I should. It's time to strea—"

"Streamline and get your ducks in a row for college." Lynn interrupted only to mock the recent campaign I had subscribed to. "I have to be straight with you and tell you, not that I'm on his side for his behavior, but did you really expect Coach Craig to wrap his brain around that on game day with Bullard? You know you could have done it the Monday before, but on game day?" Lynn's point was valid; she was the voice of reason.

"That was a dumb ass move on your part. But, he probably didn't have any other opportunity Lynn."

"Thank you, Reagan. Always on my side, no matter how backhanded it may be to get there." I'd known these two my entire stint at Pure Pines, and our AP classes had pushed the three of us closer together since the eighth grade. Most guys I knew spent their high school existence trying to figure out what girls thought or what made them tick... I couldn't get away from being told exactly what was on the minds of these two. It was a blessing and a curse.

The three of us, as individuals, had our own social positions, but it didn't hurt being grouped together as often as we were. They were both gorgeous, however the extent of our friendship had resulted in them being off-limits to me romantically... I could never think of them that way, especially Lynn. She was basically my best friend.

When our parents thought of us home alone together, they imagined us in a sandbox in diapers. Still, it was nice to see the cream of the crop upperclassmen and underclassmen alike salivate when they saw them flock toward me in the hallway.

"Are the guys upset?" Lynn pressed on.

"Honestly, no. I mean, I don't think they are allowing me the satisfaction of their disappointment, if you get my drift." Lynn patted me on the back.

"It's a long time 'til track season... But they'll forgive you by then."

I smiled a half smile. Lynn's sarcasm was more factual than she knew. I was embarrassed to admit that I was literally going to have to count on that.

"Absolutely! Once you take 'em to state in track it'll all be bygones." Reagan was motivating when she wanted to be. You just had to catch her when she meant it. "They're not mad that you left them. They are pissed because you're exposing they weren't' good enough to make it to state in football regardless. If Bullard hadn't beat us this last Friday night, they would have beat us the Friday after that or so on."

"Alright, enough." Far too flattered, I had to demand it end. "Keep your voices down, or they'll have you for high treason, and we'll all be back in that office again."

Lynn looked up at me a little too quickly on "back in that office ..." The curious look reappeared on her face. I wanted to ask when they would see July again today or say something lame like... *Is that July I saw walking with you earlier?* I had to pipe down. No need for them to be privy to my dreams all through the night. Lynn already looked suspicious, as if she saw me grab July. *Why don't I just give myself away and hand it to them on a silver platter?* This is stress and the whole football thing. That's what's happening here.

I'll admit there was something about July that did it for me to a certain degree in her JV cheerleading uniform, but for a girl that really wasn't my physical type... even I had to consider I was acting strange. I liked blondes mostly. Dirty, platinum, didn't matter. I had an affinity for all shades of that category. Well, there was always room for that one bombshell brunette with dark hair and dark eyes who is so elegant they could drown out a sea of blondes, but that's rare.

I was also... dare I say a leg guy? I liked them tallish, with a slim build. Not too tall. 5'5" to 5'8," was good. Just tall enough to have that physique. I wasn't really into short and curvy or short and cute. July was, well, I... I stood in the hallway, staring after the bell rang. I didn't even remember saying bye to Lynn and Reagan or anyone else I passed moments before.

She was not quite her full height yet, I suspected. And... the kind of girl you were curious about, as in waiting to see what turned out or was underneath. But there was something there. It was the hidden, not yet obvious part that made her seem innocent, almost, even though she had a bite to her and could go head-to-head with anyone. Trust me, I'd seen her in debate.

It was honest to say I didn't know what sparked this sudden fascination or my odd behavior over July, but it wasn't the first time I had been a little more than curious about her. Let's just say this had been the first time in a while it came back up.

JAMES HURST

THE SCARLET
I·B·I·S

The Cranberries

Monday, Monday... that word alone should be an alternate term for Hell. Even when it wasn't so bad, the anticipation it would be was. I wasn't a "Debbie Downer" or anything; I was just... tired. Pure Pines was a lot. Home was a lot. I guess I just didn't like not knowing when I would catch my next break, mentally, figuratively, or even luck-wise. Overall, I did know I was lucky.

I was grateful for many things. I just didn't like what most of them came with. Almost anything you excelled in at Pure Pines left you under constant scrutiny by both the student body and faculty. I think that's what I hated. I didn't like being thrown to the wolves every day, and I hated feeling like I was under the gun, even when I was prepared.

We made it through the uniform debacle, and new outfits were on the way, but not without those debuting on the field that night as well. Principal Sabella said they were too scant to wear them in the stands, and we had to change right after the half-time performance, but there was no reason we should miss out on doing the routine we prepared.

Our band director arrived minutes later and mentioned we could wear our matching practice shorts and tee shirts, but you could tell Sabella preferred a little NFL cheerleader pazazz to us looking like some makeshift dance line that couldn't afford uniforms. Pure Pines did not suffer regarding the elements between the goalposts or the stadium surrounding them.

As the office door was closing on our exit that day, I heard the principal comment... "Yeah, I'm fine with those on the field for tonight, just ah... make sure they look as... you know, appropriate on the rest of the girls." Our band director, Mr. McClendon's response stuck with me. "You bet. I think most of these gals are, ah, in shape. Hell, they'd have to be to kick that high! But, ah, I'll have their sponsor do a once over—make sure everybody is... proportioned, ah... anatomically correct to wear *that* on the field tonight. Anybody who isn't can probably sit this one out until the new uniforms come in next week."

Wow. I can't say that didn't stick with me up to the performance. The entire day, I kept snapping my head over to Reagan and Lynn whenever I saw them huddle together in conversation. I was petrified that one of them was prepping to reluctantly come tell me I didn't look okay in the uniform and was to be benched until next week. Instead, everything about the performance went exceptionally well. The crowd in our stands stood on their feet, applauding their new drill team, and we were already more skilled than the opposing team's dance line. They must have had twenty-five to thirty girls in their line. I guess that was the difference in elitism. Our school only took the nineteen who could perform exactly like they wanted. Well, eighteen that night...

As I turned my head to the right on a fan kick lunge, smiling through red lipstick, I noticed the girl that hooked arms with me was linked to a different girl on her right. Someone was, in fact, missing. When the drum major blew the whistle to march us off the field post-performance, I saw a tear-stained freshman wearing our team practice shorts and tee shirt freezing on the side of the track next to Mrs. Tandy and our band director. She was short. My height or shorter, and she had chunky little legs. At that moment, she reminded me of my freshman year on the cheerleading squad. I didn't remember her being too heavy or having any part of her tummy bulge over the spandex when we performed in the pep rally that day; however, that was all a blur. What was I thinking? *Surely not*... surely, she just twisted her ankle during our kick routine earlier? *Right?* I had to stop overanalyzing. However, as curious as I was... as disturbed as I was by what I heard the two men in the office deliberating over... I did not have the guts to ask Lynn or Reagan. I was a coward. I don't think my own psyche could have handled the worst-case scenario as an answer. Reagan and I both battled with weight but in very different ways. Hers never showed.

The weekend flew by, and I could tell my mom was happy the drill team had been successful. She wasn't home for the game, but my Aunt Denise had my Uncle Dean record it on his new camera. It was the same way they came and took pictures freshman year for the first football scrimmage of the season when I was a Pure Pines cheerleader. Dean was my mom's younger brother, but Denise had been blood to us since they married. She fit like a glove and loved my grandparents, Pure Pines, and all of us.

She and Dean were in love at first sight right out of college. They moved onto my grandad's land, well, the acreage he gave his kids as a wedding present, and had three boys. Growing up as an only child, they were like my brothers and Aunt Denise, a second mother-sister hybrid, anytime my mom was stuck at work.

My mom was a single parent, so that was all the time. It didn't bother me not to see her in the stands. I had enough one-on-one time with her when she was home. It was just the two of us when we weren't crashing at my grandparents' house for when we want-ed the feeling of a family around. Sometimes, it did get lonely.

I was always just as proud when Dean and Denise were there, and even more so when my grandad came. Football games were kind of our thing. Dance, twirling, globe scholars, student council, and all the rest... my mom's. If she had been there Friday night, she would have just been taking mental notes on who kicked higher between Reagan and me, and who was late on the contagion before we all fell into a jump-split.

She was amazing, wonderful, and incredible, but also critical. At least it would be a while before she had time to analyze the video. She had seen it small through the replay on Dean's camera lens, but I don't think he had transferred it to a VHS for her yet. She had already asked me why there were only eighteen girls, not the full line. I didn't have the heart to tell her what I suspected. I didn't have the bandwidth for her caveat that would follow... something along the lines of, "Well, better eat boiled egg and grapefruit and nothing else this weekend to keep on top of it and drop a few in case."

Today's Monday wasn't so bad; the first two periods had opened on a high with a handful of compliments combined with raised eyebrows over the debut of our first official drill team. It did feel good to be official, and I heard the administration was already getting calls over requirements and dates of tryouts for next year.

I had suppressed my public groping from Adrian or my public, bizarre display of affection by just standing there offering some strange form of carnal support. I still didn't know what that was.

If you could count on anything at Pure Pines, it was denial and business as usual to save face. I felt certain that Adrian wouldn't fall short of that, especially given the circumstances. Come on, quitting football and the way Coach Craig spoke to him... those stakes were way higher than his hand landing on my thigh... and then my waist for no apparent reason.

Lynn was the only thing that kept it fresh on my mind. She didn't ask me directly but kept bringing it up, unsatisfied with anybody's response. She seemed overly invested in my take on the intensity with which Coach Craig spoke to Adrian and why Principal Sabella allowed it. She point-blank asked how upset I thought it made Adrian. I knew she saw the little encounter, and I felt terrible that I couldn't answer her.

I usually told Lynn and Reagan everything. Why was this different? Maybe she was helping me out of my funk, encouraging me to say out loud, *"Weird that Adrian groped my thigh while he was getting yelled at. What am I, his mother?"* That way, we could all have a laugh about it. I didn't laugh, though. I didn't say anything ... or even acknowledge it happened, which made me seem cagey, as if there were a secret. I normally had a bold personality. You could say anything to me, and I would say anything back. Lynn was used to that.

Since cheer tryouts, failing to make varsity, I had become more and more of an introvert over things I didn't understand. Don't get me wrong, I never just expected to make cheerleader, and I have failed at PLENTY of things. I just wasn't prepared for the stigma of not making it. I wasn't aware there would be one. Again, why did it matter to other people that I wasn't good enough to make cheerleader? Why did that have to say something about me to them?

It felt like a letter was sewn to my chest, maybe an "F" for failure. Okay, that's a little dramatic, and we obviously had gotten our AP English reading list in. *The Scarlet Letter* topped it and was a favorite of mine. Of course, it was.

I just hadn't felt as carefree about expressing every little thing I thought, and I'm sure to Lynn that felt as if I was keeping a secret. *As if... come on*! Lynn was smart enough to know that she'd know something that insane before I would. Adrian was her best friend.

I tried to block it from my mind and get through third period. At least I would have Lynn and Reagan off my back until lunch. And finally, the release happened. I walked out of third period toward the history hallway. I felt a distant stare but didn't try to meet it. Just before I turned to the hallway toward my locker, my brown eyes fell on Adrian's sharp blue eyes in time to see them cut away from me before I turned. Classic Pure Pines move, and just as I had anticipated from him. I guessed that'd be the end of that.

As I headed down my hallway, which was always refreshingly quieter between the bells this period, my mind exchanged the moment of relief for a replay of his face above mine. His dark hair made his steel blue eyes stand out as the remarkably identifying feature on his face. He had an angular face with thick dark eyebrows, but they were tame and somehow kind, even when they furrowed at me. Curious looking instead of ever truly angry, although they did look angry with Coach Craig that day.

His intelligent nose and chiseled chin were contradicted by his abundant lips. *Oh my God!* What was I saying? Maybe I had just never really looked that close before. I mean, I had a silly crush on him in junior high, but that was kids' stuff. I think I was attracted to his confidence. I've now grown to recognize that element of him as being conceited and cocky. I don't think he's ever been nice to me on purpose.

The halls were almost all empty now, and I thought this was as good a time as any to stop by Mrs. Rickie's class to pick up my books on the reading list. I had fifteen minutes before I had to be in study hall. As I turned down the empty English hallway, something struck me when I looked up at the door to freshman English lit. *Okay.* Well, there was this one moment with Adrian other than our norm, but it was so long ago that I couldn't imagine it counted.

I stood frozen, staring at the freshman English room, thinking about the day it happened. The day it happened, I had just left the very freshman English room I stood in front of. I thought about that moment and that classroom and wondered what my old English teacher, Coach Timpson, would say of me now eagerly stepping up to tackle my AP reading list. To say I was an avid reader back then would be a gross overstatement. I loved books and had an avid curiosity about what I thought you were supposed to know or what others knew and I didn't. To devote hours to a book on a list for no reason or read continually was something I did not have time for. My relationship with literature was more of an isolated or serial obsession. I guess you could say a book had to find me, but when it did, I was devoted.

It's like the bookshelf everyone's had in their room since childhood. Mine was full of old or new classics that adult relatives or my mom's friends bestowed on me for Christmas and birthday presents of the significant coming-of-age years. They were all signed and dated inside the front flap: "You're turning twelve this year!

You'll love *Little Women*." "Every little girl should read *Tuck Ever Lasting*."

Or my favorite… "Hey, kid start with the classics, *Great Expectations*, it'll put hair on your chest." Love Uncle Don.

I can't say I read them at the time I received them, but the older I got, and the more I got to know those friends and relatives, some in a different light, and others, maybe even less than I had known them as a child, I began to grow curious about their relationship to the book. I wanted to understand why that particular book mattered so much to them, why it made them think of me, or in some cases, if they'd even read it.

After that, it became a personal education. A teacher would say a phrase or make a pun, then reference the book it came from. I'd tend to find and read that instead of what we were required to read for class. We didn't have Google back then, so a book was the only way to satiate your curiosity. I'd get obsessed with it for a while. What the author meant by it, why they wrote it, and why the person remembered that line or moment from it.

It was similar to when I randomly heard that Winston Churchill's favorite movie was *That Hamilton Woman*. They say he used to watch it over and over. It was an old black and white movie from the 1940s starring Vivien Leigh and Laurence Olivier. I remembered hearing that when we got to Churchill in History, and the teacher commented that he wasn't much of a romantic. *Hmmm*. To watch that movie multiple times, you would have to be a hopeless romantic, in love with Vivien Leigh, or obsessed with Laurence Olivier. I can't imagine he was watching it for the art of war. Needless to say, I must have rented it at the tape store and watched it as many times as he did to try and figure out why he liked it so much.

At that time, we were studying short stories in freshman English and were required to read *The Scarlet Ibis* by James Hurst. I didn't read it before the class discussion. Then, once it piqued my interest, I spent the class lecture reading it thoroughly. Coach Timpson assigned a two-page essay on the plot just before the bell rang. I went home and wrote a seven-page essay.

It changed me, this story of these two young brothers and what goes on in the over-analytical mind of a child. The things you think when you're a kid, how heavy the burden and significant to that moment they are. I must have read the story three more times, once even after I wrote the overachieving seven pages. English and history were my strong suit, even without reading the required material.

Imagine my surprise when I got a "C." I naturally assumed Coach Timpson was being a dick and holding me to the assignment being two pages, not seven. But then: *See me after class*! Written by it, seemed even more severe. I began to skim through my words. I had a horrible habit of not proofreading. Maybe he was punishing me for that to teach me the value of not having typos. It would have been fair.

***

Freshman Year...

As soon as the bell rang after class, so did Coach Timpson. "Miss Edwards?" I'll never forget having to unintentionally saunter up to the desk in my blue JV Palamino cheerleading uniform. It was a Thursday, and JV had a scrimmage that night. Freshman cheerleaders covered JV, so we wore our uniforms on Thursdays to show support for game days. It was ridiculous if you thought about it. A school with a dress code that strictly allowed no tank tops, spaghetti straps, or dyed hair beyond that of "natural human coloring," and the most paramount rule, no skirts, shorts, or dresses more than four inches above the knee... this same dress code encouraged cheerleading uniforms two days a week.

I'm sure you can guess the skirt was far more than four inches above my knees.

"Miss Edwards, out of seven pages I would have thought you could have landed on the story's theme at least once. Unfortunately, your grade had to reflect that you did not. Now, I hate to give you a "C" when you wrote so much and were so in-depth; you clearly read it... I'm just not certain you grasped it."

I was livid. *Did he read my essay? Did he not grasp it?* "I'm not sure I understand. I mean, I'm not sure what you think I missed or how the theme is different than what my essay suggests."

"The theme of the *Scarlet Ibis*, Miss Edwards, is that Doodle's brother is ashamed of him. He acts out of pride and that is the downfall or what ultimately makes him responsible for pushing his disabled brother so hard he finally dies."

"Wait. He wasn't ashamed that his brother couldn't walk or run as fast as the others, no more than any kid is embarrassed of their family or surrounding elements. He wanted a brother, and he wanted to turn Doodle into a brother he could be proud of, yes... but pride is different than shame. Being proud of someone is very different than themes of foolish pride or that of being too proud that we typically explore in literature... I think he just wanted to be a big brother and all he had to offer was what he knew to bestow on Doodle. Doodle lived, and had a big brother he looked up to for much longer than anticipated, and he died trying to live. They both learned from each other. I'm sorry Coach Timpson if you didn't get that from my essay, or is it that you needed me to accept the shame angle and make it the brother's fault? Forgive me but is that on some abbreviated teachers' guide over the story?"

"Miss Edwards!"

"I'm sorry Coach, but I really love this story, and I guess I'm a little upset that you don't get my understanding of it." *Ugh! This was not coming out right! And why did he care so much?* He was a coach for crying out loud. The rest of them usually just phoned in everything that wasn't on a field or court.

"July, I don't want to insult you with this, as I'm sure you didn't intend to insult me over the teachers' manual you assume I graded you by. I'll leave you with this..." He looked my uniform up and down and handed me the "C" marked essay to suggest the grade still stood. "I fear you have a very "Pure Pines" view of this story, and I urge you to look past the generally accepted scrutiny and criticism that makes up the norm on our campus. Then you can potentially see that he was, in fact, ashamed of Doodle."

Oh, my God, was this man seriously judging me for being in a cheerleading uniform? That was his second mistake.

"For example, you don't ask your friends who are not cheerleaders to adopt the uniform and skills to try out, do you? You're quite well versed in these halls, Miss Edwards; I don't see you turning to your band friends and suggesting they take on student council or whatever else may interest you. Your less academically inclined friends... do you tutor them, and insist they join GLOBE Scholars and take AP classes like you plan to? However, their differences are not as celebrated as those that do share cheerleading and student council, and—I'm simply suggesting you might see the shame he held for his brother in trying to make him become something he was not if you viewed it as yourself doing that to any of your peers, which is common among our halls."

The next bell rang. I tugged at my backpack and folded the "C" paper, declaring I would take it. I thanked Coach Timpson for his time as politely as possible. I walked away from the classroom, replaying his interpretation versus mine, chasing the idea that I had been too forgiving of the older brother, and that's why he suggested this Pure Pines point of view he thought I harbored. Assuming because I was a cheerleader, I thought it was okay or better to bring someone you were ashamed of up to your level as opposed to risking being embarrassed by them. *What? Wow.* His assessment of Pure Pines wasn't wrong, but his judgment of me was grossly inaccurate. *What a jerk.*

I caught the reflection of my short, chunky legs below my cheerleading skirt as I passed the glass-windowed hallway. It made the corners of my mouth dip down every time I saw what made me ashamed in my uniform, what didn't look like the typical thin figure that I thought would magically appear when I "made it." It must have been magic that I did, in fact, make it, as there never were fat or chunky cheerleaders at Pure Pines; at least, I had never seen one until my own reflection.

You see, Coach Timpson and I were both wrong over our assessment of *The Scarlet Ibis* because I wasn't judging the little br other... I was him. I was "Doodle," I had something off, wrong, or disabled about me that I would ALWAYS be working or striving to fix. Maybe I welcomed the brother's tutelage the way I had secretly hoped a combination of the summer, the growth spurt I longed for, and the magic of wearing the cheerleading uniform would make me look like all the others.

Turning the corner into the cheer PE room, I tried to regain my confidence. It was sign painting day. I even tried to use the fact that Coach Timpson misjudged me as a bitchy, privileged cheerleader as flattery, but that didn't work. What did work was Adrian.

I went straight to my task from the varsity cheer captain to fix one of the signs some dumbass had misspelled. None of us were artists in the group, so it sucked to be tasked with turning a mistake into something clever for our boys to run through. If you didn't achieve it, you had to repaint the whole sign yourself.

I spread the grey craft paper across the hallway. It was stunning to think someone could mess up sayings as simple as "Kill the

Hill!" for Spring Hill or "Smoke the Oak" for Red Oak. Those with nondescript mascots were typically the hardest to come up with.

This one, however, someone had gotten clever with. It had the word government in the phrase, misspelled across the top of the entire sign. On all fours, I reached over to the other side to secure the corner to the floor and begin working on it. I heard sneakered footsteps jogging up, then slowing down behind me, but I didn't bother to look, even though my cheerleading spanks were the only thing representing me with my butt hanging out under my skirt. I knew it had to be one of the girls.

It was a closed period between classes, and these halls were usually empty, but for us. There was a longer pause behind me than expected. One of the girls would have already spoken by then.

"You're missing an "N." A deep male's voice fired off the statement. I dipped my head between my arm and body to look behind me, and there Adrian stood with a sarcastic smile. An upside down smile from my angle, and a succinct view of my derriere. I wish I could say I calmly rose from all fours with tact. Instead, I plopped on my butt immediately as if the damage had not already been done. I felt wet paint beneath my bloomers and down the back of one leg. Apparently, part of a flag someone attempted to illustrate had not yet dried completely. I tried not to let it show on my face.

"I'm not missing it. I mean, I might look stupid in this very moment, but I wasn't the one to leave the "N" out of the word government. Thank you, though for the concern." A smile grew across his face, and he squinted an eye at me as he tried to take in the overall sign.

"Do you know what it means or was meant to mean?"

"Actually, I was just about to ask you the same question... you're the one who has to run through it tonight."

"One can't be entirely sure... could you maybe slide over a bit so I can see the entire display?" The hint of sarcasm remained in his voice, as did the smile that grew larger as I looked down and cleared my throat, not enthusiastic about moving.

"I would love to, but I believe that to be an impossible task this very moment." Adrian stepped delicately across the painted sign toward me and held out his hand.

"It's ah... cold isn't it." He squashed his large smile.

"Yes. Very." I admitted my defeat, put my hand out, and let him hoist me up as I felt the wet paint smear all over the back of my leg. We both looked down at the spot where my butt had smeared the paint. Our heads tilted, and then we walked backward to look... "Do you think they meant parliament? Or paramount? Is that the word they meant to write instead of government misspelled?" I was really trying to make sense of it.

Adrian still had my hand. He lifted it at the wrist and motioned toward ducking behind me to look at what was missing from the illustration. He took a half step back behind me.

"No... they definitely meant to misspell government." I punched him playfully in the arm and took my hand back.

"Darn it. I'm afraid this one's a do over."

"Well, look at it this way, if you run out of paint..." He peeked behind me one more time.

"Well, aren't you just about as clever as this sign was meant to be."

He stepped closer to me, and I felt the heat between us, but I assumed it was from my uncertainty of not knowing what he wanted, or the flirting, or... *wait, were we flirting?*

"You know, we have a golden opportunity here. You being the painter of the sign, and me being one of the individuals running through it. It is our very first home game."

"I see. Would you like me to write your jersey number across the top in bold? Or, are you here to check my work and make sure there are no further spelling mistakes?"

"Wow. You don't make this easy, do you?"

"What? Making spirit signs with finger paint?"

He moved even closer. I looked down to make sure neither one of us was stepping on the wet paint part, and he smiled confidently at my nervous fidgeting. When I looked back up, his face was looking down on mine. His remarkably blue eyes searched my face through his dark lashes and the corner of his lips played with a smile matching mine. That was the first time I realized how tall he was or that he had gotten taller since junior high. There was something different about him. I couldn't figure him out.

Our eyes met, and mine involuntarily locked on his. We were standing closer than I realized or understood at the moment. His charming smile transitioned into a nervous one. Eyes remaining transfixed on mine, the rest of him seemed to stammer. Now, he was the one fidgeting. He took a half step back to look away, and I gained confidence, taking a step forward.

"Careful." I pointed at the paint without looking down. "You wouldn't want to step on the wet part." He froze where he stood. He closed his eyes and pressed his lips until he could counter with his confident smile.

His throat cleared. "Umm, I was just going to suggest before that—I don't know—maybe you could make one for me, or make this one for me." He shrugged kind of sheepishly. "...Not my number or anything, but maybe a private, spelled correctly, inside joke."

"Um hmm." I smiled wickedly back at him. *We were flirting.* "What makes you think I can spell?"

He laughed immediately, a bit harder than he meant to. "Well, statistically... since none of you can draw or paint well, and someone else misspelled government, I'd say it's a safe bet that one of you can."

He began backing up from me without taking his eyes off mine. "I should probably..." He motioned toward exiting in general. "I'll... see you there?"

"I'll be the one with the paint all over her..." I motioned to my backside he had become so acquainted with during the last three minutes that felt like twenty. Then he jogged off toward the locker rooms. I guess I didn't realize. Or, damn it, maybe I did...

That night at our first JV home game, my first game as a freshman cheerleader, we started our walk across the track to introduce ourselves to the opposing team's cheerleaders, and I knew what was coming. I think I had just forgotten about it with that little sign episode on my mind, but I had been warned. When the JV cheerleaders meet the other squad, there is a game we play. It's an introducing game to build camaraderie with the others, but it has a fun little trick that was a Pure Pine's tradition. Every year, the freshman cheerleaders on the squad, 'the fresh bate,' would declare the guy they liked within the cheer while introducing themselves.

If you'd already moved as quickly as two of the girls there that night, you already had a boyfriend and an obvious name to say. To be fair, one of the two mentioned was actually dating their long-term boyfriend from our class, but the other, let's just say she was calling a senior's name out, and he didn't mind at all. That was the crux of it. You had to say someone, and the hope was you were hot so that someone who caught your eye would be glad you said their name. If you said someone who had no interest in you, then I'm told it felt the equivalent of being in third grade and the entire elementary saying you had a crush on a boy who didn't like you back.

The worst part was that the other cheerleaders, each with their own agenda for someone, were the biggest threat to expose or destroy you if you messed this up for them or yourself.

I had no idea what to say. I hadn't had a boyfriend yet, much less set my sights on an upperclassman. The other cheerleaders were quick to coach us on going for an upper classman being the thing to do. It was a way to exercise your power and get who you wanted to ask you out. The game was in full swing when we started our walk to the other side. It was a secluded end of the track. You would assume it was out of earshot of our team or our own crowd in the stands. They set it up that way so you would feel as if you were making that declaration to the other team's crowd. How this immature game became a tradition and still existed was beyond me.

I racked my brain, thinking of someone safe to say. Some guy friend who wouldn't care that I used his name, and we could laugh about it later. That was the thing about Pure Pines; I didn't have a guy friend high enough on the social ladder to use. The options were to link yourself purposely to someone safe, and not necessarily cool, and that was just suicide if you ever hoped to get asked out... or take a chance and say a name that may not say yes back.

The first option that came to mind was Adrian, but not because of our little moment in the hallway, just because he was the first thing on my mind after it. I hadn't had the time or the wits about me to overanalyze the situation into the possibility that the whole encounter happened because he potentially wanted me to say his name. That was the furthest thing from my mind.

"Okay. Spill. Who are you saying?" Devin Scott halted the group just to get me to tell them beforehand. I stammered. "I..."

"Come on, July, we've talked about this. We already know who everyone else is going to say, so just tell us already."

"You know, I was thinking I could just say..." *Come on, just say him! Say, Adrian. If it comes out and backfires, and he's pissed, you could just say that was your little inside joke; he probably even meant it to be.* The conversation continued in my head well past Devin's patience.

"Just set her up then." Brooke was usually sweeter than the others, but even she rolled her eyes at us being down to the wire.

"Yeah, Devin, you already said we were going to." Hanna, the other minion, broke out."

"Set me up?" I was horrified.

"Trust us, it's for your own good," Brooke added. Devin stood thoughtfully for a moment. "I know, I said we would fix her up; I was just curious who she'd say first."

There it was, that trap she set off in front of me.

"Look, why don't you just say, Corey Bower. He just broke up with Lyndsey Moore, and everyone is looking to see who he'll go out with next. It's the perfect set up. He's a newly single sophomore in line for varsity quarterback, you're a cheerleader. Trust us, he's waiting to see if someone says his name tonight. This works."

I couldn't help but notice Brooke, Dane, and Hanna exchanging looks when Devin offered Corey Bower. He was a sophomore, so it was age-appropriate, but he was on the more popular end, as Lyndsey Moore, who he had just broken up with, was a junior. All of this felt out of my league. I wasn't used to their antics yet and wasn't about to come this far just to set myself up, literally or figuratively. No way did I trust Devin Scott.

As soon as greetings were exchanged with the other team, they did a cheer to introduce us to their crowd. It was time for us to run out and start the cheer that would have us stepping out, one by one. I couldn't help but notice the water boy from our side was suddenly in earshot, as well as the football manager. *Holly shit! This was a thing.* They were all listening!

"'H" CLAP, CLAP, CLAP, "E" CLAP, CLAP, CLAP, "L" "L" "O." "HANNA IS MY NAME, AND CHEERING IS MY GAME, I'VE GOT ELLIOT ON MY MIND, AND OHH, HE'S SO FINE!

"SHE'S A FRESHMAN!" We all chimed in on cue after Hanna went first. My brain was still reeling to find a way out of this. I would just say Adrian's name. That's what I made my mind up to do. With Devin and Brooke still going ahead of me, I calmed myself, practicing his name in my head. And then I heard it out loud with the crowd roar from our side.

"Adrian Reed off the twenty-yard line, and that's—OH, HE SCORES!!! Ladies and gentlemen that's a touchdown for Pure Pines at the hands of number 44, freshman ADRIAN REED!"

The announcer's voice ricocheted over the loudspeaker, and we turned and cheered toward the field before we composed ourselves to continue with introductions to the visiting team. I don't know what happened to me at that moment. I could ask myself to this day why hearing his name over the loudspeaker suddenly made me feel insignificant or less than I already did, but somehow, hearing them say it out loud like I was about to in the cheer felt so revealing.

I didn't know Corey Bower and didn't care what he thought of me. I did know Adrian, and I couldn't set myself up for that kind of rejection should I have misread earlier that day. *Plus, look what he just accomplished. He may have girls flocking at his feet and want to take whatever that was back.* I was up... I didn't know Lyndsey Moore very well either. I had to hope she was happy with the breakup.

"JULY IS MY NAME, AND CHEERING IS MY GAME; I'VE GOT COREY ON MY MIND...," and that's where it landed.

By the time we walked back to our home side, people were still screaming Adrian's number out of excitement. The band was playing our fight song, and on a quick time out, the couple of guys that made it to the water cooler were high-fiving each other and looking our way. Corey was one of them. Brooke pushed me forward as we passed, and he shot me a wink. Okay, so that didn't backfire yet. Our torn sign over by the far corner of the track reminded me of the moment with Adrian again, that and everyone chanting his name from our stands. I did a herkey clapping toward the crowd, then turned to look toward the field.

Adrian was sifting through a succession of high-fives from the team, and just as I looked for his face to see his crowning moment, I saw him cut a glance toward Corey, then back at me. His brow furrowed as if he had just heard. Then a whistle blew from the ref, and his helmet was back in place, leading him out onto the field. My heart sank into my stomach. I tried to tell myself it was a look about something else, or even if it was over that, he might have just been surprised that I said, Corey. I couldn't think it was that he anticipated me saying his name, especially after the success he achieved. He had to be on cloud nine.

I, however, had bigger worries and should have been in complete fear of Corey Bower's wink or one Lyndsey Moore watching from the stands. Brooke and Hanna congratulated me and looked excited that their little setup played well. Devin, however, did not look so excited. She kept looking at me, then Corey, as if she was watching to see if he checked me out again after the initial reveal.

I never figured out the Adrian moment, but the Corey situation was found out that Saturday night at the infamous Tomlin Twins' party. I was automatically invited that freshman year as a JV cheerleader. I received some pretty telling intel, probably inadvertently down the pipeline, from Devin herself, so I would know... *hands off!*

Basically, Devin was interested in Corey, but she didn't want to be the rebound or put herself out there if he was still hung up on Lyndsey. Only time would really tell if he intended to get back with her. Devin thought she'd use me as bait. If Corey was curious or the least bit interested when I called his name, then she would know the coast was clear to start moving forward to pursue him. She certainly had my number from the beginning.

No way would I compete with her over a guy who was practically a stranger to me. However, she didn't have Corey... by the time we arrived at the party that year, Corey and Lyndsey were lip-locked and mugging down in a historically memorable make-out session. I guess neither Devin nor I got the name we wanted that year.

I was halfway through the Monday I'd been dreading and on to athletics, the hour and a half I'd been stewing over the most. I expected to get shit in the locker room, or just be completely exiled for a day or two, but I had no idea what was coming from Coach Craig.

When I walked in the locker room one of the guys started a slow clap until the others caught on and joined. To add insult to the sarcasm, my #44 football jersey I'd turned in was hanging on my locker ready to wear. That part was actually kind of sad or made me feel bad for them. They could have spray painted it or slashed holes in it. No, they were set to forgive me if I came back to the game.

"Bro, just tell us all you had mono or some shit, but you're better now and we can move on with the rest of the season." Billy Aiken came up behind me with his hand on my back. The fact that they were sincere made it hard not to mean something to me, but it was also the worst part. It meant they just didn't get it. If I'd gotten behind on grades and dropped out to be a stoner, nobody would give me a second look. We didn't really have that luxury in Pure Pines. That would be worse than getting arrested. This was because I was choosing another sport and ultimately myself over them. How could I make them understand that "them," the team, was only going to last about six more weeks of games if they were lucky enough to make it to playoffs. It was a fleeting moment next to the scholarship I had to land to set up my career path.

I'd been over and over this in my own head, then with coach, and now this. Even prepared for it, I wasn't in the mood. There was no way to make them understand without insulting them. How could I tell them that three or four of them, the very guys begging me to play, would drop out before two-a-days started next Fall. Or, that one or two would be injured and have no choice. I wasn't above anybody with this decision. It was a tough one to make. I was just in a position where I had to make it.

I tried to smile my way out of it. "Sorry guys. It's just something I gotta do."

"Oh, I get it, it's not us... it's you." Billy's comical jester went a little too dark to remain friendly. A locker slammed behind me.

"You think you're that fast, Reed? You fucking better be. If we lose again next week, I'm coming after your sorry ass, and you won't have to worry about a potential football injury."

My jaw tensed as I turned my eyes from Billie to look behind me at the fat linebacker of a senior that took this to a whole other level. It was hard for me not to call him "Bubba" as I slammed my locker harder and turned to face him.

"You want me to hold you to that Lance? I think everybody in here heard you. Sounds like a threat to me. Hell, we don't even have to play catch me if you can. What are you up to now, two twenty? I'd hate to make you run. Why don't you just crush my ass right here? But you better do it now, and you better finish the job, because no way will you get another opportunity. I don't do ultimatums especially waged on you fuckers winning without me." I stepped closer toward his face, letting him know I wasn't intimidated and had no intention of backing down. Lance looked away and dropped his head. I knew he didn't want to fight me.

"Look, we're all friends here, and we've had a good run of it, no pun intended." I actually did get a few laughs from my friends in the back on that one. "You don't need me out there. I make one small part of the game easier by playing my position well. That's it. That's the formula behind it. Don't sell yourselves short. You find somebody else who wants that position, or you make every other position that much better so nobody misses this cocky bastard. If you guys want to win, it's got nothing to do with me. Don't make me your lousy excuse."

There was a pause before Lance extended his hand and we hugged it out. Billy grabbed my jersey and tossed it, and the rest of the locker room jumped in to give me a sendoff. I didn't deserve it from them, and I'm certain they didn't all feel the way the collective celebration would suggest, but I won a crowning moment out of it. Or, at least I didn't have to worry about getting jumped behind the school dumpster one night.

"Hey, ass holes! You change into your tutus yet? Everybody signed Adrian's "get well soon" card since he lost his mind, I hope. Now get dressed and get on the field. Now!" Coach Craig ordered the team out.

I turned back toward my locker to start getting changed while the guys rushed past and out of the locker room as quickly as they could. I could feel Coach Craig standing and staring behind me. I had no interest in challenging him or dealing with whatever he was about to propose.

"Reed, I'm just curious what you think you're getting dressed for."

"Well, Coach, my schedule still says athletics, and it would behoove me to keep it that way for Spring and the upcoming track season. So, I guess I'm getting ready for whatever you tell me to."

"That's right son. Your schedule says athletics this period, and if you aren't playing football, you aren't in athletics anymore. You're in regular P.E. Now, last time I checked, that takes place in the special ed room or under the bleachers with the stoners. I don't think I've ever seen any of that crew in here in our nice locker room adjacent to the brand-new weight room."

I sighed audibly and dropped my head as I turned to look up at Coach Craig. "Really? Is this really what we're going to do here?"

"Well, Hell son, I don't know what you're gonna do. I would have never bet on you quittn' ball on us, but as you said it was your decision. Now, I guess you can make a decision between playing football and running drills with the team in your scheduled athletic period or you can choose P.E. and I don't want see your face in my locker room."

"Wait a minute. You can't do that. I'm in athletics, I lettered in football, track, and basketball last year. I have every right to be in athletics."

"What did you think, boy, that you'd just get to run around the track all day to your heart's content, prepping yourself for spring?"

"Well, yeah, there are dumber ways than that to go about winning state. So, you intend to punish me? You lose out on a wide receiver, so you make me lose out on track? Is that the logic behind this? You have plenty of guys in athletics that don't do football. You've got them working drills and training for their other sports, it's the way it's done."

"It's not the way I'm doing this. Now, I've got dedicated players you used to stand beside out there on our field, and they're waiting on me. I suggest you get dressed and join them or get lost. Hell, I don't care what you do if it's not on my field."

I was fuming. I knew I should leave it, but no way would this prick be my obstacle. "Hey coach, I guess that's what you meant when you always told us to "give 'em Hell."

"You smart aleck little shit. I made you out there on that field and you're gonna go reap my benefits somewhere else?"

"YOU overlooked me until I got so fast, I was invited to your party. I came, I participated, I've already fucked my knee once for you, and now I don't want to be a part of it anymore."

"I told you I would handle that, and I did. You're first-string varsity football and my wide receiver to take us all the way this year... How do you think that's not gonna get you a scholarship unless you just don't wanna play ball for a major university? I don't understand you, son? I can help you get there."

"With all due respect, coach, how many football scholarships have gone out of Pure Pines to a major university?"

"That's all before I got here... you gotta' look at my track record with players."

"Have a little faith in you, huh? It's my education. Aren't you supposed to have some in me? And, what you really meant earlier was, if I don't get injured again, that's how you can help me go all the way. That's a big fat if for a wide receiver in Texas high school football, coach." My eyes purposefully drifted down to the two gnarly scars on the coach's knee.

"Yeah, well, I guess we don't always get what we want. Your choice, Adrian. Suit up or get out."

July

"CHAMPAGNE SUPERNOVA"

Oasis

My day took a different turn after lunch than anticipated. I didn't care, though; I was grateful for any distraction from the weirdness of needing to avoid Lynn's questions and bumping into Adrian at all costs.

Reagan was our class president and student council vice president, so she was tied up prepping for homecoming votes. Mr. Mc-Clendon had stopped me in the band hall and asked that I take the drill team's measurements to Mrs. Tandy; he informed me she was in the girls' athletic wing meeting with the cheer sponsor. Principal Sabella made them order the drill team's uniforms through the cheerleading program, a sure sign we had been impressive enough to invest in.

All the band money came from the band booster parents, who held fundraisers. It was used to buy instruments and for band trips. Passing us off to the cheer sponsor meant Mrs. Tandy got us more money. As much as I was going to loath walking into the cheerleader's room, I was proud of the task at hand.

The athletic wing of the school was amazing. Instead of the high school gym separating the girls' locker room and the boys' on either side, the gym was flush against one wall with an arena of stadium seating upstairs surrounding the basketball court. The double doors in and out of the gym led to one huge athletic department. Two separate staircases gave the illusion that the athletic department was separated into girls on one side and boys on the other. However, walking down the stairs on either side would take you to your destination. The weight room was the divider. It separated everything in the middle. Walking across or past it or swinging left in front of it from the girls' staircase would lead you to the girls' locker room. There were some small dividers in between, such as cheer P.E., "the cheerleaders" room. It was mostly just for changing clothes after practice or meetings, as everything they did took place on the field or gym floor. Then, there were a few coaches' offices and the shop teacher's office in between and further down the hall.

That said, I had never seen any path crossing to the point I thought it was set up oddly or unsafe. The girls' locker room was appropriately spaced away from the guys, and even with the glass walls making the interior of the offices visible throughout the entire area, the locker rooms and the cheer P.E. room were not transparent. Plus, there was never a reason for the coaches to pass by the little section carved out for girls. Of course, we could all see the guys no matter where you stood. They had more rooms, more stuff, and larger locker rooms for football pads. Mapping this out still doesn't quite help me understand what I saw, much less experienced, but it is how it happened that Monday.

I ran down the boy's athletic steps and beelined toward the cheer P.E. room. Anyone down in the area would have been in the locker rooms, changing for class. We had a good ten or fifteen minutes before the bell. I passed the weight room, and before I knocked on the cheer room door, one of the glass window offices two down from it caught my eye. It was a scene I recognized, but Principal Sabella wasn't included this time. Adrian sat across from the assistant coach and Coach Craig. Coach Timpson, who had been my freshman English teacher those years back, stood above them all with his arms folded. Adrian's face was redder than I had ever seen, and he was working hard to explain himself. I couldn't hear anything, but I saw enough to know Coach Craig was screaming at the top of his lungs when he interrupted Adrian and lunged toward his face from across the desk.

In self-preservation, I stepped back to the cheerleading door, and my fist was knocking before I consciously ordered it to.

"We're changing in here!" Hanna announced. The old me would have barged in and said, "Nothing I haven't seen before." A sentiment that would have been appropriate now, but I'm not sure welcomed, as I no longer felt welcome with my former friends. Friends. I should apply Lynn's joke and use that term loosely when referring to this bunch.

Mrs. Palmer, my old cheer sponsor, opened the door to let me in. "Well, hello, July. It is so wonderful to see you."

"Thanks, you too."

"I saw you ladies knock 'em dead last week, it's a shame our boys didn't do the same."

"Well, then again it could be because you're not their coach!" We shared a laugh, but the joke more than hit home for me. I couldn't get Adrian's red face out of my head or the way that vulture was lunging at him.

"Ladies, we have a visiting friend of yours."

"Oh, no, I'm here for Ms. Tandy. I've got the new uniform measurements for her." I looked at the varsity cheerleaders, listening intently as they changed for our next period. I hoped they didn't think I thought I was working my way back in through this little drill team charade. Some of their faces suggested it.

"Oh, she just left. Here, let me grab the order sheets and we'll put all of these together. I'll give you a copy of what we worked on for Mr. McClendon and you can leave me a copy of the measurements. Deal?"

I smiled and nodded. I couldn't help but notice the cabinets on the back wall across the room. They had our drawers for our things, and you could still see part of the "J" where mine used to be labeled. I guess mine and last year's graduating seniors were the only ones that had to change. I tried not to stare when I read

Natalie Hilliard's name across my drawer. She was a sophomore who had made varsity this year. She could tumble well and was a very sweet girl. I sounded like my grandmother complimenting someone in my head as I tried to justify my way out of feeling the sting.

Wendy Tomlin, one of the Tomlin twins and a senior on the squad, raced by me, buckling her platform sandals as she ran. She leaned up at me on her way out the door and pecked me on the cheek, "You'll be there Saturday, yes?"

"If I make it through this week!" She took that as a yes and bolted out the door without closing it.

"Oh, come on, I'm half naked here." Devin screamed from the back of the room by the cabinets."

"Sorry! I'm late for Chem lab!" Whitney shouted back, running full speed out the door and up the boy's stairwell.

I was still waiting for Mrs. Palmer to return with the order forms, so I politely moved toward the door to shut it. I was only five feet away, but it had swung open wide, exposing all the girls changing in the room. I walked up and heard male voices coming out of the weight room. It wasn't our guys. I think it was Coach Bartlett's voice, and I could see Coach Dodge approaching me. *Wait, what?* If I could see Coach Dodge, then he could see... As I raced around to reach the open door, my eyes met Coach Dodge. His eyes were glazed over as he stared straight into the room of changing girls.

They were too far away to hear their voices and had been gabbing since Wendy's exit, so I don't think they noticed. I'm sure Devin naturally assumed I had moved to shut the door as planned. A cold chill ran through me as Coach Dodge finally brought his eyes to meet mine and realized I was standing there and saw the whole thing. How incredibly creepy. There was nothing normal or even TV sitcom funny about it. It was strategic, and I felt sure he'd stepped into it before as I noticed he was careful to walk directly down the path that gave him a line of sight inside the room.

Meanwhile, Coach Barlett, whom I hadn't seen but recognized his voice, veered toward the offices. I shook my mind clear of what I'd just witnessed, and as I heard Coach Barlett's voice trail away from the area, something came over me. I thought of the office Adrian was held hostage in, and how it was perfect timing for Barlett to walk by, only he wouldn't see it. At first, I think, I ran out to feel safe and to confirm it was, in fact, Coach Barlett out there. He was a good guy. I had him for history, and he set a clear precedent of making us all feel he put our well-being first on and off the field. Coach Bartlett was older, more distinguished, and far more intelligent than Coach Craig, Coach Timpson, and apparently young "Chester Molester" Coach Dodge. I say young... he must have been thirty-two or so, but he had a youthfulness about him, and most of the girls swooned and talked about how hot they thought he was. He just lost my vote.

Coach Bartlett was also the track coach. Even though our school was run by football, there was no question that Bartlett had more invested tenure, esteem, and a literal track record to show for it above Coach Craig. He took us to state last year in track, and he's the one who made Adrian fast by giving him his workouts the summer before our sophomore year. At least that's what Lynn told us when she would joke and call Adrian Forest Gump for an entire summer of seeing him running down their street back and forth every time she looked out her window.

When I shut the door, I realized I had committed to walking out of the cheer room and standing directly before Coach Dodge. My eyes were sharply fixed on his caught-in-the-act expression, but what I had in mind to do next took far more guts. I looked away from Coach Dodge, letting him off the hook so I could chase Coach Bartlett. It was him. A sigh of relief went off in my head, and I took a giant diagonal leap in front of his path and grabbed his arm more dramatically than necessary. I was so glad to see him. He was short-cutting to head straight down to the offices on the other side of the weight room, and if he had just taken two steps forward and looked up before changing course, he would have seen Adrian with Coach Craig and the others.

"Coach Bartlett!"

"July. Is there a fire somewhere?"

"No. I-I'm just glad to see you." I tried not to look too crazy, but there was something about my desperate energy that seemed like it would get his attention quicker. At this point, I didn't care if I embarrassed myself. How could I, after Coach Dodge. I think he won the award. My hand still tugging on his arm, I looked back toward the cheer room and the glass office a few doors down. Adrian's red face was still there, and Coach Timpson was pacing while Coach Craig continued ranting. It could have been incredibly awkward for me had they not all still been in there.

"July! What is going on... are you okay?"

That's what I meant about him. He asked if I was okay first, instead of demanding I let go of his arm.

"Um, I am, Coach Bartlett, but I stumbled on someone or something I think is *not* okay." God, I wished in the back of my mind that fucker Coach Dodge was still standing within earshot, wondering if I was throwing him under the bus. That would have been priceless.

I stepped backward, pulling him by the arm I grabbed. "I just think there is a conversation happening that you should be a part of." I looked back toward the office and saw Adrian looking at me through the window.

I can only imagine what he saw until Coach Bartlett came into view... me pleading and pulling a grown man's arm. The look on Adrian's face was a combination of déjà vu, confusion, and horror. Coach Bartlett looked at me and then in the direction I was insisting on, and he immediately got it. He stiffened, releasing his arm from my grip, and took two over six-foot-tall-man strides toward the football office. He and I were standing to the side of it, and anyone in the office could have seen us. From what I could tell, Coach Craig and the assistant were talking to Coach Timpson, and Adrian was shaking his head in disbelief. He looked back over at me. His eyes changed instantly when he saw Coach Bartlett standing there. I could only hope it was a good thing. Coach Bartlett looked down at me.

"Well, why didn't you just say so, July? It looks like I'm late for a very important meeting." He looked at me and nodded to confirm

I did the right thing. "I better get in there." He walked past me and straight into the office. I wanted to hang out and see Coach Craig's face when Bartlett laid down the law, but I didn't want to make Adrian nervous. I had one thousand percent crossed a line and felt I should leave well enough alone while I could. If I could. Let's see. So far, superhero July caught a peeping Tom and sent in relief for Adrian that he did not ask for and potentially did not need. Wow. For somebody with no real business to speak of, I was undoubtedly into everyone else's.

The bell rang, and I flew up the girls' athletic steps. I would have to go back for Mrs. Palmer's order sheet later. I needed to get out of everyone's way. It was time for Superman to find a phone booth and change back into Clark Kent. *What the hell was wrong with me? What did I just do?* The craziest part about it was that I couldn't even over-analyze why I did it.

Standing there, terrified of potential problems it might have caused, I inherently knew it was the right thing to do. I would do it again, no matter how crazy it was. I didn't understand what they were talking about, but I knew it had to do with Adrain quitting football, and I knew Coach Craig had already mistreated him for it once. Anything past what had already gone down in the office that day would have been abusive. Principal Sabella was little to no help. I just brought in the only person left who could be. Right place, right time... *right?*

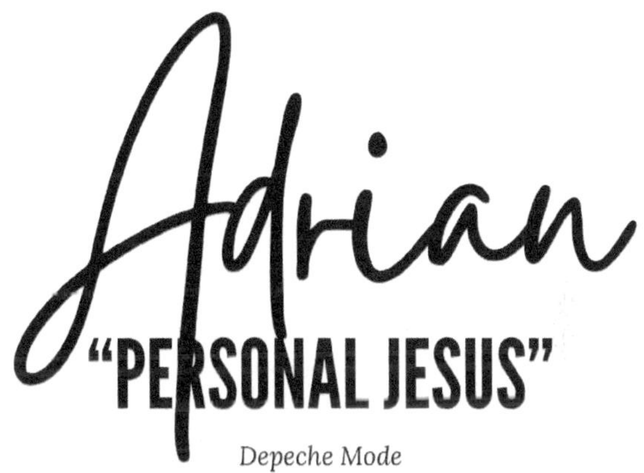

She didn't pick me. She didn't say my name. That's all I remember from that moment our freshman year. That, and... well, that ass. I was walking down the hall from an early dismissal. Like a massive dork, I didn't want to go home. I was too excited about the game, so I thought I'd head to the athletic room and focus. When I saw the painted sign surrounding, forgive me again, the most incredible ass I'd seen. I assumed it was Devin or maybe Brooke... no, it was Devin's ass.

To my surprise, a much prettier, more familiar face peeked out from underneath it. I don't know what came over me after that. It was just some stolen moment. She was familiar. But everything about her was new, *better*. I was standing so close I could smell her hair. Her dark brown eyelashes fluttered up at me. It was like seeing a deer slow and stop in front of your car instead of darting out in front of you and ruining everything. It insists you watch it cross before you, gifting you this suspension in time that no one else is on the highway.

I saw that once. My headlights across a deer's face, making its eyes dance back at me. It was the night I drove my car for the first time, with permission, but it was technically illegal to do it on my own with just a learner's permit. It was so strange, not just the feeling that I could have hit it by mistake and ruined my car had this gone any other way, but that it walked out and dared me not to. It was the deer that was in complete control of two lanes.

July was someone I'd known all my life, but she was showing me who she was for the first time. I don't know. I guess I thought she would always be who she was in sixth grade or something like that. She was daring me not to watch her, and I liked it. To say she surprised me, or I was taken aback by her that day, was an understatement.

We joked about the stupid run-through sign. I made her get paint on herself. It was childish, goofy, and foolish but sexy as hell. It was new territory that she and I embarked on that day. *We were flirting.* We had never done that before... not like that.

That night, I was so excited about the game. I just felt something in the air. I watched from a distance as the cheerleaders began hoisting up our sign. There was a comical "N" worked into where it was left out, and an arrow was drawn from it to where our paint smudge had been on what used to be a flag, but instead, it was a colossal bull's eye. I laughed out loud. I knew it was for me. Somehow, she had not only corrected the spelling error on the sign, but also found our joke by making one up to make sense of the sign that didn't. I was fueled with excitement for the rest of the game. I guess I was... giddy. So strange how something so small can make all the difference in the world.

When I looked up and saw the cheerleaders walking to the other side, I felt invincible the minute I had the ball in my hands. I knew I wouldn't let it go until I made the touchdown, and I did make it. My name was called across the game, and a few minutes later... I don't know what happened. I can't remember if I looked up, hoping to hear if she said my name, or relieved when I heard she didn't. I just scored the touchdown; I could have had any one of those girls, and Corey...fucking sophomore Corey Bower, the best of JV. Please. He would have been on varsity if he was as good as I was as a freshman. Besides, I may have earned my spot on the varsity team in that moment. They didn't notice me before... *How do you like me now?*

Regardless, my name was called on the loudspeaker, not his, and I knew she heard it.

I came back to the present. I must have been sitting in the coaches' office for forty-five minutes when Coach Bartlett finally returned alone. Thank God. I'd had enough of those other assholes. Bartlett was a better man, an actual educator. He knew the way this went down was immature and inappropriate, to say the least. He also knew that if he was going to rip anybody a new once, it wouldn't be in front of me like Coach Craig had talked to me in front of Principal Sabella and all the other coaches. They would never understand Coach Craig didn't just disrespect me; he disrespected them, too.

"Alright, Adrian. We've got it all sorted. That bastard. Why didn't you come to me? You know what they're like. Hell, son... did you think he'd throw you a party?"

"Well, I thought it was my own decision, so I was prepared for a reasonable amount of consequence." The Coach shot me a look.

"This is Pure Pines, that'd be your first mistake. Plus, you know how good you are. That's his fault not yours. Sign of a bad coach. Somebody who can't afford to lose their best player is somebody who doesn't know how to coach anybody else to be the best."

"I guess I was banking on that. That maybe being a coach is what he was here for, not his own accolade for taking a team as far as he could."

"Uh-huh." Coach Bartlett's eyes twinkled at me with a load of sarcasm as he tossed a toothpick in his mouth. "I think that outta' tell you right there why I don't coach football. Son, anytime somebody tells you that something is everything... that's the first sign you better start looking for something else. And, that you did. I've got to hand it to you."

"That's exactly why I didn't come to you with it. It was my decision; I didn't want you implicated. So how did you work it out with Coach Craig?"

"Let's just say I implicated myself and made it between me and him. He thought you were his star wide receiver, and I let him know real quick you were my state track champ. I let 'em think I was an old man and needed the win, then I left him with the challenge of not being a good enough coach to survive your exit. Better for him to be in a pissing contest with someone closer to his own age. It's really the only kind of competition he understands."

"That rudimentary and barbaric?"

"Oh, come on son... surely you remember my social studies class, and if you don't, a comic book works too." We chuckled at the Neanderthals that made up Pure Pine's finest. "So, you report to me in athletics. Now, I don't have that period this entire semester. I won't be with you daily until track season obviously. But same as we set it up last summer... I leave you the training drills, you do the work. Coach Craig will still observe you on the track and be responsible for your grade until Spring, but you won't have any more problems out of him."

I nodded in acceptance and was grateful to be under his jurisdiction. I slid my chair back to stand up, stretching to leave. "I don't know how to thank you for coming through for me. It was looking bleak."

"Well, I guess you really don't have to thank me... you never asked for my help. You could thank a pretty unforgettable con-cerned citizen. Good God son, she nearly broke my arm to get to you in time." He studied my face for a reaction. "I just think that's a good damn deal to have one like that looking out for you. I'm not sure how you achieved it, but I wouldn't mess that up if I were you. You don't get too many of those in Pure Pines."

I half smiled, super confused. I think I even zoned out a second. The coach rose to exit as well. I felt a supportive hand slap my back.

"Reed? Don't think about it too much, son. It'll hit ya right one of these days, if not, it'll hit somebody else. Boy, I'd hate to be on the loosing end of that mistake. See you on the track."

The coach waved as he exited. I stood in the office, exhausted and dumbfounded from what felt like an all-day event. That, and Coach Bartlett's mention of July. I recalled looking at her from the office and seeing him standing beside her. I'd never felt so relieved in my life. Not just that, but the fact that it was her. It was overwhelming in a good way I can't really describe. Having someone know you needed something that you didn't even imagine available to you. It was a kind of awareness or discernment for another person that a lot of perceptive people have, but don't put themselves out to act on. *I guess she just did... for me.*

Still, that freshman game night, when the cheerleaders returned to our side, Corey got a high five and threw July a wink. I felt sick to my stomach for a second. Funny how things work out. I'm sure I remember him being back with his girl by that next week.

I didn't expect her to pick me, at least not the day before or even that morning. It's not like I planned our little paint sign moment. It just happened. Even if I felt a twinge of relief not to be tied down to anyone after my small moment of glory, I couldn't help but feel empty-handed that night. I just kept thinking. She didn't pick me. She didn't say my name.

BEE
THE RIGHTE
YOU'VE LOST TH
Verve

July

"LOSING MY RELIGION" PART 1

R.E.M.

It was finally Friday. I had managed to dodge everyone I needed to. Lynn had an insane chem quiz and relatives visiting from out of town. Reagan was taxed with the Student Council and Honor Society, and we were all trying to get it handled before the party of the year. The Tomlin Twin party was finally happening on Saturday.

I hadn't seen Adrian since I led coach Bartlett to where he could see him that day. That is, other than glances in the hallway, which I tried to avoid. I didn't have to worry about lunch because fall golf had picked up. I had to do Bio 2 lab during lunch just to make it on time to practice all this week for tournament prep. Things would all settle down once debate started. Who was I kidding? They'd get a hell of a lot busier, but at least I wouldn't be alternating a bio lab with everything else on my plate.

Adrian worked at the Pure Pines Country Club, which is attached to the golf course. He waited tables some summers at the Nineteenth Hole, an upscale bar and restaurant casual enough for golfers to lunch or have a highball in their golf cleats. Lynn had mentioned that he was picking up a few shifts there since he dropped football. She said he'd probably work there until debate and track started.

I had steered clear of the golf course's only restaurant all week to avoid bumping into him. How do you go from never thinking of a person and not caring what you say to him to having him occupy your mind all the time?

Adrian and I somehow had nothing whatsoever to say to each other when there was a risk of walking past or being in the same room together. Yet, there was so much more to say than had ever been said.

Even though I was grateful for being busy and not coming head-to-head with this, whatever this was, I still couldn't seem to shake it. The moral support-groping in the office that day and me coming to his rescue with the coaches, appeared to have all died down without explanation. I didn't ask him for one after grabbing me that day, and he didn't ask me for one for my involving Coach Bartlett.

I was glad it disappeared, but I was not happy about the residue it left. Constantly thinking about him, wondering where he was or what *he* was thinking. I felt like I was in junior high all over again. *What was the matter with me?* I was a junior in high school and had never had a boyfriend. I laughed to myself. That's what this was. He stepped close to me, and I smelled him... it's human nature.

I would have thought nothing of it if I had been dating somebody. This was nothing. However, not having a boyfriend yet might have been a bigger problem than having Adrian on my mind more than I could understand. *So?* I was so unbelievably busy. I had never had time for a boyfriend. That was it, right?

I immediately thought of the girls at our popular table. *Was it them that kept me from having one*? Had I not gone out with anybody because *they* didn't assign anyone to me? *Ridiculous.* Or was it far worse... no one from my class or the surrounding student body had asked me. *Yikes. That one hurt.*

I wouldn't say I was naïve or a late bloomer but in so many ways... I really was. I knew nothing about the mechanics of sex other than you shouldn't have it until you are married, according to my grandparents and church. My mother's birds and bees speech consisted of two sentences. "Sex is a wonderful, beautiful thing shared between two people who are married." Then, when I was eleven or so, the movie *Dirty Dancing*, the original with Patrick Swayze and Jennifer Grey, came on cable one night. As we neared the end, my mother turned to me and said, "See, she slept with him and now he's leaving."

That was the extent of my sex education, combined with Pure Pines abstinence campaign, which was... if you do it, just don't get caught. Most of us knew each other's dating history and the level of each other's carnal knowledge simply by who we had dated or if we hadn't dated at all yet. But by junior year and age sixteen morphing into seventeen, it started to get a little fuzzy for some.

We were all well-versed in locker room talk. It was quite an education from the upper classmen. That, and you'd have to be blind not to catch someone making out in the parking lot at some point and understand that's not where it ended. Still, I don't know what I would have done on a date or alone in a room with a guy I liked. I was clueless. I don't even think I could say I'd had a proper kiss yet. Not one you could count anyway.

That Friday night was another home game. Lynn, Reagan, and I were practically going through withdrawal from each other, so Lynn invited us over to get dressed at her place and talk party prep for Saturday. It was a big deal to figure out how to get to the most coveted underage drinking party that had been scheduled for months. It took strategy. Luckily, we were Globe Scholars. Having a high IQ comes in handy in these situations. I digress.

Our new uniforms hadn't come in yet, so the slutty Smurfs would ride once again. I still hadn't asked Reagan or Lynn about the one girl on the sideline last week. I guess I would know today if it's something they were keeping from me. The Adrian and Coach Bartlett situation had become the first thing I never told them that year, if you don't count the groping in the principal's office. I was trying not to. The fact that Coach Dodge was a Peeping Tom, I was absolutely going to tell them about, we just hadn't seen each other.

My mom pulled up to Lynn's drive, replaying the weekend's events and wanting to know exactly where I would be. She was flying to Salt Lake that night for a work convention. I would miss her this weekend, but pulling off the party with her away was also easier. She had been told I was spending Saturday night at Reagan's, so my grandparents had already been briefed. I couldn't lie to those two if you paid me. I was grateful it was already worked out.

"So, you'll come home to grandma and grandad's from the game tonight, you're at Reagan's on Saturday night… are you're going to work on debate?"

"Mom, can I please focus on one activity at a time. I've got a game tonight. Plus, I'm going to miss you. I wanted to hear more about your work trip plans on the way over here."

"Well, you know they are far less exciting than your stuff."

I meant it when I asked about her, but I couldn't help that my eyes drifted to Adrian's house as we pulled up to Lynn's drive. I wasn't worried about bumping into him. It was a Friday night. Minus football, he was probably working at the country club tonight. My mom noticed my distant stare.

"What's Adrian up to these days?"

"How should I know? Mom, I don't see him much. Debate hasn't even started yet."

"Well, you know what I always tell you girls… he is *so* good-looking. Far cuter than the riffraff you three pine over. Speaking of riffraff, do I need to worry about anybody this weekend? No new boys? I say that as a question and a statement, July."

"Mom! Why do you make it so hard to wish you a nice time and mean it?"

"Come here." I grabbed my bags from the back, and my clarinet to play in the stands with the band. I leaned in and hugged her back tightly. I always made a memory of the smell of her perfume every time she left. It's a game I played as a kid, and I would get so excited when I would smell her walk in the door on her return. I watched her drive away and tried not to look at Adrian's house as I topped the hill of Lynn's driveway.

Lynn's parents were super successful. They had a big, warm house that was always full of people. I would cherish the moments spent with her family for the rest of my life. The overwhelming and delightful way the house was often full of relatives and strangers, and those rare moments when we got time with just her momma and daddy because her older sisters were out. Some people just feel like summer or Christmas. Her family always felt like Christmas. It was just wonderful to be there.

Without grilling us or standing over our shoulders, her parents instinctively knew what was happening at school. We blamed her older sisters. After all, they'd been through it three times already, and although Lynn was quite unique, I doubt she had any tricks up her sleeve that her sisters hadn't already pulled. Truthfully, I think it was her mother's silent intuition.

She was reserved until she smiled. Her smile lit up three rooms at once, just as Lynn's did. She never scolded or told us not to do anything per se; she just asked a question or two about our plans and nodded when she got the answer she already knew. It was as if she watched over us from afar with this resounding wisdom that made us think twice about pulling anything on her watch. She had a lot of grace that way. It was contagious.

Needless to say, we wouldn't be lying, leaving, or sneaking away from her house the next night. Tonight was rare as we had her house to ourselves for the first time ever. Lynn's parents had gone out to dinner before our game with her dad's work friends, and all her older sisters, well, the ones that still lived at home or came home nearly every night as if they still lived there, were out and about or at work. I don't blame them; I don't think I'd ever want to leave that house if it were my family.

I think it was wild being there by ourselves, for Lynn, too. The three of us raced through the house like children and slid in our socks before time demanded we start to get dressed. Lynn was funny by nature and always full of surprises. Although her car stereo played obscure Southern and East Coast Rap from Master P to local artists the guys she dated had recommended to her, she had a vinyl record player in her house she would often use to catch us off guard.

While Reagan hogged the hot sticks and curling iron in the bathroom, I began to do my eyeliner in a mirror in Lynn's bedroom. Lynn had put a "Best of the Bee Gees" record on and was in the back room digging through her older sisters' closet for something to wear to the Twin's party the following night.

"Look, I know we'll pick up Devin, Brooke, Hanna, and them, that's not quite all sorted yet, but let's just do our thing. They can come in with us, but we're not responsible for them, and

July..." Reagan yelled loud enough for Lynn to hear her in the back bedroom from the bathroom. "Don't get involved in Devin's bull shit. I know you two go way back, but she's a shit friend."

"If one could even call her that!" Lynn chimed from her sister's closet.

"Guy's, I've barely talked to Devin twice this semester. We're giving them a mercy ride as far as I'm concerned. There are way more upper classmen there with allegiance to us. The party is not Devin's homecoming court, it's our party more than theirs."

"Here, here! Nicely done. Just, we're not letting her fix any of us up or going for that crap when she says somebody's into one of us or tries to play match maker, deal?"

"Reagan! You're preaching to the choir on that one. I've learned my lesson with her. Besides, you're the one she hasn't tried to fix up in a while. Careful there, I think they've lost interest in me." I finished my mascara and moved on to our signature red lipstick.

Lynn yelled from the back, "They don't ever pull that crap with me or try to fix me up 'cause I'm a black girl! They wouldn't know what to do with me."

"Date one of their guys and they would." Reagan's quip was unbeatable. I laughed so hard that I almost choked. The needle moved on the music we'd been shouting over, and "How Deep is Your Love" by the Bee Gees began playing on the record player. "I love this song!" I announced. "Can I turn it up?"

"YES." They both replied in unison. "*Familiar eyes in the morning sun,*" I repeated the first words of the opening verse out loud to myself as I got up, barefoot in my flesh color tights and sporting my makeshift NFL nightmare of a dance uniform. "What a great lyric." I turned the corner from Lynn's hallway at high speed to slide on the carpet in my tights to the record player.

I was already running before I saw something tall blocking me at the end of the hallway. I couldn't stop until it stopped me. Before I could take a breath or scream anything to prevent it, I slid and smacked into Adrian's chest. We hit with such great force, I knocked him onto his back. A slight growl of surprise gurgled out of his throat as we hit the floor together, and my head bounced onto his chest.

I don't know how many seconds went by, or what exactly happened to my brain and body during the most humiliating fall of my life. However, I felt arms tight around my waist, a hand bracing my back from the fall, and my legs were tangled in his. I looked up toward the record player to get my bearings and perhaps, I don't know, attempt to fly off him? He looked down at me and then at what I was looking at. "Yes, this is a great song."

Oh. My. God. There was no telling how long he had been listening.

"I... I am so sorry." I stammered, trying to get up from where my chin rested on his chest, almost touching his neck.

"Up until this point I would have said you've been trying to avoid me."

I felt his voice vibrate through me, and I knew he'd noticed. His smile was dangerously effective as he looked down at me lying on his chest. I could smell him again, consuming my senses in ways I wouldn't admit.

Since willing myself off him from that position had not proven to work. I decided to roll off him to the side before I literally inhaled and visibly sniffed him the way a dog goes in for a whiff of bacon.

Get up! Oh. My. God. Get up before Lynn comes flying in here and sees this, and it becomes another... thing! I was up. I think. I also could have jumped out of my skin. I wasn't sure what was happening. "I am truly sorry."

"Apology accepted. It's not often I'm greeted with that kind of gusto. Lynn's family usually just says, hello."

I stepped back and looked up at him. I guess he was a little taller than I remembered from that day in the office because I was shoeless. He was smiling wildly at me. I wasn't sure how to respond to him.

"How are you?" His face was more serious when he asked. His blue eyes dazzling. I looked down at myself, partly to make sure the limited amount of Spandex was still covering something between vital organs and my dignity.

"Ah, blue, looks like very blue," I said with a smile re: the uniform. I looked up at his neck, and to my horror, he was covered in my red lipstick... not kiss or lip shapes. When I fell on him, my mouth must have grazed those spots on his neck and cheek. *Wow. It just keeps getting better.*

"Yikes."

"What?"

"Umm... you are very red in a few—" I stepped closer, on tiptoes, to point and reference where. I touched my lips to make him understand. "I think I must have gotten you with my lipstick. Umm..."

He seemed to welcome me reaching out to show him, so I continued and tried smudging them off. I stepped back, surveying him, and pointed to his face.

"Should I..."

"Of course, unless you think it looks good on me."

He bent his face toward mine so I could reach better as I used my thumb to wipe my dark red lipstick off his cheek. I was holding my breath as I was so uncomfortably close to his face, but the lipstick was not coming off as quickly as it had on his neck.

I'm afraid when I finally had to exhale slowly, releasing my breath, it gave off a different impression on his neck. My eyes and nose were by his cheek, leaving my mouth open slightly and breathing down his neck. I felt him jerk a little when that happened.

His jaw clenched in that sexy thing men do when they are thinking, withholding something, or about to get serious. He cut his eyes down his cheek to meet mine as best they could, and I saw his chest rise and fall in a deep, tense breath.

"July..." he whispered slowly, almost inaudible, and I felt the side of his hand graze the hand that hung at my side. Warm tingles ran all over my body from the flip of my stomach. *Okay... can't ignore that.*

"My, my... Is this another showing of what we witnessed in the office?" Lynn was standing behind us. This time, I did fly off him. I turned to explain, confident I had a perfect excuse.

"Are you crazy? I basically tackled him to the floor while running to slide across the living room to your record player." When I mentioned the record player, I realized the original song that started it all was over. I hadn't even noticed the next track was playing.

"Yeah, I quit football only to realize having July at your house was far more dangerous!"

Excellent work, Adrian... that didn't sound loaded. We both tried to fake laugh. Reagan descended from the bathroom on cue. "What happened in the office other than Adrian dropping football?"

"I guess Lynn thought I was attacking him the way Coach Craig did." I took the win and went for an even deeper cover.

Lynn rolled her eyes and went to the kitchen to grab something to drink. I knew it didn't bother her because nothing was going on to upset anybody. It's just that it looked like there was. Murphey's Law, I guess. It bothered her that she thought there was something I wasn't telling her. That would frustrate me, too, if the roles were reversed.

I did want to talk to Lynn, but what would I have said? I would look like a fool or look the way I felt, like a kid with a crush. I couldn't like Adrian that way; it wouldn't make sense. And Lynn was his best friend too. It wouldn't have been a fair conversation.

"Hey, grab me a coke if you have one?" Adrian picked up on his friend's response to the situation and resumed his normal behavior.

"Are you done plugging your items into every available outlet? You think I could get in there?" I turned my attention to Reagan, not knowing what else to do. Thank God she picked up on the tension and didn't force the issue or quip back. She watched Adrian's every move as she followed my lead.

"It's all yours. Just use my purple ones in the roller bin. They're already hot." I headed straight to the bathroom to finish getting ready, hoping that was the end of the impromptu visit and an additional awkward notch to add to the Adrian belt I seemed to have buckled around me.

Nothing got past Reagan and Lynn. It was wonderful to have intelligent friends, but even on an off-occasion when they were being selfish, petty, or making something all about them... you could still bet they wouldn't miss a beat.

I started wrapping the ends of a portion of my hair around a purple hot roller. They were hotter than I expected, but I didn't flinch as I clasped the end of my hair with my fingertips, pressing it into the heat until the curl locked and rolled up evenly. I held it in place longer than I should have, the heat burning the pads of my fingers as I stared into the mirror in thought.

Avoiding him, huh? Last I checked, Adrian had made no effort whatsoever to track me down. That was an odd thing for him to say. He was suddenly kind and jovial?

I wish I could have shot back with the truth: The only thing I had been avoiding was getting chewed out if I had made a mistake by bringing Coach Bartlett in. Once I felt in the clear for that, it was dodging his distant stare before my eyes met his, and he cut away from me. I'd say that was business as usual since the sixth grade.

I put the voices in the other room out of my head. I couldn't help but overhear something muffled about plans for Saturday night and whose car was taking who. Then I heard footsteps heading out the front, and there was no longer a distinguishable male's voice.

The beginning of the game flew by, and halftime came and went. I looked for the chunky little freshman on the sideline but did not see her. She wasn't in the kick line, either. I guess she wasn't at the game at all that night.

When we got back in the stands, now fully dressed in our team dance pants and zip-up jackets, our high from just coming off the field from a great performance was lowered by the numbers on the scoreboard. By the fourth quarter, we had lost all hope of winning. I couldn't help but secretly hope we might win for Adrian's sake if only to get the world off his back. Again... *not sure why I cared.*

Out of the blue, some strange commotion erupted from the top bleachers of our band section in the stands. We heard a tuba, and maybe our base trombone started a downbeat. It was a total surprise as the entire band looked behind them to see what was happening. A lone trumpet stood up from the back of our band and started playing the melody of *You've Lost That Loving Feeling.* The cheerleaders turned from the sidelines where they stood facing the field, calling out chants.

It was Jessie Hines on his trumpet. The hot, alternative, part grunge, part musician, truly too cool for school without trying to be, bad boy with a heart of gold, and an exceptionally skilled trumpet player. He was one of the most sought-after seniors in our school and the one who saved us by making the band cool just by being in it. He also got under senior varsity cheerleader Savanna Baker's skin, and rumor had it a whole lot more than that.

Savanna was with Drew Bishop her entire high school career. Drew graduated the previous year, and in true Pure Pines fashion, they continued to date long-distance while Drew was off at college. You had it made if you were a Scott, a Childress, or a Bishop in our town. Savanna had it made by dating Drew, with all salivating over the power couple. Maybe there was more to her than we thought. The unthinkable happened when she fell for Jessie.

I'm not sure what surprised the student body more, the fact that she was tempted by the polar opposite of Drew and found something in Jessie, the fact that he fell for her, or the fact that they acted on it while she was supposedly still in her long-distance relationship with Drew.

Savanna and Drew were preppy and the epitome of what Pure Pines represented. People used to say someone should have painted them on the water tower.

Jessie was a very good-bad boy, and he had every student and teacher charmed without even trying.

No one knows how long their little fling lasted, but it ended quickly once word got out. Drew's mother worked in the administrative office at the school... she was our Mrs. Bishop. Savanna did what any red-blooded American caught cheating does... deny, deny, deny. To Jessie's shock and dismay, she cut things off immediately and completely once they were found out. She could do the crime but wasn't willing to face the time.

Rumor was that Jessie was a bit torn up about it, although you'd never know it by his actions. He had rocked her stuck-up little world; she had been the un-gettable get. The situation had become a stalemate for the past month and simply was what it was until this moment. The bass line supplied by our senior tubas and trombones was light, and the song's first verse was almost undetectable. However, by the second verse, Jessie had the baseline plus some others on their feet behind him, and his trumpet filled the stands with an undeniably recognizable melody.

I couldn't see for certain, but I'm pretty sure my buddy Sarah Weems pushed Savanna forward toward the band section. All the cheerleaders surrounded her, facing the serenade. By the time Jessie's trumpet got to what would have been the "You're trying hard not to show it..." lyric, the drum section, including a triangle, and every upperclassman that knew how to play by ear stood playing the song for Jessie.

The home crowd in the stands even sang it for him when he ran down to kiss her on the chorus. With all that resistance, she didn't even make it through the chorus before allowing his lips on her in public, at a game, where Mrs. Bishop was most likely in the stands with Drew's dad and siblings.

It was the most memorable moment we'd ever witnessed at a Pure Pines football game. This was Texas. We'd seen a lot... a heart attack in the stands, and the game played on as the ambulance rolled away with a dying man. A fight with a rival team that resulted in the entire stadium's electricity being turned off. Literally, the whole place went black, and all our guys could hear was the sound of the other team coming toward them to kick their asses. We had seen it all, but not that. It wasn't the movie-like moment that surprised everyone.

It was the front-row seat to the unabashed truth of the rumor. Even Savanna couldn't deny the charms of the underdog any longer. Someone else had prevailed over a polo shirt and a name, and it felt exhilarating. It was also unique to see true love like that. Two people with an itch they couldn't stand not to scratch, and before it's ignored for too long, one of the hottest guys on the planet demands she acknowledges it... Brilliant.

It didn't even matter that we lost the game. Everyone left the stands and walked out of that place on a high except Drew's parents, I'm sure. Public humiliation is not well received in Pure Pines, not by those who can do something about it.

"Ready to rethink being set up?" Lynn turned to Reagan and nudged her as we watched the two forbidden lovers walk off together. Savanna waited outside the band hall for Jessie that night. It was strange for all of us to see her there, but it felt right.

"Please. I doubt they'd set us up with someone like that. You know the rules, if they don't have the guts to ask someone interesting out, you're not allowed to. No way do I want to see who they'd have in store for me."

As Reagan drove me home from the game, I kept thinking she'd never had a boyfriend either. Sure, she had dated around when a decent upperclassman had asked her out or done her due diligence when the in-crowd had suggested she and whomever would make a great couple.

She really hadn't said much about who she liked or what she wanted. Reagan was a shit and a rebel just to be one. She made straight A's, held the perfect attendance record, and looked like some angel cherub in a painting that came to life. I never knew if she hated what her parents had created and designed her to be, or if it simply wasn't enough for her. Maybe she needed more attention.

The perfectionist in her never faltered, but her behavior got increasingly more erratic as we got older. She'd lay it all out on the table to prove a point and push the envelope, but she was astute at not showing all her cards. I had never known anyone with such control and restraint who was also so impulsive and self-destructive. I don't understand why she felt so restricted and on display when the reality was that she probably could have gotten by with anything.

"You okay?" I had to check. She had barely said anything since popping off about the serenade moment.

"Yeah. Just tired."

I knew she was tired of Pure Pines. It was a lot of pressure. So much so that even an incredibly fantastic moment like the one we just witnessed was a bittersweet reminder that it wasn't the norm. That feeling when Jessie stood up in the stands and defied the system to get the girl... that was an anomaly.

Normal was three hours of sleep a night (if you're lucky) after cramming, being told who you can date, can't date, and who you can ride to the party with (if you're invited). Sliding across Lynn's carpet in our tights like we didn't have a care in the world, that had been a rare moment, too. We all had family dramas on top of the Pure Pines pressure. Yeah, I totally got it. It was fun to witness, just not our reality.

I grabbed my stuff to say goodbye.

"Hey…" Reagan called after me. She turned the music down and smiled with her head tilted in curiosity. I knew she was going to ask me about Adrian. There was a halt instead.

"Never mind. I'll catch your act tomorrow." She smiled, turned the music up, and sped off through my neighborhood. I think she withdrew the question to allow me to keep my secret.

I didn't know the art of restraint. I used to tell EVERYTHING I knew. I think it was an only-child thing… Craving communication with others. For the first time, I believe she sensed I hadn't said anything about something going on with me, and I think that was her way of letting me keep it. It was encouraging, and I felt we were all growing up a little.

July
"LOSING MY RELIGION" PART 2

It was Saturday night, and I don't think we had ever anticipated a party as much as this one. The key was to have as few cars on the road as possible. That wasn't a problem for me. I didn't have one. That was another box I had failed to tick, I suppose. Of course, there were others without cars, even in the elite group. They just had better ways of not broadcasting it. In other words, if you were popular enough, they overlooked that and you rode with them. In a way, I suppose that's how I was with Lynn and Reagan, and I was damn lucky for it.

Lynn parked her shiny yellow and black Jeep at the top of the driveway at Reagan's house to stay there all night. It was less than a year old and already one of her trademarks. We probably should have taken her Jeep with so many to pick up, but again, the trick was not to seem obvious.

Reagan's dad had just moved them into this larger house. It was a new two-story with an attic on top of Reagan's room where she got to hang extra clothes and store shoes, and they also had a pool in the backyard. Her mom, Cynthia, decorated like a professional. The place was gorgeous.

Cynthia had frosted blonde hair and crystal blue eyes like Reagan. She wore black eyeliner like the woman on the show our moms watched, *Dynasty*, and we had never seen her without her false eyelashes. People often suspected she had work done, but the truth was, she was just that pretty. She and Reagan had that doll-face gene. She really didn't need the eyelashes and all that makeup. When Reagan got mad at her, she'd pop off and tell us about how her mother had been nothing but a poor hick from Arkansas before she met her dad, and she'd been climbing ever since.

We wanted to think she exaggerated, but the evidence was all around us. Large, framed pictures of a six-year-old Reagan in a rhinestone-covered twirling costume posed with two batons, a literal foreshadowing of JonBenet Ramsey. A beauty pageant win each year marked her age, and decorated the hallway, the way most parents would represent your height on the wall.

One picture always disturbed me. It was the first one. A four-year-old Reagan with long platinum blonde locks crowned in a pageant dress with a banner across it that read, BEAUTY. Reagan and I met at that pageant when we were four years old. That's how our mothers were acquainted as well. She won "Beauty," and I won "Talent." I must have looked comical next to the miniature blonde bombshell.

My brown hair was curly when I was little, the ringlets surrounding my head hadn't dropped, grown, or straightened far past my ears, and my brown eyes were larger than my face. A poor man's brown-eyed Shirly Temple.

I didn't continue in pageants much longer. It was the early '80s. It's what you did back then. Meeting and competing so young had given Reagan and me an understanding and a sense of normalcy about what went on at Pure Pines.

Take Jessie, the trumpet player, for example. He wasn't just a hot stoner who liked to headbang to heavy metal and terrorize the jocks with the threat of his grunge appeal effortlessly taking their girl...That was just the one thing he had going for himself. And then there was the rest, like going to state as this incredibly gifted trumpet player. The guy was a musical genius.

It was so odd, this set up to push us as if they were preparing us for something greater beyond Pure Pines, yet this reverse logic that Pure Pines was the best. Why did they want us to excel past it if it was so great? None of us minded that part. It was the only motivation to complete their impossible tasks... the chance to put as many miles between us and this place as possible.

Maybe they had to maintain the perfection part for the people who went through the program and didn't fly the coop. The ones that bred more little Palominos that looked just like them and lettered in the same sport they once did. Maybe that's what the contradiction was for.

Ninety percent of our class knew how to read and could count to a hundred before we started kindergarten, and most of us could write in complete sentences. It was simply expected. My mom did not receive child support from my deadbeat dad. That's what they were called back then. If you got a divorce and the dad couldn't hack it or stick around, and especially if he broke the law and didn't uphold child support from the custody agreement, he was a deadbeat.

By four years old, I knew how to swim and dive. I could do a back dive as well. My mother, who didn't like to get wet or play in the water, taught me, well, made me, even though it scared me. I was always afraid I would over-aim and hit the side. I had been in multiple beauty pageants and had several talent acts. I had my first tap, ballet, twirling classes, tiny black ballet shoes, some that mom spray-painted gold for a recital, two pairs of tap shoes, and two batons. In addition, my mom paid for a private school the year before I attended kindergarten. I could count to a hundred in Spanish and sign milk and apple. My mom made sure I had the best for school, and if she couldn't achieve something, my grandparents made it happen for me.

I vividly remember Vacation Bible School at church, playing with the neighborhood kids across the street, and blackberry picking in shorts and flip-flops with my boy cousins who did not warn me to wear jeans. The only thing I can surmise is that I had summers off, and that must be when my mom worked two jobs to pay for all the other stuff.

I didn't pretend to know Cynthia or what it must have been like for Reagan, but I certainly understood. As much as I know how much our mothers loved us, there was something Pure Pines bred and brought out in everyone, and there was a hint of it in what motivated them. It was the same double standard the faculty at school facilitated: education, merit, tradition, values, safety, achievement, and status. Social status. It was an expectation that would not be ignored. Keep your grades up and don't get caught with your pants down, but *do* be a part of whatever gets you votes. If you can't impress your peers, how can you expect to make your mark on the rest of the world... seemed to be their logic.

All the sneaking around to get to the party of the year... If I thought about it, Reagan probably could have walked right up to her mother and said, *"We must go to a house party. There will be no parents there, and plenty of underage drinking. People will lose their virginity, and some will just get high, but we won't drink and drive. The Tomlin twins are throwing it at their mini-mansion. If we don't go, we will lose some of our social status and be less popular with the in-crowd. Is this all okay with you?"*

She could have delivered that speech, and I'm willing to bet Cynthia would have helped her do her hair and told us she just put a fresh tank of gas in the car. But no, we had to do it the hard way and keep up appearances.

"What time are we picking those bitches up again?" Lynn asked as she handed me the smokey plum lip color from her makeup bag. She thought it would be better with my shirt.

Reagan leaned into the mirror, curling her eyelashes, and mumbled, "Should we just not and say we did?" She was back to her old self. Nothing like a party to get Reagan's juices flowing.

I laughed, seeing the moment clearly in my head. "Can you imagine their faces Monday at school if we played dumb and pretended we drove by and waited but never saw them?"

"Damn. That's how you do your friends? You do you, Boo." Lynn jokingly swiped her lipstick back.

"Oh, don't act like you haven't thought about it. We're the ones taking the biggest risk here. It's Reagan's getaway car. When have they *ever* done anything like this for us?" I suddenly had a backbone again and appeared to be taking a stance.

"Reagan, she's getting political on us, and it's about to be a party."

"Lynn's right July. We're going to pick them up as planned, in my car, and we're going to get them to the party simply because we are better at it, and everyone is expecting to see us. I'm not sure they can bank on the same." Reagan smiled at the truth in what she said. Lynn reached over to high-five her above my head.

"Remember last year when Hanna didn't get to come because her mom caught her sneaking out the window? Brooke and I had to go all the way back and get her and got caught too." I was glad I had examples to remind them.

"Oh, I remember clearly," Lynn shot back. "I was the one stuck with Devin the rest of the night and she threw up in the back of my jeep when I drove her drunk ass home."

I looked at Reagan funny. "Where were you?" Reagan looked down a second, pretending to let her mascara dry. "Oh, that's right. You had already gotten a ride!" I tried not to be too sarcastic.

"I let him drive me home. That was it. He was still with that whore, so he was of no use to me. You both know I don't share. He stopped by the party, I let him drive me home. That was all." Reagan ended the discussion.

"How do you just stop by a party you weren't invited to?" Lynn pushed the issue. Kane Frater was our age and an elite from the larger school next door in Prairie. We didn't play them in sports. They were a 4A school. We went to Prairie for almost everything else. Reagan met Kane on a teen night in one of the clubs in the nearest city. I guess he saw something from our side of the Piney Woods he liked.

She gave him her pager number. Yes, Reagan had a beeper, just like a drug dealer. Contrary to what I said about Cynthia earlier, all of which was true, she was also an overprotective mother. An oxymoron, I know. The pager was so she could keep tabs on Reagan at all times.

Kane looked just like actor, Jonathan Brandis. He had the same kind of charm and alternative thing our Jessie Hines had, only combined with Prairie's popular prep status. He was with his long-term girlfriend, Candice, someone we had never met but heard about through the grapevine. Apparently, she was a dirty blonde self-destructive nightmare, the daughter of a coach in Prairie who didn't quite have it together as well as Reagan did and wasn't nearly as pretty. She just held all the social pull in their school group. These boys sure did have their own types.

Kane was attractive; we had to give her that, and his personality was unique. You almost felt sorry for him being stuck with that awful Candice chick until you remembered he obviously had free will to do something about it. We didn't hear too much about the infamous Kane. It was an off-and-on thing between fights and breakups with his steady girlfriend. Reagan didn't give anything away to make her look stupid, but we did witness it ourselves on occasion, like the night they met. Since then, Lynn and I had been painfully aware that it could become a "Kane night" almost every other time we went out with Reagan.

That was the best example of her destructive personality. If she had chosen to shit where she laid and mess with someone else's guy here in Pure Pines, we could have handled it better and almost helped her. But that was the thing about Reagan. *Go big or go home, baby.* She wasn't about to infiltrate herself in front of these tiny townies like Devin Scott and her minions. If Reagan got caught, it would be on a larger scale, and she'd go down in a blaze of glory just to prove she did it better than them.

I had no idea what to expect at the party that night. When Reagan's beeper went off, and she announced it was Adrian saying he was going to head over in an hour, I got an overwhelming rush of fear and anticipation, as well as the depression I had recently become acquainted with since school started. A flood of thoughts and emotion ran through me... That chunky little drill team freshman who wasn't at the game. She missed the epic movie moment in the stands that should have been her right-of-passage to see. My freshman year, when Devin screwed me, and she and I walked in to find Corey, the object of *her* affection, and my setup, back with his girl Lindsey. My old friends in their varsity cheerleader uniforms walking down the track without me, all the other old friends that weren't invited to this party. Then him... When Adrian's face settled on me, and the way it felt when his hand grazed mine and he whispered my name just the day before. Other than the flutter of butterflies, the rest of me calmed down. I looked up just in time for Reagan to throw me a dress and motion Lynn out the door with the family cat.

We were in our pajamas as part of the plan's first step. We had gotten undressed and eaten a late-night snack of toaster strudel with her mom, only to excuse ourselves to go watch a movie in Reagan's room, which would really be us getting dressed for the party. Leaving our pajamas on, we started with our makeup, knowing there was a strong chance her mother would come up to check on us. Lynn hadn't washed her makeup off from earlier yet, so we sent her down in her pajamas with the family cat.

"Hey, Cynthia." Lynn found her dozing on the couch, false eyelashes and all. "I think this one is missing its momma."

"Come here, Mr. Alabaster, snowball baby, poof tail." Cynthia cooed at the cat, offering every nickname in the book as we watched Lynn operate from upstairs. "Thank you, darling. I'm about to head to bed. I'll keep this one in our room so he doesn't scratch at the door and bother y'all all night. He's just a little ladies' man with a poofy tail, aren't you, Alabaster baby." She returned to the fat, fluffy white cat that looked like the one in the Fancy Feast commercials. "You girls knock if you need anything, and don't stay up too late, you'll burn tomorrow!" She threw an arm around Lynn and pinched a dimple on her cheek.

"Good night." Lynn awkwardly half-hugged her back and then bent down to love on the cat in her arms. Lynn hated cats, but she was a pro at handling Cynthia. Reagan and I were terrified of her mother. She could see right through us and always called us out.

Lynn yawned as she strolled back up the steps toward us. The downstairs bedroom door closed behind Cynthia. Lynn's hips started shaking vigorously to each side in a mock Hula dance until she landed in front of us on one knee with jazz hands.

"Get up, turkey!" I whisper-shouted. "We haven't gotten out of the house yet!" It didn't take long to get dressed after that. We were high on adrenaline. I wouldn't wear the slip dress Reagan tossed my way, and she knew it. It was automatically going to be way tighter on me, and if I knew her at all, entirely too short for me, who was, in fact, shorter than her. I squeezed into some Calvin Kline's; I was grateful they zipped. I wore a black belt and set myself up for any top Reagan recommended. Set myself up was the key... She handed me a dark purple long-sleeve body suit. It only had a Brazilian half-butt in the back and alluded that it was a thong if your jeans rested too low on your waist.

"What the Hell?"

"It's a throwback, and just trust me. Go put it on with those jeans and you'll see."

"A throw back to when, 1993, or 86'? It looks like what that actress wore in Crocodile Dundee!"

"Just put it on July." Lynn chose a side. "And take your underwear off. The whole point of the body suit top is not to have an additional panty line." Lynn was happy to explain. I went into the bathroom and removed my jeans to contort into the literal onesie.

"Gross. It goes up my butt crack. I hope this thing is clean."

"Is it?" I heard Lynn's aside to Reagan through the door. It sounded like Reagan threw a pillow at her in response.

Once I figured out the mechanics via where it snapped at the crotch, I could peel into it from the waist up. It was an understated material, soft to the touch but perfectly fitted for style and shape, and it was a gorgeous color of deep purple. A dark plum, the same as Lynn's lipstick. I had to wonder if they didn't plan it.

The body suit neckline was rounded but dipped down into three small white buttons at the bust, giving the illusion of a Henley but on a feminine build. I didn't dare unbutton any of them. The fitted neckline already acted as an automatic push-up bra. I wasn't sporting cleavage or anything, but if you looked at me from the side, you could see the tops of two conspicuous mounds without using any imagination. I was always self-conscious of having a bigger bust than Reagan and Lynn.

I slid my jeans and belt back on and looked at the final product. Lynn had flat ironed my hair, and it looked significantly better than when I simply blew dry it straight. I had to admit, this was a great color for dark brown hair.

When I turned to the side, I noticed when I raised my arms or moved a little, you could see the top of the thigh-high bodysuit rising above my belt and jeans...

"I can't wear this like that!" I flew out of the bathroom, pointing to my exposed hip.

"Wow! YOU LOOK HOT!" Lynn completely ignored my valid concern.

"Shhh! You'll wake my parents up, and yes, you will absolutely wear it. That's how it's supposed to go." Reagan slapped the back of my hand hard, which was pointing to my hips, then covered my mouth so I wouldn't scream. "Let's go!"

Lynn wore dark navy designer corduroys and a cropped baby blue cashmere sweater. She looked so stylish. Reagan threw on the dress she had initially laid out for me, and it was way shorter than I had suspected.

"Wow. Why don't you just wear our drill team uniform?" I couldn't holdback the suggestion.

"What's wrong with this?"

"You'll freeze to death!"

"So will your tits and hips and Lynn's midriff. Now let's get out of here while we're still young!"

July

"LOSING MY RELIGION" PART 3

R.E.M.

Reagan's red Audi Cabriolet had already been moved to the bottom of the driveway so we could start the ignition undetected. We piled in all silently wondering where the Hell the others were going to sit. The others...

So that thing about being one of the three big names in our town, or a varsity cheerleader, one could also add, came from the fact that the elite founders and their descendants owned profitable businesses if not most of the businesses in town. However, the working founders, like my grandfather whose grandfather before him settled here, and owned land, always found that made for an interesting game of adult monopoly.

Since it was hard to point the finger at who had more power, the people who wanted it most made up their own rules to the game. It started with church. This was the Bible belt of East Texas after all. The old adage about the two things you could count on more than anything, being church and football, was a stereotype we absolutely represented. THE church to go to was determined, and after that, all schoolboard members, or anybody who wanted to be one, the chamber of commerce, local teachers, small business owners, and all the popular kids attended that church.

My family didn't get the memo. We had gone to the same church my entire life, and my mother's life before that. It was full of laughter, love, and kind older ladies who baked cookies for vacation Bible school every summer. We sang old fashioned hymns, prayed on Sunday, and shook our neighbors' hands. Every second Sunday of the month we had a potluck in the fellowship hall after church. It was always a big deal to my grandmother to make sure we "fixed something good to take." That was usually her pineapple upside down cake, or fresh baked yeast rolls. I can't imagine it was much different than any other church that offered a food pantry to those in need. It never even crossed my grandparents' mind to change churches or find their religion with the masses.

That's one social club we were automatically left out of. I don't think I was even truly aware until I got to Jr. high and realized that for all those informative years, the people I thought I was friends with, were better friends with each other from going to the same church together all those years. Although, I think it was fair to say we were not picking the others up to take them to Sunday School that night.

"A: It's freezing so don't you dare put the top down, and B: I spent over an hour on July's hair." Lynn set the one rule for the evening, and we were off to Hanna Lewis' house to pick up the varsity cheerleaders in our class. We pulled up exactly when and where we pre-planned, and three girls came running out to the car like it was the most thrilling adventure of their lives. Devin Scott was the only one dressed for the party. Hanna and Brooke looked like they had their sleep shirts on over their jeans.

"Amateurs." Reagan whispered before they opened the car door. Lynn and Reagan were in the front, so Devin shoved me to the middle and Hanna sat on Brooke's lap on the other side of me.

"Ladies!" Hanna shouted in excitement. "We're doing it! Have you been yet, or did you come get us first?"

"Is she drunk?" Lynn asked frankly.

"Well, she started early." Brooke answered as politely as possible. Devin just looked annoyed and kept looking out the window.

"Real smart. Strategic, Hanna." Reagan turned the music up annoyed as well.

"Whatever. It's gonna' be fun or at least I'll be fun!" Have you talked to anybody who got there yet?" Hanna continued.

"Adrian just got there. He said everyone's there, plus some." Reagan offered more politely than before. Reagan loved a party more than anybody, and on second thought could care less about being Hanna's mother.

"Ugh, Adrian." Devin's voice interrupted from the back seat.

That bitch. How dare she say his name like that. She'd do best not to say it at all!

"What's wrong with your boy, Lynn?" Is he out to kill our season? Did somebody hurt his feelings on the team, so he thought he'd take his barbies and go home?" Devin apparently had more to say.

"God you're such a bitch." I whispered half under my breath.

"What did you say, July?" Devin looked over at me letting me know she heard.

"I just think its obvious that he didn't quit to hurt anybody, and it's probably hard enough as it is without people spreading negative gossip. Maybe if everyone focused on making the team we have better, you guys wouldn't miss Adrian on the field."

"Oh my, well I thought I had asked Lynn. I didn't realize I got his girlfriend. When did this start up?" Devin turned her eyes to Reagan and Lynn who were speechless over what had hit a little too close to home.

"Oh, that's mature. So standing up for someone earns the response of an elementary student? You know I have nothing to do with Adrian."

"I don't know... Remember sixth grade when she had a crush on him." Hanna hiccupped as her sentence dropped.

"That's right! I remember that!" Brooke joined in.

"Well, well, I guess my rudimentary assessment was only off a few years, July." Devin turned to face me in the back seat as best she could. "Pray tell, just what is it about the illustrious Adrian Reed that has you so bent out of shape? Does he know? Is there any way I could be of assistance."

"Don't be ridiculous, Devin, you know they're just friends." Reagan took the heat off me.

"Actually, no, I don't. I don't think I've ever seen them... too friendly. Maybe we're embarking on a new phase for those two. Is there something I missed that you all would like to make me aware of?"

"Yes! That people should be able to make decisions without it affecting you, Devin. Can't we just all grow up and accept when somebody quits football or switches classes or—"

"Or doesn't make it?" Hanna's voice interrupted mine with words that silenced the entire car.

"HANNA!" Both Brooke and Lynn screamed in my defense. There it was. The awful truth we all knew that only someone drunk would cop to.

"Yeah, Hanna, you are absolutely right. I can't tumble as well as you all do, and I wasn't good enough to make varsity. That's something I had to accept. Good example." My words stung my own throat and I wished I was the violent type.

"Did you though? I mean, you couldn't just retreat with your tail between your legs, you had to go and make the world start you a drill team so you could still have a piece of the limelight." Hanna was on a roll. Reagan stopped the car.

"Hanna, you're a lousy drunk, and you don't have any rhythm sober, which is why you only made the squad because you could do a standing back flip. I heard on good authority your cheer dance score was a four next to all your nine's and ten's on everything else. I also know that July's cheer score was higher than yours, so you might want to kick it up a notch the next time you're out there." Lynn said a few things you can't come back from.

"Y'all, she's drunk, she'll apologize tomorrow. July, I am sorry for Hanna and for Devin." Brooke looked over at me sincerely.

"You know, y'all win already. If you want to try out for drill team, please be our guests. You know we aren't trying out for cheerleading; we don't do gymnastics. But, then again, y'all didn't twirl either, and last I checked the toe-touch is a very different kind of a split than what we fall into on both legs. So I guess I'm just wondering what makes you so fucking special." Reagan started the car back up and began driving.

"She's right. Y'all sound like a bunch of jealous assholes." Brooke was sober and sweet.

"If you guys think its lame that I'm on the kick line, then I guess I can just quit for you, since that seems to be how we make decisions around here, based off other people's needs." I couldn't help but shoot a glance toward the plotting Devin.

"No, July, you know I support you, and you ladies were great. It's really impressive we have a competitive drill team now, and I mean that sincerely." Devin would have done well to leave it at that. "I just also want to support you in all endeavors, including your happiness. If you like someone, you shouldn't waste any time."

"Knock it off you two! It's supposed to be a party." Reagan turned onto the street of the twins' house.

"And this is one of four times this year we are all supposed to pretend we like each other. You think we can get that right tonight? Only one year left after this one..." Lynn was always the voice of reason.

Devin turned her attention back to the window, watching the party ahead as we approached.

"Hey, speaking of, before we go in... where's Shelby." I asked sincerely. Shelby North wasn't a cheerleader. She'd never had to try out for anything a day in her life, but she was one of them. She just happened to be abnormally gorgeous. She had a 5'7" model body of a figure on a five-foot frame. She had somehow coined the combo of being gorgeous and cute, and all the guys nicknamed her "Cosmopolitan" or "Seventeen Magazine" behind her back.

"She's kind of thinking of seeing Billie. He asked her to the party, so she went with him, but no one is supposed to know yet, because she hasn't quite made up her mind." Brooke seemed keen on explaining.

"Well they know now, Brooke." Devin fluttered her annoyed eyes.

"Could we please get the fuck out of the car, I'm about to hurl." Hanna had the last word before we parked and embarked on the adventure we had all looked so forward to.

The house was alive with action, and you could tell it was busting at the seams with people. The Tomlin house was a phenomenal treat. Most parties were just kegger's in a field somewhere or smaller get-togethers in someone's basement, but this one—Every year the twins' parents took a trip and left them home alone for a week. It usually took them the rest of the week to clean up after the party.

As tense as the ride over was, we all couldn't help but smile at each other with anticipation as we saw all the cars parked and the sheer number of people. The events of the football game had been nothing compared to this. There were alumni who had graduated a couple of years before. It was insane. We scanned the parking lot for cars we recognized as we walked up the drive to the house.

My heart skipped a beat when I saw Adrian's 1967 Mustang GT350. His grandfather, a car enthusiast, and so much more, had it restored for him, and it was a beautiful piece of classic machinery. I felt sick for a second over what Devin thought she revealed. What hurt the most was the truth of it, that Lynn and Reagan must have suspected. In terms of Devin getting wise to me... It was such bullshit. I didn't care what she thought.

Adrian and I had mutual friends and we were on the debate team together, and that's where it ended. Past that we tolerated or had nothing to do with each other. I would have stood up for stupid Corey Bower or Billie Akin had it been them getting dumped on for quitting football. *Wouldn't I?* How I could explain the abundant, recurring butterflies he gave me... I couldn't, but that was none of her business.

I'd already been humiliated over the issue that challenged me most. The cat was out of the bag over their scrutiny of me not making cheerleader this year, and all I had to do was bury my shame and humility and move on. Adrian was not a factor in my life, and

Devin wasn't about to make him one. It was a party. It was time to act like it was one.

There were several small groups and larger groups gathered in spurts outside drinking. They waved at us as we approached the front door. Something we couldn't quite make out started running toward us. We didn't see it in it's full glory until it bumped into Reagan, giving her a bear hug that almost knocked her to the ground.

"Beckett! Save me please. You must! You have to! Give me your keys!" A wasted, Angel Alvarez was wobbling in front of us in a pair of white long johns and purple and teal Umbro brand soccer shorts over them. His dark hair gelled straight up like a Calvin and Hobbes character and his eyes blood shot. He was holding a beer in his hand unsteadily.

"Angel, what the Hell?"

"Dudettes, you have to give me your keys."

"Come again?" Reagan needed clarification for this insane request.

"Not to drive, silly pretty girl. I need to sleep. I have to sleep this off. I'll go and sleep in the back of your car and come back and hang out with you guys on my thirdly wind."

"Go ahead, its unlocked. If you puke in there I'll call the police." Reagan grabbed his beer and turned him to the direction of her car, pushing him along.

"Thanks Reagan hot Becks!" He called out behind us. Angel was hilarious. He was rich and the only Latin guy my class had let into their little bubble. The bastards. We didn't have much diversity to begin with, but it can't go unnoticed that Rafael and Esteban, two second generation Mexican American classmates of ours who had been with us since kindergarten had been treated like second class citizens. Angel was also second generation.

He moved here in the sixth grade. He wore the right clothes, didn't have an accent and the chickens flocked to him like he was a God. I liked Angel, he was a friend. I was glad he got the attention he deserved. I just didn't like the way they treated Rafael and Esteban. You would think you could show some respect to friends you've known your entire life as well. They weren't cruel to them, they just didn't include them, which is perhaps the cruelest you can be.

I heard the music blaring from inside. Lynn and Reagan looked over at me like it was about to be Christmas, and we opened the door. I have to say, there were definite perks to standing next to those two. Devin had stepped to the side to go check on Hanna and Brooke who was probably holding her hair, so I knew when we stopped the room on our entrance, those looks weren't for her. Wendy Tomlin ran up and gave us hugs.

"Get in here and get a drink, you're late! But what a way to make an entrance, you bitches are hot! You're showing your seniors up!" Hurry up and get a buzz going, I'll come back and tell you who's too far past their limit to bother with! Oh, and who's DD?" I raised my hand. Reagan high- fived it out of gratitude, then I felt Wendy's hands on my cheeks.

"Awe, pumpkin... I think I'm disappointed. I guess I wanted to see you tipsy just once before we left this Hell-hole. Although, looking like that tonight, I'm glad you're not drinking!" Then she was off. Two small things happened immediately after, and simultaneous, that may have changed the course of my junior year, no matter how subtle they seemed. I leaned against the island in the middle of the semi-crowded kitchen waiting for Lynn and Reagan to get their drinks when I felt eyes burning through me.

I looked up toward the entry way in front of me and there was Devin standing in the open-door frame looking past or above me with the most conniving smile on her face, as if she had just caught someone. I sheepishly looked from side to side, then finally turned around. Adrian was propped in the opposite doorway leading to the kitchen, eyes fixated on me... well I guess it was more fair to say my ass in that moment. As I turned toward him, we made eye contact and he smiled, shaking his head at me like he was surprised and impressed by my outfit.

His face lit up and stayed on mine as if we were the only two people at the party. I know I was blushing. Something moved inside of me, and I wanted to see what was next with him more than anything, but we weren't the only ones at the party. I knew he couldn't see Devin diagonally across from him from the angle he was standing. I didn't think it was fair to him.

I looked down and away to dissolve the moment as quickly as possible. Just then Lynn turned toward me with her drink in hand, only to fall into me when someone shoved a little too hard from behind her trying to reach for a mixer.

"Damn it! Watch out." She screamed. It was too late. The DD already had booze spilled down her shirt.

"Awe, July, I'm so sorry!" Lynn grabbed a napkin.

"It's not your fault. Here, let me run to the restroom and handle it, this will leave paper lent all over the shirt." I moved past her toward the doorway that Devin was still guarding. I leaned into her ear carefully.

"Devin, we've been friends for a very long time. Please don't make me have to ask you to Fuck off!"

"I knew it. A hundred dollars, you don't have, says as soon as you pass me he follows you past this door to check on you, and if he does... you lied to me. And you're right, we were friends for a long time. I don't think I deserved that."

"Fuck off Devin!" I pushed past her without making it obvious and headed to the bathroom. My hope was Adrian would get caught by Reagan and Lynn. He would have to say his hellos, and knowing Lynn she'd ask him to hold her drink while she came to the restroom to find me. That's the most logical thing to happen.

Just don't look back, don't look back, I kept thinking to myself. I stopped. A feeling stopped me and I turned to look behind me. Devin smiled back at me from the doorway. She was waiting for me to look. She had her foot blocking Adrian casually as she chatted him up.

Great. He had come after me, and she raised the bet by stopping him, telling him God knows what. He looked agitated and as if he was in a hurry to get away from her. *July, for the first time in your life... do nothing. It's not your problem. No one asked you, just go fix your shirt.*

My eyes were stinging. I was ready to cry. I decided to keep walking to the twins' parents' bedroom to use their bathroom for privacy. The twins usually kept it off limits during the party. Adrian had just walked into a vulture's nest without knowing it. Depending on what Devin said to him... If he didn't hate me already, he was going to be repulsed by me now.

Why did that hurt so much? Why was I worried about his feelings above my own. I had never cared if Adrian Reed hated me. What would it have mattered? This did sting though, and I didn't want any part of it. I just want to go home to my grandparents' house and... I swung the ensuite bathroom door open.

"Oh, I'm sorry!" I slammed the door back and there was a pause on the other end before I heard another friend of mine puking for what obviously wasn't the first time. It was Robyn Maze.

"Fuck, Trent! I told you to keep the door locked!" Spencer Pearce yelled forcefully at Trent Childress. As I said before, if you were a Scott, a Childress, or a Bishop, you had it made. Spencer Pearce and Trent Childress had already graduated. Spencer was supposed to be at the University of Texas, and I don't know where Trent was supposed to be.

I just knew that was Robyn, and other than puking her brains out with her eyes closed and limp arms, she looked unconscious. I took a deep breath to open the door again. Replaying the situation in my head, Spencer was holding her up above the toilet and Trent was sitting on the side of the jacuzzi with his head in his hands. Robyn was in her underwear. The door wouldn't open. It was already locked. I pounded on it screaming Robyn's name.

"We got it! She's fine, just had one too many." Spencer's voice rang out. Try a million too many, and why did she look so disheveled. I didn't mean from throwing up or being on the verge of alcohol poisoning, I meant her clothes, or lack thereof. They didn't even seem put on her right. Those were an interesting choice of words I had put together in my head. Something definitely wasn't right.

I raced out of the massive bedroom, looking back over my shoulder to notice the bed unmade and the rest of Robyn's clothes tossed about. There was a torn condom wrapper on the ground in front of me that could have been from anybody. I just kept running. I went through the other wing of the house, I anticipated to be empty, to get my head together and bump into the least amount of people possible until I could get to someone sober enough to help me.

I made it to a quiet sitting room and noticed long black locks of hair leaned over a couch cushion beating it. Cool blue eyes and a pale face shot up at me in fury. It was the other twin, Whitney Tomlin. Whitney was the more dominating twin, and until this moment I had forgotten all about the twin cheerleading debacle. Whitney was not a cheerleader this year, her senior year, while her sister Wendy was.

They had both been varsity cheerleaders throughout high school, and both tried out for their senior year. With the tumbling situation so competitive, and neither one of them doing that level of gymnastics, I guess the judges determined they could only go with one twin. The strongest one. So my drawer wasn't the only one replaced that year. *Wow.* That's how easily Pure Pines covered the mistakes they couldn't fix.

The thing was, Whitney was by far the strongest cheerleader of the two, but they were identical twins. It would have been easy to confuse them when going down final score cards and attaching points to each girl. The early gossip had been that the judges got them mixed up and the weaker twin made it while Whitney did not.

Once school began, they acted as if Whitney had just been so busy with academics and all other activities that she decided not to do cheerleading this year. But seeing her face and remembering the gossip through my tear-stained moment of not having my name called, I knew that happened.

I stood in front of her trying to wipe the stigma of my thoughts off my face and go back to the emergency at hand.

"There are people getting high in my house, there are people fucking in my house! There are people fighting in my house." Look at this place!"

"I'm sorry Whitney." I could tell she was on-one and there wasn't much I could do to solicit her help. "Have you seen Presley?"

Presley Maze was Robyn's older sister and I just thought she'd be the fastest most effective person to find.

"What?!"

"Never mind." I left her to stew over her housekeeping and started to run toward the traffic of the party as quickly as possible. Thank God it was a small world. Big house, but small world.

Secrets we had plenty at Pure Pines, but they were hard to keep. Evidently someone else must have barged in on the scene, or one of the guys had gone and gotten her sister.

I looked up to see a fully clothed Robyn with one arm over Presley's shoulder and the other on two different guys carrying her out. They were taking her through the side toward the garage to avoid the masses. Robyn was a good person, I wasn't sure what happened, but I was so glad to know she was safe. As relieved as I felt at the moment, I did think it strange not to see Spencer Pearce or Trent Childress anywhere around.

"July?" A voice I recognized, and could not avoid, called out to me over Robyn's shoulder. "Could you take my keys and go unlock my car for us? We're going out the garage. I don't want anyone to see my sister like this. Just kind of check for me on your way out that the coast is clear, yeah?"

"Of course!" I grabbed Presley's keys trying to think back to my freshman and sophomore year to remember what her car looked like parked in the drive at Robyn's house. I hadn't been in it much. Presley was way more popular than her sister and I back then, and she was always out with someone leaving her ... silver-ish?... *Eclipse, yes that's it!* It was a dark silver, not quite grey Eclipse, parked in their drive all the time.

My God, was the Superman emblem showing on my chest? I didn't mind helping, at all. I just wanted everything to be okay, and I didn't like having a hint of suspicion that it wasn't, especially over something that wasn't my business. I found the car and waited with the door opened and a path cleared.

I saw Reagan and Lynn from a distance up on the porch balcony looking for me. I was glad they hadn't looked down to see this, along with the mob of people that could have looked over at any moment. It didn't look like Adrian was with them, but I could see from where I stood his car was still there.

I wondered if Presley would say anything to me or ask me anything about her sister. Instead she and the other guys got Robyn in safely and took over. Presley thanked me and then shrugged and said, "Sorry, I guess she had one too many." Then they were gone.

I couldn't help but feel miffed at her words, not only that, but the irony of them after what I had just seen. Now I worried Robyn was in worse hands with her sister's denial. What a messed up night. I made my way back through the crowd to reach my friends. Reagan was looking down at her pager and Lynn saw me from a distance and ran over.

"Where the Hell have you been? We've been all over the party looking for you. Adrian said you ran off."

I didn't know how to answer Lynn. I was still shell-shocked at what I'd seen, and...

"I bumped into Whitney. She's pissed, I think she just wants the night to be over." I tried to deflect as best I could.

"I don't blame her, have you seen the amount of people here? This party was out of hand before we arrived." Lynn was slurring a bit and talking louder than usual.

"Anything fun happen?" I asked more to try and determine how they had drank so much so fast. Reagan seemed too far gone to relay anything. Lynn opened her mouth to try, and was cut short by a group of guys who threw her over their shoulder and carried her out to dance.

"Just a minute July, we'll be back! Hey, watch her!" Make sure she doesn't leave with anybody." Lynn gave me a tipsy, two finger snake eye and pointed toward Reagan. I thumped Reagan to get her attention.

"Bitch, why did you leave us?" Her words were really slurred. "We had to listen to that asshole all night ask was' you where ... Where you went... What you wearing..." She laughed at her word mix- up. "Hey did I tell you that's my mom's body suit. I take-et-ed' it from her closet. It looks really good on you."

"Reagan, I'm going to stab you. Which asshole was looking for me?"

"Dudn't matter. His' okay now. He's been busy with them. Hey, asshole!" She called out across from us where I saw Adrian in what looked like a meaningful conversation with Devin and little Natalie Hilliard, the sophomore varsity cheerleader whose name was on my drawer. Her light strawberry blond hair was half up and she smiled cheerfully at everything he and Devin were saying. As if those two had shit in common.

He looked back at us after Reagan yelled, just before she stumbled in place a bit.

"Let's go somewhere else!" Reagan shouted. Adrian rushed over and lashed out at me. "Where have you been?"

"What?"

Adrian grabbed Reagan in front of me who was starting to look like she needed help standing.

"And where's Lynn? I can't believe you let them drink this much. You know, if you didn't want to be here with everybody, you didn't have to come."

I looked up at the mob of people dancing in the large den when I heard Lynn's famous giggle. Then I looked back up at Adrian holding Reagan up.

"Go. Just go get her." He demanded.

What was happening? Was it a full moon? I grabbed Lynn and excused her from the dance floor.

"Hey, I think we should go." I started leading us toward Reagan and Adrian, who still had a scowl on his face directed straight at me.

"What did you guys drink?" I tried to make Lynn focus.

"Not a lot of cups."

Wow. This was worse than I thought. Lynn exhaled a deep breath with her eyes partially closed.

"It's hot in here. Did you find your man?" As we stopped in front of Reagan and Adrian, Lynn continued. "Cause this one here's been looking for you all night. He won't tell me why, just like you don't. Hmmm. And don't we all wonder what that's about?"

Adrian shook his head and looked away from me. "Let's just get them to the car. YOU haven't been drinking, have you?

I scowled at him instead of dignifying it with an answer.

"Then what *were* you doing?" A female, non-tipsy voice joined our group, picking up were Adrian left off with an instigating smile. It was Devin.

"Fuck you Devin, I told you to stay away from me tonight after the shit you pulled." I didn't mean to lash out like that, but Reagan and Lynn were drunk, Adrian was yelling at me for no reason, and I'm pretty sure I witnessed a friend puking after being raped.

"You know me so well. That's touching and reminiscent of our good ole days, only you don't know what I've accomplished yet."

Adrian was a few feet ahead of us dragging Reagan carefully along as I walked Lynn. I didn't know if he could hear Devin or not, but he did look back several times.

"By the way, you owe me a hundred bucks, although I don't think I would make that wager again. I don't think he'll be barking up your tree anymore." Devin was toying with me and made no effort to disguise it. I don't know what happened to me. I just saw red. I stopped and set Lynn up making sure she could stand on her own, and then I turned to Devin fully intending to aim for the smirk on her face.

I wasn't a violent person, and I had never punched anyone in my life. Let's be honest, the best anyone was going to get from me in that moment was probably a solid slap...

"JULY!" A voice that sent chills up my spine stopped me before a hand was raised to touch a hair on the infamous Devin Scott's head.

"What is going on?!" Adrian demanded, looking put-out from having to drag Reagan out of the party we were supposed to be enjoying.

"Yeah, July, why don't you tell him what's going on?" Devin was relentless.

"Oh, I think you've said plenty." I stood up for myself. I didn't look over at Adrian. I was too ashamed of what Devin could have possibly said about me, and I was also furious at him. *Could he please drop the dad act already?!*

"Would someone please tell me what's going on? I think I'm the one sick of being the last to know." Lynn looked at me in the eye and then at Adrian.

It was about to get ugly on that end as well. And then, something miraculous happened. Whoever said "cheerleaders are awesome" that one time at cheer camp, certainly had my vote. Before I could make a move I looked up at a stampede running toward me.

"I'm so sorry!!! I'm so very sorry, July! Please forgive me. Please, please. Please!" Hanna ran up out of nowhere with Brooke trailing behind her. Her arms thrown around my neck squeezing the breath out of me.

"I was so drunk! I didn't mean a word of it, and I'm so sorry I made a mess of things. Please forgive me! You look soo gorgeous tonight and I was jealous in my stupid tee shirt. Then I thought of you not cheering with us this year but being with Reagan and Lynn and what fun you'd have, and how good you guys are. You are all right about me... I can't dance! Never could!" Hanna did not release her hug. Brooke's arms were around me next, and she was apologizing with the same gusto.

"My God, are you two high?" That was all I could muster as I peeled their arms off my neck. I smiled at them and forgave them, for what I wasn't entirely sure, but at least in the moment they made me look good. If nothing else had gone down, and they hadn't seen Adrian all night, and this had nothing to do with Devin's plot… These two had just lent me a hazy explanation for my disappearing act, as well as made me look far better in front of Adrian than if I had in fact slapped Devin as intended.

"Let's get out of here." I rallied the troops. I didn't look up at Adrian, but I thought I saw a small smile of relief on his face as he threw an arm around Reagan and led the way to our cars. I know for a fact I saw Devin roll her eyes.

"Hey, guys, can we get Shelby home or back to Hanna's house with us at least?"

"Of course." I stepped in confidently before Adrian could. *Who's your daddy now?*

"Where is she?" I asked.

"We left her by a tree." Brooke explained.

"You left her by a tree?" Adrian asked with sufficient cause and a demand for answers in his voice. *My God, with everything going on that would be like leaving a combination of adolescent Brook Shields and Kim Basinger in the boys locker room for the taking.*

Thank God she was visible before anyone could get alarmed. She was leaning against a tree right by our cars. Shelby looked as drunk as Reagan and Lynn, which was odd because she really didn't drink. What was going on with everyone tonight?

"So I guess Shelby decided not to go out with Billie after all?"

"No, we wouldn't let her go off with anybody like this." Brooke was at least level headed drunk.

"Good girl." I winked at her and Adrian and I walked over to Shelby or "*Seventeen Magazine,*" as the boys called her. Something had certainly hit that five foot nothing empty stomach of hers. Never mind we were in fifth grade together, I'd known "popular" Shelby as long as I had known the cheerleaders, and I'd never seen her so much as tipsy. This was crazy.

Adrian tapped her shoulder. "Shelby, it's Adrian and July." Wow, I had never heard our names put together like that, so casually.

"Are you okay if we take you home or give you a ride to Hanna's house? Whatever you like?" Adrian was so patient with her. She nodded and walked over to the cars with us. I wouldn't expect any less from him on his worst day, but still, seeing him in action was impressive. He looked over at me. His face still patient as if he was trying to make up for lashing out moments ago. "So I guess Lynn goes with me, and I can take—

"No, sorry, Lynn has to go with me back to Reagan's where her jeep is and she's supposedly sleeping over right now."

"Oh, right. So then, you've got you, Reagan, Lynn, and I will take the rest?"

"Actually, I'm not going back to Hanna's. I'd just rather head home." Devin changed the plan. *Great.* She'd be with me then. There's no way all the other girls could fit in Adrian's Mustang.

"In that case, if you don't mind, Adrian, I guess you'll take Hanna, Brooke and Shelby back to Hanna's and I've got ours and Devin." I confirmed the obvious, maybe just to keep a little of the power I had gained.

"Can you two be in the car together? Adrian asked looking to me alone for the answer. I just rolled my eyes. Devin opened the back seat of Reagan's car and sat down on two giant Nike Air Jordans hanging off a pair of white long johns.

"Hey!" Angel screamed as he woke to surprise us. We all started laughing. We had completely forgotten he was sleeping it off back there. "Is it time to go back to the party?"

"No, Angel, it's time to go home." That was something I could assure him.

"Move over, we'll take you." Devin informed him as she shoved him up right to make room for Lynn. Lynn seemed easier to maneuver than Reagan at the moment, so she sat down in the back seat and shut the door. I opened the passenger side door of Reagan's car and Adrian slid her into the seat protecting her head. She was almost asleep on us. Then he turned to Hanna and Brook and unlocked the car for them to get Shelby settled. He walked over to the driver's side before I got in.

"You sure you didn't have anything to drink?"

"Adrian! If I said I didn't, I didn't."

"Well, I didn't know where you disappeared to for nearly an hour, so I guess you could of—" He looked down realizing. "Look, I really just meant to make sure you didn't have anything at all, not that I don't trust your judgment, it just doesn't take a genius to figure out something went wrong here. So as long as you didn't have so much as a sip of what they all had..."

"Yeah, something was definitely in the water."

"You can handle this group? *Ours*?" He smiled at the reference I had made moments ago referring to Reagan and Lynn as ours.

"Plus Devin and Angel? I kind of feel like we should switch gro ups..."

"Yeah, but then that's more backtracking and how would I get back..." We both looked at each other as if something might suggest he drive me home or back to Reagan's. I spoke up as responsibly as possible. "No backtracking, and the least number of cars on the road—"

"To minimize the risk." He finished for me. On that note there seemed to be a lot of commotion, people and cars dispersing up on the hill near the side of the house.

"We should get out of here and get them home. Will you let me know when you girls get back and settled?"

I looked at him funny.

"How could I call without waking anyone?" He smiled a smile that gave me butterflies.

"Umm, I have my own private line." He said it in a way that could only be perceived as cocky, but his voice was low, and he said it quiet, for my benefit. It wasn't for the entire party in the car.

"Of course, you do." I immediately felt stupid and naive. I moved to open the door and get in. Adrian lingered above the door he held open for me, as if there were more to say. He looked at me a second without saying anything. His eyes meeting mine and locking me in place. His gaze made me feel nervous and exposed.

I drifted my eyes down from his to try and stay in charge, only they landed on the silver watch around his left wrist. Subconsciously, it had become another indelible mark of his, as he AL-

WAYS had it on. It had never made my heart skip a beat nor my stomach turn a summersault before.

However, after the experience in the office with him, I found my mind wondering to that moment Friday night at the football game when I thought of his watch and moved my hand to the side of my leg where he squeezed my thigh. There was a little snag in the dance tights where the chain of his watch must have caught. I wondered how long it would stay there as my little reminder before it tore through and became a runner.

Ignoring the fluttering in my stomach, I tugged at the door to pull it shut. I was met with a strong resistance. I brought my blushing face back up to Adrian's as my hand remained pulling at the door he held in place. Both corners of his mouth raised into a slow, knowing smile. *Fuck.* My flushed cheeks did not go unnoticed. It couldn't have been more than a thirty second exchange, but that felt like the most intense ten minutes of my life.

Adrian shut me in and stepped back for me to drive out. For that long moment I forgot everyone else was in the car, much less who. Devin opened her mouth to speak.

"Don't Devin. He was just making sure you guys were safe. It had nothing to do with me."

"Shut up July. I'm not going to hug you and make a fool of myself like Hanna and Brooke, but I do owe you an apology, and I really am sorry."

I looked over to see if anyone else was hearing this. Such luck... they were all passed out.

"The party blew, and I guess I just got carried away out of boredom. You just made it so easy. Well he did too."

He? Were we talking about Adrian as my "he"? My stomach flipped in fear and anticipation wondering what she was going to say next. Even with the unknown element of what Devin had done, I still felt warm all over thinking of him as mine in that second.

"My God it was obvious at the mention of either of your names. And this good Samaritan act the two of you have down, making sure everybody's safe, blah, blah. Well anyway, I'm sorry if I fucked it up for you. I knew there was something there, but I didn't realize you two losers were made for each other until this pathetic display."

As I drove down her road and turned off toward her drive, I began to wonder if I should be terrified that I had no idea what she was talking about.

"Just know you can date up. So, if not Adrian, we'll get you a senior. Hanna's right, you look good. She should be jealous." And with a sardonic smile she was out of the car and my hair. I watched to make sure she made it to the door with her key and went safely inside.

What on earth did she mean, *if not Adrian?*

Adrian

"FRIEND IS A FOUR LETTER WORD"

CAKE

She didn't call. Sure, that next morning, I heard from Reagan and Lynn when they called to play detective and figure out what the heck was in their drinks. I think they both mentioned something about having to go straight to bed or being afraid they'd wake her parents, or July couldn't wake anyone to find my number. Whatever it was... She didn't call.

I waited up. I lay by the phone, hoping to hear her voice before I fell asleep. I was going to ask her how she knew to get Coach Bartlett and where she was all that time at the party. Did she walk away from me? *And what was going on with Devin?* Why was she trying to set me up? I just didn't understand the motivation. Did July know or encourage it? *Enough.*

I felt stupid. I waited for her call, but it didn't come. I looked down at my nightstand and saw a crumpled piece of paper ripped from Devin's day planner. It was Natalie Hilliard's number. Devin shoved it in my pocket after introducing us. I knew of her, sure, but Devin did an official introduction, "set-up style." No doubt, it was why Devin called her over. I just didn't understand the motivation. Don't get me wrong... I should be reason enough for a varsity cheerleader to want to stake her claim if I do say so myself.

In all seriousness, with the whole football situation, I was prepared to spend the rest of this semester in exile. I'm not going to lie. It felt good that Devin took an interest in setting me up. It meant I was still on the list and hadn't burned all bridges the way I did with my team. It wasn't a list I cared to be on, but it was part of the dog-and-pony show here. If you weren't excited about it, *they* could find ways to make you less excited about something else.

Devin was the worst, although I have to admit she was in rare form at the party. Devin Scott ruled our junior class, and probably a bit more than that, with her being a Scott. Something tragic happened to her end of the Scott family when we were kids. I don't even remember what, but the whole town's been putty in her hands since. Why they feel the need to make anything up to her or them, I do not know. Her family already had everything.

Devin was always a difficult girl to get to know. She was gorgeous by everyone's standards. A bit of a brunette version of Jennie Garth from *90210*. Being bossy as she was got her what she wanted, but it also made people step back. She had only ever dated upperclassmen of extreme status. I think everyone our age was too scared of her. Sometimes, she was right and seemed more mature than the rest of us. Other times, she was just a supreme bitch. I once saw her talk to one of our junior high coaches in class like he was a degenerate. I sat at my desk staring at the train wreck in awe of how a man like that, who destroyed us on the field, could sit there and take it on the chin from an 8th-grade girl. She didn't even get written up.

The strange part about it was - that it never happened at Pure Pines, not even at the High School level. We just didn't talk back to teachers or faculty. It would be a cardinal sin. Once in a blue moon, a rebellious skid or dump kid from in and out of juvie tried his hand at it, but it would be the last time he tried... and we had so few of those.

What a dick I was to July! I even looked at her like she had two heads for being so hateful to Devin when it was sort of hot. I don't think I've ever seen July that mad or frustrated unless it was at me during debate last year. What was I doing acting so pious? Everyone knows that if anybody had reason to talk to Devin like July did, she probably deserved it. I guess I was sensitive to burning bridges.

I didn't know the cheerleading tryout details other than the rumor about the Tomlin twins. But that dissipated before anyone could get to the bottom of it. I didn't know what happened with July or why she didn't make it, but even from a dude's perspective,

I knew it would be a sensitive subject. I guess I was worried everyone had been drinking, and July might say something to "Queen Bee" that she couldn't take back. That, and our school, was zero tolerance. If someone hit you and you pushed them off to defend yourself... you both got suspended. We weren't on school property, but I can only imagine the consequences for anyone who laid a hand on Devin Scott.

Great. There I go, protecting July again. I had to put an end to this strange fascination. First, I couldn't be involved with anybody who occupied my brain and everything else as much as she did. I simply didn't have the time. Second, why would I waste time on someone who played so hard to get, pulled disappearing acts, and last time I checked, before I lost my mind over her... we despised each other!

I hadn't dropped football to take a break and pine over somebody. This year was crucial, with grades, faculty, scholarships, and everything this deplorable place had set us up for. I didn't run with the rabbits and howl with the wolves so successfully thus far just to go out a social pariah. I wasn't about to get dropped from anybody's list. Besides, if I got lonely, here was prospect number one. Sweet, kind, tall, and blonde with ballet dancer legs, Natalie. July wasn't even my physical type.

Monday came in strong, with news of the party being busted up after we left. The county sheriff was called on dispatch, and he sent a couple of cop cars over from Prairie. They had jurisdiction when they needed it. Thank God we got out of there when we did. Although, that's the funny thing about Pure Pines... the gossip says the party was busted by cops; meanwhile, that's where it ends? Two cop cars didn't call in back-up and arrest the multiple underage drinkers or the twenty-two-year-old college guys that gave the booze to them? Nope. No one was booked. We couldn't have anyone at Pure Pines having a record, now, could we?

After first period, I was on a mission through the hallway to find Lynn and Reagan. An entire group of alumni had been there, home from college for whatever reason... in the middle of October? It was obvious. They spiked the punch big time. They may have even brought roofies in. We had never had that happen. The bigger question was, why? And why were SO many of them back for this party? They didn't even go to the same universities.

We knew Nach', SFA in Nacogdoches, was a party school. We'd heard about kids from Prairie driving the hour up on the weekends to score ecstasy or coke. We just didn't have that in our arsenal. Underage drinking, partying, and making each other miserable were hard enough to handle simultaneously with AP classes, multiple electives, Globe scholar requirements, and, I don't know, showing up and breathing every day.

Weaving down the hallway, I finally caught Reagan at her locker. Lynn approached behind her before I did and whispered something in her ear. The look on both their faces was alarming.

"Hey, I was thinking about the—" Lynn put her hand on my mouth, and Reagan shook her head, warning me to say no more. I squinted at them, wondering what changed between yesterday and first period. A different classroom door swung open down the hall from us, and a swarm of students poured out of it. I knew July would be one of them. I tried not to look up. Then, something stopped us all.

"May I have your attention, please? Would Reagan Beck ett..." Reagan's eyes widened at the sound of Mrs. Bishop's voice echoing through the intercom system. "July Edwards..." I couldn't help it. I looked up, and my eyes were on hers as I watched her freeze in the hallway, holding her books.

"Hanna Lewis, Shelby North, Brooke Pender, Devin Scott, and Lynn Stokes, please report to the library." There was a throat clear on the intercom mic. "Also, Angel Alverez and Adrian Reed. Before your next period classes. Thank you."

All our eyes were wide now. July walked over to join us, and everyone stared down the hallway at each of us as the space diluted to the people whose names were called. Nobody said a word to speculate what this could be about. We just started walking in a big group to our fate.

I did notice July looking at Devin as if she wondered if she had anything to do with this. Their tension was palpable. It made me cringe at the reminder that they were in the car together after we separated, and July drove her home. I couldn't help but wonder if Devin had debriefed July on my potential Natalie situation, and it made me more uncomfortable than wondering what our fate would be in the library.

We all entered the library like we were about to walk a plank. To our surprise, neither Mrs. Bishop nor Principal Sabella were there. Instead, the very familiar face of our favorite librarian stood, eyeing us with a devious smile. It didn't take long for most of us to assess she had called in the getaway cars.

At first, it was tongue-in-cheek when the fifty-something, almost hot, not to be creepy, Mrs. Crawford kept up the ruse by asking us what we all did over the weekend. Lynn kicked Reagan and said, "We had a slumber party." Mrs. Crawford's eyes swung to Angel and me.

"Obviously, she meant all of us girls." Reagan smiled as if that would solve everything.

"I see. And whose home did the slumber party take place at?"

"Mine!" Hanna volunteered, excited as if she got an answer right. I saw Devin pinch her for it.

"Well, actually, it all began at Reagan's, and then we headed to Hanna's and finally, Devin's house." *Way to go July. Damn.* I had to hand it to her. She was good on her feet. Obviously, Mrs. Crawford had been made privy to all our stops. It only made sense to acknowledge them. "It was sort of a treasure hunt type thing." July continued.

Reagan took over from there. "We saw these two shooting hoops outside Angel's house on our way to pick up Shelby, and the rest is history."

"Interesting. I was curious how the group of you missed out on all the fun the rest of your friends were having. I can't imagine you all weren't invited." She was being facetious. She knew we were there.

"Oh, well we'd had our little meet-up planned for a long time, so..." Brooke stepped in to confirm our story.

"Um hmm. Lynn, the jeep your dad got you last Fall, it holds quite a few people, yes?"

"I suppose it does, Mrs. Crawford, would you like a ride after school." Lynn smiled back as we all laughed.

"Yet, you all took Reagan's two-door to...

"Hanna's." July jumped in on cue.

"Right. And... Adrian, your beautifully remastered Mustang can't hold more than three comfortably; if that, wouldn't you say?" I smiled and nodded at our librarian playing *Colombo*. Angel stepped in before I could do more.

"Come on, Mrs. Crawford, I know I'm a tall guy, but the Mustang had plenty of room for me, Adrian, and a basketball."

"And you jumped in the car with Adrian from your front yard to..."

"Grab something to drink. We got thirsty out there."

"And your green Geo Tracker was with you the entire evening?"

"No. No, ma'am, it was not." We all looked at Angel, who possibly held a link to our puzzle we didn't know was missing.

"I didn't know where it was." We shot a collective, dumbfounded glance at Angel, questioning his reasoning.

"I mean, I had loaned it out."

"And you were happily surprised to find it this morning left for you on the practice field?" Mrs. Crawford revealed what the rest of us did not see coming.

"Yes, ma'am. That I was."

"That's a good friend to return to you what you didn't know was missing. Well. I see despite the gossip your peers seem to be the subject of, the nine of you have made it through the weekend unscathed. Tell me, I'm so curious who dropped whom home and how you all fit between the two cars you made available to yourselves, but all in due time. I commend your clever efforts. I do hope you'll explain further and entertain my curiosity one day when you feel the coast is clear. But for now, I have to say, I'm equally entertained at how you pulled it off. I believe you were the only ones successful at it this year. Quite the magic trick. Okay, get to class. If anyone asks, we were getting the library's favorite Juniors' pics for the annual."

Everyone else took the win and dispersed to class in case there were prying eyes in the office. It was right next to the library. Lynn, Reagan, July, and I carelessly stood right before both doors.

"We taught you well." Reagan punched July's arm.

"Nice work, you little deviant! Lynn's praise followed. And I... I said nothing. I saw July's eyes float from them up to mine. I cruelly almost dared them to with my mind, knowing I wouldn't make eye contact. Reagan and Lynn looked at each other and then back to me. July just glanced around the hall and fumbled with her books.

"Well, you were awesome, and how wicked curious is Mrs. Crawford?! What the hell? The woman just wanted our alibi." Lynn broke the awkward silence.

"No, she wanted details about the party. That's just the only way she could ask!" Reagan was probably right, knowing the noscy administration at Pure Pines. "And thank you again for thinking fast enough to give us that alibi."

"Well, Devin didn't deserve it, but it all worked out." July said this quietly as I tried not to look her way without being too obviously childish.

"What's with you two anyway?" Lynn asked.

"Yeah, I think you're both going to have to fill in some blanks from that night for us, 'cause there are SO many." Reagan had grouped July and me together in her request, and Lynn called us both out, and I still couldn't look her way. I was determined to make her feel like I did when waiting for her call. *What was I, five?*

Our little pow-wow broke when we heard keys jingling and footsteps running our way. It was Angel. He tossed me his keys as he passed us, running toward the front double doors. "Bro, help me out?"

"What?"

"You drive, I'll hold the gate open."

Then, a sudden realization on my part: "You didn't know your car was on the practice field?"

"Nope!" Angel continued his sprint out the front school doors, and I followed him. When we made it down to the practice field and jimmied one side of the gate open, there was not enough room to drive the car out. It dawned on me who was doing this. Angel's dad was a cop over in Prairie. This was obviously an effort on his part, combined with the office administration, to teach Angel a lesson. I had to hand it to them; it was way more clever than what we thought we'd gotten by with.

Soon, the entire student body was watching out of any classroom window they could. At one point, they all started cheering us on. It was awesome. It was the most fun I'd had at school since the football-quitting nightmare. Everything I typically loathed about Pure Pines wasn't so bad at that moment.

The Cranberries

The week back from the party had been tormenting, and it was only Wednesday. I was glad we had escaped the news we heard of the party being broken up, as well as Mrs. Crawford's part in the prank the administration pulled on Angel. I guess when the cops came, they found that Angel's car had been left there at the twin's house. His dad was privy the entire weekend. He kept it from Angel, just casually asking every once in a while where his car was. Angel kept oddly saying a buddy borrowed it. He should have known something was up when his dad accepted that as an answer.

I was caught up on all my assignments. Adrian was back to business as usual, ignoring me. I didn't have anything too out of the ordinary to worry about other than Robyn's face haunting me when I replayed her vomiting next to Spencer Pearce. How unconscious she looked, thrown over some dudes' shoulders as her sister helped them lead her out.

I felt guilty. We sure got over the disturbing parts of this failed party quickly. *Come on.* Lynn and Reagan were WASTED. That may be par for the course for Reagan on occasion, but it wasn't like Lynn. She never drank to get wasted. I guess many things went down that night that somehow got swept under the rug, and in Robyn's case, I needed to know if she was okay. She didn't show up to school on Monday, but I'd seen her the following days.

It was classic. She seemed withdrawn and depressed and not as dressed up as usual. I couldn't get the ordeal out of my head. My mom was still in Salt Lake. Her meetings were extended, which was great. It meant she was sourcing out to more clients, but I really needed her. I wanted to tell her about Robyn. She would know what to do.

The only good part of the party was Adrian. I don't think our friends gave him enough credit for what he did for everyone. Even though I hated him that moment for ignoring me, I had to admit his actions at the party were something I'd always admired and counted on from him.

He wasn't a designated driver that night. Sure, in the sense that he drove, so he really couldn't drink all that much, but he could have thrown caution to the wind and gotten a ride from someone.

Instead, he came, rallied, and then made sure everyone we knew got home safely.

He was always responsible like that. He didn't ever take advantage of being gifted that incredible car. It's like he knew what a privilege it was to own it, so he treated being able to drive it that way.

Ugh, what was I going on about? He had been brainwashed by Devin, and whatever anyone thought was starting to happen between us had stopped. That, or I needed to wake up and stop blaming Devin for the actions Adrian had shown me throughout our history together.

We were not friends. He wasn't into me that way, and it would be beyond weird if he was because we didn't even like each other. The reality was that Adrian had always thought he was better than me, and I was better off when I let him think it instead of letting him in my head.

It was almost the last period, and I had to focus on getting to the country club for golf. My grandmother was working tonight, and my granddad said he'd try to be back before I got home from practice. He had a water main to go check just outside of Corsicana.

I could call Uncle Dean for a ride, but it would just be quicker to get one. I stopped in the girl's restroom on the way to my last class to fumble through my backpack and make sure I had everything. We didn't have practice last week, so I quickly realized I had taken my practice bag out at home and had no extra golf clothes.

The bathroom door swung open to reveal Reagan popping in on me.

"Hey, Wendy's going to wait for you after last period. She's going to golf practice tonight, so you can ride with her." Wendy Tomlin, the funny, nicer twin who did make cheerleader, usually only showed up to golf for actual tournaments and picture day. She played with her dad on the professional course he had with his work membership. She didn't have much use for our school's golf program, and they let it fly with special permission.

"She like, never comes, so I didn't think to ask."

"Well I did, and don't you forget me for it."

"Hey, will this work to play in?" I had worn a vest that day over a fitted white turtleneck, reminder... it was the '90s. I took the vest off to see if the turtleneck flew on its own.

"Um, yeah, if you're careful not to cut anybody with those things!"

"What?" I turned to look in the mirror to see my boobs at attention and two darts sticking out of them.

"Good God, are you not wearing a bra?"

"Of course, I am! Apparently, it's not a good one. Can nipples grow over night?! What the Hell?"

"Oh relax. At least you have them. Some of us are still waiting for more to come. Maybe you just had a little growth spurt there, and that shirt is translucent, as well as your bra, and you are incredibly cold?"

"I can't wear this."

"Yes, you can. Just grab some Band-Aids from the nurse on your way out.

"Band-Aids?"

"Yes. You put them over your nipples, and you'll look fine, better than fine... you'll look amazing in that flimsy bra and almost see-through shirt.

"Reagan, I'm going to the golf course, not the "Chicken Ranch." It's fine, I'll just wear my vest and look like a dork out there." Reagan grabbed my vest off the bathroom countertop and took off running.

"Band-Aids, and don't forget Wendy's waiting out front for you after class!" She shouted behind her as the bathroom door swung back and the late bell rang.

I made myself late to stop by the nurse's station on the way to last period. There was a note on the door that the nurse had already gone home for the day and to please go to the office if you had an emergency. My nipples were not an emergency I wanted to share with Principal Sabella's staff, so I went to my last-period class, holding my backpack in front of me and clinging to it as if I didn't feel well.

Once the bell rang, I escaped the hallways as quickly as possible. I knew Wendy got out before I did, and I didn't want her to have to wait too long for me.

"What's the matter with you?" I dropped my backpack onto the floorboard of her passenger side and slid into the car.

"Woah, momma! You want me to turn the heat on for you?" Wendy noticed right away.

"Is it that bad? I don't understand. Did I get new nipples after lunch? I swear it wasn't like this when I got dressed, and I had a vest on all day."

"Maybe you threw your vest on before you looked in the mirror this morning. Are you even wearing a bra?"

"Oh my God! Of course, I'm wearing a bra, at this point I'd be arrested if I wasn't. Tell me you have an extra t-shirt back here or something." We both looked back into the messiest, most expensive car I'd ever seen.

"All that and no shirt, huh?"

"Please. You sound like Whitney. She says my car is disgusting."

"It is!"

"Well, she and I shared a womb and a face; we do not, however, share a car!" We both laughed as she peeled out of the parking lot. The sky became super cloudy. It was instantaneous, and we saw lightning strikes in the distance.

"Hey, you might get lucky, and we get rained out. If not, you can run in the club house and buy a jacket." I didn't say anything to curtail her optimism over what she had just assumed I had in my wallet, but no... I didn't have sixty to ninety dollars in my purse for a windbreaker or hoodie with the Nineteenth Hole's logo printed on the back.

"What are you showing up for today anyway?"

"Coach said I had to at least pop by one practice before every tournament to tee off and play nine holes with everybody. Something about team spirit, although I think you've brought enough for the both of us today!

"Thank you. That was lovely."

"Hey, I might cut out early if coach lets me. I've got a huge quiz tomorrow. You have a ride home?"

"Oh, yeah, I'll figure it out."

"I'm sure you will with those things!"

When we got out of the car, the clouds covering the golf course had turned even darker. I walked up to the clubhouse to check out my clubs and, in my peripheral vision, saw Adrian's car parked in the next lot over. *Damn it.* I forced myself to relax. The last practice I had while he was working in The 19th Hole Restaurant was a non-issue. I didn't bump into him at all.

Our little side entry of the clubhouse was practically empty today. I wondered if I wouldn't get lucky, and it would be just the girl's team playing, and just a few of us at that. A few minutes later, Dane Lewis and Shelby North showed up, followed by some incredibly shy senior who rarely spoke to us unless she was paired with one of us at a tournament.

There was a note that Coach Mellis wasn't going to be there. One of the girls said she had to pick up her kid or something. As we pulled out our clubs, I saw Wendy in the distant parking lot waving for my attention as she ducked out.

"Dibs!" Dane Lewis shouted behind me.

"Dibs second! July's it!" Shelby demanded with a polite apology in her tone.

"Oh, come on, I wasn't even paying attention." I had to push back. This had already been a shit day.

"Nope, you are cart duty. It's only fair. Dane did it last time."

"Okay." I could see I was defeated. A small voice attempted to interrupt us from outside the clubhouse. It was Kathleen, that silent senior.

"I, uh, already checked one out. With just the four of us today, we can all fit, as long as one of you takes it back for me when we're done."

"She will!" Dane and Shelby fired that one off in unison. I smiled and nodded sarcastically in agreement.

"By the way, what are you wear—"

"Don't ask. Just avert your eyes and try not to get cut." I wasn't sure, but I think even painfully shy Kathleen chuckled. At least there was that.

Halfway through our assigned nine holes, the bottom fell out of the sky. We gathered our balls and clubs and flew into the cart, with Kathleen driving us as quickly as possible through the pouring rain. I was glad the clubhouse was pretty much deserted when we pulled up.

People in the cars in the parking lot were mainly on the restaurant and bar side of the country club. This meant I could duck for cover as I dropped the cart off and be seen by as few people as possible in my brilliant white turtleneck and the bra from hell.

In all the commotion, I had forgotten I didn't have a ride home. My clubs were the last ones out of the cart, and by the time I walked inside to my bin, I saw Dane, Shelby, and Kathleen running for the parking lot, holding their jackets over their heads. They weren't being jerks. They knew I had to drop the cart off.

The entire point of calling dibs on not doing that was that you got to leave and didn't have to deal with signing out. Sometimes, the clubhouse was packed on busy golf days. Obviously, the high school kids from the golf team had to wait behind paying customers and club members, so I don't blame them for running.

I was at least optimistic it wouldn't be too bad or busy today with the rain. Over half the people in the parking lot when we arrived were gone. I double-checked that everyone's clubs were locked up and stepped out the back door to walk around in front.

Everything was closed, and a fresh sign read: "Closed due to rain. Drop any remaining carts at the 19th Hole/they will sign you out." *What. The. Entire. *%#?!*

I looked up to the adjacent parking lot, and, of course, Adrian's car was still there. At this point, I just wanted to scream or give up. I didn't even care. It was literally raining on my face. I hopped in the cart and drove down to where I saw a row of carts parked by the restaurant.

A busboy was packing up the outside bar tables as quickly as he could, and one last ditch effort had me hoping that Adrian had gone out the back and I just missed him. No such luck.

I opened the door to the dark, dimly lit neon signs that shined against silver and gold trophies and tournament cups proudly displayed on high shelves. Adrian looked funny with a black apron and bar rag hanging from his waste. He didn't "look" funny as much as it was peculiar to see someone like him working.

He was flipping the chairs over on top of the empty tables. One older golfer was settling up and finishing his Old Fashioned at the end of the bar, and from what I could tell, the kitchen staff was still in the back.

I was soaking wet from the rain, and it was chilly outside despite my white turtleneck faux pas, so it was perfectly appropriate for me to cross my arms tightly and cover my, excuse me... high beams. I saw when Adrian looked up at me, but I had already diverted my eyes to my saving grace at the bar.

It was Ethan, the bar manager. I had dealt with him several times at the clubhouse, and he was nice enough. He was rough around the edges but an attractive man in his late twenties, and I knew he would recognize me as one of the high school golfers. *Good, I can just sign and run.* I would worry about getting home as soon as I was out of Adrian's eyeline.

"Hey, I was hoping it didn't take you guys out up there! Judy said about four of you headed out two hours ago or so. What hole did ya'll make it to?" The seasoned bartender was relieved we hadn't abandoned the cart and ran.

"We got nearly six holes in before the bottom fell out on us."

"Nice. I didn't factor you all might breeze through faster with hardly anybody else out there." Ethan picked up the clipboard and grabbed a pen from behind his ear. "I think you ladies were my last cart out. Did you see any stragglers on your way in?"

"There was a rogue player... it looked like he was across the green from us on the 8th hole." Ethan put the pen down on the sign-in sheet in front of me, then moved to the back of the bar to reach for a set of keys.

"Adrian, why don't you check her out and sign for the cart? Then you can head out of here for the night. We're not gonna get anybody else in this storm. I'm gonna go check on our straggler.

He's probably played out by now and headed home, but better safe than sorry in this weather. Ole' Jack will hold down the fort til' I get back." He tapped the bar, and the older golfer raised his old fashioned in agreement. "Night Adrian. Night, young lady. You all be careful heading home."

My heart froze.

I tried to just look for Kathleen's name and our cart number as quickly as I could so I could just sign, hand him the keys, and run. He had walked up to the bar where Ethan left me and was standing in front of me before I could grab it.

"Where are the others?"

"They already left. I was stuck with the cart."

"Wait, how'd you get here? Do you have a ride?"

"Well, yes, of course. We just got rained out early, so I was going to call home at the club house." *Why did I have to defend myself to him?*

"And, how'd that work out for you... being that the club house is obviously closed?"

"I don't know, Adrian, I guess I'm pretty resourceful, and I was going to figure it out. I'm sure there is a phone here your bartender boss wouldn't mind me using when he gets back." Adrian scoffed at the idea of me waiting here until Ethan returned.

"So, you'd rather ask a practical stranger for a ride than me?"

"I wasn't going to ask anyone for a ride, Adrian! I was going to ask to use the phone. I'm not completely unfortunate."

"What's that supposed to mean?"

"Nothing. Where do I sign? It's under Kathleen's name."

He looked me over before moving to the clipboard.

"You look like a drowned rabbit; you didn't bring your jacket?"

Then, to my complete and utter dismay, a Texas-sized rumble of thunder shook through the bar. It was so loud my arms flew uncrossed, and the lights behind the bar flickered.

"Woah!" Adrian said out loud. In those few seconds, I felt confident that his exclamation was about the thunder as he quickly looked back at the old man down the bar from us to check that all was okay. However, when he returned his gaze to me, much quicker than I anticipated, his eyes were on my infamous white turtleneck. Only the white turtleneck was additionally soaking wet.

I looked like I had shown up for a wet t-shirt contest for some bizarre Oktoberfest. Not to mention the fact that my nipples were frozen into standing at attention apparently for the entire day, I'd worn a shirt and bra combo that offered no coverage whatsoever. And then, he confirmed I was right with his second exclamation.

"Woah." Yup. His eyes were on my girls, not the old man at the end of the bar anymore. "Sorry. It's just... You're SOAKED."

"Yes, I'm fully aware. Now may I please sign and get the hell out of here?" Already exposed, I took the opportunity of having free hands to reach for the clipboard and pen and sign away. I dropped the keys on the bar and walked out as fast as my legs would carry me.

The rain was still pouring down like an avalanche, and it was deafening on the patio awning I stood under. The door swung open and shut behind me.

"What are you doing?" Adrian screamed to be heard over the rain.

"I'm going to wait for that guy to come back and use the phone."

"No way in hell are you waiting here like that for Ethan. I'll obviously take you home."

"Well, I certainly wouldn't want to put you out." My response was ruder than I meant, having to yell over the pounding rain.

"Wait here." He turned toward the door, then paused and turned back to me. "Why are you like this?!" It must have been a rhetorical question as he went right back through the door and continued inside without waiting for an answer. He returned with a pile of clean bar rags he covered under the blue and white Palomino letterman jacket he was now wearing.

"I don't have an umbrella either... want to make a run for it?"

On three, we took off. I thought that meant he would run as fast as he could separate from me, but he locked his arm around my waist and took off with me by his side until we made it to his car. It was pouring, and there was no undoing the water dripping off both of us.

He opened the passenger side of his vintage Mustang for me and pulled out the bar rags as quickly as possible to put down on both of our seats. I couldn't help it, but I almost burst out laughing. I think I would have if the intensity between us wasn't so thick. All of this going on, and *that's* what he thought about... *his car seats*? Typical Adrian. He was such a perfectionist.

The sky was crazy when he started the ignition. It had clouded up and started raining before it got dark, so it looked like it was in some transition between day and night that didn't involve the sun. It was light grey and almost lavender all around. Even though it was darker out, you could see the lightning and the massive droplets of rain as clear as day as they pelted toward the windshield. It was undoubtedly dangerous to drive in, but it was phenomenal to see nonetheless.

We drove down the winding drive of the Country Club in silence. I didn't want to say anything to disturb his focus navigating the rain, and the truth was, I had nothing to say. I saw him glance over at me a few times, then he reached to adjust the air.

"Are you cold?"

I tilted my head and bit my bottom lip, stifling a sarcastic reply.

"I didn't me those—that! I didn't mean that," he corrected. "I was asking if you wanted the heat turned up."

After that, anything he said sounded like the beginning of a dirty movie. *Was he nervous? Surely not.* I took a deep breath and looked out the window. There it was again, that scent. The smell of... him. I thought I had policed that out of my head already, but it was magnified in the close quarters of his car. Every part of my body responded to taking it in.

"You never called me that night."

"You've never given me your number."

I saw the corner of his lip raise into a partial smile toward his window, and with that, the car was full of heat. There was an electric charge between the driver's seat and mine, and it was so intense I had to turn to look out the window to release myself from it.

When I turned back, peering out of the windshield, I was instantly aware of every breath I took, where and how my hands were folded in my lap. I almost forgot about the rain. Adrian seemed lost in thought on the road, too. I never felt such a heavy pull toward someone in my entire life.

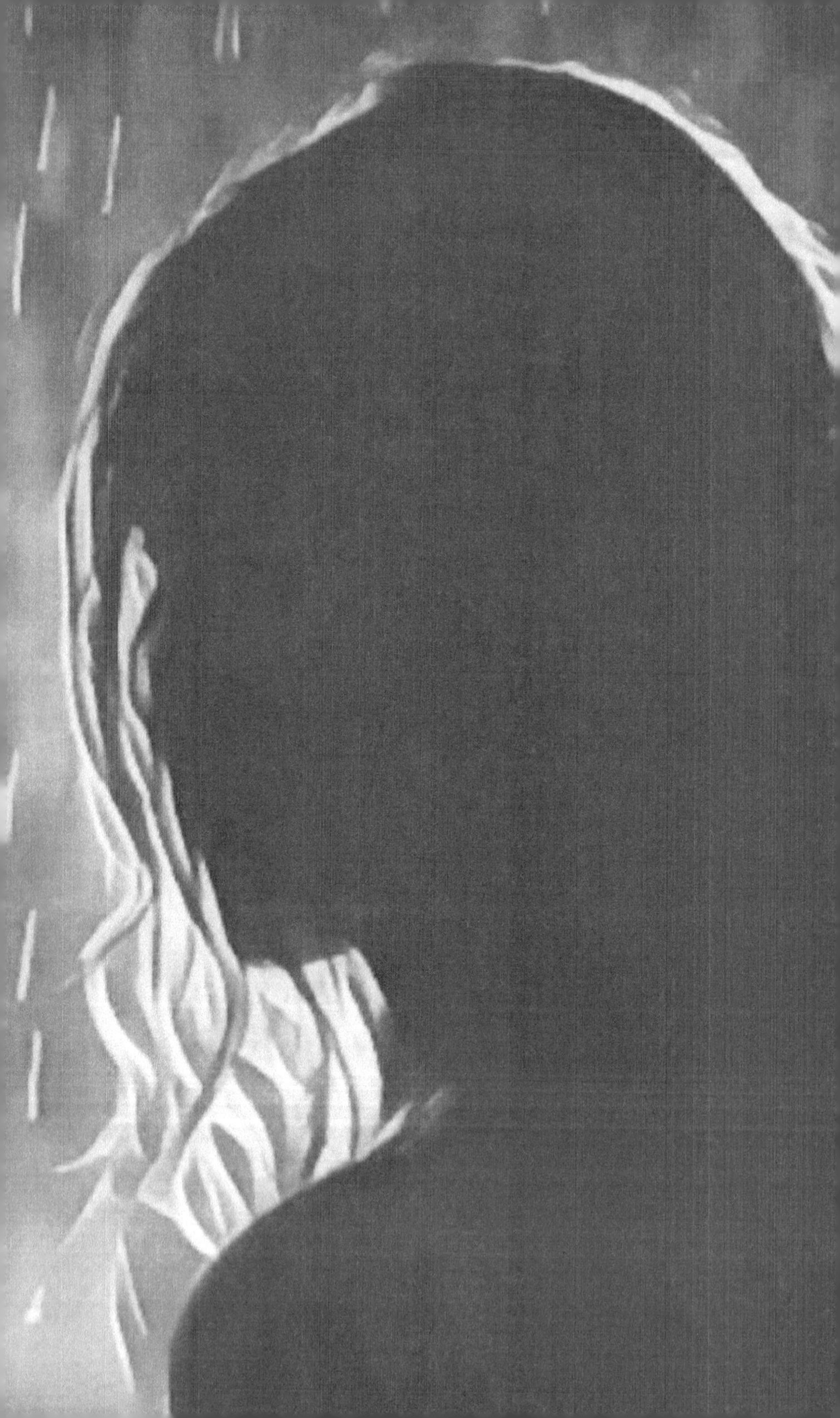

The rain was still pounding steadily on my windshield. The storm made the sky look deranged in a brilliant way, and it felt like the entire town was deserted.

I would have thought our driving in silence was an extension of our new norm. All week, we had aspired to ignore each other, pretending the party never happened... among other things. I thought there'd be a comfort or familiarity in that...but there was a familiarity of a different kind present.

Sitting next to her in the intimate space of my car, getting to be responsible for her for a moment... It evoked the same feeling I'd come to experience every time I caught her eyes on mine down the hallway. The way I felt when I grabbed her that day in the office because I needed to at the moment... I needed *her* for some reason I couldn't explain.

It was how I felt when she weighed heavily on my mind because I hadn't seen her in a while and didn't know how soon I would see her again. And the air we breathed in my car was profuse with that feeling.

I turned onto her street slowly and became disappointed I was already there.

"I'm sorry. I haven't told you where to go." Her voice came out much slower and softer than when she was angry or sarcastic with me.

So did mine. "I know where you live, July."

"Right. So that house, but three houses down instead, if you don't mind dropping me at-"

"Your grandparents'?"

She turned and smiled at me, nodding to confirm. I liked that smile. I couldn't tell if it was a smile of surprise that I knew that was her grandparents' house or if it was just how she looked when she talked about them, as if she was excited she was about to see them.

"My mom's on a work trip, so no one's home down there. The house is empty." I knew what she meant by that. She was simply informing me, but I couldn't help replaying her soft words in my head as the rain continued to beat down on the driveway we approached.

An empty house and two people who avoid being alone together at all costs. Although I had not yet consciously admitted the reason to myself, it was becoming abundantly clear at the moment, and possibilities of the empty house continued to hijack my thoughts.

I pulled into their drive. No other cars were there. "Are they not home either?"

July looked around at the empty drive and securely closed doors and windows. "I guess my grandad isn't back yet. He was coming from Corsicana earlier today. My grandmother is still at work. I hope they're all okay in this rain."

It touched me that she seemed worried about them.

"Shoot. Reagan!" She said it, flustered as she began searching through her backpack.

"What?"

"She has my house key. She took something... ugh, my vest! It had my key in the pocket. It was when she left me with... the turtleneck that just keeps on giving." She took a deep breath, and her hand was on the door to go.

"Wait. What are you doing? You're not waiting out here in this storm."

"I can go open the side window. No big deal. It's fine, and thank you, Adrian. Thank you for giving me a ride home in this weather. I really do appreciate it."

The way she thanked me was so sincere, yet I was also confused as to why she was in such a hurry to leave with no way in the house. "Look, I'm not leaving until you get inside."

"Okay. I'll come out the front and wave once I make it in. But you don't have to wait." She had the car door open and closed before I could respond, and I watched her running until she disappeared on the other side of the house.

The first minute or two made sense, but the thunder roared again as loud and startling as it was at the bar earlier, followed by an even heavier downpour.

I kept looking for her, squinting through the rain to see if I could see her waving from the front door or coming back from the other side of the house. Maybe she couldn't get it opened. I was beginning to worry.

Lightning struck and revealed a tall TV antenna on that side of the house. I knew that couldn't be safe to stand next to. I raced out of my car to find her. I turned the same corner of the house I'd watched her turn, and there she was.

She stood there less than four feet from that stupid metal antenna, struggling to push the window up. She stopped to look over at me. She was soaked through and through. Her questionable turtleneck was rendered obsolete.

I froze at the corner, staring at her. She was so determined to do everything in the hardest way possible. She gazed back at me from the window frame she'd had no luck with. Water dripped from her hair, eyelashes, and lips. I wondered what she was thinking of me at that moment. The thunder rolled around us, signaling more lightning.

"Get away from that antenna! You'll get struck by lightning! I screamed it as loud as I could, but I may as well have been whispering it; the rain was SO LOUD. I took a step toward her and screamed her name.

"JULY!" I demanded. She ran toward me as a shotgun bang of thunder shook everything around us. I couldn't say if she was planning on stopping just as she reached me or melting into my arms the way she did... because I grabbed her. I caught her and pulled her to me.

Water dripped off her face onto mine, and before either of us could think better of it, my mouth was on hers. I kissed her hard, the way I had wanted to for a while but hadn't acknowledged.

My heart was pounding in my chest as I held her close to me. I couldn't get enough. I wasn't even sure she was kissing me back at first; I just knew it felt like something I hadn't expected and had never experienced. I loosened my grip slightly to look at her, my face still above hers. Her eyes were dark and stared through me when they opened. I felt her take an uneven breath, and I leaned in, slowly moving her lips apart with mine until my tongue found hers.

She responded with her own against mine with slight trepidation and discovery that almost immediately transitioned to something sensual. It felt insane. Her lips were so soft. I was tasting her mouth, and I was kissing her like I'd never kissed anyone before.

I pulled her tighter, even though we couldn't be any closer. Just the impulse to... I couldn't contain it. I know she felt my hands gripping her tighter, my arms wrapping further because she began kissing me vigorously back. I was out of my mind pursuing her mouth in mine, and my entire body, which was soaked from the rain, felt on fire. *What was she doing to me?*

The rain slowed as abruptly as it started, and the last drops trailed down. The sky stayed its strange color and felt too bright to be as late as it must have been. Every slight tug of her bottom lip from mine, every chase of my tongue after hers, was something I wasn't willing to emerge from. I'm not sure how long we stood there engulfed in each other, in a kiss that seemed it wasn't meant to end.

With the rain gone, it felt like someone turned the lights on us. The sound of a truck pulling up in her grandparents' drive confirmed they had.

We pulled away from each other. I'm embarrassed to admit I think I missed her immediately. I turned the corner to see her grandfather get out of the driver's side of the truck, now parked in their driveway next to my car.

No matter how nice I'd heard he was, the six-foot-three gentle giant was not someone to be reckoned with. An instant wave of respect flew over me, and all I could see behind me was his drowned rabbit of a granddaughter in that ridiculously see-through turtleneck.

I thought as fast as I could and threw her my letterman jacket. I could say I don't know why I didn't think to offer it to her before. But that would be a lie. July swung into the jacket and zipped herself up as she turned the corner behind me. We approached the driveway toward her grandad, and she raced ahead to grab his keys.

"Your back!" She smiled up at him with that same smile from the car and held her hand out, pointing to his pocket. "I left my keys, and we were rained out at the golf course." With one eye on me, he tossed her the keys. She turned up the front sidewalk toward the house, shouting over her shoulder.

"Thanks for the ride!" Then she vanished into the house to get changed and dry. I couldn't blame her for that. *But did she not want to introduce me to her grandad?* I saw him smile as he approached my vintage Mustang. I liked the guy already.

He was a Robbie. Joe Robbie, to be exact. I remember my dad mentioning that they were good people. He said they'd been here from the beginning and owned land. He said Joe was fair and honest and didn't dabble in all the hype around Pure Pines. He didn't have to. He owned what he needed of it from hard-earned work.

He leaned against his Black Ford F1 50 truck and took his cap off, surveying my car. He wasn't intimidating as much as he was self-assured.

"67?"

I nodded proudly in response.

"That's ah' nice roadster you got yourself there. Looks like it got a good wash in the storm today." He stood up and extended his hand.

"Thank you, sir." I attempted to dry my hand a little on my shirt. "I think I did too." I smiled and shook his hand firmly. "I'm Adrian."

"Reed?"

"Yes Sir."

"Uh-huh. Your daddy does a good business over at his shop in Linden. He's a good man."

"Thank you, Mr. Robbie. I've heard him say the same of you."

"You're in debate with July and her swimming buddy, I believe." I was confused for a moment and not used to someone older taking an interest like our parents did.

"Oh, yeah, Lane. He's my debate partner. I forgot he and July lifeguard together."

"Every summer since they could. She's a quite a swimmer." He took a second look at my car as he walked past me toward his house and raised a charmed smile. "I'll bet she enjoyed riding home in that one."

I looked behind him at his truck. *Oh, right... a FORD.*

"We're kind of Ford people around here. It was the best car you could get back in my day. Good to meet ya, son. Appreciate you gettn' her home safe."

I watched him walk into the house without looking back at me. Wow. It was like talking to a rare giant. He was kind and sincere and scrutinized me all at the same time. Her grandad was sharp. I smiled as I drove away, hoping I'd made a good impression and the guy liked me.

The man barely said three sentences, and the conversation only lasted thirty seconds. Yet, he already let me know that if you drive a Ford, you should respect his granddaughter, that he knew who I was and when I would be spending any significant amount of time with her, which was debate, and that my own debate partner, whom he knew better than me, would obviously be looking out for her when it came to debate season just as he does every summer at the pool. Oh, yes, and he knew my dad and where he worked.

I shook my head, smiling again. That man was awesome. I hoped to be the same way if I ever had a daughter, although I doubted I could pull it off as relaxed and easygoing as he did. You could tell a lot about July after meeting him.

Obviously, she thought her grandad hung the moon, but he felt the opposite. He knew she did. My own grandfather was a pivotal figure in my life. We just had a very different relationship than that.

As for that moment on the side of the house... it hit me like a ton of bricks when I replayed it. I could taste her sweet mouth and feel her soft lips on mine. I knew this would drive me crazy until I saw her again. Then I remembered my jacket. Bold move me leaving it with her.

The ball's in your court now, July!

I didn't see her at all the next day. I had forgotten Reagan, and Lynn said the band had some marching thing in Mt. Pleasant. I hadn't heard from July either. To be fair, we'd never exchanged numbers, per her pointing out, but still, after the exchange outside her house in the rain, I think that warranted finding a way to get in touch.

School sucked without finding Lynn and Reagan between classes. I realized how much I relied on their friendship. It was funny that we had never discussed July and I, or whatever may or may not have been going on.

She'd be with them at the band thing all day... I wondered if she would say anything. Or, maybe she'd just walk in like a baller the next day wearing my jacket and leaving it for all of us to figure out. *That'd be hot.*

Still, what the hell was I thinking. We hadn't even had a conversation, and midterms were coming up, a pre-semester switch to debate prep, and the start of track training, all before Christmas break. I had to keep my head in the game.

"Adrian! There you are." Devin approached my locker with a slew of her minions not far behind. "God, you're so hard to track down these days now that you're not in football. I wasn't sure if I could unearth you without finding Reagan or Lynn first." She did that on purpose. I'm sure she wished she was likable enough to have a true friend of the opposite sex who wasn't after her clout.

"What's up Devin? Ladies." I nodded and smiled at everyone.

"I just wanted to say thanks again for having our back last week at the party."

"Don't mention it."

"And especially for having mine with July. I can't imagine why she was so upset with me. Honestly, Adrian, I've never done anything but support her in her endeavors. The worst part is, we used to be good friends. We were as close as she and Reagan are."

Okay, this just didn't get weird fast. "What do you want Devin?"

"I was just checking in on you. Have you gotten a chance to talk to Natalie yet? I thought you guys really hit it off at the party. Anyway, let me know if you need any help with that. Or maybe you can lead a palomino to water, but you can't make him drink... See ya around."

Wow. Devin and Coach Craig should have started their own think tank. Who knew a bunch of broads would be worse than the guys when I quit football. I looked up and around for Natalie. She was sweet, and I didn't want her innocently put in the middle of whatever was going on with Devin.

I shot some hoops with Jed and Angel after school. I didn't get to do that very often, but it was a rare night with no real homework. Billie and a few other guys from football joined in when they saw us.

I could tell they were reluctant at first, but everything felt back to normal after ten minutes of letting them score. That's the thing about Pure Pines; on their own, as individuals, these weren't bad guys; they were my friends. And Devin wasn't that bad when she had no score to settle or beef with someone.

I waited for Lynn to pull up from getting off the band bus that night. When I saw her jeep in the drive, I was relieved to see she was alone. I thought I'd run the Devin thing by her to see if she could make sense of it. I didn't really care; I just didn't want there to be a problem.

My real motivation was to find out if July had said anything about the kiss. Just the reminder gave me a physical reaction, and I wanted to know what she was doing that very second. Was it weird that I was hoping she spilled the beans to Lynn? That is the kind of thing girls tell their best friends, right?

Lynn yawned and took her contacts out on her vanity. She was the most unique individual I knew. I was lucky to have her.

"How was it?"

"It was band. Actually, it kind of blew worse than usual because of Jessie. He was so off, and a dick to everyone the entire trip. Oh, wait... you didn't go to the game that Friday."

"No, but I heard about him serenading Savana across stadium lights while our boys were slaughtered on the field during the fourth quarter."

"You would hear that part over the epic love story!"

"What's that supposed to mean?"

"Nothing. It's just, you know, you tend to keep your head in the game instead of getting sprung over someone, and when you do, you don't ever do anything about it."

Was I that obvious? Funny, she threw my own words at me. Again, Lynn knew me well.

"Anyway, Savanna and Jesse barely made it through that weekend. It turns out Mrs. Bishop had the administration put some "silent pressure" on her. It was enough that they got her point across. They laid out for her that Drew was coming home Thanksgiving, and if she knew what was best for her, she'd have this Jesse thing dead and buried. Nobody knows exactly what was said to end it so severely. As in mic dropped, all ties cut, just the whole thing set on fire and burned all to hell—"

"Yeah, I get it."

"Well, anyway, it is over. Jesse's in a dark place. It just goes to show that Pure Pine's prevailed. Again. We couldn't even have that little piece of fairytale last. In the end, they made her choose what was best on paper, and the underdog never wins."

"You don't think Savanna chose the one she wanted?"

"Please, Adrian. You can't be that naïve or pragmatic. You sound like July. Speaking of..."

Lynn yawned again as she reached across her dresser and pulled my letterman jacket off the nob it was hung on. I hadn't even noticed it was there.

"July gave me this to give you. Said you left it at the golf course or something like that. She figured I'd see you before she did."

She tossed me the jacket, and the disappointment landed before it did. So that was how it was going to be. I thought there was no going back or sweeping it under the rug after that kiss. Was it Lynn and Reagan? Were our friends the problem? Were we afraid of what they would think?

I couldn't imagine it was that for either one of us, yet... looking over at the exhausted Lynn, it occurred to me I hadn't made an attempt to tell her. Not even when she probed me after the office incident. I was either waiting for July to seal her fate with our friends, or I was keeping it from them, too.

I exhaled a heavy breath and stood to leave. I was hurt and angry over nothing. Over what exactly? Nothing had happened. I hadn't heard anything from her. Maybe that was it. Maybe she was trying to make it clear that she didn't want anything further to happen.

"Go to bed sleepy head, but hey... quick question. What do you think of Natalie Hilliard?"

"Blonde doe-eyed sophomore who's got a wicked crush on you?"

"What?!"

"Oh come on, don't pretend you haven't' noticed. It may be a Devin inspired infatuation, but it's real all the same."

"Yeah, that's what I'm worried about. Not Natalie... the Devin inspired part."

"What's wrong with it if you think you could be into her? The optics are better if it's a set up in case it's not great. If it doesn't work out, then the powers that be were wrong about the match, no harm no fowl."

"Sure, tell that to Jesse and Savanna."

"Get out of my room you dork!"

I could still hear her chuckling as I closed her bedroom door. But in the silence of the night lit by a single street lamp, I began my walk across our lawns with a sinking feeling. Why did I feel like it was over before it started? I raised my jacket to my face and got a whiff of July's perfume on the collar. It was hard to admit, but I automatically felt better, and all shreds of doubt dissipated.

July

"DON'T SPEAK"

No Doubt

F inally, it was Friday.

I hadn't stopped smiling since the storm. I didn't know what happened and didn't care; I was just glad it did. I had never kissed or been kissed by anyone like that. *What happened? How did it happen?* These are the questions I focused on that night and throughout the marching competition. The one thing I did know was we could no longer ignore it. It felt amazing to know how he felt about me. The speculating and overanalyzing had been making me crazy.

I also hated feeling like it was my fault or my misunderstanding. There was no possible way to misunderstand the kiss *he* instigated.

It was on a whole other level. I didn't know you could feel like that from just a kiss. Anytime I almost forgot or tried to downplay it, my stomach flipped in consecutive somersaults, and a warm feeling made me crave seeing him again.

I had to get a handle on this before I shot off like a rocket through the hallways. It was already evident to people like Devin at the party. I could only imagine what my face would give away now.

It was hard not to say anything to Reagan or Lynn, but it was personal and private. *If there were ever a time to hold my fire and keep my mouth shut to see how things go, it would be now.* I was confident we had crossed into new territory that would most likely require a conversation. Still, I also had to be realistic about how Adrian had presented thus far.

His jacket. That was difficult to figure out. It wasn't 1950. He hadn't just pinned me at the malt shop. What was I supposed to do, skip down the hallway wearing it? The most logical thing to do would have been to bring the jacket to school and simply return it to him like a normal, sane person. Logic suggests that if he had his tongue in my mouth, swapping spit for a good five to ten minutes, he wouldn't mind if I simply gave him something that belonged to him.

However, every time I played that scenario out in my head, as I smiled toward him, met him at his locker, and passed his jacket off to him, all eyes were on us, wondering why I had it in the first place. I could see that being a nightmare for him if he didn't want this or was embarrassed by me.

I wasn't being hard on myself. Several things led me to think this way, like his behavior after every other encounter and the phone situation or lack thereof. Adrian had never tried to call me or even asked for my number from Reagan or Lynn.

That was strange.

Also, other than the speculation those two arrived at from their own eyes, neither Reagan nor Lynn had asked me in private about Adrian. That lead me to believe he told them nothing about us from his end.

I thought he might appreciate having his jacket back with no fuss or grand display. He might have even needed it sooner than later... I didn't know.

I walked through the side double doors toward the main hall. I breathed in that nerve-wracking smell of Pure Pines High School and loved every bit of it for the first time that year. I could tell I was excited to see him, and I'm sure a smile had already spread across my face just thinking about it.

Even so, I tried to brace myself as I got closer to where most people hung out by their lockers together... I wanted to prepare myself to be strong if he ignored me and turned his eyes away as I passed by.

I saw something I could never have been prepared for when I entered the main space. Had I kept Devin's threat in mind, I might have been prepared. *No, I don't think so.* Even with the assumption she was partially to blame, I could never have anticipated this level of betrayal from him.

In between a crowd of varsity cheerleaders, football jocks, and the entire in-crowd to speak of stood Adrian beside Natale Hilliard. It must have been 1950, after all, as he had her first-period books cradled under his left arm. It was Friday, so she had her varsity cheerleader uniform on. And it was a cold Friday in late fall, so naturally, she was wearing his letterman jacket, too. The very one I had just returned.

I think I kept walking at the same pace. I can't be sure. It felt like slow motion, but I kept moving forward. I couldn't even look at him. And I didn't. I just kept going, waiting for the release of having passed by them.

As I approached the group at the spot I would have spun toward them to say hello in my cheerleading skirt the year before, I slowly angled in the opposite direction as if I needed to turn down the other hall. I would still have to pass by them, but this gave me a solid purpose that didn't look like I was ignoring anyone.

I had almost made it in the clear when a black, high-heeled ankle boot shot out in front of me, catching my foot and tripping me. I flew. I literally slid down the hall on my face for all to see. My books were everywhere. The owner of the black-heeled boots raced toward me and stopped where I lay defeated in the hallway. My eyes rose to find Devin Scott squatting down to whisper in my ear.

"I told you not to lie to me July Elizabeth Edwards. See what you've done? That could have been you. And you thought you were going to hit me?! Know your role before I have to show you again."

She rose without helping me up. I'd either skinned or busted my chin on the hard concrete floor. Not that I gave half a shit anymore, but to reduce my humility while lying on the floor, I began looking for my books. I don't think Adrian actually saw the fall. He certainly saw what followed, as did the entire student body that walked closer to see what happened.

With no Reagan or Lynn in sight, I could do nothing but think how to best peel myself off the floor in front of everyone. Before I could get up, two muscular arms were hooked under mine, pulling me off the floor as several students began retrieving my books. Sarah Weems and Wendy Tomlin had lifted me onto my feet.

"What the fuck, Devin?! Sarah screamed for all to hear.

"Did she trip her? Did you fucking trip her?!" Wendy got louder and in Devin's face. My former friends who hadn't seen the fall and were curious about what was happening gathered behind Devin. Soon, more of the student body led by the upperclassmen's elite were all standing behind me, including Savanna Baker, who typically couldn't be bothered to say hello since I hadn't made varsity.

Whitney Tomlin, the other twin, beelined over from her own locker. She darted right up and stood between her sister and Sarah, who were in their cheerleading uniforms, and she also asked Devin what the hell was going on. When I looked up at Whitney standing next to her peers in all their varsity uniform "fly skirt" glory, it was the first time this year I'd seen her back to her usual self and next to Savanna, Sarah, and her twin, Wendy. It felt like she crossed a picket line for me, at the risk of acknowledging or reminding everyone she didn't make varsity cheerleader either.

It meant a lot that she came and stood by me and them when there was a sting for her to be next to all the varsity cheerleaders without being one anymore. I obviously knew the sting all too well. A couple of our popular senior guys handed me my books and stood next to the girls beside and behind me.

I looked back, and there were band friends. Lane, my swimming buddy, as my grandad calls him, and Anna George, my best childhood friend and lifer who grew up a backyard behind me, were also standing there. I didn't need anybody else that day to make it right. A day late and a dollar short, I may have always been at Pure Pines, but my merit stood, and over half the student body was standing with me.

Devin didn't say a word. Her eyes stayed glued to mine as if this wasn't finished. Hell, I didn't even know what had started. *Hadn't she been the one to mess with me?* I hadn't done anything to her that I could think of.

Teachers and administration came running down the hallway, mainly because of the crowd size. Mrs. Rickie made it first, and Mrs. Bishop swooped down from the office before others arrived.

"Who do I need to remind that this is a zero-tolerance school?" Mrs. Bishop pulled office administration rank.

"Break it up, guys. Nothing to see here, let's get to class." Mrs. Rickie was our fun teacher. She was debate and English AP for juniors and seniors. She knew this shit wasn't necessary, and she just wanted the day to move on. Nobody moved, though. All eyes were on me and Devin.

Billie Aiken walked up to the middle of the group and stood between Devin and me. He nodded behind him to Russell Shirley and Graham Dowds, our two most popular senior jocks who had lettered in every sport since their freshman year. They slid past Sarah, Savana, and the Tomlin twins towards us.

Russell was hot and had the personality to match. Graham was quieter but equally intimidating.

"Thanks, Mrs. Rickie. We're all good. July just tripped, so I thought I'd walk her to class and make sure she's cool." Russell grabbed my books and held out his arm for me. Wow, I obviously knew Russell my entire life but hearing him say my name out loud, publicly... I couldn't help but be surprised he remembered it.

Billie Aiken spoke up, following his lead. "Yeah, don't worry Mrs. Bishop, I think Devin slipped and almost tripped herself trying to help July. Graham will walk her to first period if that works for you.

That was one bonus of the whole Pure Pine's taking care of their own mentality, and it wasn't lost on these elite upperclassmen. The "zero tolerance" policy could ruin you if you were on the wrong end of it. It was probably more terrifying than the cops busting up a party. At least there was a slim chance for the cops to call your parents and try handling things... with Pure Pine's administration in charge, it was all politics.

Mrs. Bishop's son Drew, the one Savanna was linked to, was good buddies with our current senior football players, Billie, Russell, and Graham. They were a year behind Drew and grew up raiding her kitchen cabinets after school with him. She was absolute putty in their charming hands. She frowned skeptically, then winked at them. "Okay, boys, just make sure you walk yourselves to class after that." The crowd in the hallway chuckled to break the ice and began dispersing.

I was blown away. I never dreamed anybody at Pure Pines other than Lynn, Reagan, or Anna George would stand up for me like people did. *Did they see her trip me? Is that why?*

Either way, I had bigger problems than the pain in my stomach from my heart sinking into it when I saw Adrian with Natalie, and bigger issues than the piece of skin I felt tear off my chin while sliding down the concrete floor... Somehow, without intending to, I had waged war with Devin Scott. I wasn't sure this would be the end of it after the support just shown to me.

Great. The day almost the entire student body stands by you against the most popular girl in school... it still bites you in the ass?

I walked out of first period in our usual hallway to meet up. Reagan and Lynn had an early lab that morning and may not have heard the gossip. I could see it all in slow motion before it happened. A million stares would warp in my direction, watching my face as I walked out of the classroom.

Lynn and Reagan would already be pow-wowing by Reagan's locker, having no idea what happened but wondering why everyone was staring. Then it would be a battle of who approached our friends first, me or Adrian. The battle that always caused the other to first look away, then change the course of their direction. If I was lucky, he'd be waiting for his precious Natalie after the bell instead.

I turned out of class with all eyes on me as anticipated, and I breathed a sigh of relief when I saw Reagan and Lynn standing by themselves.

"Oh my God, did you hear?" Lynn went first. Reagan stood wide-eyed, raising her eyebrows, ready to jump in and relay the scoop.

I just looked at them. I was lost and confused. I couldn't handle anything more exciting or traumatic than I had just experienced.

"What's the matter with your chin?" Reagan's alarm made me aware it had gotten a little worse than it felt in the last hour. I hadn't even gotten to look at it yet.

"Oh, I guess you didn't hear." I halted their enthusiasm. "It doesn't matter. Just, what were you going to tell me about?"

Reagan stared at me, trying to figure me out. Then she looked over at Lynn, who was about to say what I had already witnessed.

"We were just going to ask you if you'd heard about the latest setup with Ad—" Reagan punched Lynn's arm and gave her a look. Lynn realized immediately. I guess she saw it written all over my face, plus whatever was wrong with my chin. My eyes swelled instantly with tears, and I couldn't breathe.

They were my best friends. How could something have gone this far without them knowing? I needed them. I needed to— My eyes shifted above their heads as I saw Adrian approaching behind them like clockwork. He was alone, and he had a concerned look on his face.

I couldn't breathe or feel my legs, and I didn't know how much longer I could stand there without wanting to cry a river into my friends' arms right in front of him and everyone else staring. I spun around faster than I thought possible and took off in the opposite direction.

"JULY!" Three voices screamed my name, including Adrian's. It was too late. I had already slipped around the corner into the masses, and my face was about to be covered in tears and mascara. I couldn't let the student body see that, especially not after they came to my aid. Sure, they were all staring at me out of morbid curiosity, but that didn't mean they wanted me to crumble.

I passed two bathroom opportunities on my way down to the band hall. It would be much safer to disappear into the old majorette room, now our drill team changing room. I hoped maintenance had left it open. They were sloppy about it during marching season as we were annoyingly in and out of there more times than they cared to go back and lock it.

I desperately wanted Reagan and Lynn to find me. I wanted to explain why it all had been so weird and how it somehow got weirder with Devin. How could I have explained then? In some bathroom for all to overhear and spread more gossip? Plus, I wasn't sure I could divulge anything in my state without revealing everything to them. And I just wasn't ready to do that.

When I ducked into the band hall, I heard a few people clambering around in the instrument room and saw that Mr. McLendon was out of the office. No one noticed me go in and lock the door. I leaned against the wall in the dressing room and slid to the floor, balling.

I had never felt so stupid in my life. The most conflicting part was trying to discern what made me the biggest fool, Adrian, or the night of the party where I suddenly got balls and thought it was my right to stand up to Devin as if it were allowed.

All those years I knew Devin, especially during cheerleading, there wasn't a time Hanna, Brooke, or Dane stood up to her. We had all seen her run Brooke and Hanna through the mud, and they still didn't fight back. Dane, a strong personality who often stood up for people outside the crowd, never suggested Devin take it easy on one of them.

Ridicule was Devin's for the taking; everyone stood by and watched. Until today. I had to admit to myself something had changed. Our elite group of friends shifted, and the observing student body that looked at me on the floor said, "Enough." I can't think that I was powerful enough to be the catalyst, but maybe she'd pissed somebody else off, and I was the last straw.

I was also honored to be championed by three senior jocks that ruled the school. When Billie escorted us to class by Russ and Graham, that was a scene no one would forget. Still, I couldn't help minimizing it in my mind.

The fact remained that we were a zero-tolerance school, and Pure Pines took care of their own. One could say they were making sure no slaps or punches were thrown to make Devin's reputation suffer. However, she wouldn't have needed their help. Devin could get by with anything. Maybe I had maintained enough status to be "one of their own" after all.

A knock on the changing room door startled me. I opened it to find the most familiar face I could hope for. It was Anna George, my childhood bestie and a true blue for life. Anna and I had opposite schedules since high school started. Having no random freshman and sophomore classes together was cruel. She went the choir route... and so on. Our only saving grace was that she was a backyard away from my mom's and grandparents' houses. Her house was a street behind in between both houses, making it diagonal from either house I walked over from.

"Good Lord, I thought I'd never find you. Do you know I haven't been down here since we got to tour it in Jr. High band and here I am breaking an entering for your ass. Remind me again why we don't hang out on a daily basis?" She held her hand out to help me off the floor, and I jumped up and hugged her.

"Take it easy. I don't want any part of whatever violent delinquency you have going on!" We laughed and I play punched her arm. She was standing in her favorite jean skirt and her Palomino letterman jacket.

It stung when I saw another blue, white, and maroon jacket after what I had just been through. However, the sting dissolved when I noticed an additional music note patch she must have earned this semester. Even through my tears, I was proud of her and even more proud that she was the one who found me.

"Okay, will you tell me what is happening here? Should I be worried about you? I *saw* Devin Scott trip you!"

"How bad is it?" I raised my chin up at her.

"You look like you have lesions or got scabies and scratched way too hard, but... only from your chin down. Just don't look up at anyone and I think you'll be fine."

I rolled my eyes and couldn't help but smile. All of my friends were sarcastic, but Anna's sardonic wit was record-breaking and always what the doctor ordered in a crisis.

"Yeah. So, I guess I had that one coming. I kind of challenged her at the Tomlin party."

"You went to that this year?!! I heard it was insane. I can't believe you didn't get grounded for life or... *dead*. I can't believe they didn't kill you. My parents would have dropped me off on the side of the road somewhere miles from home."

"Well, caught. I didn't get caught. Anyway, I have no idea what I did to get on her bad side."

"I'm surprised. As mean as she is, out of all the girls on varsity I still would have thought she'd be the most compassionate when you didn't make it. Did you remind her we have pictures from when we were little of her playing dress up in your grandparents living room and my mom's sewing room?"

"No. I thought I'd save the incriminating physical evidence of true friendship for the next time she assaults me in front of the entire student body."

"Some assault. I'm afraid it backfired on her. Did you see everybody's face? They were looking at her in disgust and the people who didn't see her trip you were on your side automatically. I'd say if it was a fight... you won."

"Well, not entirely. If you're right, I'm sure she's embarrassed and will retaliate until everything works in her favor. Tripping may be the mildest part of her sinister little plan. She... well, she kind of –"

"Natalie Hilliard?"

"How did you know?!"

"Well, I don't know what Devin had to do with it, but I can only assume. Everyone saw Adrian coupled with Natalie in the hall this morning. Devin made sure of it. As much as I never understood your adolescent crush on your mortal enemy, I still know you like the back of my hand. I never assumed that the well ran dry.

"Anna—"

"Nope, I was there during freshman cheerleader round up. Thirty minutes before kickoff a mini you in a very large hair ribbon pulled me out of the stands and asked me if it would be appropriate to say Adrian's name in your introduction. Not for nothing July, I was just as taken aback when I saw Adrian with Natalie followed by Devin tripping you. Do you see the common denominator in both those scenarios?"

"Adrian?"

"Umm.... Yes and...,"

"Devin getting in the way of someone I liked."

"*Ding. Ding. Ding.*"

"God, I can't believe that didn't cross my mind!"

"Now you just have to figure out why.

"You're right. I have to figure out her motivation. Either way, she got the win, keeping me from Adrian. At this point, I don't think either of us would touch each other with a ten-foot pole. I'm truly dreading debate season this year. Hey... did you really skip class to come save this wayward soul?"

"No, but I am fifteen minutes late for choir. Tell me you are not going to spend the rest of this period crying your eye makeup off, then find some nasty drill team girl's dried up tube of mascara on the floor and end up using it to motivate yourself back into walking the hallways with dignity. Because that's gross, July, it's really gross."

"Get outta here! Actually...do I look okay? Are my eyes too puffy?"

"I think you'll need to start looking for that mascara." Anna smiled and headed out. If it wasn't for her, I think I would have walked straight out of the drill team room to the band hall exit and left the school premises without checking out. I needed that.

I needed my friend. I hope she knew how grateful I was for her kindness and insight, that her tardiness was not in vain. Anna was not a rule breaker. It put her against her better judgment to hunt me down and check on me. *That* gave me the strength to pick up and move on about my day.

When something happens to you, and it implicates someone else or puts them out, that's enough. Anna was more important than any of this bull shit, and she just had to waste her time with it. I was better now. Having a friend like Anna, and even Reagan and Lynn, who were still in the dark, superseded an enemy like Devin and the humiliation of Adrian.

I grabbed my books and tried to escape into the band hall. I knew there would be no class or rehearsal, but anybody could be in a practice session. As I poked my head out into the large, empty space, I took a deep sigh of relief. No one was around. I heard a familiar voice from the instrument room, half whispering. "I don't know! I can't remember! Please stop asking me. I told you everything I can remember about that night!"

"Hang on, I think someone's out there." Another familiar voice interrupted the girl who was whisper shouting. I turned on a dime to hide behind the band-stand cabinet. It was taller than me.

"I don't see anyone... go ahead."

"That's it." The original voice spoke more confidently and in less of a whisper. I recognized it immediately as Robyn's. I froze behind the cabinet and wished I could throw up the entire day. This was my last straw.

"That's all I can remember. It wasn't until I woke up the next morning, went to the bathroom and realized that my underwear was on inside out, and I was sore where I've never been before. I asked my sister for all the details and she had a reasonable explanation for everything. She didn't seem worried at all and even suggested she was with me nearly the entire time."

Well, she wasn't with her when I saw her.

"Well, she wasn't with you the entire time then."

Jinx. Whoever this girl was, she was a better friend than me. Robyn wasn't a super close friend of mine, but we became close shortly after she moved here. She was gorgeous and had an exotic look about her. She was very different than your typical Pure Pines girl, and the fact that she came from a bigger school with more open-minded, perhaps kinder people showed.

One flirtatious look from a slew of upperclassmen our freshman year, a date or two from interested elite guys, and the in-crowd tore her to shreds like vultures. They never did anything to her outwardly, but a heavy, unwritten rule accumulated around her.

Suddenly, everyone tagged her as a bit too wild for their taste. It was obviously jealousy. Someone striking came in and stole too much thunder, so they had to behave like something was wrong with her.

The first time in my high school experience that I was ashamed and disgusted with myself was my sophomore year when she came up to talk to me during a break. Surrounded by all the other cheerleaders and elite assholes who all had a specific spot of rank... she had just walked right up to say hello to me and ask me what we should do after school that day.

She was a genuine, charming breath of fresh air next to those insecure sociopaths, and I froze up and let myself be embarrassed by my association. I was lucky to have an association with someone who knew exactly who she was. That is why they despised her. She was noticeably more attractive than many of them, and more impressive than that, she knew who she was. They only knew who they thought they were supposed to be.

The chickens pecking the new chicken nearly to death had settled well before the recent Tomlin party. Still, I never forgot the indiscretion that made me stoop to their level. Even though I didn't say anything rude, even though I wasn't directly mean to her... She felt the cold shoulder as she walked toward the shark tank, and I will never forgive myself for mine being one of them.

"You have to tell someone!" Whomever her real friend talking to her was, they were insistent. I couldn't see them. The instrument room had no doors on either side. It was a long shotgun hallway of a narrow room with large square shelves for our instruments lining its walls. Robyn was in the band with me, and I could only assume the other familiar voice was, too, even though I hadn't made it out yet.

"Tell them what? That I think I got drunk and raped at the biggest party of the year. Although I'm not sure who I slept with, I can tell you the names of the two people I remember being in a room with and I don't think you're going to like it."

The bell rang for the next period, and I fled from the band hall into the hallway with the masses. I no longer cared about the stares I was getting from this morning's nightmare.

A much worse night mere had happened to someone who didn't deserve it. At this point, I was sure I was already a part of what would help suppress it for the system. That was a much more significant concern than anything else. My stomach ached, and Project "Get over Yourself" was in full swing.

Adrian

"SOMETHING IN THE WAY"

Nirvana

T hird period felt like a year. I needed to see if July was okay and find out what the fuck actually happened. Lynn and Reagan had pulled a disappearing act.

In their defense, I think they ran after July. The question was, why did she run? I know she saw me standing next to Natalie, but we weren't walking down the aisle for crying out loud. I didn't understand what happened between now and the other night in the rain.

If I thought about it harder, a part of me understood. It was the same push-pull that started that day in the office. Although I couldn't acknowledge it then, I was as much to blame, if not more, than she was. I was the one who made the immediate return of my jacket mean something. Also, the fact she hadn't told Lynn or Reagan. I took it as a sign she rejected what happened between us.

Honestly, nothing about my situation with July had been orthodox. Why would this be the deal breaker? Did I make it one by appearing to take Devin up on Natalie? All I knew was there had to be a way to fix it.

Catching up with Reagan and Lynn after the bell finally rang was an act of Congress. I arrived just in time for Reagan to swing her locker door open in front of my face. Lynn turned to walk away from me.

"Hey! What's going on with you two? I've been trying to get to you all morning. Have you found her yet?"

"Oh, I think we can speak for her when we say you're the last person she wants to see." Reagan was fuming.

"Frankly, you're the last person we want to see right now." Lynn surprised me by seconding the motion.

"Why, did she say something?"

"She didn't have to." Lynn whisper-shouted at me, looking furious. Reagan grabbed our arms and pulled us back toward her open locker.

"Okay, I don't mean to bulldoze over any potential... did they or didn't they like each other and why didn't anybody think it appropriate to mention it to their best fucking friends, but I do need to interrupt to ask *what the hell happened to her face?*" Reagan stepped into me, demanding an answer.

"I don't exactly know. I couldn't get over there fast enough to see before a mob of people surrounded her. I was on the other side of the wall by the lockers when she walked past Devin." I tried to explain what I didn't understand as best I could.

"Oh, that's rich. Something you weren't fast enough for." Reagan retorted.

"Hey, just tell me if she's okay!" I hit Reagan's locker above her head, slamming it shut, and prying eyes down the hall met ours immediately. "I'm sorry, I've just...been on edge the entire last period, and she probably shouldn't be walking around by herself right now anyway."

Lynn glanced between Reagan and me. She could help me out or be the voice of reason. Instead, she stepped in front of Reagan and got in my face. "Don't you already have someone to walk to class? Isn't that what started it all? I wouldn't keep her waiting if I were you." Lynn stepped away, then came back at me with one last hit. "From what I heard July had better men than you come to her aid."

Reagan remained in front of her locker, waiting for my full attention.

"This, whatever *this* was or wasn't with July, that neither of you thought to tell us about... If you know her like we do, you can bet it's over." She spun away from me.

They could have let me explain.

I could have told them that I walked down the main hallway that morning the same as July did, only a mere ten minutes earlier.

Fewer people were roaming the halls as it was still early, so it didn't feel weird when Devin singled me out and called me over.

What I should have noticed is everyone gathered around Natalie's locker. She was a sophomore, so that wouldn't have been a spot that begged everyone's attention. All the varsity cheerleaders from our junior class gathered at her locker. Shelby North, Angel, and my other buddy Jed were there, so it felt more natural than it looked or vice versa. *Hell, I don't know.*

Before I knew it, Devin had me in a conversation with Natalie, and a comment that it was cold in the hall turned into her wearing my jacket almost immediately. I don't even think Natalie mentioned she was cold. It was all Devin. I took the books out of Natalie's hand when she reached back into her locker for something she was having trouble finding. *That's it.* It was that innocent until more of the student body filtered in to stare, and July walked in at the perfect moment. *Wow. I guess that would be what one would call a setup.*

***

I can't say how long it really was. It may have only been two weeks, but it felt like a month that Reagan didn't return my call when I paged her, and Lynn wouldn't come to the phone or stop by. Devin persisted daily. She wasn't stupid. She didn't keep pushing Natalie on me as much as she included me in the group that surrounded her.

I was on autopilot. In truth, I didn't protest as much as I probably should have to work my way back into my friends' good graces. Instead, I appeared to fall into the trap.

I needed it. The distraction. Anything to keep me from looking down every hallway for the face I couldn't get out of my head. And, not to sound like a pussy or anything, but not having anyone to tell about it because my best friends had chosen a side... Stupid.

Looking back on those few weeks, I don't remember seeing them much around July either. She was distancing herself from us all, which made me want to go after Natalie more out of spite. If I couldn't have what I wanted, I wasn't going to lay down and die. I didn't like being made out to be the bad guy. I may not have handled everything that well. Her. I may not have handled *her* well, but she didn't exactly rise to the occasion either. She could have gotten my number from Lynn or Reagan at any point, and she knew where I lived.

This didn't have to be as cryptic as we made it. It was exhausting. Maybe that proved it wouldn't work. The fact that it was all so surreptitious. I toyed with the idea that we set ourselves up so covertly because, subconsciously, we both knew becoming involved was a bad idea.

I needed to entertain the situation with Natalie. She was kind and easy to talk to. I wanted to get out of Devin's web of bullshit and see if there wasn't something actually there.

Natalie was great, and she didn't make me crazy. I wasn't up all night in knots over what she thought or didn't think. I didn't *need* her. I wanted to hang out with her and see where it could go. That felt promising because it was attainable. More-over-*containable*. She fit into my schedule way better than the vice that was July. I could date her, have a typical high school relationship without drama, and get myself in gear for the work I had ahead. I could have fun.

The end of fall had come into full fold, and it was downright cold out. My stepmom sent me to the grocery store for a loaf of bread. My stepbrother lost his jeep privileges, so I was designated errand boy. I didn't mind. I'd been reading our English AP list for Mrs. Rickie's class, and I needed a break from Hester Prynne and Arthur Dimmesdale. *Now, they were exhausting.*

It was almost seven o'clock, but if I hurried, I could roll up to Pure Pines Market before it closed instead of driving to Prairie. Our only grocery store supplied the basics for a pretty price. My stepmom griped that a can of cherry pie filling, notebook paper, or whatever was more than five bucks. That and they closed remarkably early. The doors would lock at seven sharp.

I hit the brakes in a parking spot up front and raced in before the cashier could reach the door with her keys. She smiled reluctantly and gave me a go-ahead nod.

A single loaf of wheat bread was in hand, and I was in one of the only two lines available, waiting to check out with the other last-minute shoppers.

I took in the local drawl of the place, literally. The cashiers' accents were so thick I could barely understand them. I understood their inflection. Each sentence ended with them calling you or the person in front of you "Honey."

I stepped forward in my line toward the only person left ahead of me. As I looked down to grab my wallet in preparation to check out quickly, I smelled a hint of a familiar scent. It was so faint and hardly stood out above the aroma of the grocery store, but it was enough to still my heart for a second.

I knew it was her. I couldn't look over. I couldn't move. I casually cut my eyes to the line beside me an aisle over.

There, July stood with a gallon jug of milk. She was sent for one item, milk, as I was sent for bread, to ensure our household worlds continued revolving. She didn't notice me. If she did, she played that she didn't exceptionally well. She wore dark denim jeans and an old college sweatshirt cut off on one shoulder. I couldn't see the college, but I assumed it was her mother's. She looked hot. Kind of had this relaxed, 80's Debra Winger thing going on, but with Melanie Griffith's boobs.

"You're up, hun'." The cashier interrupted my potentially dirty thoughts, and I looked away from July and stepped toward the checkout. The guy in line in front of her grabbed his receipt and headed out as well, so I knew she would be standing right behind me, one aisle over. No way she couldn't see me standing in front of her at my checkout counter. I didn't want to turn around and make it obvious I'd seen her, so I waited until she called my name.

She didn't. July not only refrained from calling my name but she said nothing as I walked past and in front of her toward the exit. I got in my car, started the ignition, and waited there. I was full of heat and nerves. My head physically felt hot. I wasn't sure what was happening. I watched from the large front store windows as she headed out the sliding automatic doors and straight to her grandad's truck without flinching when she saw my Mustang in her peripheral vision.

Why didn't she say anything? Was she suddenly mute? Okay, living the best, worst John Hughes movie had to stop. Maybe it was my fault. I guess I missed the moment. For what? To say... *"Hey, remember when I drove you home in the rain and mauled you outside your grandparents' house and if no one had come home, I'm not sure what would have happened? Because contrary to me being seen dating another girl, it's all I think about... you're all I think about."*

Yeah... that. That would have gone over well.

July

"IF IT MAKES YOU HAPPY"

Sheryl Crow

"Look, I'm not going to lie and tell you it's okay and you can wait and tell us when you're ready, OR, it didn't hurt our feelings that—" Reagan was really on a tear with her speech until Lynn interrupted to chime in and take her crack at me.

"Or never ever tell us which was apparently what you were going to do while we watched it blow up in your face, literally."

Wow. I didn't know Lynn could be that harsh.

"Okay, that was a little harsh." Apparently, Reagan felt the same way. I was grateful she jumped back in. I preferred her version of schooling me over Lynn's at that moment. "I am sorry about your chin. Let me see it. How is it healing?" I rolled my eyes away from Reagan's attempt at mothering.

"It's been weeks. You can barely see it anymore."

"We're just hurt. *Can't you understand that?* You didn't come to us and that's really messed up." Lynn was starting to sound more reasonable and like herself.

"I still don't know what went on between you and Adrian, if anything, and I'm afraid that hinders us in getting to the bottom of this Devin thing. Trust me, July. You know I speak from experience when it comes to her."

It got quiet momentarily as we mulled over the reality of a prior situation. Fortunately, Reagan had more clout with the administration than Devin did. That was an anomaly within itself, but one brought on by Devin's bossy attitude she had exercised far too many times with authority figures. Let's just say the pendulum swung Reagan's way when she and Devin went head-to-head, whereas I would not have enough clout to achieve the same results.

"It's my fault." Lynn broke the silence. "The night before she tripped you Adrian asked me about Natalie. I told him she had a crush on him, not that he'd do anything about it. I basically challenged or shamed him into pursuing her. July, I said that to Adrian having no idea what was going on between you two and the truth is, I still don't! But, you know I saw him grab you in the office. You know I noticed and practically begged you both to enlighten me without coming right out and asking you. Now I have to ask myself why I would push him on her to unwittingly fulfill Devin's fucked up plan."

I could tell this really upset Lynn. Compassion and fear that she had something to do with Adrian going after Natalie outweighed her anger with me for not being forthcoming.

"July, I was so tired that night from the band trip and I truly just answered his question. I guess I subconsciously thought... if you never said there was something going on, then there wasn't, and he was fair game."

"It's not your fault, AT ALL. *He* asked you about Natalie. He did that on his own and she is obviously who he wants to be with. Plus there is nothing going on between us, so you were right to answer him honestly. As for Devin, I just want it to blow over. Let's just start this part of our junior year over and forget this non-issue."

They exchanged glances as if considering my proposal, and their eyes lasered in on me. Contemplative.

"And stop ignoring your *other* best friend!" *Yup.* That was me defending Adrian. "It's mean and hateful. Just because I have a personal beef with him doesn't mean he deserves that from you guys. Please fix it with him, or I will feel worse about the whole thing. This is all a Devin ordeal escalated way out of proportion. No one that she didn't intend to target deserves that. I was her target, not Adrian, and not Natalie."

That was the last conversation I had with Reagan and Lynn over Adrian. After that, they rallied and picked up where they left off with us. They eliminated the *"What's going on with you and July?"* fascination. And I'm sure Adrian piped down on the, *"Is*

July okay... have you seen her today?" Everything seemed to go back to normal except for Adrian and me. Whatever our normal was.

***

A sophomore with almost a foot of height on me and a better metabolism. How insulting. It had been nearly a month and a half of them dating, and I still had to remind myself that I liked the girl and it wasn't her fault. Of course, I knew her from school and cheer tryouts, but I'd also seen her at my grandparents' church a few times. Her parents, like mine, were divorced. When she stayed with her dad for a few weeks out of the school year, she came to church with him. We never spoke, really; we just gave each other that nod of recognition.

There was something sincere about her that I'm sure Adrian was attracted to. But it must have made him crazy that he would feel guilty for pushing anything too physical she wasn't ready for. I knew this from years of watching her hold the hymnal for the elderly member in the pew next to her so they could see it better; meanwhile, she had all the verses memorized.

Sometimes, you can just tell things about people. She was a walking secret that exposed everything about herself. She was nothing like the little bitches in her class and the class below her.

We called those girls the "freshman cult." They were just a few years younger than us, but they felt like an entire other generation. They are the ones who decided they were too cool for school. Sports, cheerleading, and academia were too lame to be bothered with.

They showed up on campus to basically fuck the elite senior guys, pissing off the in-crowd's junior and senior girls, just for entertainment. They were way more rebellious than any Pure Pine's class surrounding ours had ever been, and the funny thing was... It was a rebellion of Pure Pine's own making. They weren't heroes for the underdogs or crusaders against pretension.

They were ruthless. They thought their shit didn't stink like they were the most special Pure Pines ever bred. I knew I wouldn't want to look back once I left this place, but I had to admit, you didn't need a crystal ball to know their senior year would provide the faculty and town top-notch entertainment.

This genuinely kind, conservative sophomore snatched up by the elite on her climb for social hierarchy was no match for the Freshman cult coming in behind her, no matter how much she wanted to be. It would have been easier for me if she was one of those little demented bitches. I could have hated her for sport. But she was sweet and a person you wanted to root for.

It also made me feel sorry for Adrian, in a way. It was as if the pecking order deemed she was the one for him, as opposed to elites from the in-crowd.

Come on. If you weren't going to match him with me, match him with someone I could at least be jealous of. I'm sure that's what Devin thought she was doing. A sophomore that made varsity cheerleader above me. An innocent, trustworthy friend type instead of a foe.

Someone you wish the best for instead of trying to ruin their happiness was sure to help the hurt last longer. A pale blue-eyed strawberry blonde with thin limbs and an angelic walk for her height. She was the opposite of me in that regard and harmless. Natalie was really a harmless creature. I didn't quite get that part. It felt as if it served my cause more that she wasn't a force to be reckoned with. Wonder why Devin went the safe route? My only guess was Natalie was easier to control.

As for the Adrian of it all... I hated two life statements: "Lesson learned" and "Time heals all wounds." However, in my case with him, I hoped they applied and were in full effect. I just wanted it to be dead and buried. He already haunted my thoughts, and as much as I hated to admit it, he owned large chunks of my heart.

I couldn't have him haunting me at school. That was apparently Devin's job, as well as whatever had happened to Robyn at the hands of Spencer Pearce.

Debate was starting soon. I would have to be cordial for any chance at a successful season. Reagan was my partner. My swimming buddy, Lane was Adrian's debate partner. It was too intimate a group. The stakes were too high. We'd never advance in competition if there was any malice between us. If he could pretend nothing ever happened, so could I. I hoped his plan was to show me that mercy.

I'm ashamed to admit that my concern over Robyn is what kept me strong in distancing myself from the grief and drama of Adrian. It helped me keep my head down and out of Devin's way. I became obsessed with finding the right moment to talk to her and tell her what I saw at the party... ask her if it helped or if there was anything I could do to help her tell somebody.

Sadly, my chance meeting with her in the girl's bathroom did not go as planned. She seemed upset that I was one more person who knew about it. She asked me which list I wanted to help her make. The list of the additional people in and out of that room all night, or those who knew about it and didn't care. I knew she was hurting. My God, how could she not be. But I couldn't pretend to understand what she was up against.

Bad stuff isn't supposed to happen in small towns. At least, that's what people will tell you. They say, "Oh, that would never happen around here." No, I guess it wouldn't. It would be much worse. The first time we all realized we weren't infallible at Pure Pines was when an upperclassman coach's daughter was implicated in a serious scandal. It involved a crime, a courtroom, and another girl. It was Adeline Morgan, and the only crime she committed was being herself. We didn't know what it was or meant to be a lesbian back then at Pure Pines.

We were all painfully ignorant about things they didn't want us to understand. It was the one opportunity that someone from the in-crowd could have made it okay to be who they were, even if that was different than what Pure Pines had dictated. Instead, they outed her, turned it into a scandal beyond her control, and then made it disappear. I remember the day Adeline's mother, Coach Morgan, left class to appear in court.

It was so strange... Everyone knew why she was dressed up and where she was going, yet no one said a word. They just watched it on the local news, then returned to school and pretended with the rest of the horses in the corral. I guess they thought Adeline couldn't be a lesbian if the word didn't exist.

The fact that I don't know who or where Adeline Morgan is today in her life makes me think it caused her to disappear as well. *That* is what Robyn Maes was up against.

For everything I didn't know, I knew enough that it kept me up at night worrying about her. And I knew I hated Spencer Pearce, and if I ever saw him again...

I often replayed when I tried to hug her and tell her I was there if she needed to talk. I thought of it in my head or during class when my mind wondered. How she looked at me, her eyes burning in anger, and said, "Sure thing," dryly as she escaped the bathroom and my judgment. I must have seemed so patronizing to her after what she'd been through, and me especially, after the way I treated her that day a year or two before. I hated Pure Pines.

Yet, there I was on "Spirit Day" with all that hate, officially posting the academic awards for mid-semester. Thanksgiving had come and gone, and we were all in the thick of our final exams for block scheduling, prepping for a new course load in spring Semester. I was standing on a small step stool on the tiled outer wall of our auditorium, negotiating sticky tack and trying not to wrinkle anyone's certificate or knock down the office administration's poorly hung Christmas garland. A few other junior and senior cheerleaders, band members, and annual staff who had been solicited were bringing more stacks of cards as the student council printed them.

Every year during Spirit Week, there was some form of mischief in almost anything we did. It was in good fun and encouraged by the faculty because they cracked the whip so hard on exams. They were innocent pranks. For example, a bunch of the guys approaching me and tossing the alphabetically stacked certificates into chaos or just taking off with the entire stack below my step stool. We'd have to go find them somewhere. I should have expected as much when I heard the double doors open and a slew of sneakers squeaking and shuffling quickly toward us.

"Get 'em hot off the press, ladies and gentlemen!"

"Ahh!!!! Don't you dare!" Russel picked up Sarah Weems and dragged her off the stool, controlling her hand like a rag doll and making her toss the pile of certificates she held all over the auditorium lobby. She laughed so hard that she gave up and started throwing them herself. Everyone else picked up boxes and ran as fast as they could not to get them confiscated.

"Ju-ly... you're awfully high on that stool." Before I could jump and run, Billie grabbed me off the stool. He let me down to try to grab my certificates, but I fought hard and began running in the opposite direction toward the auditorium. Reagan turned the corner to join us with a fresh box of certificates.

"Uh oh! Reagan, you're up!" Billie and several others who had just come through the double doors started running towards her.

"Hey! Get July... she went that way, and she still has her stack!" Billie shouted to someone running behind him as he ripped Reagan's box from her. The auditorium door slammed shut behind me. *Shit.* I knew whoever it was had time to see the door swing and would follow. It was dark, though, abnormally pitch black for a day when we would have an assembly later. I decided to halt and squeeze against the back wall, hoping they would run past me and further into the auditorium, not seeing me in the dark. Then, I would run right back out.

The door swung open, casting a small amount of light. I hadn't anticipated that. Whoever it was could see my shoes. In a mere second, I was being held against the wall. One wrist was above my head. The other was held at my waist in pursuit of the certificate stack it clung to.

I froze, and my hand holding the certificates stopped trying to twist out of the grip that sustained it.

I smelled him. The face of the silver watch I must have memorized glowed by my waist as it was worn by the wrist that sustained my other hand. The butterflies in my stomach did not miss a beat, nor did my broken heart as it began thudding in my chest in almost echo-like beats, alarming my entire body of who was standing so close to me. It was Adrian.

My shocked, wide eyes met his steely blues. They were all I could see other than the face of his watch in the darkness. Something changed on his face from the glint I initially caught of him casually going after the certificates for the fun of the prank.

His blue eyes darkened as he looked down from above me. His studious brow furrowed as if he didn't expect to be thinking so hard. His eyes shifted to my chest, rising and falling to my thudding heartbeat. Then his breathing changed, and he stepped closer to me. His body pressed mine against the cold, hard wall; in contrast, I felt the warmth of his breath on my face.

I moved as best I could to shove the certificates toward him without saying a word. I was just giving up, and the plan was he could have them rather than think he could have anything with me.

He didn't respond to the certificates I pushed toward him. He was so strong. His forearms held mine in place. He had no problem keeping me there. It didn't help that my body responded so quickly to his touch, like a goddamned magnet. After a long moment, I felt sure he'd let me go. Instead, he brought his eyes back to mine and his face closer, and his stare burned into me. Voices approached the auditorium stage below us. Footsteps walked toward the main podium.

"No house lights yet! Keep them dark. Just bring the bottom footlights and main spotlight on us." Mrs. Bishop called up to the booth. This was obviously rehearsal for the assembly later. Adrian moved me in one motion to the other side of the swinging door we came through. It was separated from the house seats by a partition. We saw from the sides when they brought their stage lights up, but where we stood remained in the dark. We could only be caught by the swinging door if someone else entered the auditorium from where we did.

He dropped his nose above my face and smelled the top of my hair, burying his face in it. Then he traced my face with his and looked down at how rapid my breaths had become. He closed his eyes and pressed his cheek next to mine. I raised my free hand to the back of his warm neck to try and form the strength to pull him away from me.

"Okay, you. Four. Step up after the initial applause, and Natalie, let's have you and Alexa stand on this side. Good." Mrs. Bishop's voice rang into our ears like an anthem of everything that sucked about life, this school, and our situation. Of course, we both heard Natalie's name. I felt Adrian's jaw tense on my cheek. Then he brought his head down on my shoulder as if in despair.

I pulled his head up and started pulling it away from me to peel out from under him in what I assumed would be an easy, if not welcomed, gesture under the circumstances. He pushed himself back on me, pinning my right arm back above my head the way he originally had it...like he put it there because he wanted it there. He traced my neck with his lips, shaking his head as if reminding himself to be careful and not go too far. He brought his lips to the other side of my face that had not experienced yet. He slowly and softly traced that cheek with his lips until they trailed down to mine.

I couldn't move. I couldn't move away from him, but it wasn't because he had me physically trapped. However, I wouldn't move to participate or potentially do more than intended in the renegade moment that, by anyone's standards, was cheating. I knew he wasn't going to kiss me. As much as I hated him, as wrong as this was, Adrian had standards. He didn't want to hurt anyone *other than me, apparently.*

I dipped my head down a bit to cut him off and remove myself from his lips resting dangerously close to mine. He nudged my face back up with his in what oddly was so intimate and erotic with all that word could encompass. My stomach turned a deep flip that made me weak in the knees. I took in a slow breath to try and contain myself. He brought his lips back to tracing mine. This time, he traced them one at a time, pulling my bottom lip apart from my top. Then he slid both his lips between my parted lips, slowly in a confident manner that still honored refraining from an actual kiss. I tried not to move, but an uneven breath leaked out of me onto his lips as I trembled from his touch. Goosebumps rose across my entire body.

Thank God we heard familiar voices much closer to us as the guys chased someone still holding certificates back down the hallway to the auditorium lobby. Adrian moved to press his forehead to mine. He looked at me as if he just wanted to stay a moment longer. I fought to push my hand between us and handed him my certificates.

Okay. Enough. What was I doing? What was I thinking? *I wasn't.* That's what it was. I did not hunt her down for... *that.* I was just messing around with the guys. Even when I saw it was July Billie asked me to chase after, I still didn't consider anything past the fun of it.

If anything, I had a flash of hope when I began chasing her that this could get us back to the innocent, playful banter we always had on debate team. Anything but silence. Ignoring her was killing me.

I'm not sure what happened when I grabbed her like that. Maybe it was how close we were standing. Her face inches from mine. Maybe it was the way I restrained her. It truly was meant for sport. But then I felt her soft, determined hand twisting in mine while I raised her arm above her head, holding her captive by her wrist. How barbaric of me… that must be what did it. That or her scent. God, did I literally drink her in?

Maybe it was when she went still; I felt it when she realized it was me. I didn't even really know her, not that way, but somehow, it felt like I knew everything about her. Somehow, standing above her, watching her catch her breath while I inhaled the scent of her hair, I was reminded of what I had been missing ever since that night in the rain.

Okay, so I knew some part of me had it bad for her, especially since that kiss, but that was just hormone stuff, right? I kept returning to the fact that she wasn't my type. It's not like I picked her out intentionally. And even so… I wasn't supposed to lose my mind over her. It was a battle, being around her without being *with* her… In ways I'm embarrassed to admit to myself. She must have thought I was insane! Why didn't she say anything? *Why didn't I say anything?* That's just it. There were no words to describe it. It was just me proving my insanity. However, she wasn't completely immune to it. Every part of her body felt warm and inviting. Even when she froze, she never went stiff or closed herself off. I saw goosebumps rise over her at my touch, and I couldn't ignore her heart beating wildly on my chest. It did something to me I can't explain.

Her breath grew unsteady when she worried I might kiss her, and she most likely would have turned away to be respectful, but she didn't have to. She trusted I would only go so far. That's what made it so intense. Knowing I wouldn't, she dared me to cross a line, which made me crazy for her.

Whatever was happening at that moment, I couldn't stand to be without it, and I couldn't pull away. Not when people entered the auditorium threatening to expose us. Not even when they called Natalie's name, revealing she was one of the people on the stage below us.

Shit. Natalie.

No matter what, this had to stop now. I really liked Natalie, but "liked" as in was fond of and attracted enough to, was where it ended. I know I hurt July, and I had no right to think past that. But I had an obligation to end things with Natalie that had nothing to do with July, and I wanted to make this move right.

I wasn't going to talk to Reagan or Lynn about it. I didn't want to announce it to the school or the Devins of the world. It wasn't that I didn't want to give July the satisfaction of knowing she was the reason... Trust me, after the auditorium, she knew. However, this wasn't a cheap shot to get her back. Or to get her, I should say. This was a mess I made, and I needed to make it right for Natalie with a respectful breakup that was free of rumors. I would do the kind thing and wait until after Christmas. I didn't mind buying her a gift. She deserved one.

Then, I needed to make it right with July. Somehow. But that shit in the auditorium... That could not happen again. I don't know how she had that effect on me, but we were about to be working together in debate. This was messed up from the beginning. First, the office, then all the mayhem that followed. Surely, we both learned our lesson by now. I knew I needed to make better decisions. I had to accept that I couldn't be alone with her, which would solve a multitude of problems.

***

I called Natalie one January night a few days after New Year's before school returned. I asked if she could meet me for coffee at "Good Jives" in Prairie. I knew she would sense something was up when I asked her to meet instead of offering to pick her up. It was around six on a random Tuesday night. The place was popular with college kids cramming and high school kids wanting to pretend they were in college. It wasn't my scene. Still, they had great virgin granitas, and the atmosphere seemed right for something like this.

It went as well as it could have. In the end, she said she expected it, which was kind of sad as much as it was a good thing. It meant she also noticed there was no chemistry where there should have been. I hoped I was clear with her that I had enjoyed our time together and was available for anything she needed. I think she got that I was still her friend and had no interest in making a big thing of this.

The first day back, it was already common knowledge. What did I expect? It was Pure Pines. The girl gets broken up with and, in a classic move, dresses up that week to look confident and unfazed. Her friends flock to her, and she eventually has to explain whether or not she needs consoling.

Yeah. It would spread like wildfire.

I knew Lynn and Reagan would be upset that I didn't mention it beforehand, especially with things finally returning to normal. The breakup with Natalie had so many July implications surrounding it... I just thought it best for all parties not to mention it to them. They'd have to get over it.

Like so many unspoken things between us, July seemed to get it. I could tell she was sensitive to Natalie's feelings and somehow intuitive that I had not done this to immediately go after her. Part of me thought that was super sexy of her, emotionally or intellectually. The other part of me wondered, *what the hell... Shouldn't she be rushing into my arms*? She didn't say anything to me about the auditorium moment or the breakup with Natalie.

I hadn't seen her much those few weeks after we returned from Christmas break other than passing in the halls. The four of us had just started to come back together for chats by the locker like we used to.

July wouldn't address me directly too much, but she did make an effort not to treat me like a complete asshole.

Late nights between reruns of *Cheers,* followed by *Night Court* (the original), took more of a toll than seeing her and avoiding her at school. Since the auditorium, I hadn't been able to unwind after work or study with the TV in the background like usual. Instead, my mind slipped off to her face, her deep brown eyes. It was like a succession of glances down the hallway, all the seconds I waited for her not to look away too fast so her eyes would meet mine, mixed with the auditorium and how she looked up at me part shocked and angry... part as entranced as I was.

I never knew what was more maddening, the fact that I didn't know what she was thinking or what she wanted (and quite frankly, didn't have the guts to ask)... Or, that I didn't feel this crazy, unshakable desire with *anybody* else. All of that, and it hadn't gone away. It seemed progressive.

I considered that she may not have these feelings at all for me, or anything past the physical attraction we both seemed captivated by. Then I'd remember what she did for me with Coach Bartlett and how she put herself in jeopardy for me because she knew I needed it.

I'd tell myself that's just who she was, that she would stick her neck out for anybody. But no, that was so specific to me and for me...

I don't know. It was personal. It felt personal that July did that, and it meant a lot to me. Maybe she did have feelings for me, but I ruined my chance, appearing to choose Natalie instead. That would be reasonable on her part. *Would she ever forgive me?*

I would mull things over multiple times and then lay there and wonder like a coward why she never called, came by, or pursued a conversation.

Then, I would try and feel relieved, like before.

July
"LOSER"

Beck

I couldn't get Mom before she went to her next conference. I had needed her earlier, but by that point, I moved on. I was glad not to have to divulge what was making me so upset. I couldn't have explained it, even if I was willing to tell her about it.

Snuggling into my warm bed at my grandparents' house felt good. It just felt like home, no matter how shit the day was. I rolled to the middle of the full-size bed, pulling the cotton sheets and quilt around my neck. I lay on my back, staring up at the patterns on the ceiling.

I could hear the dog from a street over. The owners left him tied out back sometimes. He'd bark all night as if calling out to someone far away. It never bothered me that much, other than wanting to go untie him and bring him in with me. He sounded so forlorn. His barks were distant, muted, and more elongated, like moans. He cried out steadily all through the night, and I wondered who he was calling for. I felt sorry for him, but I also envied how vocal he was. He may have been lonely, but he had the guts to let the world know. I wish I could have given a voice to the way I felt.

The following day, I woke to my grandparents scurrying in the kitchen. I could smell sausage frying, and I heard my grandad talking about where the water lines would take him that day as he opened the fridge for the gallon jug of milk. There was a pause, and then I heard my grandmother say, "What was that darn dog barking at last night?"

"The moon I guess." My granddad said with a level of certainty.

Is that all it was? I couldn't help but smile. Poor "Forlorn-ed" and me. Even if you did tell the world, there wasn't much they could do about it. I laughed to myself as I pushed out of bed. It was much colder out that day, almost freezing. Maybe the groundhog saw his shadow after all, and we were in our "6 more weeks of winter phase." I didn't care, though... it was time to shake things up and start living again. If "Forlorn-ed" could do enough about it to keep the whole neighborhood up while on a chain, so could I.

I ignored the temperature and went to my sock drawer to the specialty side, where all of my tights were folded securely in one of Mom's lingerie bags I had swiped so they would remain snag-free. I loved tights. They had been my favorite stocking stuffer since I was a little girl, and I had just gotten a bunch for Christmas, so they were there with me in my room at my grandparents' house. I'd wear tights and a tee shirt everywhere if I had my way. I found a black pair of opaques dark enough for the season but the perfect texture to show off whatever good leg parts I had.

Tights were a texture thing. I did not own any thick ones that added an extra layer. My mother was an expert on hosiery, and if there's one thing I got proper from her with my short leg challenges, it was that the sole purpose of tights and pantyhose is to elongate and smooth. Anything past that is just a fashion mistake or a choice to be tortured for no reason. If you could allow yourself any expensive vice, it should be fine hosiery from the specialty store that may cost more than your outfit.

In terms of the outfit, well, I had my designs on a skirt and top my grandmother bought for me at Dillard's last Valentine's Day on an after-Christmas sale. There had been only one size left. It was a size smaller than I wore then. Like my mother, I was optimistic about the right outfit. "If it was going to look better on you thinner, then buy that size and lose into it." I'd hoped I'd trimmed up a bit since last year as I pulled the tags off the collar.

The top was a fitted black knit button-down with a black, grey, and maroon plaid collar and cuffs to match. The plaid matched the A-line schoolgirl skirt and pleated on one side where it buttoned. It was an outfit, to say the least, and gave off a total Alicia Silverstone-Clueless vibe.

Sooo... it fit for sure, but the skirt was also proof I'd grown an inch or two, as it was a bit shorter than I remembered. Let me just say it was pushing the "ruler rule" of the school's dress code, but I didn't think anyone would notice with the right tights.

I slid into the black penny loafer heels I got for Christmas and, *Dang!* Talk about elongating. This worked out far better than I anticipated. It felt good to want to walk the halls of Pure Pines for the first time in a while. Devin seemed to have backed off a bit, and we hadn't purposefully put ourselves in each other's paths recently.

All I wanted to do was get started on debate and get Reagan and me to place at our first meet. I had been worried about her a bit. Since the holiday break, she had become withdrawn and not her usual self. She did that sometimes, which usually meant issues at home. Her parents applied a lot of pressure to be the best, bringing out Reagan's worst. I hoped she wasn't under the spell of that Kane guy from Prairie. He was always a bad decision.

Given the recent event I'd withheld, I had no right to ask her about it. I guess I hoped this outfit and my attempt to join the land of the living would remind her that we needed to make plans to go out and have a little fun!

Debate had been going better than expected. Reagan and I had prepped our affirmative case over a few all-nighters during the break, and for the most part, I hadn't had to deal with Adrian. We chose a unique "squirrel case," Mrs. Rickie thought it would be best to have us work separately from the boys in the initial prepping so that we could spar with them and have our case be a total surprise. Then they could have our brief after to study before the first meet. We would not be competing against each other, but someone else they competed with could have this same case. I was relieved I didn't have to work with him daily, beyond small talk in the hallway.

When I walked through the double doors that cold Monday morning, I got the reaction I hoped for. Several heads turned away from the girls in sweatpants and frumpy jackets who had decided to bum it in the cold that day. Hey, I needed the win, and my friend did, too. I immediately found Reagan and Lynn, which was new this semester. Last fall, they both had an early morning lab that kept us from meeting up just before first period.

"Ow ow ow!" Lynn shouted and tried to whistle.

"Wow. Who finally pulled your string?" Reagan added. I reached out and gave her a massive bear hug and squeezed her ribs until it was painful... Something she would totally do to me.

"You did! We need to go out on the town. We've been acting like somebody died since before Christmas. We will only be seventeen once. I for one am sick of you losers moping around. It's really starting to cramp my style."

"Sarcasm is the lowest form of wit." Lynn interjected.

"Oh, somebody's reading Oscar Wilde in AP English." I retorted.

"What did you pick?" Lynn started peeking through my backpack.

"Do you have to ask her?" Reagan dug deeper into my backpack with closed eyes and pulled out a paperback. She continued with her eyes closed to announce the title.

"The Scarlet Letter. Lynn, how could you not know she'd pick the most tortured unrequited love story known to man. It's not even a love story. It's a massive sadomasochistic mistake that only highlights gender inequality and women being punished above all."

"Well, I learned from the best." That felt a little too real at the moment as Reagan turned from us to grab the books she needed from her locker. I didn't mean it about her and Kane, but even Lynn looked at me funny.

"Seriously though, we haven't been out in ages, let's go!" I was oddly loud and encouraging, so obviously trying to fire them up.

"Go where?" The only familiar male's voice that could destroy my excitement instantly butted in as Adrian appeared in front of me, throwing his arms over the backs of Lynn and Reagan's shoulders. I quickly looked to Lynn to save me and tried not to be too obvious about not wanting to make eye contact. I think he was grateful for that, as I could see him looking me up and down from the corner of my eye. It was so apparent that Lynn had to clear her throat dramatically to get his attention before answering. "We were just saying we haven't been out in a while and should go. July and Reagan have been working so hard on their case that some much-needed fun is in store."

"Count me in." Adrian demanded.

I wanted to flee before any plans were solidified. Thank God the bell rang and saved me.

"See you guys." I took the opportunity to relay that to the group and keep up the ruse. It was difficult to be around Adrian, but I did this for my friends' sake.

I made my way into theater arts, and there was a sub. Half the class hadn't shown up. I guess they got the memo. I sat at my usual desk as the substitute handed out some BS theater history worksheets to occupy our hour. This was a waste of a great outfit. I looked at the sheet that could be finished in three minutes and pulled out my trig work instead. I could use all the time in the world on that one and still not be up to par.

I pulled a pencil sharpener out of my backpack and began sharpening. There was an empty seat in between me and Darrell Neely. He was what the faculty called a "dump kid" behind their back. The disparaging label usually meant they were lower income or didn't care about any particular subject, much less our elevated curriculum. Basically, they didn't drink the Pure Pines Kool-Aid, wear the right clothes, or got caught smoking in the boys' room one too many times to be of interest, so they "dumped" them in whatever class was available.

I didn't even know how old Darrell was with the rumor that he had been held back so many times. He was quiet and always got in trouble for drawing in every class he was in. Darrell was also most likely a genius and only dangerous because he had nothing better to do and nothing to lose. He slid into the empty desk beside me and asked if he could borrow my sharpener. I passed it to him and watched, fascinated, as he sharpened one of his drawing pencils.

It had a different number etched on the front of it from a standard number two. He let all the shavings fall on the blank piece of notebook paper and smeared them around it, letting the lead smudge and darken the page. Then he flipped that sheet over again and handed me my sharpener back. He drew a stick figure on the new sheet of notebook paper, like the game hangman, I guess. The pieces of the man were left unfinished, and there were no spaces for letters to form a word.

He finished an arm that angled up to the man's face and slid me his pencil and paper. I wasn't sure what he wanted me to do, so I drew a book in the man's hand on a whim. Darrell raised a half smile, and I slid it back to him. He drew a cigarette hanging from the stick figure's mouth with smoke flowing past the book our stick figure was engaged in. It was fascinating how the circle turned into a head-facing profile toward the book when he drew the cigarette at the perfect angle.

Darrell added two stick legs and returned the drawing and pencil to me.

"I hope everyone is completing their worksheet. I must pick those up at the end of class." The sub eyeballed the two of us. I looked down at our little fellow on the paper and drew the first thing I could think of... A ball and chain linked around his ankle. I slid it back to Darrell, and it was met with a full smile. He ripped the page out of his notebook and gave it to me.

"Thanks for the sharpen." Darrell whispered to me as he nodded and moved back to his original desk one seat over. I stared at the man smoking while reading with a ball and chain around his ankle.

It might have been the coolest drawing I'd seen if I said so myself. I slid it into the back of my notebook and glanced back as Darrell opened his to the page darkened by the pencil-shaving lead. He began drawing something else. His theater worksheet had fallen to the floor incomplete. I couldn't help but look over my shoulder periodically, wondering what he was drawing next or if I'd get to see it.

Gin Blossoms

I sat through AP English watching the VHS tape Mrs. Rickie recorded of *The Scarlet Letter* from PBS. It was the version that came out before I was born. She had vetoed us watching the Demi Moore movie, not because it was too explicit for school, Mrs. Rickie was pretty cool that way. She hated it because they deviated so far from the book in the end. As a reward for our essay writing, we were punished with the movie companion of each book on the list. I like to think she was just giving us a break from a class lecture. At this point I wasn't sure which one was worse.

I don't know why I chose *The Scarlet Letter* for my essay. I guess it appealed to me in some way. Maybe it was because Hawthorne writes about a world surrounded by puritans in New England, and I lived in the bible belt of East Texas in Pure Pines. It felt appropriate.

"Okay, that's it for today. Stay tuned for when Dimmesdale squeezes the pus out of the letter "A" he carved on his own chest." Mrs. Rickie laughed at her joke as she hit the power off. Collective disgust rang audibly through the classroom as the bell rang for lunch.

"It's true, they back it with a sound effect and everything." Half the class was at the door on that one. "Oh, Adrian, could you hang out for a few minutes? I hate to cut into your lunch, but I'm very excited about this and I had to speak to you guys."

"No problem." I put my notebook together and headed towards her desk. When I looked behind me at the exiting class, I saw July standing in the doorway waiting to come in. She was in that school girl skirt outfit I saw this morning that I had already saved multiple images of. It's not like I expected her to change clothes, I guess I didn't expect to see her again this morning. There is only so much a guy can store in his memory bank before he explodes, if you know what I mean.

Watching her enter the room a little longer than I should have, I assumed this was about debate. Only, shortly after it wasn't Lane or Reagan who came next. It was Brandon Powell. He was third in our class and a total dick.

"Hello July, thanks for coming. Don't you look nice today? Brandon, come on in. I don't want to keep you all too long, but I did want to run something by you. There is an essay competition over the classics, and we can only send in one from the junior class for a small scholarship award. It's not much, more on the merit end." Mrs. Rickie looked us all over and continued.

"Anyway, you three were my top essays. Now, it took me time to really deliberate on this. I mean, you all know the rest of the AP juniors had free rein over which classic to write about and many chose other titles. I felt a bit odd that my three best came from The Scarlet Letter, and I had to question myself as to whether this was a biased decision over my personal favorite. The thing is, Hawthorn offers a great deal of symbolism, critical analysis, and possibly one of the most subjective pieces of literature. I think the proof is in your three very different essays." She walked back behind her desk and began fumbling through papers.

I couldn't help but look over at July. I was so curious what her take on it was, and how we differed in our understanding of it.

"It's a huge bummer I can only send one, because you each touched on some interesting points that made me reconsider my own understanding of Hawthorne's intention. I thought what might serve is a small discussion where we share each of your takes on what you three differed on. Your original essays will stay the same, but I'd like to assign an amendment to them. We'll just have you tag on a final section that either confirms your opinion after you've heard the other points of view or justifies theirs as well in some way. So, you can agree with one of your fellow essay writers here, or deny their theory, or justify your own against theirs. I just need to read it." She pulled our essays and began sifting through the flagged pages.

"Some of the major themes I want you guys to touch on, I'll just read right out of your essays... July, you wrote of the minister, bachelor Dimmesdale, that his biggest downfall was his insult to Hester Prynne in that: *"He didn't even include her as his partner in crime."* Mrs. Rickie looked up from July's pages to find me shaking my head.

"Yeah, but that's because he thought it was HIS FAULT. He took full responsibility." *Wow.* That flew out of my mouth fast. I was oddly protective over a fictional character.

"That's it! That's what I'm wanting this discussion to bring! Thank you, Adrian, for jumping in. You each have such valid points that have long been in the discussion over this piece of work, and I want you to challenge each other with them." Mrs. Rickie looked back and smiled at Brandon. "Nothing ever really gets heated here Brandon... these two are on the debate team together, so you'll just have to jump right in with them."

"Well—" Brandon stammered to come up with something to say until he was cut off by someone who did have something.

"He most certainly did not." July snapped toward me. "I'm sorry, Brandon... Mrs. Rickie. But the idea that Arthur Dimmesdale took any form of responsibility when Hester Prynne spent seven years enduring public ridicule. She was exiled from society and her only contact with them was to be punished by them with no word or explanation from him what so ever! Meanwhile... She stayed there for him."

"She should have just left!" I directed that a little too strongly toward July. I tried to dial it down some. "Instead, she tortured him by staying." I continued down the list. "She kept secrets from him. She let him be tormented by her psycho husband!"

"Yes, and when she told him, he wasn't going to forgive her at first. He said he would forgive her, but he didn't!" July shouted back in my face.

"He was angry! She deceived him!" We were face to face yelling.

"No!" July declared firmly. "He even says, "Hester, I have not your strength." He admits it!"

"Admits to what?" Brandon tried to chime in at the wrong time.

"BEING A COWARD!" July and I both shot back at him simultaneously. Her eyes were burning at me and her little top lip quivered a bit. I was very close to forgetting we were in public.

"There you go." Mrs. Rickie stepped in. "Do you see how two exceedingly different opinions over their behavior came to the exact same conclusion? Brilliant you two! Now, to your thoughts about the ending... Again, all three of you had different conclusions."

"It was clearly a tragedy." I spoke up to state the obvious.

"July..." Ms. Rickie paused to flip to the last essay in her pile. "Adrian's essay does a remarkable job of explaining the tragedy these to figures suffered together, yet, I flagged where you wrote that the ending was a waste. It was very interesting that you fell in love with these two and wrote so eloquently about what they must be experiencing and then called it all a waste. Now, Brandon, and Adrian, you two did have similar ideas towards the ending being tragic, but what about July's idea of it being a waste?" Mrs. Rickie looked at the three of us excited.

"Wow. That's a powerful choice of words, especially if we consider most tragic characters in history are long suffering from their own torment or fatal flaws, whereas the true definition of a single tragedy encompasses distress, great suffering and destruction commonly from a natural catastrophe, or serious accident. Just different imagery there I encourage you all to explore when you read the notes I've written on each take. We sort of have one of you suggesting it was the fault of in our stars; be it fate, society etc. One of you suggesting it was both their faults collectively, and the other suggesting their individual fault in the circumstances."

I saw July's face drumming up something. "Yes. It was Hester's fault for waiting for him and believing it was love, when he only felt guilt or compassion for her being caught. He didn't love her past their moment under the sun no matter how much we want to believe in their love story. In a way, Adrian is absolutely right, had she left town when given the option, he would have gone on about his business and been the climbing, successful minister he had originally intended to be."

It startled me when she said my name, and gave me credit. So much so I failed to realize she was using it against me.

"July, are you saying that had he not been forced to watch her suffer he would not have made himself to suffer along with her in secret?" Mrs. Rickie looked truly intrigued with her head cocked toward July.

"Yes, and I'm saying he was a coward and did not choose to out himself the way she was forced out, for that same reason. He wasn't in love with Hester Prynne. He was in love with his career and the social status of his own ambitions. Add religion and you get the guilt, shame and compassion he felt he had to punish himself with for his moment of weakness with her." July really nailed that one in a way I had never thought about, but I didn't care. *She was wrong about me!*

"No." I fired back. "He did love her and that was the problem. It was his torment. She was the one thing that would get in the way of everything he knew and ultimately wanted. He couldn't throw away what he had worked for his entire life for something that went against every fiber of his being and was ultimately the unknown with her. No matter how much he loved her. It would be insane."

Brandon shook his head and whispered something under his breath.

"What did you say?" I called him out.

"I said get a room." Brandon called us out.

"Sure, we'll get you the Cliff Notes over what happens." I shouldn't have said that. Brandon was cocky and arrogant and obviously didn't like being ignored, but whatever he put in his essay was clearly subpar to ours, and he had nothing to offer the conversation. That wasn't lack of debate skills, he simply hadn't read the book as thoroughly as his essay suggested.

"Okay, guys take it easy on Brandon. This isn't debate, just a healthy discussion over Hawthorne. Brandon, I apologize I didn't mean to fuel the fire with July's essay, but I was very intrigued by how her point of view differed from your essays. Something to consider on the last patch you all write. Now get to lunch or what you have left of it!"

July smiled at Mrs. Rickie and flew out of the room first. I guess that was her solution, to just leave like I said Hester should have left. Words she would no doubt punish me for. There wasn't enough lunch remaining for me to bother going to sit with everyone. I just unwrapped something from the vending machine. As I moved toward the trash can I saw a crumpled piece of paper hit the floor. "Yo, man you dropped this." I called after Darrall Neely, at least I think that's who was hidden under that large flannel shirt.

"Nah, man. I'm done with it. I don't ever keep my drawings." And he was off.

What a weirdo. I picked up the crumpled notebook paper to toss it in the trash bin and was face to face with the girl who walked away from me. She wasn't in the hallway or standing next to me. Her face was the drawing. The image had such a likeness that my chest tightened as I held it in my hand. The dude had drawn her face. The hair and eyes were a bit lighter, but it was undeniably July's face. I folded it into my pocket as the bell rang before anybody could see me with it. I hoped at that moment I didn't look as crazy as I felt.

Later that day I met up with Lane in Mrs. Rickie's room. She wasn't in there. It was her conference period, but she let us use it during study hall for debate prep. I don't know if it was being there after the great *Scarlet Letter* throwdown or the face on the drawing that was burning a hole in my back pocket, but I couldn't stop thinking about the things July said. Then my mind would drift to that skirt, those legs... I'd never really noticed her legs before. Did she get taller? And then I'd think about that guy, Darrell. How did he draw her like that? It was good. It looked just like her, but did she pose for him in class or something?

"Earth to Adrian. Bro, are we going to win our case with silent treatment? Lane waved his hand in front of my face.

"Sorry man. I was—somewhere else. What were you saying?"

"Just that if we keep our case as is and have a rebuttal for each of the known squirrel cases that—" Lane was laid back and smart at the same time, but there was something goofy about him. Word was the girls from our class would say he was hot until he opened his mouth. He was a good guy though, and an excellent debate partner.

"Anyway, I was thinking if we win at the first meet and go on to regionals... wait, when does track start up for you?" Lane finally landed on a question for me to answer.

"Training starts next week, but even if we go to state in both, I already checked the calendar. This year they won't conflict. Why? Are you not running track?"

"Umm, I may do cross country, but everything else gets in the way of the pool starting up come May. I'm better at long distance and stamina above speed anyway if you get my drift." Lane raised his eyebrows suggestively.

"Shut up, man!" I laughed. "Hey, you work with July at the pool, right? You two lifeguard together in Prairie?"

"Yup."

"Is that... weird working with her in the summer and then seeing her at school or in debate?"

"Are you asking me what it's like to see her in a swimsuit when none of you guys get to, then come to school and see her in regular clothes and pretend I haven't handled looking at her stuff for years?

"Well, that's a way to put it."

"Why, you want to know if they're real?"

"What?"

"They are. For sure."

"Wait. No—I didn't ask you about her… and what would make you think they weren't real. This isn't Beverly Hills."

"No, but it is Pure Pines, and if you don't have something someone else does, you go buy it. I can point out a few fake ones for you."

"Maybe some other time. Back to how you know July's are real."

"Oh, well I haven't seen them completely topless, but I've spent summers since we were kids on swim team with her, and then last year sitting next to or across from her every day both wet and dry in a swimsuit. Anyway, when hers came in and she got her nipples, they do the perfect round on the bottom before they dip up thing. Fake ones don't do that, they just sort of have the round and a dot in the middle that's normally too centered. And a lot of real ones that don't have the perfect round, have completely awkward shapes."

"How do you know all of this? And wait, what's the "perfect round"?"

"They dip up. Perfectly round on the bottom like a tit is supposed to be and then it dips up at the middle. That's the kind you want. Sort of the perfect handful with the nipples pointing up. Perky, I guess is a better word."

"I can't believe we're having this conversation."

"Why, you into her? I can tell you more."

"Are you into her? You seem to know an awful lot."

"Nah, man, I had a crush when we were kids, but I'm into quantity over quality. She's quality. Come on... don't look at me like that. I spend the entire summer staring at babes in swimsuits. We are only young once. Quantity is the way to go."

"On that note. Wow. But... what do you mean she's quality?"

"You know. That egg would take a whole lot of work and time to crack open. But it's not just who she is or how smart she is, I mean physically too. Trust me, she gets more credit for her looks in Prairie than we fools give her here. All the girl guards are pretty top notch, except the bitchy ones. Let's just say the one thing they all have in common might keep you up at night if you know what I mean."

"No." I shook my head at him. "I can't imagine what you mean at this point."

"Bro! You have got to get out more! You don't bang chicks at the country club after work?"

"What? Do you at school or work?"

"Oh, yeah, I've been laid, and no, realistically it doesn't happen every day, but that's why I say quantity over quality. Girls are like slot machines. Getting a yes is a numbers game. The quantity system is putting a quarter in the slot knowing eventually it will pay off, whereas with quality like July, well, you can keep your quarters. A prize like that you gotta' wait for. Except for that one thing she has in common with the other guards. It sometimes makes me wonder if she may not be as prudish as I know she is."

"You're killing me bro. Just what do they all have in common."

"Well, the girl guards, the ones that came from swim team, which includes July… they shave all their pink parts. Religiously."

"You mean… no—anything down there?"

"Scout's honor. Smooth as a baby's butt."

"Well, the baby thing is not entirely an appealing thought."

"Oh, trust me. When you do get laid… it is. Clean shaven is da' best!"

"Okay, sorry. At risk of me putting myself yet again in the best, worst, John Hughes film… What makes you think July is… or doesn't have any um… down there?"

"Wait, what… Ohhhh, *Sixteen Candles*. Good one. Dude. On the swim team, even the guys shave their legs and sometimes their heads if they advance in a top heat and it comes down to seconds in a race. For girls, it's more of a convenience thing. Speed is always the excuse between girl talk among the swimmers, but they mostly do it because they are half naked every day of the summer and it's just easier not to have to worry about your junk poking out of a swimsuit. So, they shave everything off to be smooth as a whistle in their suits."

"And July…"

"Oh, right. Well, I knew this about her from swim team, but how do I know she is currently clean shaven and as smooth as a baby's butt as we speak?"

"Would you please stop making that reference..."

"Anyway, last year in the guard room when our suits came in, the guys changed in the locker room, and the girls changed in the guard room. We could hear them talking through the vent clear as a bell. The pool was empty, there was no music or outdoor noise. Literally every word they said. One of the new rookie guards that never swam on the team said, *"Ugh, I hate this material it gets all caught up in your..."* Then our head girl guard said, *"That's why I shave my shit. So you don't have to worry about it."* The new girl said, *"Yeah, but isn't it a nightmare when it grows back, and hard to shave again?"* And... wait for it, that's when July, plain as day, said, *"Well, you just keep it up and don't ever let it grow back. It's easier that way."* And that is how I know."

"Okay, well, today has certainly been enlightening. On that note, I've got to get to next period.""

"Anytime man. Sweet Dreams." Lane raised his eyebrows. "Oh, but don't say anything. I mean, if you tell her I told you, I'd have to mess your face up. She may be hot, but we go way back. She's... my friend."

I gave a lazy salute to him above a very confused look on my way out. *What the Hell just happened in there?* First of all, I learned far more about my debate partner than I ever desired to know. Second, IF I needed any more in the vault on July before, I did not now. Her outfit today was already killing me. Now I knew what was under those tights, and it was really hard for me to be furious about the things she said in the essay discussion which I was still upset about. However, it didn't mean I didn't want to take her tights off on Mrs.

Rickie's desk and-- "Hey! Darrall. Wait up." I couldn't believe it. There was that kid again in the flannel. If I had tried to find the guy every day for a year I wouldn't have seen him once. Or, to be fair, maybe I never looked before. "What did you mean you never keep your drawings?" He looked up at me a little startled. "And why did you draw her hair lighter and her eyes a lighter shade? She has darker brown hair, not sandy brown, and her eyes are deep brown."

"If you say so. I just draw what I see. There's a girl in my class a seat over from me. She let me borrow a pencil sharpener, and I liked the way her hair and eyes glowed under the fluorescent lights when she looked back to hand it to me. She looked curious and sad, so I drew it. That's it."

"But you threw it away?"

"I told you; I throw all my drawings away." Darrall jetted off from me toward another hallway, but his persistence in leaving did not stop mine in asking.

"Why?" I shouted after him.

"Because you're only as good as the last thing you did."

And that's when I had my mind blown for the third time that day.

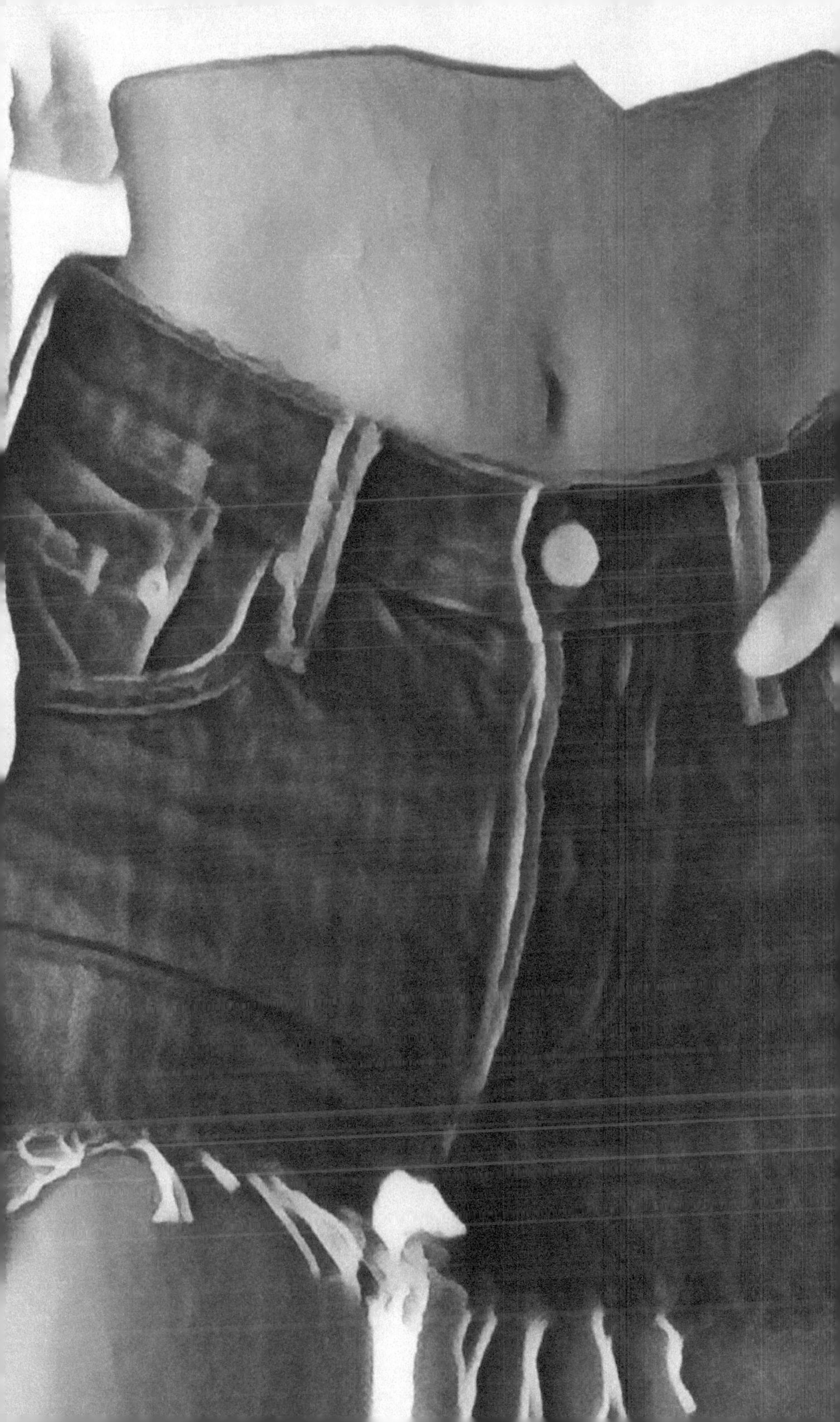

July

"CRASH INTO ME" PART 1

Dave Mathews Band

Strange, the bubble we lived in East Texas, nestled behind the Piney Woods curtain. Everything we did, worked towards or hoped for was for somewhere else beyond these pines. At least, that was our understanding of greatness. Yet, we were contained here, almost suspended in our own little universe. It was often so surreal that it took a great tragedy to shake everyone out of it and help us realize it was real. Even the bad parts. I never could quite grasp something going that wrong. How it happened on their watch, who was responsible, and worse when it was an accident or random tip of the hat.

There wasn't room for that kind of thing in a small town. It reminded me of a book I read in elementary school about two boys on bikes that go down to the river, and one drowns. I mean, really dies. I always remember that feeling of having to flip several pages back to make sure I didn't miss something. I couldn't comprehend that someone would let that happen, not just the boy who survived, but the world, the author, or whatever. What was the benefit of learning from this type of tragedy... the fact that they happen? Or, maybe, don't go swimming where you're not supposed to if you're not good at it? Even then, the lesson felt daunting.

As a child, I couldn't think past what a waste it was and how severe the consequence. The entire honesty and integrity part was lost on me, maybe because the kid who drowned was lost forever in that book. Pretty shitty and permanent lesson if you asked me. I would never knock the brilliant piece of literature it was meant to be... just how it made me feel. It haunted me. I suppose that was the point.

Years later, when something tragic or too real happened in Pure Pines, I had to remember flipping back through those pages to confirm it did, in fact, happen. I felt I flipped the pages back to double-check when Adeline Morgan was thrown to the wolves in a scandal and called out for being a lesbian in a school that pretended they didn't exist, so she was forced to get noticed in some other way.

I flipped back the pages when I saw Robyn with Spencer Pearce in the bathroom at the Tomlin party, and again when she told me people knew but didn't care.

I felt I had to flip the pages back after Adrian kissed me the way I didn't know anyone could and then chose someone else, but I didn't do it. Metaphorically speaking, I didn't let myself flip back to confirm it was real. My heart crumbling to pieces was evidence enough.

However, when Lynn called me that sunny day in May and told me the news... about Adrian. He spent an extensive day training for track, hitting some of his most brutal intervals yet, and was a success at each one. Beating his time repeatedly when Coach Bartlett had him go one last time. There's never been someone more prepared to compete. Reagan and Lynn were beyond excited for him, and I had to confess, I couldn't be prouder he had stuck it to the bastard football coach. Only, on his final sprint of practice, he leaped towards the finish and stopped abruptly, excited to see how many seconds he had shaved off.

One moment, one stupid wrong footing abruptly halted his body weight, forcing all the strength and momentum from his sprint to come down on his knee. It popped. He collapsed on the track. His ACL snapped in two. I had to flip the pages back in my mind to confirm that one was real.

My heart sank to my stomach, and I hid my watering eyes from Lynn and Reagan when they came and picked me up that day. We all headed to Reagan's to mourn our friend's crushed dream and the irony that made the whole incident sting more. We knew Lynn would need to check on him as soon as the initial shock wore off and all had been handled, but we weren't sure when he would want to see anyone past that.

I gathered, with all the turmoil and conflict going on in his mind, not to mention the physical pain he was in, I was the last person he would want to see. I stayed away.

***

It was officially the start of summer, not that school had gotten the memo. We had a week and a half left and two more final exams to take before I could leave this institution behind for one I thrived in.

Last May, my mother dropped me off at the city pool in the town over from ours, where I spent my first summer as a lifeguard. It was more like paying my dues. A rookie guard is up early in the morning for the worst swim lesson slot, teaching four-year-olds who are afraid of the water. The seven-hour shift that followed in the Texas heat, rotating from the deep end to the shallow, was only completed by working the night pool parties the senior guards didn't want... and I loved every minute of it!

As May faded into June through our last few days of class, I would be a returning guard at the Prairie City Pool. It was a feeling of social status I could never have imagined within the walls of Pure Pines High School, where hierarchy and merit were mandatory but relative to the powers that be. For one who wasn't that into summer, I had to admit I had a pretty stellar gig. It may have been the one thing I got right.

My grandad took me swimming every day of summer since I could walk. There wasn't a sunny day at the Pure Pine's pool that hadn't been attacked by my bare feet racing to the deep end. Later, that time at our small community pool turned into swim team practice at the larger city pool in Prairie, where I was getting ready to drive to. It was our initial guard meeting of the summer. *Yes, I said drive.*

My grandad was working on-site for the next three days and would be riding with his work buddy, Mr. Young. That meant his beautiful, brand-new, shiny, black F150 truck would just sit in the driveway next to my grandmother's minivan. Although I had the unfortunate pleasure of occasionally borrowing her vehicle, I was certain this moment warranted the truck.

My grandad had been a recreational swimmer in every pond or watering hole Pure Pines had to offer his boyhood. It was fair to suggest he was proud of me and what all those years of mom dragging me off for competitive swimming had led to. The smell of sunscreen and tanning oil was in the air, and I was ready for the only part of summer I loved.

Maybe I needed it, this distraction so big it got my head out of the haunting halls of AP classes and the constant judgment that roamed them. It was a distraction from any unfulfilled moment that lingered into an intrusive thought that reminded me of the last time I saw Adrian.

I had spent the past month looking for him down every hallway, even though I knew he was home with his knee injury. Still, the chamber without him was a torture of its own. Maybe even worse than the torture his very presence inflicted on me. It was evocative to look down the hallway between classes every time a bell rang, anticipating a glance from the only person who could provide that rush. I was frankly exhausted from it.

My grandmother wasn't home yet. Thank God that meant the grey minivan was not an available option. As I suspected, my granddad had left the keys to his prize possession on the end of the bar in the den. They were sitting on an envelope he had written a note on.

"Be careful. Back roads in the daylight, interstate at dark on your way back. Don't go anywhere else. If you need to call in, your Grandma will be home shortly, and I will see you tonight. Have a good first day. Love, grandaddy.

I tossed my books, grabbed the keys, and ran to the truck. I drove three houses down to my house to get ready. Mom was away, of course, but most of my summer stuff was in my bedroom closet. I pulled a small gift sack out of my bag with a shirt from Reagan on loan and flew inside to try it on.

I had a pair of cutoffs from my favorite jeans Mom had cut and shagged exactly the way one wanted them. I didn't have the heart to tell her they were a bit snug when she did them for me, and she wasn't around enough to notice I hadn't sported them. This summer, I had high hopes of squeezing into them.

I knew I had lost inches, but still worried about my stomach. If the shorts were too tight, they could pinch my skin or, worse, give me a fat roll hanging over, which would absolutely defeat the purpose. This would ruin the midriff debut Reagan had no doubt planned for me. It was risky to promise she could dress me for my walk into the lion's den of new and returning guards, including the rookies under me.

Every year, we got a few college lifeguards from the junior college in Prairie. It was a big basketball school, and despite having a pool on campus, the Prairie City Pool was larger and run by the city's Who's Who. This meant the city lifeguards were protected from most speeding tickets, and the head guards were paid handsomely compared to the campus pool.

It was a rite of passage for anyone on the Prairie City Swim Team who could pass the guard test and make it into the summer draft of returning guards. A few rookies from Prairie High School were promised a slot due to politics, and the coveted head guard positions usually went to the college guys. Lane and I were the only two from Pure Pines. We had been on the swim team in Prairie since we were in junior high.

There was that. Lane. He was the one attachment to Pure Pines that kept me from completely going off the rails as a different person, not that I would be entirely capable of that. He was just a fraction of judgment that kept me on my toes throughout the summer. But for the most part, he was easygoing, had his own agenda, and didn't torment me or get in my business at the pool.

When we were younger, I relied on having a buddy from school on the team with me. Sort of a familiar friend to be in the trenches with. I didn't need him as much once we got through the tough part of our rookie year. The older we got, I wanted to separate myself from the world we came from.

We had both worked too hard all those summers not to recognize the value of what WE *got* to do away from the jurisdiction of what settled beneath that ridiculous water tower with the blonde horse painted across it. Even though he was Adrian's debate partner, we had a remote understanding. I never worried he would tell some crazy summer gossip or out me if I got in trouble with our pool manager for some ridiculous reason.

Okay, this was, in fact, the top I suspected Reagan would send me, but was it shorter or less material than I remembered? JEBUS! I couldn't wear that! What was I thinking?! Even if the cutoffs fit, I hadn't ever shown my belly like that. Ever. *Was it flat enough? Was I tan enough?...* Okay, I was definitely tan enough. Thanks again to Reagan.

That was the thing about having a friend you know so well who equally knows you. There was no way Reagan would pack me something too scandalous or even as outrageous as she wanted because she knew I wouldn't wear it if it was too terrible. She wasn't there to force me, so logic had to prevail in her wardrobe choice for me.

Reagan was already halfway down the interstate in the opposite direction, heading to Marshall with her mom. She had forced Reagan to work some event she had. This usually meant her mother wanted to show her off. Like most of us, who never had a moment of downtime, Reagan had even less. Looking back, that should have explained some of the stunts she pulled.

Reagan knew this guard meeting was important to me. It was the first time I was able to order a two-piece. Her wardrobe choice was meant to keep me brave and honest, so I wouldn't chicken out.

She was brilliant and thoughtful that way, a way she often didn't get credit for. She's the kind of encouraging comrade that put that shirt in there, thinking that even if I were a coward, they may just assume I wanted a two-piece from the outfit I had on and order it for me anyway. That would be the ultimate compliment after all she and I had been through with weight issues. We didn't discuss it much, but we knew when we struggled. I was the kid whose mom put a can of frozen Slim Fast in her lunch box in fourth grade.

I didn't live that down until junior high. Reagan had one fat phase where she was chunky for one year. Since that moment, she had doubled up on her mom's thyroid meds or found a way to borrow someone's ADD medication when she could. Anything to suppress the appetite. During our freshman year, she taught me little tricks like how to privately chew what you wanted to eat and spit it out before you swallowed. None of that made the mentally and physically healthy list, but I would be a liar if I didn't cop to it... That or the fact that Pure Pines had gotten so stressful at times that I had relied on a few of our antics to keep me from going off the rails with gaining weight. Believe it or not, those ridiculous damaging tools felt like our only agency or control over our growing, changing bodies under the watchful eye of Pure Pine's perfection seekers.

Cutoff jean shorts, check! They fit better than expected. Maybe I had grown half an inch. I looked taller. I left the mirror to check the time. I had plenty of time. "Take it easy. You'll be an hour and a half early at this rate. Show a little restraint." I shut down, talking to myself in my mom's empty house. It was one thing to be abnormally anxious, but I couldn't add going utterly insane to the list. I dug through the bottom of my closet for the right shoes.

I had to go low-key the rest of the way, so I didn't look like I was trying too hard or dressing up. I didn't want wedge sandals or anything strappy. It was like fishing through a river of adolescent memories. There were so many clothes, shoes, and costumes from junior high and freshman year when my mom was home, and we stayed there more regularly. It was strange to see the reality of the situation that way, but I couldn't think about that.

I redirected and went back to Reagan's shirt I'd laid out on my bed. It looked like there was more in the bag it came from. I shook it out over my bed to find a black lace push-up bra and the second note from a loved one I'd received in one day. Pinned to the ridiculous bra, a yellow Post-it read, *"Bitch, I don't pretend to know what size you trap and hide those massive tatas in, but it's time you let the world know you have them. Just wear it. It will give you confidence. It's the gun in your handbag today. Don't leave home without it... you can take the padding out through the little slits on the sides. That's our compromise, now put it on!"*

A giddy smile rose across my face that frankly surprised me. I took the padding out immediately and tried it on. It fit, and so did the shirt. An old pair of white Keds in the corner of my room caught my eye. They must have been from some twirling contest sophomore year. They were perfectly broken in, yet still clean and white.

I slipped my bare feet into them without untying the little laces and walked to the mirror. *Perfect.* I was sporting some serious Jennifer Grey from *Dirty Dancing* vibes, but I didn't mind it at all. This came together way better than I anticipated. I was excited to walk into the lion's den, also known as the guard room.

The curls in my hair from early this morning had fallen a bit. They looked relaxed, like I slept on them or unraveled them from an updo. I liked it looking a bit unkempt and less obvious. Messy curls.

I don't know if the feeling of absolute freedom was due to no parental figures hovering over me at either residence or the anticipation of the summer I was about to embark on with the black truck outside to take me there. Maybe it was my midriff showing for the first time in public. Either way, it was exhilarating and a chance to break free of the mind trap I'd been in with Adrian for the last nine months.

I poked my head out of the bathroom when I thought I heard my mom's home phone ringing from the kitchen. At first, I let it ring out. Then I worried it could be my grandmother checking on me if she saw the truck in the drive on her way home. I ran to answer it. "Hello?"

"Finally! Where the Hell have you been?!" It was Reagan.

"Calm down, I'm wearing it already!"

"No, that's not why I tracked you down. Man, it took me FOREVER to get ahold of you! I couldn't get anyone at your grandparents' house before I left home. Luckily, I remembered your mom's home phone when I got here. I've got to hurry, I'm in the back on a kitchen phone and my mom's already sent six people to come find me. Look, I need you to bring Adrian the calculous notes and his assignment."

"What?! No way! Can't Lynn run it by?"

"You weren't leaving this second where you?"

"No. I –

"Listen carefully. I did leave the notes for him with Lynn after school, but she got called into work, so she left them in a notebook on the porch."

"So let Samuel or his stepmom or somebody walk over and get them."

"You don't understand. I forgot his assignment from Mrs. Keagan. We have our final tomorrow. Lynn and I won't even get to study much less walk him through it. He just needs the notes, and then his one-page assignment on Mrs. Keagan's desk has the equations she wants him to look at for the exam. That's it. It's that simple. She's there right now in tutorials. She'll be there until five. You don't have to leave until 6:30 and you'll still be more than on time. Can you please just go do it?"

"You want me to go back to school and get Adrian's assignment from Mrs. Keagan, then drive to his house, run up to Lynn's front porch and grab the notebook... then go over to Adrian's house to drop off the notebook and the assignment?"

"Yeah, you got it. Bye!"

"Wait, does he even know I'm coming?!! Is Mrs. Keagan expecting me? Reagan!!!! I didn't say I'd do it!" The dial tone responded for her, mocking me and confirming that I had, in fact, agreed to this according to Reagan's demand.

I rolled my eyes, grabbed my keys, and headed out. The feeling of freedom had dissipated, and a heavy weight cemented in my chest as I drove past the water tower and saw the high school rising to meet me. I wasn't angry. I had time to do it. We were all friends. This is what we did for each other.

Well. Reagan, Lynn, and I were friends. Reagan, Lynn, and Adrian were friends. Adrian and me? I didn't know what *we* were.

I parked in the back by the old band hall and slipped in the side double doors toward the math hall. It was hushed as I approached Mrs. Keagan's room. I peeked through the door and saw a few students hard at work. One was in my trig class and I'm sure had scored better on our last quiz than I had. *Yikes.*

It's funny the things you allow yourself to slide on. Math had always been the sacrifice in my case. I just didn't take to it the way I had my other advanced classes. It didn't bother me to have one major subject I didn't excel in. I wished I had shared their enthusiasm and study sessions for calculus, but college-level trig and analysis was where I drew the line. And it was a fuzzy line capable of lowering my GPA significantly.

"Did you change your mind?" Mrs. Keagan's voice was sharp and clear, and although it was a fair question, I could decipher a hint of sarcasm in it.

"No, sorry, I probably should have, though." I gave her a half smile as I sheepishly ducked into the room. She looked my outfit over with slight contempt.

"My, you've shaped up for the summer." I looked down, incredibly embarrassed at my attire, but felt relief when I saw a genuine smile grow across her face. She had a glint in her eye of woman-to-woman pride as if she knew what a triumph it was for me to be able to wear something like that. The fact that she seemed proud of me made me think I might have looked okay.

"Sorry, I'm headed to the pool for guard training, I ..."

"Yes, yes, summer is calling. First, I lose you all to Student Council, marching band, athletics, debate team, and what was your latest endeavor with tournaments every Monday last Fall and Spring? Oh yes, golf."

She moved toward her desk to fumble through a stack of papers. Dear God, please don't let her pull up last week's quiz and force me to stay here and lose my job.

"I'm just suggesting if you'd hung out here a little more or given my class half the time, I think you could have excelled as well as your buddies."

"Actually, I came here to get—" She handed me a collection of papers stapled together with *Adrian Reed* written across the top.

"Oh, did Reagan..." Cutting me off, Mrs. Keagan shook her head.

"I knew you ladies wouldn't forget him. It's their final." She passed me the papers and guided me through all the notes to relay to him. I thanked her quietly and headed out in the hallway to avoid further disturbing her tutorial students.

"You know he could help you…" Her voice called me back as she leaned out her classroom doorway with a knowing look. "If you had the time, Miss Edwards." Her eyebrow was raised. "Adrian's one of my best calculous students, even with his absence from class, and trig was a breeze for him. You should ask him to show you a few pointers when you drop this by."

She held her hand up for me to wait and appeared seconds later with my quiz. It had an "F" circled across the top in red.

"It's not as scary as it looks, although you should be terrified. It was a small quiz. You got the first half correct, but that second half was worth all the points. I've taken the opportunity to mark the equations you should rework and be able to factor before the exam on Thursday. I trust you'll need more than a "B" plus to bring this one up? Ask him. He'll help you."

I smiled at her, grateful for her interest and faith in me, even though I had exhibited no interest in her subject. She was a good egg. She was an educator who was worth the prestige and hype of Pure Pines because she was a good person who genuinely cared that we got it. It wasn't just for show or accolades on her end.

Ask him??! As if my pride could EVER allow him to see an "F" on any body of work I'd done. Honestly, Mrs. Keagan and I knew a "C" minus was the best I could hope to muster for the semester. The class was ridiculously hard. The only "A" I made was after staying up all night reading over Lynn's notes from her previous year in class just to crack out one quiz with flying colors. To ask *him* for help, I'd have to rewrite the test questions she marked for me to study so he would never see that grade on my actual quiz, and I didn't have time for that.

I flew down the two-lane highway past the school and toward Lynn and Adrian's. My banner day had been ruined by a guilt complex over a subject I had written off as my one freebee not to feel guilty over. It was a compliment. She was asking me to live up to my full potential even in a subject I did not excel in.

Why couldn't I accept that and move on? And what did she mean, *he* could help me? How did she know if he would have done that or if we were friends or... Wow. Even Mrs. Keagan felt she had a better clue about what *we* were than I did. Ugh. *Could I just drop this off and be in Prairie signing up for guard shifts already?!*

I pulled up to Lynn's empty driveway. Out of pure habit, I couldn't help but notice the house next door that haunted me every time I was over at Lynn's. Even though I was about to have to muster the strength to knock on its door, I still couldn't help but glance over. As Reagan said, the blue notebook was sitting on the porch swing. I added the stapled assignments to it and walked over to Adrian's. It suddenly struck me what I was wearing.

I got incredibly nervous. Any other time, I would have felt confident in this outfit endeavor or any ensemble meant to impress, especially if I showed up at a party where he was supposed to be. I knew it would guarantee he noticed me across the room. This was different. I hadn't seen him since before his knee injury, and I was barging in on him. Odds were, I was Reagan's one phone call, and he was expecting Lynn to drop this over, not me.

Surely he wouldn't think I wore this getup for him? *Ugh.* The thought made me want to turn around and race home. I felt uncomfortable parking in the guy's driveway, much less knocking on his door. I hated how this demented attraction demanded such an investment of my mind.

His house was alive and warm, with kitchen lights glowing and two cars parked in the drive. *Good, other people were home.* Maybe his stepbrother Sawyer would be there, and I could just hand it over, and he'd run it upstairs to Adrian. At this point, I just needed to talk myself down. This was a drop and run. Then, I would be out the door and on my way to my original destination. My hand was shaking as I raised it to ring the doorbell. This was a mistake.

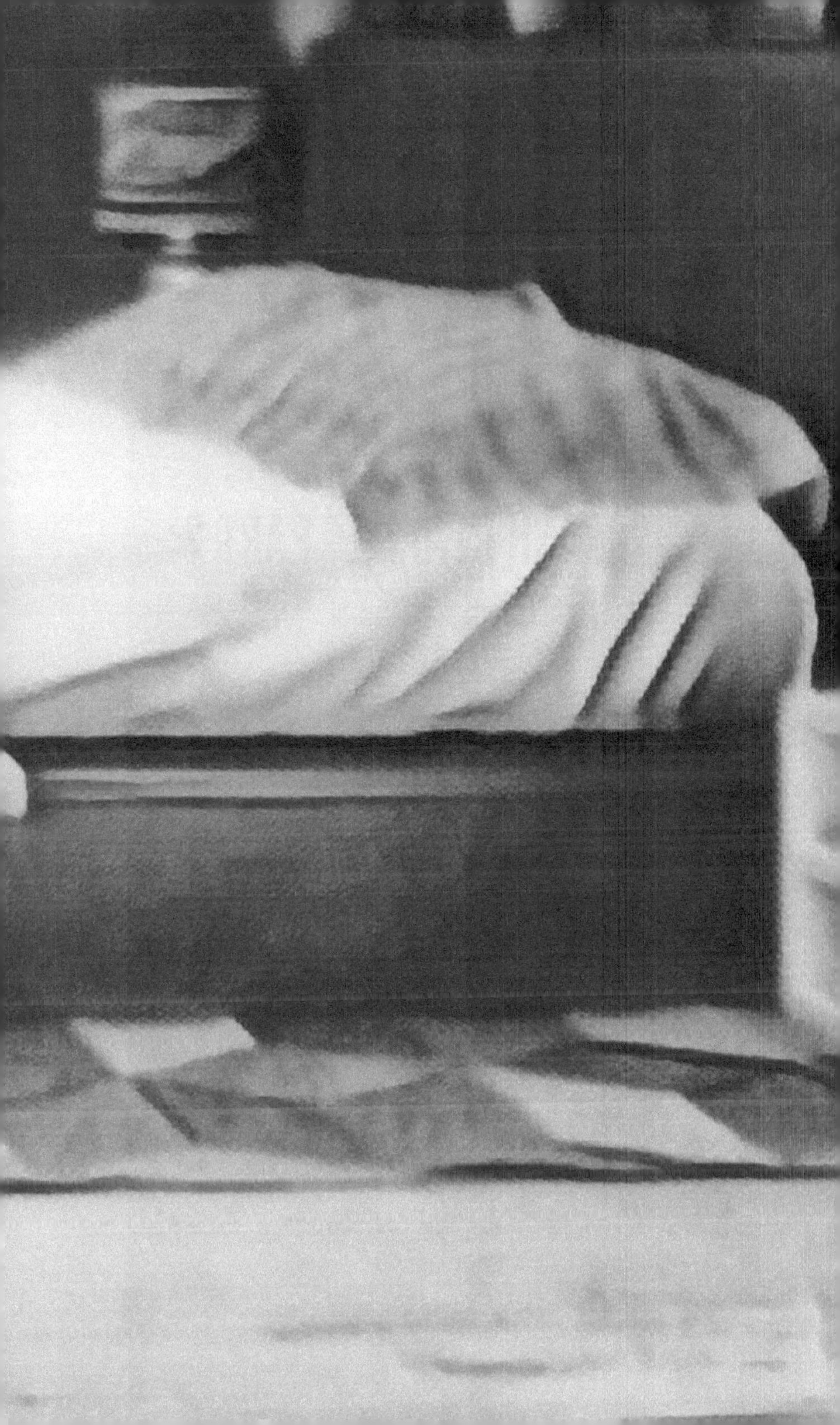

July

"CRASH INTO ME" PART 2

Dave Mathews Band

"Come on in! July? Is that you?" Beverly Reed's voice traveled through the front room from the kitchen. I opened the door and headed inside. Adrian's stepmother stood between the kitchen and living room, holding a dish towel. "July! I thought I saw you walking from next door. Why didn't you just go through the garage?"

Because we're not friends or neighbors, nor am I his girlfriend, and I'm shocked you know my name?

"Oh, I wasn't sure who was home, I just—Reagan asked me to pick up Adrian's assignment and—" I stopped talking as Beverly looked at me oddly. *Oh my God. She was just as shocked as I was that I had come here. What was happening?! Could this be more awkward?*

"My, we have certainly slimmed down and filled out in all the places, haven't we? Goodness, you... are quite the head turner." She looked me over suspiciously. "Ahh, to be that tan. I used to get so dark in the summer. I loved it. I could wear anything."

"Ah, sorry. Forgive my attire, I was just headed to Prairie Pool for a lifeguard meeting when Reagan got in touch to send this over for their exam." *It's just a stomach! Jesus, what was so surprising, the fact that mine was finally flat???* I felt stupid.

"Hey!" A male's voice broke up the weirdness. He was approaching from behind Beverly. I couldn't see who it was yet, but the voice was jovial and far too excited to see me to be Adrian's.

"What are you doing here?!"

Thank God it was his younger stepbrother, Samuel. He could take this stuff to Adrian, and I could be on my way.

"You look awesome! Don't tell me you're here for that loser!" Samuel motioned upstairs as he grabbed his cap and keys.

"Sam! Out! And, please, be careful. I want you back before your dad gets home or you won't take the truck again."

"Later!" Samuel smiled back at me as he bolted to the garage. He was a year and a half or two younger than us and much nicer to everyone in general than Adrian. *And... now he was gone. Great.* Beverly looked at me and shook her head.

"Learners permit. Be careful on the road when you see him coming." She opened the oven to check a casserole. Maybe she would just let me leave the notebook with her.

"Well, I won't keep you. I just needed to drop this by. Mrs. Keagan left Adrian's assignment with a few equations marked. I can show you the ones she mentioned." The oven door shut, and Beverly looked at me strangely again.

"Are you kidding? If you think I could relay the Greek that woman has you all speaking to each other, well then, I'm flattered. Go on up, he's in there. He can't really go anywhere else right now." She chuckled at her own bad joke, then made a pity face.

I took my time up the stairs, trying to control my nerves. I had no clue what to expect. I took a deep breath, crept down the hall, and tapped on his door.

"It's open." My heart skipped a beat at the sound of a voice I recognized. *Just act naturally, whatever that is with him.* I stepped through the door and met his eyes. He was sitting on his bed against the headboard in boxers and a t-shirt with his freshly scarred knee straightened out. A large brace lay open beside him.

"Hey." I threw out the first word. He stared back at me as I stepped further into his room, motioning toward the notebook in my hand to immediately establish why I was there. "Reagan didn't get to pick up the assignment before she left, and Lynn had already left for work, so..." *Steady. Keep it professional, friendly, but professional.* I steadied myself through a beat of silence and no response from him. He was still staring at me.

I couldn't help but notice how meticulous his room was. I knew he was a perfectionist, but good God, did a teenager really live there? It was spotless, apart from a change of clothes tossed on the floor between the door and his bed, but I didn't think that was the norm. He obviously couldn't pick up after himself with his knee. Everything else was in strict order.

Usually, when you walk into one of your peers' bedrooms, you glimpse what they were like as a kid. An adolescent poster on the wall, ribbons, and trophies from random activities you didn't know they were involved in. Horses, teddy bears, and medals, at least girls still held onto a lot of that memorabilia.

Adrian's room looked like it belonged to an adult. A seasoned bachelor, if you will. Everything was organized. Even his bookshelf was sexy. It didn't have stray sheets of paper sticking out of books that they were trapped between or random knick-knacks cluttering the spare spaces. I had to look away from it before I lingered too long and learned it was in alphabetical order.

He had no distractions other than a TV. This was obviously why he was so successful at everything he did. I felt inferior, thinking of my room or rooms since I straddled two houses. I had my own bedroom at my grandparents' house and another a few houses down, in a house Mom and I were seldom home to occupy.

Compared to him, I lived in chaos and complete disarray. It was cozy chaos, though, and I handled it well. I always knew if I had one earring at my grandparents' and another at my house or if the missing curler to my hot rollers was in a drawer in my grandparents' guest bathroom from when I changed there for a football game.

Still, I had a sinking feeling that this might be why I was such a "Jack of all trades, master of none."

"What are you wearing?" Finally. It was shitty, but at least he said something.

"I have work. I was just on my way there."

"What kind of work?" He was relentless, and I was visibly annoyed with his disdain for me.

"The guard meeting at Prairie City Pool where I work if you must know. What does it matter?"

"You'd go to a job interview dressed like that?"

"I already have the job, and it's a swimming pool, not a law office or nursing home. Everyone there either just got out of the water or is about to go in. No one's in a suit and tie, trust me."

"I trust this was Reagan's idea?"

"This? What's this... me going out of my way to make sure you get these?" I waved the notebook to bring us back on topic.

"No, the getup for your meeting. Isn't that the shirt her mom made her change out of when she went to wear it that one night?"

For someone who seemed to forget I existed, he had an impeccable selective memory.

"Her mother asked her to change because it was the middle of winter, and she was wearing it with low rise jeans and heels. It was inappropriate for where we were going as well as seasonally inappropriate. It's now summer. I'm wearing it appropriately."

"Come here."

I walked closer to him on his demand.

"Turn around."

"Absolutely not!"

"Don't you want a guy's opinion?" He smiled as he looked me up and down.

"I already got Mrs. Keagan's opinion, so I'm good." Again, bringing it back to the reason I came.

"Wait, you walked into her math lab in that? So that's it, summer's already here?" He sounded slightly taken aback. My eyes drifted to the massive scar on his knee, and I felt awful for him for a second.

"Apart from a week and a few finals including yours in calculus tomorrow, I'd say that's a fair assessment."

The half smile dropped from his face, and he looked away from me, then spoke coldly. "Why do you always have to be such a smart ass?"

Me? He was the one who spun smartassery into a profession every time we spoke. "Is it not clear that I simply respond to you with whatever you dish out?" There was a scary truth to that statement that made me wish I could swallow those last words. I looked away from him and down at the floor.

"So this is what you're doing? This summer?"

"I'm sorry? I literally just made a pact with myself to not be a smart ass, but I have to ask... As opposed to what? Flying a jet, robbing a bank...?"

"I guess I was just asking if that's what you will be doing... if that's where you'll be all summer."

"Yes. July. Lifeguard. At. Prairie. City. Pool." I delivered my response in a robotic, cavewoman-like tone.

Adrian sighed, and then I felt his hand grab mine. It was unexpected, as were the cascade of tingles that ran up that arm and down my spine. He pulled me to him.

"Sit. You're making me nervous."

I admit my heart nearly jumped out of my chest before I caught on that he was simply leading me to sit on his bed next to him. I looked back at his injured knee, opting to be extra careful as I realized I was being led to sit beside it.

"So, what did Mrs. Keagan say?"

I reached to open the notebook. Adrian closed it, still staring at me. "I meant about your attire."

"She asked me where I was headed..." I left out, *as opposed to her tutorial.* "Then she told me I was really looking good with a thoughtful expression of elegant pride instead of her usual frown of disapproval."

He smiled, mulling over my facetious rant as his eyes floated from my exposed midriff back up to my face. "Elegant, huh? That's what she said?"

"Well, you know Mrs. Keagan is quite a dish for a woman her age. There is a succinct vibe to the way she carries herself in three-inch pumps while writing harrowing hieroglyphics in chalk across four walls of a classroom. All would suggest the woman used to be hot." *Okay, we were playing now.* It's what we did best in public. "Thus, I value her opinion as much as I'm sure you do over your calculus exam tomorrow." I pushed the blue notebook toward his chest.

"You are one sick ticket." He opened the notebook without looking away from me.

Maybe I could get out of this unscathed without jumping out of my skin in front of a guy with so much power over me, even when he could neither stand nor walk alone.

"I don't know anything about the previous notes in the binder. That's all you, Lynn and Reagan, but she marked your problem areas on the—"

He ripped his assignment out of my hands and flipped it to his last quiz with a grade of ninety-nine and a smiley face marked on top.

"Um, problem areas?" He waved the A+ in front of me. "I can only imagine Mrs. Keagan took, what was it? 'Elegant pride' in drawing a smiley face on my next-to-perfect arithmetic."

Stop it! I was blushing, and that thing that happens to children when they can't hide their ear-to-ear smile was starting to happen to my face. *Just get up and leave, dumbass. You have no business in a crop top, and you're not even supposed to be here. Go to your meeting! Take some power back and exit.*

Without planning it, I reached toward his nightstand to grab a mechanical pencil I saw sitting by his phone and post-surgery meds. This innocent maneuver put my face and upper body dangerously close to his. I did not linger.

"So let's just say she circled the parts of your previous quiz that would be on the test so that you could make a hundred." I clicked the mechanical pencil so I could write. "Either way, she said you have to watch for the basic quadratic equation within the last two derivative equations. It obviously can't be solved using differentiation only, just like the others. Only on this one, the constant multiple rule applies before the final sum of two functions. It's kind of a basic algebra two trick within the equation set to throw you off. One you got correct, but this one she has marked you did not. From what she implied, she's most likely going to do a bonus question and use the last grouping of that quadratic equation to …"

"How did you know that one was a quadratic equation?"

"Because it is."

"Aren't you only in trig?"

"Come on, you know I don't take calculus. Stop trying to find something you can beat me at. This is an obvious win for you. Anyway, just watch the last three elements, those are the ones she's going to apply, and I think you reversed them in that one problem." He pulled the test away to look at Mrs. Keagan's notes.

"And she told you that when she explained?" He grabbed the pencil and reworked the section where he had gotten points marked off.

"No, she didn't say that exactly, but it became obvious to me when she pointed out those two equations. They are the only ones with the same three factors in the same pattern at the end, and you got the one reverse when she changed the element. It was just the last two steps you reversed."

"How do you know that? That's almost correct, I think... I mean, I need to put it in the calculator, but I know that's right. How did you see that so quickly?"

"I didn't. I told you I was paying attention when she walked me through it so I would understand how to relay it to you. I know this is your final, and it seemed important to her, almost fun for her that you would potentially get this part correct. Now you can get a hundred plus or the bonus or whatever you freaks need to celebrate."

"No, it's just I don't know that I would have gotten that from her notes, and I'm really surprised someone who is not in calculus did."

"Careful there. It'll sound like you're trying to compliment me."

"I certainly should be thanking you… In terms of the complement, I'll have to see if you are right first. Can you grab my graphing calculator? I think it's on the shelf up top."

Gross. Something I understood even less than the scribble on Mrs. Keagan's chalkboard was the TI-82 graphing calculator.

"Yeah, but then I have to go."

"Oh, right, your job interview."

I looked to the right above him, where he gestured for the calculator. "I told you; I already have the job."

I wasn't an expert on the layout of Adrian's room, much less his bed, but he appeared to have pointed to the shelf four or more feet above his headboard. His queen-size bed was flush against the wall on the other side, so I couldn't walk around the bed, and even if I could, I don't think I could have reached that shelf. His leg brace was also open and ready to be put back on. Some apparatus, which had to be part of his physical therapy, commandeered the other side of his bed.

"You're just going to have to step across. It's fine, you can step on the bed."

I stood up from his side, trying to figure this out. I saw the calculator's light blue case peeking between his calculous book and a spiral notebook. *Step across?* I wasn't going to stand on his bed. I looked down at his fresh scar.

"I would get it myself but..." He was obviously amused by this challenge.

"I'm getting it. I just didn't want to put my shoes on your bed." I bit my bottom lip, placed a knee on one side of him, and swung the other over. Okay, now I was straddling him, upright on my knees. I wasn't sitting on top of him by any means. *How did this just get weirder?* I stretched up and over as far as I could and tried to ignore the fact that whether he liked it or not, he had a spectacular view of my "outfit."

I stretched my right arm toward the shelf as far as it could reach, and my hand was almost on the calculator. Keeping my knees and stance above his waist rigidly intact in my humble efforts to protect his injury at all costs, I turned at my waist. I extended my left arm as well, trying to flick it down.

I felt Reagan's formerly awesome shirt open at the bottom, exposing the parts above my midriff that it was, in fact, meant to cover. *Just keep going, and get the damn thing.* I ignored the fact that I might be exposing more than I intended and that his view just got elevated if he were looking.

Although I'm sure, this unbelievable shitshow only lasted about three seconds, reaching for that calculator felt like an eternity in slow motion, that is until I felt the heat of two hands on my thighs. Startled by the charge of electricity that shot through me like a rocket, I made a last-ditch effort to pitch it down with my fingertips.

I knocked it down, alright. The calculator, textbook, spiral notebook, and other books above it tumbled onto the bed.

We both ducked for cover, or I guess it's more accurate to say I covered him. I crouched down to a seated position on his lap and laid my chest on his chest as the books and calculator landed, one by one, on top of his knee brace on the side of the bed. *Awesome.* Now, I was sitting on top of him.

There was a slight pause before I could figure out how to maneuver the situation. I don't know if I was waiting for him to yell or laugh or... I pushed off the bed to lift my chest off of his. I couldn't look at him. I had to figure out how to get off of him first! I was straddling him.

As I peeled upright from laying on top of him, I felt something holding a part of me in place. I felt *him* underneath me. Yes, he most certainly had a reaction to the view, and I was positioned right on top of it.

I did not look at him. This is when a sane person would figure out how to leap off the bed, apologize for the falling books, and pretend it didn't happen. I would have to do that for the pride of both of us.

Still concerned about his knee, I peered at it behind me over my left shoulder. The back of my shoe was right beside his large scar. I couldn't just jump off. I needed to raise up on my knees, the way I began, then swing my right leg off the bed and away from him.

This was taking far too long.

Why hadn't he pushed me off or said anything? He was probably wondering why I hadn't jumped off him yet! As I raised myself to stand back on my knees above him, I did not feel the space between us I was trying to achieve. Instead, I felt the two warm hands that had pressed against my thighs seconds before. They had moved to my hips just below my waist and were securing me in place.

I looked at Adrian. He was looking up at me. His eyes locked on mine. I had never felt a stare so intense, nor had I ever felt the intensity I was feeling beneath me. I don't think I had ever experienced an erection before, never grazed one with my hand, and truthfully had never been aware if I had given a guy one up until that point. There were so many things I was naïve to and had not yet done, and there I was, positioned like a pro... Our eyes had not deviated from their fixation on each other, and I felt he was burning through me in more ways than one.

He didn't move his hands from where they were pressed into me, but I did feel his fingertips slide further down toward my butt. His hands were strong. I'm not even sure I felt it at first when he slid me forward and down the length of him. It was such a smooth transaction.

I couldn't breathe. I just watched Adrian watching me. My hands fell softly onto his strained forearms that held us together. Then, he slowly pushed me back, reversing the motion. His hands continued to control the movement of my hips on top of him, and his eyes continued to hold my gaze. My heart beat so rapidly that everything felt crazy, and heat ignited inside me. I couldn't contemplate my gratitude for the thick jean material of my cutoffs or even consider what lay beneath his thin boxers. It was all I could do not to close my eyes and arch backward.

My body got a clue much quicker than my brain, and before I knew it, I was no longer waiting for his hands to slide me down toward him and push me back. My hips began to rock forward in the rhythm he started for us, and my breath got shorter and shorter as they rocked me back. I felt even more of a firmness underneath me, as if it could possibly get more intense on his end, and he let out an almost inaudible moan. His breath was getting shorter as he stared up at me. His eyes had still not separated from mine.

I started rocking faster. My hips dragged me down him, then back.

"F-U-C-K." He whispered out of a low moan, his intense blue eyes now dancing at mine.

The doorbell rang downstairs. It was muted in my mind or from the distance, but we both absolutely heard it. With his eyes on me, watching every rocking motion I made above him, he did not pause nor loosen his grip on me. I continued moving from the waist down but tried to catch my breath. I had to consider— the doorbell just rang, and although I was fully dressed and our lips hadn't even touched, I was, in fact, riding him!

"Adrian! Physical therapy is here!" His stepmother's voice rang loud and clear from the kitchen.

I forced myself to shut down whatever was happening inside me, but I couldn't break eye contact, and neither had he. I moved my pelvis forward to rise up and off him, but something about the way

I moved caused an additional response in him. I swung my right leg over, and I was off the bed immediately.

"I'm sending him up!" His stepmother warned us from below. As if the magnitude of lines crossed had not been enough, something came over me as I exited the scene. Remembering the day Adrian threw his jacket toward me for cover in the rain, I grabbed the shorts I passed off the floor. I tossed them over my shoulder toward him without looking back. I had a strong hunch he needed them.

I passed a balding, slightly heavy man in scrubs and sneakers that squeaked even on the carpet as I walked down the hallway toward the stairs. That was a nice snap into reality, but how would I get past...

"Did you two get it handled?"

I choked a little, then forced my voice out as strongly as possible. "Yes, ma'am." *Keep walking. Just keep walking straight out the door.*

"Thank you for bringing everything by for Adrian. Good luck at the pool!"

The screen door popped behind me. I ran across the lawn to Lynn's drive and flew into the truck faster than humanly possible. My legs were shaking. My body tingled all over. I looked in the rearview mirror to check my face; my cheeks were as red as apples. *Oh my God! What happened back there?*

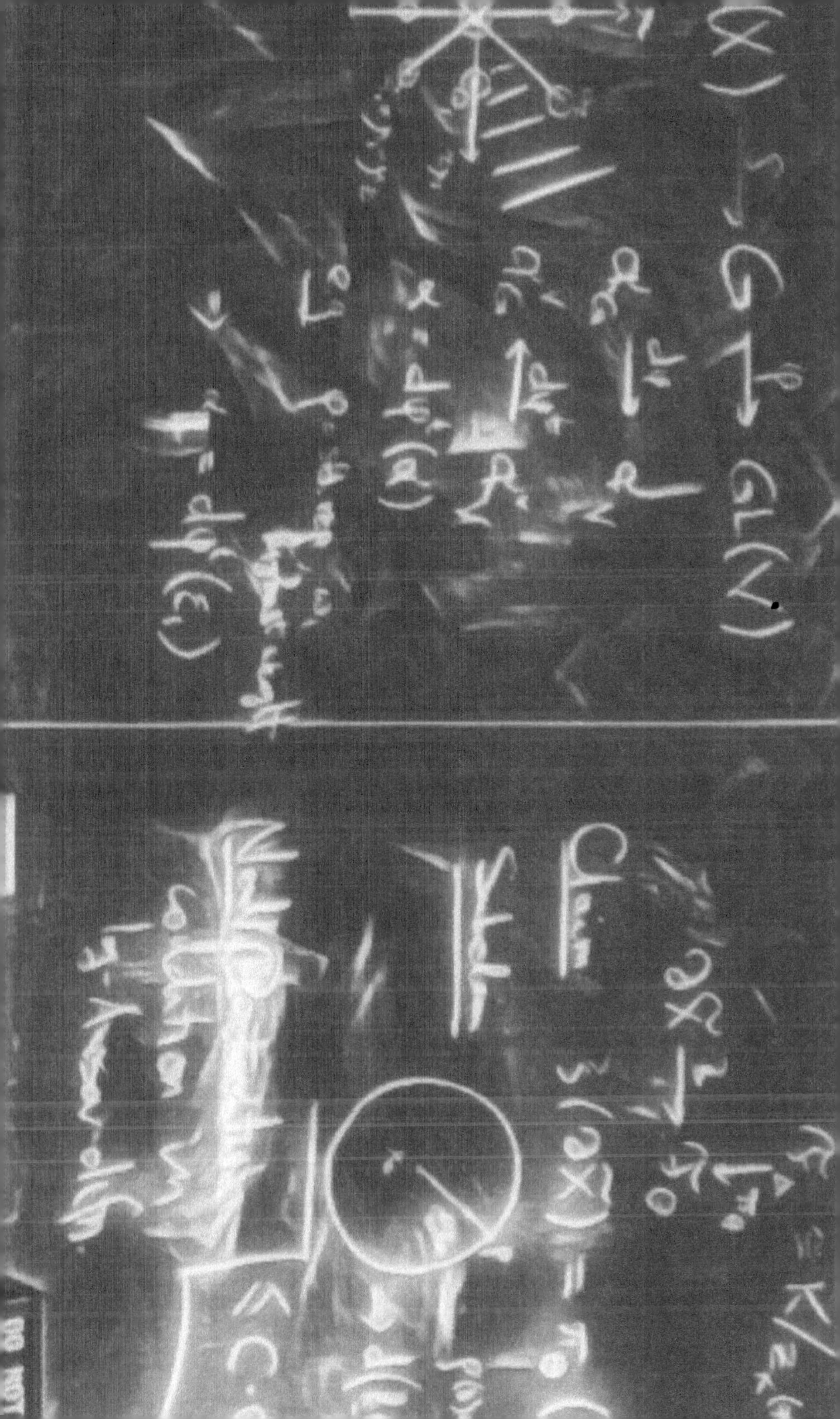

Bush

The door closed on my PT's exit, and secure in my brace, I swung my leg back over and collapsed on the bed. I could still smell her in my room. The sweet smell of hot candy, roses, and something light but sophisticated in her hair. It was so subtle, but that smell of her hair lingered every time she passed and was what got to me the most, no matter what perfume she wore. *Jesus!* The fact that I knew when she wore a different perfume. *What the Hell just happened? What did I do? What did we do?! Jesus!*

She—she came into my room. She was so ridiculously hot. Her skin was hot, her legs, her ass in those shorts, her stomach. I had never seen it before. I had never seen *her* like that before. Even with

328

this *thing* we obviously had... Okay, she's always had this appeal about her I was drawn to for some reason beyond my understanding. But, today...

She was never my physical type. We often disagreed wildly. I like taller, very trim girls. This was the list I always went down when I tried to reject my actions toward her and put things back into perspective. She's curvier, but fuck if not in all the right places now. Was she smaller, and taller now... slimer? Not like that mattered, it just blew compartmentalizing her as not my "type" out of the water. Maybe she truly wasn't my type — she was fucking hotter! I... she was always the GOOD one you didn't think of as... Well, that's a lie. I had fantasized about the July I knew privately in every possible way since our freshman year when I saw her in her cheerleading uniform.

We went from eighth-grade frenemies in social studies arguing over historical references, and one summer later, it was like bumping into a new girl. Yet, there was still that familiar thing about her; it sounded, felt, and smelled different when she passed in the hallway. I told myself at the time it was just the allure of the cheerleading outfit. Anything past that was just, you know, guy stuff, whatever does it for you. Which, if I was honest... more often than not, *she* did.

I denied a lot, most ruthlessly all our encounters this year, but I couldn't ignore this one... Not even if she planned to. It was the third time I lost my mind with her if you ignored the office situation early that Fall. *But what was she wearing???* It was like her shorts just teased below her belly button, demanding anyone who looked to ask for more. *What was she even doing here?! In my room?*

Was this a Reagan concoction? I had never been so turned on in my life. I think I would have continued in front of my PT had she not fled or had I not, to be frank... well, finished just in time. I'm afraid those shorts have met their retirement under my bed. How's that for physical therapy? *God, the thought of how physical we were. What was I doing? What was she doing to me?!*

I thought we left this in the auditorium that day. Especially after things got back to normal. Then, when she never made an effort to visit me after my surgery. I guess I thought she'd at least stop by randomly with Lynn one day as a friend... I hoped she'd come by. There were moments throughout the ordeal when she was the only person I wanted to see. I put that out of my head, though. It wasn't the reality of our situation. Her absence the entire time I've been trapped in these four walls solidified that.

We were just having fun. It got a little flirty, as it always does, but that was just our thing. It wasn't supposed to make me force her on top of me. I spent a nearly three-month relationship policing myself through making out and kid-glove petting with Natalie. I was never tempted to do *that*. I sat poolside by one of *the* hottest bodies of our class to date, Shelby North. She was even in a red bikini, bouncing around our pool deck with no one home, and probably would have let me try anything on her in her just-out-of-a-breakup state. I didn't attempt a move. I rubbed sunscreen on Shelby's back, which was a joke compared to what happened to me when

July reached above me for a calculator. I had to get out of the house!

All I know is she leaned over to reach for that damn calculator, and there was a *black lace bra*? I'd never seen her, forgive me, tits before, and God, *did I need to now.* Lane described them well enough for me to want to break his face. But seeing them up close... *What was she doing wearing that?* It affected me immediately.

Who am I kidding? I was aroused the moment I saw it was her at the door, walking into my bedroom right as rain, as if she belonged there. And then that outfit.

The black lace bra was just the straw that broke the camel's back. *She* would never wear that?! But how could I know what she wore underneath anything? I'd avoided that at all costs, and now. *Wow. What did we just do?* What would she say the next time we saw each other?

I looked over at my phone on the nightstand, then out the window. The sun had just gone down. It wasn't even completely dark yet. *Focus.*

What caused this entire hiccup was an effort to get me to ace my calculous final, an accolade I deserved. I opened the notebook she brought me. I had to stop thinking about her, how she moved on top of me, how she moved me. I had to get how she looked right through to my inner thoughts while she rocked back and forth on my lap, breathless as I pressed us together.

I glanced out the window again. It was finally getting dark. *Where was July? Still out at that stupid pool meeting with Lane and all the lifeguards? Wearing that... Wearing what we did?* That shot a spasm through my core and had me ready for round two. I liked the idea of her having me on her when she met her summer coworkers, but I didn't like worrying about who she was meeting or what she thought about what we did.

Did I make her do it? Was she mad at me? I wasn't sure what haunted me more: wanting to have her that way again or fearing I wouldn't get to. Or her. How she felt about it all. How she felt about me. Would she say anything? I wanted to know what she was thinking... I wanted to know *her.*

I pulled the stapled assignments out of the front of the notebook and sifted through them to hit all of Mrs. Keagan's notes. The last page was crumpled and folded in half. I opened a circled red "F" with "*July, these were on the third chalk board. If you didn't get them down, or fully understand the second half of the equation, you should have come to tutorials. The ones you missed will be on your Trig final...*" written in Mrs. Keagan's handwriting.

What? Why was July's paper in Lynn's notebook or with my... *Ah,* Keagan must have given July her last quiz when she picked up my assignments. I picked up her Trig quiz and started reading through the red marks. I wasn't trying to invade her privacy. Okay, that was rich after what just happened here.

An "F." That wasn't like July. I mean, I know math wasn't her strong suit, and all of Keagan's classes were college-level, so no doubt Trig and Analyt were difficult even for the above-average math enthusiast. *What did you miss July?* I wondered as I reworked her mistakes in my head, going through each step.

She was showing her work on everything. Couldn't Keagan see where she went wrong, ironically, the way July saw where I had? I got to the page where she stopped showing her work. Weird, she should know these. This simply came down to the variable she wasn't seeing.

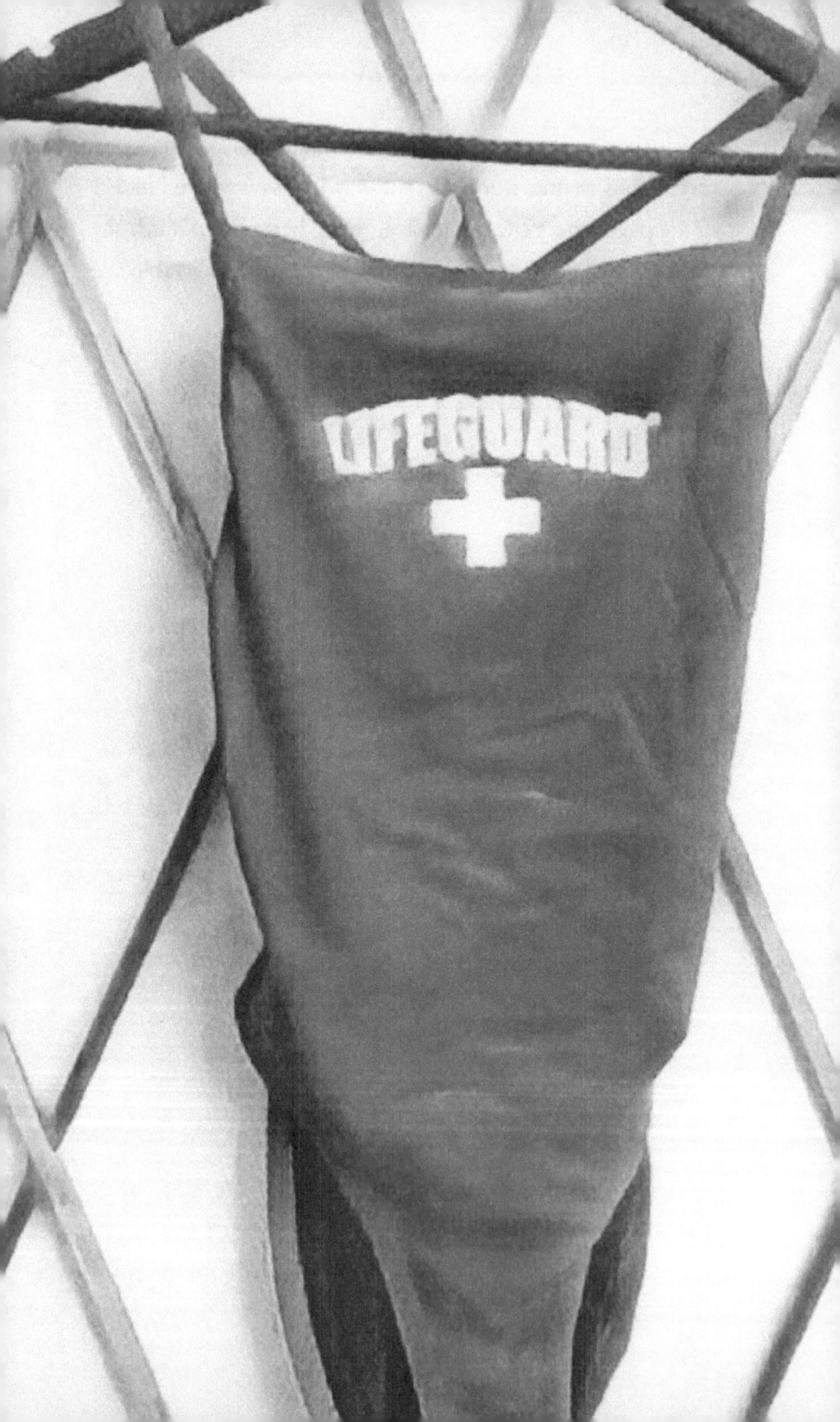
LIFEGUARD

July

"SMELLS LIKE TEEN SPIRIT"

Nirvana

I smiled as the pool manager handed me my guard shirt and first week's schedule. It was a crowded room. There were more of us this year than last. A lot of faces I didn't recognize.

I felt a few eyes on me earlier when Cleta introduced her veteran guards to the rookies and three incredibly tall college guys I had never seen before. Cleta was a tough boss, but we liked that about her. She ran the pool with an iron fist; the stricter she was, the more fun we had in our off time.

She had a wild streak and never shorted us on well-earned play. Cleta worked for the Prairie City dispatch and thus had easy access to her guards in our free time, should we be up to any unsavory shenanigans. She owned us during the summer, but again, the perks made up for it.

I knew Lane was there. When I pulled up, his car was already in the parking lot. In my state, I honestly don't know if I saw him or even bothered to glance at him before we ended up standing side by side for the introductions. Sitting there in such a thick haze was so strange. Just hours before, the anticipation of this meeting alone had me bouncing off the walls and ready to arrive an hour early. I was glad my mood had altered. Sitting through the meeting like a sane person, calm and almost mellow, felt good. Those were two looks I had never successfully sported.

I felt Lane's stare as if he was trying to get my attention when we all separated into groups to sign up for the first month of pool parties. I was in such a fog that I noticed too late and walked right past him. It was odd. Maybe the comradery we relied on in the lion's den was no longer necessary, or the pecking order somehow switched. He was an outsider high school guy trying to maintain his second-year lifeguard status among the big dogs, and I was... dare I say, *one of them?*

I was fresh bait with status, and the college guys were curious about who I was. Is that all it took to have the upper hand? Look great, keep your mouth shut, and people start noticing. *Ridiculous.* It was Pure Pines made over, and I couldn't care less that doing nothing could potentially make me one of the ones who mattered.

A clipboard was shoved in my face, and Cleta's niece, Stacy, snapped me out of my daze. "Blue or red this year?"

I looked at the checklist of an order form titled *Women's Guard Suits*. "At the risk of looking like Bay Watch wannabes, I like the red."

I heard a few chuckles from the small crowd.

"Okay, Yasmine Bleeth, I'm out voted. Red it is." Stacy shot a fake scowl at me as she tossed me a pen to fill out my suit order.

She was wild, fun, and tough. Her aunt Cleta's worst nightmare and spitting image. They were alike in so many ways, and their antics were a fun city pool staple you could count on for summer entertainment. Stacy was bossy but in all the good ways. She and I had always strangely gotten along. I don't know how. I was a goody-two-shoes compared to her. She either had a curious fix on helping corrupt me or recognized the fellow daredevil within. I never had any problem standing up to Stacy at work and always did my job. I think that's why I had her respect. She, indeed, was a chip off her aunt's block.

My hand hovered over the check box for one piece while I stared at the descriptor next to it: *Two-piece midriff racer back high cut bottom guard suit*. Stacy stepped back toward me to grab the clipboard for the next guard when she saw I hadn't checked a box yet.

She snatched the pen from my hand. "Nah, girl, this year we're getting two pieces. I'll let all my shit hang out before I have to wrestle like a stuffed sausage every time I need to go the bathroom. It's hot as hell out there. These losers get to drop trow from the waist down with their swim trunks. They don't have to think *twice* about going to the bathroom." She nodded at the new college guys, initiating them to the guard room with her brash tongue. "I'm not holding it for six hours in the heat because it takes my entire break just to peel spandex off a sunburn so I can pee and go back on rotation."

The guys stood and applauded, cheering in support of Stacy's rant. "Yeah, two pieces!" The new college guys certainly acclimated fast.

Okay, so we were getting two pieces. It hadn't happened as glamorously as I expected, but it happened!

"Relax, you'll get to keep that tan!" Stacy pinched the side of my exposed stomach and winked as she passed by. *I was one of them! I was one of the regular trim girls who didn't have to think twice about checking the box for a two-piece!* My small bubble burst slightly when I noticed the three cheerleader rookies from Prairie High School had already automatically checked two-piece. Great, the truth was, I *was* the only fatty holding us back. The others had probably never worn a one-piece in their lives.

I don't mean to be judgmental, but they just looked like little bitches. What can I say? I learned from the best; at least two were mirror images of Pure Pines' finest. I forced myself to look away from my summer buzz kills and trailed the room to find Lane.

A pair of green eyes searching for mine, startled me. A haphazard smile coiled on one side of my face when they held my gaze. The stray green eyes belonged to the tallest of the new college guards and the one Cleta introduced as one of our new head guards. His sandy brown hair was almost the same color as his suntan. He wore a modest gold chain that must have been significant in some way because, on first impression, he didn't seem the type to wear a guy's version of fashion jewelry.

He smiled an almost dirty smile I would have found offensive from another stranger, but somehow, his smile was curious and exposed my own curiosity. *Hmm.*

"Well, well, look who finally decided to grace us with his presence!" Cleta's voice interrupted the chatter across the small groups still holding clipboards.

Oh no. Great. There goes whatever social status I thought I had garnered at the workplace.

I somehow knew it was too good to be true. Enter Spencer Pearce. He was Pure Pines. His mom was on the school board, and he was a Senior when I was a freshman. Apparently, he'd been away for a while in college, which was how I missed working with or under him in prior summers. He was legendary, not just in his own world of Pure Pines but here in Prairie as a guard. And he was recently familiar. As in he was the one I saw in the bathroom with Robyn Mayes and Trent Childers.

Spencer high-fived the tall, green-eyed guy who'd given me the curious hello with his eyes. I could consider that a goodbye under Spencer's tutelage. Spencer would no doubt be the additional head guard, and his memories of Pure Pines High either held me as a chubby dork or were nonexistent, confirming I was not part of the in-crowd. There were rumors he'd graced an upperclassmen's intimate party or two with his presence once or twice since he'd left for the University of Texas. If so, he knew I was not a part of the current Pure Pine elite invited. I saw all I cared to be reacquainted with him at the twins' party.

"Court! You ready for this summer, Bro?" My new green-eyed acquaintance laughed and shook his head as Spencer slapped him on the back and surveyed the new rookies in the room. Apparently, his name was Court. I guess I hadn't paid much attention when Cleta originally introduced him. I looked away and tried to stay far from Spencer's radar. Cleta tossed Spencer a guard shirt and continued with the meeting. I shook my head at how I ended up in this moment. Small towns certainly had a wide radius when you simply tried to step out for a moment.

I folded my schedule in half and moved to slide it into one of the back pockets of my jean shorts. I immediately felt those hands that pressed me into his lap just an hour and a half before. My stomach flipped, and a million butterflies circled in a frenzy. I worried I might be blushing. I had almost forgotten my minor indiscretion. As if I could ever forget *that*. It was strange, that reminder of my dirty little secret. It was as equally comforting at the lion's den as it was exciting and nerve-wracking.

Who cared about Spencer Pearce potentially bringing Pure Pines to the guard room?

I had the first problem of the day yet to be solved. *What had Adrian and I done? And what did it mean?*

Foo Fighters

I woke up with July's quiz on my chest and everything about her on my mind.

I must have dozed off. It was finally dark out. Lynn had to be back from her shift at some point. I had to talk to her. I'd tried Reagan, but she didn't answer. I was sure she had enough on her plate with her mom tonight.

I guess I just really needed Lynn's voice of reason. I was going nuts not being able to walk out the door and make sure everything was still standing and right in the world.

Where was she?

Had she gotten back from that damn lifeguard thing, and what was she thinking?!

Was she thinking about what happened? I had to know; I wanted to see her. I wanted to ask her. I wanted to tell her that I ... That I what? *Holy shit! I wanted her.*

Whether I was coming to terms with it at that moment or not, I had never been so absorbed with anyone. *Ever.* So... I chose to ignore her? No. This time I should tell her that this thing, this recurring *thing* between us, I just couldn't shake it no matter how hard I tried, and ultimately, I didn't know why I would want to.

What if she thought I crossed the line or forced her to do that? Had I gone too far with her, and now she'd despised me more? This was so bizarre. I'd never been in this position before and wasn't sure what was next.

I saw Lynn's headlights pulling up her drive. I flashed my bedroom lamp multiple times to warn her I was calling. She had a private line in her room. Still, I hated the idea of waking her parents up with aimless rings.

My phone rang before I could dial. It was Lynn.

"Did you get your assignment?!! Did Reagan get it to you before she left with her mom?"

She didn't know, which meant she hadn't stopped by July's or heard from her. She knew nothing of what weighed on my mind, chest, and other places every time I saw July's face in my head or caught a whiff of her in my room.

"Yeah, no worries, I got it." I paused on the line for a moment. "Actually... July ended up having to drop it by."

"Oh, thank God! I never heard back from Reagan, and I worried my whole shift that you were just sitting here, unable to study."

That was a fair assessment.

"Wait, July dropped it by? She had to go back and pick it up from math lab? I thought she had her first day at the pool?"

"She just dropped it by before she left, I guess Reagan caught her on the way out."

"Oh, *I see.*"

"See what?"

"Nothing. It was just a really big day for her, that's all."

"Well, *I* didn't ask her to bring it by." I usually never had any trouble reading Lynn. Still, I didn't understand her tone, especially if she wasn't privy to what happened here.

"Not everything has to do with you and your knee you big baby. I just meant I was surprised she made time to drop it off. It was a really big night for her."

"I thought she already had the job."

"Exactly, she's a returning lifeguard, she's a boss, and look at her now, she's gonna knock em' dead this year! I was a little anxious to hear about her night. I heard a rumor at work that Spencer's back for the summer."

"Spencer Pearce? He works there?"

"Did, work there a couple of years ago. I think just the summers of his junior and senior years. That's how he got to plow through Prairie's finest and then some." *Great, and that would be her summer. Awesome.*

"Don't you remember he always had these obscure hot girls he brought to parties or prom as if the bastard was too cool to date his own kind? Like somehow going to the school over and dipping in their stock made him a God."

"No, I don't. Jesus, Lynn, we must have been in the eighth grade when he was a junior." I actually did remember. He was a God. "What, you were invited to those parties back then?"

"Shut up! I got invited plenty. I was a hot freshman!" July was a freshman cheerleader that year, so she would have been invited, too." Lynn just casually threw that last part out there.

I couldn't help wondering the significance of Lynn's obsession with Spencer's homecoming, and I HOPED it had nothing to do with July.

"Anyway, a couple of the guys came in tonight and I heard Jed and Angel say he was home from UT for the summer and going to work there. I didn't get to warn her, that's all."

"What's it matter?"

"Umm, nothing for July other than I would imagine he can't help but run that place like he did our hallways. I know she wanted a break from all that. You know, Pure Pines scrutiny. It kind of sucks to be under the gun all of the time. Not all of us got an extended break! No knee pun intended! Spencer's not as bad as his rep. I just hope she wasn't intimidated and got to hold her own that's all."

Trust me. If you'd seen what Reagan had her wearing... she held her own.

"Look, she can't have a break just yet. She's got her trig final this week, doesn't she?"

"I don't know. What are you, July's dad? If you want to run over ours, I'm good for another thirty on the phone before I have to crash."

"No, um, I'm straight, unless you need a refresher before tomorrow, but I figured you had the notes for a bit. I actually need you to help July on hers."

"Trig final?"

"Yeah, I think it's Thursday; at least, that's what her quiz notes from Keagan say."

"Did she tell you that or say she needed help?" Lynn sounded tired and defensive.

"No, she just left her quiz in the notebook, or when Keagan gave it to her it was stacked on the back of mine. It's not good. She needs to nail this one or it could hurt her final average."

"I'm sure if she needed our help she would have said something. What's the matter with you?"

"What? I'm just saying she needs to rework these equations before her exam, and no, she would never say anything to me. You know that." I could tell Lynn took a moment to contemplate the relevance of what I said.

"She probably wouldn't have said anything to any of us."

"Look, Keagan obviously marked them for her to review for the test, which is a gift as you know."

"Okay. Alright, you're saying you just need me to pick it up from you and get it to her so she has time with it before Thursday..."

"No! I mean, yes, but we should help her... YOU need to *help her*. She knows how to do this; she's just not recognizing the exceptions. Those last groupings of equations she stops showing her work on. She's not acknowledging the exceptions to the rule. It's like she doesn't recognize them, but she's shown she knows what they are on the previous page. Those last few have multiple exceptions, and I think she just stopped. Will you work them with her and show her the steps she missed? I already reworked and marked them."

I waited for Lynn to land into me or ask me what this was really about, as she intuitively did when it came to any concern on my part for July. I had to admit, it would seem slightly psycho, my pretending she didn't exist, then suddenly demanding information about her to make an effort to keep her GPA up.

"Hello?? Lynn!"

I heard a yawn on the other end of the receiver.

"Yeah, I'll give it to her or you can give it to her or tell her I... I'm so tired. Tomorrow." Lynn hung up.

I stared at the phone as I hung up the receiver, wishing I had the guts to make another call or hoping it would ring with a voice at the other end that had never called.

A door slamming and some commotion down the hall interrupted my silent wager with the phone. *Had Samuel just gotten in?* No, he was home for dinner, and I don't think he left again.

"I don't want to hear it. Just get in here and shut the door before you wake the boys up. And, don't slam another door! They have exams tomorrow." My stepmom's voice chimed down the hallway as if she and my dad had been arguing over something. I didn't hear a response from him. "Or don't you remember?"

That was the last thing I heard her yell, but it was strange to describe it as yelling. There was something odd in her voice. It was full of concern more than anger. I wondered what they were fighting about. They never really fought about anything.

My dad was pretty spectacular and unique that way. He had that quiet, stoic thing about him, but it was much more thoughtful than brooding. The opposite of the silence that drove most women nuts. He listened first. Then he offered sage advice that mattered. I loved that about him.

It was a level of kindness he offered and genuine patience as opposed to something strategic for his own gain. They rarely fought, if ever. Maybe he had to work late and forgot to tell her. This was his busy season, and he had been coming home later and later.

He'd also been super forgetful with all the stress. Come to think of it, it was unlike him to not check in on me before a major exam. And, just in general, when he got home late and missed dinner with us. We were close that way.

He didn't ask me about my finals to follow up and make sure I studied. He knew I was always prepared. He checked in over genuine interest and curiosity about what I had going on. He was the polar opposite of his own father. My dad didn't *make me* do anything. He cared that I had what I needed to succeed and was striving my best at what I wanted. That is why I worked so hard. His excitement over my interests and achievements made me want to aim higher for him.

I wondered what had him so occupied at the shop and if it was my fault for being of no help with the knee. Usually, he would knock on my door before going to bed, especially lately with me being trapped in my room. The hallway had quietened, and their door closed softly. I left it that we'd catch up when he took me in for my calculus exam.

With one last glance toward the phone on my nightstand, I turned my lamp off and succumbed to the loneliness of my room. It wasn't that lonely, not with the smell of July surrounding my sheets and my thoughts of her replaying in my mind.

I took a deep breath in the dark. I marveled at how the unexpected invasion of July to my mundane day felt more like home to me and even made my room more... mine than anything constant or missing from my current routine had.

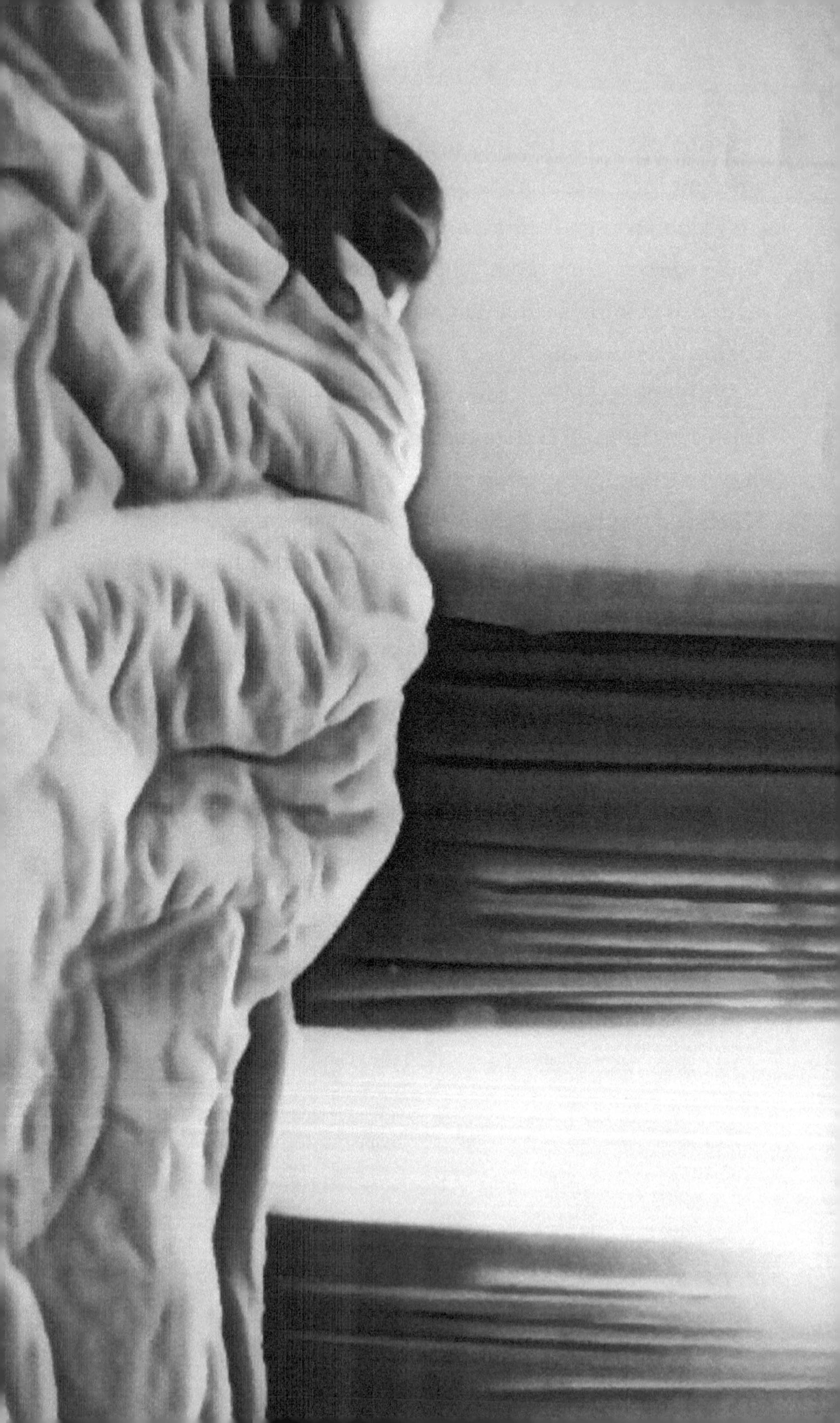

July

"FADE INTO YOU"

Mazzy Star

I woke to the sound of my grandmother unloading the dishwasher. Her early morning ritual had been my alarm clock for as long as I could remember.

I should have felt like a million bucks. It was going to be an interesting summer, that's for sure. Even Spencer Pearce hadn't thrown that much of a wrench into my reign of the two-piece.

I was still excited. I should have been. But my stomach flipped when I replayed those blue eyes burning into mine for the hundredth time since last night. *Relax!* It's not like I would bump into Adrian in the hallway. Honesty, I wished I would.

Passing by him with no nod of recognition over what we'd done... as if all were normal under the umbrella of Pure Pines' would have honestly felt better. It would have given me a catch-and-release, the way I imagine people addicted to pain must feel. The idea of the devil-you-know, or some messed up shit like that. *Ugh!*

Not knowing if what happened in his room between us meant anything or if it mattered to him was pure agony.

That, and how do you go from being the most innocent of all your friends to an act that curiously teetered on slutty? He wasn't my boyfriend. What base even was that? Third? I had been on proper dates, sure, not many, but none had ended in so much as a good night's kiss, much less that position.

Was it weird or worse of me that I never wondered if he did this with anyone else?

Maybe I was just naïve to think it was something reserved for the two of us. Was it odd that I wasn't ashamed or didn't feel like a freak? It felt natural with him, even though basic human requirements like a conversation or general respect didn't.

I made it through my first exam period. It was AP English, and I already had an "A" plus. Again, I should be happy.

"Hello! Earth to July! My God you're hard to track down. I looked all over for you this morning at break." Lynn joined my maneuver through the hallway with the enthusiasm I should have had this morning.

"I went straight to the English hall when I got here."

"Well, spill! What happened?!" I stopped— dumbstruck— staring back at her. It was all I could do to keep from saying, *which part?*

"Reagan said you got the two-piece, and they let you vote with the other head girl guards! Way to make a baller impression! Also, was he there?"

Again, *who?*

"Spencer Pearce?! Last night I heard he was home for the summer and would be working with you."

"He was there."

"Sorry I couldn't warn you. Did he recognize you?"

I opened my locker and tried to focus on the rest of the day as I answered idle questions. I had to admit, I was relieved she knew nothing about yesterday. It was closer to home and more interesting than the elusive washed-up Spencer Pearce.

"I don't think he did, or if he did, it was no more than knowing I'm from Pure Pines as a face he'd passed in the hallway."

"Oh BS! You're so dismissive, I'm sure he knew exactly who you were." Lynn adjusted one of her books about to fall. I tried to change the subject.

"Do you have more exams today? Oh, wait! How did calculus go?! Did you guys kill it?!" At that moment, a wave of students poured out of the math hall, and I couldn't help but look over Lynn's shoulder as the double glass doors pushed open. It was a pathetic habit.

"He's not here." Lynn's dry tone and unenthused look made me suddenly aware of how pathetic and telling of a habit it was. "They let Samuel drive him home immediately after the test."

"I wasn't looking for—I was looking for Mrs. Keagan."

"Um hmm. For this?" Lynn held up a familiar "F" circled in red.

Oh my God! Wait. Did I drop it in the math lab, and Keagan found it? No. I absolutely looked at it between leaving the school and the truck. *Oh my God!*

"How did you get that?! Did Keagan give it to you?"

"No, Adrian. He said he reworked your mistakes and wrote notes on the back. He said you'd know what he meant on the last problem. Why didn't you tell me you needed help? I gave you my notes from last year, I could have explained everything to you." Lynn seemed surprised or offended.

I was between confused and mortified, thinking of every remote possibility of how my epic fail had ended up in her hands and more over the hands that had passed it to her.

"Well if you must know, I sure as hell didn't ask Adrian for help either! How did you guys get this?" I took the paper from her and stuffed it in my notebook.

"You didn't give it to him yesterday when you stopped by?"

"No." It suddenly dawned on me. One, I must have left it attached to Adrian's assignments, and two... *stopped by. Good*, she knew nothing of our encounter. He had shared nothing except my "F," apparently. I didn't know if that was a huge relief or an insult to the act itself. *However, what did he say that had her so riled over my final trig grade?*

"I must have not realized it was stuck to his assignments when I stuffed everything from Mrs. Keagan in your notebook for him."

"Well, either way, July, you should have told me you were struggling. This was the last quiz before your final. Are you going to be able to bring your grade up to passing?"

"First off, you don't know how good or bad I've done on every other quiz. I can't believe you would assume it's as bad as it looks! I'll be fine. I always am."

"Adrian seems to think so as well."

"What?!!"

"He says if you just go over the rework and understand the note on the back you'll get all the others right, no problem. Still, as your smartest friend…"

I cut my eyes at her.

"Okay, fine, as the best one of us at math, can you see how this makes me look bad that you would go to Adrian for help instead of yours truly."

"I didn't go to him for help!!!"

"Relax. You should have, with a grade like that. You know any of us would have helped you, right?" She ducked her face down to mine to observe my response. She was sincere, but I knew the question was more than that.

Lynn was always the most conscious of my silent crush and the bizarre friendship she and Reagan had with her neighbor. Thanks to Keagan's university-level calculous antics, the bond outside of our girls' group had grown more and more exclusive since Adrian's knee injury.

Lynn was honest to a fault. I knew it was hard for her to spend time with Reagan and Adrian apart from me. It made sense they'd have their own version of math club-like hangouts to study with him. He was missing entire lectures Lynn and Reagan would have to relay to him. In turn, they benefited from the automatic study group.

They were like three super-hot nerds who could exchange notes without even talking math shop. They ended up putting their heads together about everything else instead, and it didn't bother me that their friendship grew as a trio. How could it? Three of the people that interested me most in the world growing closer. It was kind of unique if you looked at it from a distance.

However, standing right outside it, you couldn't help but feel the distance. It was like a punch in the gut.

I knew Lynn felt the burden of the situation, excluding me. She was his best friend, so she had the least to feel guilty about. Still, she was the first to eighty-six inside jokes she and Reagan would recall from what they had shared with Adrian out of the blue.

I think Reagan often blurted them out purposely in an attempt to include me. Explaining them was awkward; the reality would be the looming pink elephant in the room... July and Adrian. Reagan dealt with my absence on those occasions by making it up to me after. You had to love friends like that. From what I could tell, they never infringed on either of our privacies. I think they were aware of how difficult it must have been for me that they got to see him outside of school when I didn't get to see him at all.

As much as I appreciated that, I often wondered if it wasn't because they knew something I didn't. Maybe Adrian had declared to them that he had no interest in me. Maybe he had simply said enough for them to understand he didn't.

The bell rang, and we both realized we were late for our next testing cycle. Lynn slapped me on the rear, pushing me toward history. "Luck! I'm out after Chemistry. Talk to me later!" I turned over my shoulder and gave a half smile as she sashayed away.

"Maybe." I gave her an entire smile and turned back down the hall.

"Oh, hey! Adrian said Keagan wants you to stop by and see her after classes today. She's got a final tutorial session, and bring the quiz with his notes, he said!"

I halted, listening to her shout after me, but I did not look back or respond. Now my mind was racing back and forth between the humiliation of leaving my big shiny "F" for Adrian to see and know that of me, and how it had gone from him to Mrs. Keagan to Lynn???

Since when have I taken his orders via our mutual friends and faculty? *What the entire "F"?!* Did the whole student body know of my Trig quiz? Were they all rooting for me or waiting for me to fail in the background.

This was ridiculous! He had no right to talk to Mrs. Keagan about me! I was angry. I already felt sub-par in our friendship for all the obvious reasons, and I certainly felt beneath anyone Adrian desired to date publicly, or at all for that matter.

What was this? *Sorry we dry-humped for no reason, but then I found out you were stupider than I thought, so I'm trying to help???* Is that what his note on the back would say? *The note.*

I retrieved the infamous quiz from my backpack as I raced into history and slid into my seat, nodding as politely as possible to Coach Bartlett. He frowned at me but continued his pre-exam speech.

I quickly flipped the front "F" page to reveal the last stapled page. I needed to go through the motions to maintain some dignity of keeping my math failures from prying eyes... although at that point, who hadn't seen my "F" of a fucking quiz?!

My heart sank into the pit of my stomach when I saw that the last page had been folded in half and stapled into itself. Across the clean white folded part of the page was familiar handwriting with *July* gingerly written across it. I closed my eyes and saw Adrian's face, his eyes burning into mine from the evening before, and I froze.

It took me a long moment to peel the folded page away from the attached staple. I saw all of Adrian's math written in a blue pen beside my original work. He showed each step of how he arrived at the correct answer and the order in which one would HAVE to work the equation to get the correct result.

I read it to understand and then stared at the meticulously written numbers. Even using ink, he hadn't missed a beat. His handwriting was perfect. That somehow made me angrier. My eyes raced to the very bottom of the page where he had written an explanation of the exception to the rule and when OR when it did not apply to the history of those two numbers used together in the equation. It was finite, textbook as if he'd copied it from Keagan's mouth and regurgitated it onto my quiz as impersonally as possible.

I flipped the entire quiz over to the back, where there was nothing but blank space. *No note.* No "Hi, "bye" or "kiss my ass." Nothing.

I warned myself to relax and prep for the current exam being passed out. Come on, what did I expect? A profession of love, an apology, a dirty joke... something as filthy as what we did? We were on school property; the quiz was Mrs. Keagan's property. What would he do, write something to incriminate me more than the big red "F" seen by all he passed the test through?

Couldn't an "F" just mean an "F," and this was just an exchange for me trying to help him? And, maybe, he felt like he owed me for dropping by his assignments. Couldn't that be all it was? Why did I need an actual note from him? Why did I need an explanation of us or him, or why we did that? I had never gotten one before.

Forty-five minutes later, the last one in the room was the first one out. I grabbed my Scantron and test booklet and headed to the back of the classroom, where Coach Bartlett leaned against a stool, bored to tears.

"Really? Edwards, are you sure? I hope you didn't skip on the essay section."

I tilted my head and gave him a look. History was my favorite subject, which showed even on my worst day.

"Who am I kidding? I HOPE this means you did me a favor and didn't write a novel over the Dust Bowl."

I raised an eyebrow and confidently handed him his test booklet back.

"Get out-a-here!" He slapped my arm with the test booklet. "And, have a great summer, kid!!"

"You too, Coach!" I whispered over my shoulder as I bolted out of the room. The hallways were mainly empty. A few dispersed students who had completed exams or were coming early for their next one wandered between the lockers and classrooms. *No note?*

I couldn't help replaying the messed-up situation in my head. Stupid. How could I expect one? I went from humiliation to letting myself believe there would be an apology. Or a *'meet me somewhere, I have to see you.'* I felt ignorant for thinking there would be anything from him other than what it had always been. No phone call. No note. He returned the test to Lynn, not to me.

What did he want from me? I paused by my locker. From a distance, out of the corner of my eye, I saw Natalie Hilliard heading down the hallway with a few of the varsity cheerleaders. The image of the uniquely polite sophomore locking arms and giggling toward the gym with the juniors and seniors who had been my former best friends since the 8th grade was more nostalgic than I had bargained for at that moment.

That was it. That was what Adrian wanted from me. Nothing. He did nothing to pursue me. He asked nothing of me. I could continue through graduation and leave the godforsaken Palomino water tower behind. He would want nothing from me nor know where I went.

My great-aunt used to say that if someone is not asking anything of you, it is fair to assume they want nothing from you. There it was. The answer I longed for all this time had always been this clear. I slammed my locker door as the cheerleaders exited, Natalie's strawberry blonde hair blowing when the breeze hit it. When he wanted to date her, he did. And those few and far-between moments with me could only mean one thing. *Was I his dirty little secret?*

I walked mechanically toward the math lab in a daze, almost forgetting why I was going and who sent me there. I felt cold inside and stunned. The butterflies that haunted my core for the past twenty-four hours had fled. *Adrian truly did not want me.* I must have been convenient, around at a moment of weakness, or potentially his dirty little secret, as I had just deduced. Much worse than that... I was an unintended one. I wasn't even worth pursuing consistently as an indiscretion.

I just happened to strike his fancy once or twice, and he acted on it when he could. *Wow.* I couldn't even suggest he was using me. Again, he didn't want or attempt to do that on a regular basis. To make matters much worse, anyone in their right mind would think that of the situation. It was the appropriate assumption, and I must have known it. Otherwise, I would have told my two best friends about it.

I often wondered why I never told them. Was it because they wouldn't understand this freakish tryst we had the same way I didn't? Or because I knew they would think me pathetic or being used by him? Maybe I feared they'd push him to make good on it, then I'd never know if it was by his own accord that he chose me or something he felt obligated to oblige for a while.

As I approached Mrs. Keagan's open door, the sight of the familiar hallway and the smells of the dreaded classroom, yet beloved teacher, wafted toward me. I felt warmer, although a room that could give me an "F" should make me feel entirely on edge. Instead, I was struck with a feeling of comfort. I couldn't allow myself to leave yesterday's encounter at the dirty little secret assessment. *That wasn't the truth.* Even I had to admit, as I walked into *his* academic domain, it was more than that. I knew that much. At this point, I just had to be okay with not knowing what.

"GOOD"

Better Than Ezra

I was worn out after the exam. When I finally woke up, it was just after dinner, and it was dark outside. I had to jump through literal hoops on my good leg to get them to let me take the final in person.

I would be off the crutches and out of this room in less than a month. I was sick of crashing midday and waking up in the evening just in time for everyone else to go out and have a life. I shifted to find the remote. As finals ended, with nothing else to study, I was looking for any distraction to occupy my mind.

The truth was, only one thing had occupied it for the last twenty-four hours, and she was the only thing I was interested in outside these four walls. *Where was she?*

Surely, Lynn gave her my notes, and Keagan told her about them. I set her up to get an "A." She set herself up if she just took the note and did what I said. I couldn't believe I hadn't heard from her.

Did Lynn give her the quiz? Did she go to tutorials? Or was she back at that damn pool already?! *What was the matter with me?*

This had to be the four walls talking. The solitude of my bedroom had finally gotten to me, and it would only get worse with summer. The girls were all starting work.

No more study nights.

My track buddies would be starting their famous train-by-day, party-by-night combo.

Meanwhile, I was facing some post-injury psychosis after losing everything I'd worked for on the track and fixating on the only girl who does it for me. A girl I forced myself to believe I didn't want...

Psychosis. I clearly had not gotten out in a while.

I wasn't upset. Not like I was the day the knee happened. I wasn't bored, I just...

Truthfully, anytime I felt trapped, I knew it was for good reason, or let's just say I had enough ambition to push through it. I never got stuck. That's the one thing I got from my grandfather besides the car: the ability to reassess and move forward.

I had no choice with the knee, but I did have an option with how I felt. Or so I thought at the time. These four walls weren't going to have me trapped forever. I could be back to normal in no time.

Still, the solitude of my bedroom and July being the only outside disturbance that played on a loop in my mind, even my dreams haunted me. It must have been subliminal, but I kept dreaming about when I saw the deer I nearly hit.

It was when I first got my car; shortly before, I should have been officially driving it by myself regarding a permit vs. my license. But this was East Texas. We had more back roads than highway patrol.

Overzealous and with adolescent excitement, I had been taking my car out at night and pushing it to its limit down two-lane highways. In hindsight, one of the most dangerous activities a teenager can participate in minus alcohol or sex, or the combination of all three.

I look back now and wonder if I wasn't testing my limits. I had never been reckless like Billy, Angel, or Reagan. My behavior with July is the most reckless I could cop to other than pressing the gas to its limit those nights on the highway alone.

It was stupid and asinine in terms of the car itself. If anything had gone wrong... if it had gone differently that night...

I had pushed the gas through this area famous for winding curves and prided myself on how fast I could take them in the pitch-black night without streetlights.

Thank God I was going up a hill and naturally slowing instead of having to hit the brakes on the way down. To this day, I still don't know how I knew to stop or what made me. I know I hadn't seen it coming until it walked up to my windshield and stared me down.

It was a deer. I think a doe, actually.

It's common to hit one in East Texas, and it's idiotic I hadn't accounted for that. It ruins your car. A deer runs out of nowhere in front of your vehicle; you hit it, kill it, and that kills your car. It's not good business on either end. Usually, it happens so fast that both parties are left not knowing what hit them until they see the aftermath of the vehicle, or the wild animal laid out across the street, or, much worse, physically stuck in the dash.

Again, I don't know what made me stop or how I could stop that fast without destroying my new brakes or skidding into it, but I did stop. I heard my car at full speed, then my brakes, then silence, and suddenly, my headlights illuminated the creature. It was startling and magnificent how its eyes shone at me, and its coat glowed.

The large doe was not afraid or in a hurry to flee. It just walked across the highway and stopped when it got in my high beams... and looked. It looked up at the lights as if looking right through me. Funny, if you think about it... for the time it stayed there looking, we were both trapped.

It was spectacular and scary. I could have hit it. I never forgot how it looked at me so curiously and subjective to its own thoughts. They are typically petrified, spastic, or appear caught. The whole "deer in the headlights expression." I guess I was the one that felt caught in the situation. Caught, and lucky we all were spared... me, the unusual doe, and my car.

People often hit deer. That had been my only encounter, and I was dreaming about it. I guess I felt trapped in that bedroom, only... was I the car or the deer?

When I did get out to take my exam, I was finally among the living the entire morning, and it changed nothing. I still looked for July down every hallway. My goal in calculus above my own final had been to speak to Keagan about July. *My God, I guess I was trapped.*

The following week, the results of our finals were available in the office. Reagan had offered to pick up everyone's and bring them to Lynn and me if she had time before work. She was never on time, so I admit I anticipated that July would knock on my door that day.

I was disappointed when Reagan and Lynn appeared.

As they compared our scores, it ran through my mind how she hadn't called. And, again, obviously knows where I live. I'm the one cooped up who can't go anywhere.

Maybe that's what this was... she was toying with me. Maybe she was just getting me back for the auditorium. Maybe this behavior was second nature to her, and she wasn't as innocent as I thought... *STOP it!*

I couldn't do that to her. I couldn't even entertain or think that of her. *Never.* Selfish as I was with her, I could never be so self-centered that I would let myself believe something false of her just to pacify my own bruised ego.

It was already selfish enough to know what we did together was, in fact, just for me...

How did I know?

It was electric. We learned from each other the same way it had been that day in the rain by her house and again in the auditorium. She responded to how I wanted her, and we were both so receptive. No matter how skilled at each other we became in our mere minutes together, I saw it in her eyes and felt it when our bodies attached so naturally. This was new to her. The physical act was organic and an absolute first, as the intensity and aching for her was for me.

It didn't feel dirty, as if an agenda was behind it. The act felt right as rain. It was insanely personal. Between us... and it was real. That's why it scared the living hell out of me.

Once I found out, she aced her test... I never doubted her; I was left with only one concern. Did I scare her away? What we did... Was she upset or afraid of me? Is that why she hadn't come around again? Did she like it? Was it the last straw, and she finally had to expose us as a dirty secret to Reagan and Lynn? *No. Not the last one.*

I looked up at Reagan and Lynn cackling over some end-of-year happenstance, and there was nothing on their faces to indicate she had shared our secret. I may not have known what July thought, but I knew she would never betray our personal moments. Deep down, it wasn't as much about the secret we kept as it was about what it meant to both of us to keep it. Trust. We may not have been able to communicate that to each other, much less our friends, but we had upheld each other's trust.

I don't know... I think that meant a lot to me somehow. Maybe more than it should have. It made us even more personal. My chest tightened just thinking about it, and I fought the twinge I felt below the belt. I focused and jumped back into Reagan and Lynn's end-of-year gossip.

LIFEGUARD

"FOOLISH GAMES"

Jewel

I aced my test! I wasn't sure how or who to celebrate with. Did I owe him a thank you? Would he be happy to know I made an "A?" Would Lynn or Reagan tell him? I was so confused. I shouldn't be.

This was his M.O.

However, even though he hadn't called, and we had both fallen back into the dangerous trap of not including Lynn and Reagan in our extracurricular activities, I couldn't help wondering if my test wasn't his grand gesture.

Granted, it wouldn't have been enough. After what that boy put me through, he'd have to beat me over the head with his caveman club and drag me by my hair to his campfire in front of everyone for me to fully understand our status quo had changed.

Still, it had me questioning quite a few moments from our past. The additional things we never discussed were probably more paramount to unravel than the physical moments. Coach Bartlett, when I forced him into that football meeting or when Adrian gave me his jacket, should I have kept it?

The Devin and Natalie of it all, me not saying his name freshman year... and much worse, not visiting after his surgery. Had this been my misinterpretation of things?

No, I had enough confidence to know he'd find a way to let me know if he wanted me. When someone is genuinely into you... You aren't left to wonder.

I got dressed and grabbed my tote bag for the pool. I was excited to see everyone. All but one. Spencer, of course. And in terms of holding on to Adrian for the summer or letting him go... My mother always used to say that anybody who would risk losing you didn't want to keep you that bad in the first place.

My mother was full of antidotes and sayings to live by. Things like, "Don't let your left hand know what your right hand is doing," or "Don't tell everything you know, it's unattractive," "It's easier to get a job when you have one," and perhaps the truest of all time... "Men notice you most when you are attracted to someone else or have gotten another's attention—it's as if they smell it on you."

I turned into the city pool parking lot. I had my grandad's truck again and was looking for the best parking spot when a spectacularly red GMC truck slid beside me with its passenger window down. It was the tall, green-eyed guy with sandy brown, almost dirty blonde hair. I think his name was Court. "Nice truck."

"Thanks. I like it."

"It's ah' August, right?"

"Yeah, just call me that." I knew he knew my name. He had a friendly but naughty smile.

"I guess I'll see you in there then." He gestured his arm out, signaling the parking lot was my oyster, and he was allowing me to go. "Ladies first." I wasn't sure what came over me, but his banter quickly brought it out.

"I wouldn't have it any other way." I winked and drove past him into the front spot.

***

Spencer paced the front of the guard room by Cleta's desk like he owned the place. Everyone was there, including Lane, who I pulled my chair up next to. The small guard room was well past crowded.

"Although Cleta appreciates your gusto in eagerly signing up to guard the first wave of pool parties listed, she wanted me to remind you rookies that the senior guards have first dibs, even if you put your name down first. I also have to remind you all that we have jurisdiction to move things around a bit depending on how large the party is, and so on. Some parties will simply require a head or two senior guards, and of course, rule of thumb, no two rookies scheduled to guard a party alone. You guys will always be paired with a head or senior guard."

Spencer picked up the clipboard and began going through the sign-up sheet. *Yikes.* I had been so occupied with the trig final and overanalyzing Adrian that I had forgotten to sign up for any. *Great.* The rookies would have all the best slots; worse, I'd be paired with them.

The pool parties were private events after hours when the pool was closed. People rented us out for everything from birthdays and church functions to their own version of a nightclub with diving boards.

They were intimate events for us because it was just the two guards working it, not nine more guards like during regular hours, and no cashier or concession workers. It was just you and one other guard. If something went wrong, you called the cops or the ambulance or Cleta to come. The parties were a lot of fun to work on if paired with a guard you could stand being around; if not, they were boring or torture.

"I have to apologize right away for these first three or four changes. These are massive parties, and each have a special request or something that has to be delt with, so no rookies on the first three Friday night parties and that one Saturday highlighted. Those of you that signed up already, go ahead and mark that off your calendar, and I need some veteran guards. Show of hands if you're available or interested..."

Almost every qualified hand popped up as the rookies sulked.

"July. I don't see you down for many just yet. I know Pure Pines got out a little later than Prairie with finals, so you may not have been around to sign up. Let's get you on some of these."

What? Why was he being so nice to me?

When the clipboard came my way for me to sign by the ones I was scheduled, he had me down for three of the four. "Cleta wants a head guard on the majority of those as well. I've got a few, and Stacey is on the others, but I still need those we just redid." Spencer moved on as if he hadn't just given me all the parties in front of the others who raised their hands.

"I'll take them." Court's deep voice was laid back but enthusiastic as he looked at me, reaching for the clipboard. I leaned his way to hand it over and watched him smile as he initialed each party I was on. *Okay.* That was bold. Wow. Every party I was signed onto for the upcoming month was with Court, Spencer, or Stacey. Mostly Court.

Way to be one of them! What was going on here? I wasn't sure what I had done to deserve this, but it was awesome. Maybe Cleta or Stacey vouched for me and told Spencer I was a good worker. *Weird. Or, maybe he's being nice because he knows I saw him that night at the party. Maybe he remembers, and he's trying to get on my good side, so I don't bring it up at work. Wow.* That got dark fast. Either way you play it... it was going to be an interesting summer.

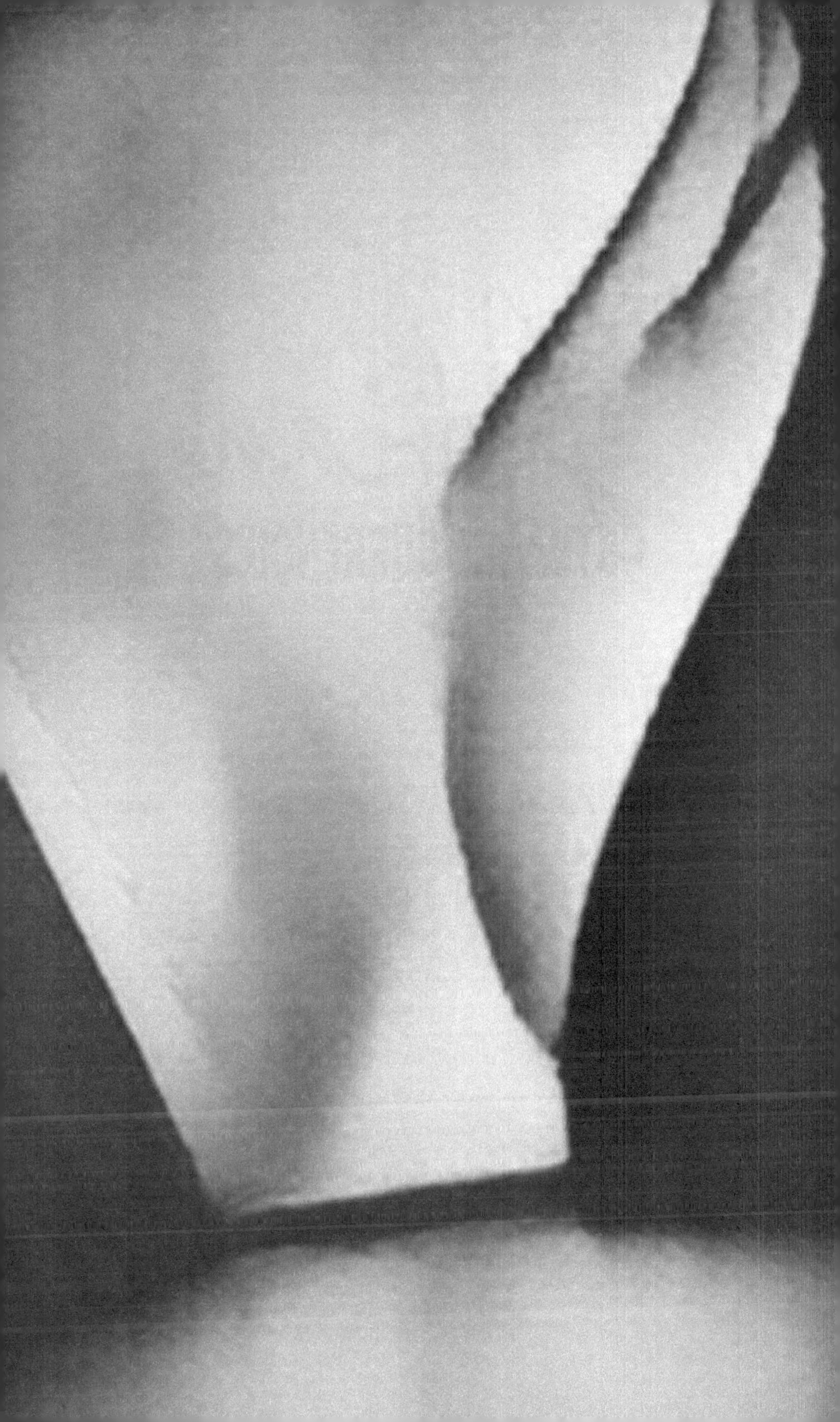

Would I stop by and check on her? What was I, her mother? It really was unfair of Reagan to ask of me. She knew I would. She knew I couldn't help myself.

Whether or not I had openly admitted that July's absence from our group and what she was up to all those hours at the pool drove me mad. It was hard to say who knew me better, Reagan or Lynn. They just dealt with what they knew differently. Lately, whether that had more to do with their allegiance to July or me was getting hazier.

This was the longest time I had spent away from her in the last two years. And I'd never thought of her more. Even when I tried to ignore it, July came up in everyday conversation. It was like I couldn't get next to her, but I couldn't get away from her, either. I'd been sure it would pass once I was back on my feet and out of the house, but it hadn't.

"Come on, Lane might be working today, and I know Spencer's there. It's not like you won't know anybody. Just ask for her up front at the concession."

"Thank you, Reagan. I do know how to enter a public place and communicate with other human beings. I haven't been couped up that long."

"A. Yes, you have, and B… I thought you might be a little nervous to go see about her. You know?"

"No, I don't know. Why would I be nervous? It's a favor you're asking me to do, a favor you or Lynn can't do for one of our mutual friends; what would that--- why would that involve me being nervous?" I could hear Reagan rolling her eyes as I hung up the phone.

Apparently, July jumped into the shallow end during their morning swim lessons to catch a runaway kid and misgauged the depth, smacking the top of her foot as it bent and caught her fall. I guess she couldn't go home between shifts or get her foot checked out. Knowing July, she didn't mis-gauge anything. She would have broken her foot to catch or save a kid.

Her mom was out of town, of course, and her grandparents dropped her off this morning on their way to some outing with the church. Her mom called Reagan from her hotel and asked her to check on her and make sure she didn't need to have it x-rayed. I assumed she was worried that since July didn't have a car that day, she would be less likely to leave even if she truly needed to.

I took a little longer than usual to decide what shirt to wear. Come on, it was nearly a hundred degrees outside, what did it matter what I had on. Just getting there and getting it over with was all I could reinforce in my head.

What I really meant was to get to her. I was dying to see her.

Pulling up to the massive city pool, I killed the music blaring off my speakers and parked at the closest spot. There weren't that many spaces left. I didn't remember it being this busy from when I was a kid. Occasionally, we had come here when my parents wanted to take my younger brother and stepsiblings.

It was easier to go over here than the tiny pool at Pure Pines, where you knew everyone you passed by. Prairie's pool had a high dive if my childhood memory served me correctly.

When I stepped out of my prized possession, I was beyond grateful to be driving again; I noticed my car was not the only treasure in the lot. A brand-new Camaro sat a few spaces up, obnoxiously taking up two spots. I didn't have to guess who it belonged to because the plates read PEARCE on the back as I passed.

Douche.

I looked around but didn't see Lane's car anywhere. Guess he wasn't scheduled that day. Selfishly, that felt good. I wasn't sure if I could justify my "checking on" July to my debate partner.

I trotted up the steps toward the entrance, and a strange feeling came over me. It was kind of mischievous. I was excited to see July's face when she noticed me instead of Reagan. I was curious about what she would say or how she would behave. The shoe was on the other foot, and I was about to ruffle her feathers in her domain... or so I thought.

Small and large wet feet pitter-pattered around me in line for the cashier at the entrance. The one line must have serviced both entry and concession. A small boy was running the girl up front crazy over how to make his suicide drink. He wanted two pumps of Dr. Pepper first, then Sprite, then the rest of the way up with Big Red, and to top it off with a small splash of Root Beer. Gross, but I couldn't help but grin and miss the days when something like that was the most important thing in the world, as opposed to what I would be asking of the front cashier.

"Ahh, so sorry about that!" The cashier, a girl who had to be my age or a year or two older, apologized to me as she wiped the soda that dripped from the young patron's cup off the countertop. "Just one?"

"No. I'm ah, a friend of July's. I just stopped by real quick to check on her foot... see if she needed anything. "

"Yeah, she got it pretty good this morning. It swelled up quite a bit, but we got ice on her before the pool opened, and I think the swelling went down enough. They just had to bandage the top part where the concrete scraped her." The girl looked me over, tilted her head, and smiled curiously while smacking her gum. "How nice of you to come to check on her. Are you—? She was only curious because she hadn't seen me before.

"A friend."

"Oh, of course!" She smiled flirtatiously. "No, I just meant are you from here or you go to –"

"Yeah, I go to Pure Pines with Lane and July."

Wow. That just said A LOT. A friend? Lane and July... As if I couldn't suggest I was solely there for her. What was the matter with me? Ever the politician. This is *exactly* why she fucking hated me, or maybe it was why I despised myself.

"Cool. What's your name?" She pushed up from her swizzle chair at the front counter and started walking out of the concession room.

"Adrian Reed."

"Nice to meet you, Adrian. Wait here, I'll take you back." She looked over her shoulder at two tweens behind me with beach bags full of magazines and their parents' bath towels. "I'll be right back with you ladies!" Her accent was thick but friendly.

"I go to Prairie High. I didn't think I'd seen you before. Let's see if she's on break or still out on rotation."

She led me past the restrooms and down a light blue concrete hallway to a big red office door. The door had a white square, a red cross painted inside, and vinyl stick-on letters that said Guards only. I stood to the side as she knocked. It was loud in there. A fan was blowing, and it sounded like there had to be about thirty people in that tiny room laughing and cutting up.

She knocked again louder. "Sorry, they're a bunch of children." She cracked the door open. "Guys! Hey... is July in here?" She opened the door all the way to look around. I was standing where I couldn't see anything in there, but I could hear everything.

"She's on rotation." I heard a girl's voice volunteer. "She's about to come off if Court will get his lazy ass out there and relieve her."

"Who wants to know?" A male's voice stood out above the chatter, and the room seemed quiet as if all were awaiting the answer.

"You guys are so immature. She has a visitor, assholes. Try not to eat him." The cashier shrugged and walked past me. "Good luck, and nice meeting you!"

I saw a male's head poke out of the doorway. He immediately walked out upon recognizing me.

"Reed! What's up, dog!?? Why didn't they tell me that was you?" Spencer Pearce smiled through his UT cap as he low-fived me. "Long time, Bro."

"Yeah, how's UT? Blowing up out there I heard."

"You know, it's the same shit, only this fish in a big sea, but ah, I hold my own."

"Yeah, I heard you were back this summer."

"Hey, tough break on the knee, man. My dad told me about it when it happened. Dude, I'm so glad nothing like that ever happened to me. Sorry about the track team. They'll never get to state without you, and then you've got to start all over now."

No shit. To be clear, Spencer wasn't known for his compassion. The fact that he was talking to me as one of his bros was classic Pure Pines. Sure, I was impressive in track, even as an underclassman to Spencer, who I beat as a varsity freshman. I earned this conversation through merit, but the honest truth was, the Pure Pine's elite were notorious for turning an acquaintance they may or may not say hello to while passing down the hall on a good day into their long-lost best friend when found outside of Pure Pines.

It made them appear more popular to their new constituents. It was the summer camp syndrome. You know, someone you wouldn't give the time of day to in your class, but then you go away to a big bad summer camp and don't know anybody, so you immediately form an alliance with that one person you know.

It's something like a survival of the fittest, law of attraction, or birds of a feather kind of thing. That was what he was doing to me at that moment. The question was, who was he trying to impress?

"How's PT going? Will they have you starting back up this fall?"

"That's the plan." Spencer patted me on the back to lead me down the hall, and I assumed out to July. A large shadow hit the wall as the guard room door popped open, and a very tall guy suddenly loomed over us. *Who was this guy?* He was half a foot taller than Spencer and me and, for some reason, as curious about me as I him. He looked me up and down, and then at Spencer as he towered over us in the hallway.

"Court, you're late. Get your ass out there, man, before you have those ladies dripping in sweat." Spencer patted him on the back and pushed him past me. I could tell they had some sort of inside joke going.

"And, ah, tell July to come on in, she's got company. This is Adrian, Pure Pine's track. A finer sprinter than me, that's for sure." I loved how that was now somehow a dig.

"What's up." I nodded at the six-foot-plus giant looking down at me.

"Prairie basketball. He's here on scholarship from Knoxville, one of their finest."

"Court." The stranger muttered a low, unenthused voice as he nodded back and gave me another once over. Then he headed out the hallway and up the steps I assumed Spencer was leading me toward.

It was bright out there, and the sounds of summer and the smells of sunscreen I had not yet experienced drifted into the musky concrete pool house we stood in. Something started to excite me above the complete mockery and bullshit I was putting myself through. It was what I came for, and it felt worth it in that flicker of a second. *She* was about to stride down the steps.

Only Spencer stopped me on the first few steps.

"Hey, what's Lynn up to these days?" I keep trying to get July to have her come by one Friday night. We're having a guard party at my parents' place on Lake Cherokee. Maybe you can put in a good word and come through, too. Every time I mention it to July, she acts like I have leprosy or I'm some kind of a criminal."

He laughed and punched my arm as if we had an inside joke. "I don't know, man. I wonder why..." He looked me over intently, searching for an answer.

It was as if he knew there was one, but he didn't know if I'd been told. I couldn't be entirely sure what he was fishing for. He was bouncing back and forth so fast between two people I care about most in the world, so forgive me if I was a little short on decoding his very forthcoming yet cryptic inquiry.

"What's with July anyway? She's hot now. Is she still a prude?"

If he only knew.

"It's a shame though. You'd think she'd grow out of it once she grew into a body like that!"

What was he even talking about? I thought he was asking me about Lynn.

"Don't get me wrong, between you and me, bro, even back in the day, I thought she was one of the hottest JV cheerleaders on the squad. The only one who never let me touch her... I guess that made her hotter. Well, that and the face. Of course, you may be here today because you know that already. From my experience, a little baby fat on a gem like that almost always turns into premium curves. And I certainly wasn't wrong about that one. Damn. I almost didn't recognize her when I saw her here on the first day."

That first day. That was my day with her. The day she came to my room. I swallowed the daggers ready to shoot out of my mouth, and tried to release my clenched fist as I looked him dead in the eye without blinking, his new Camaro being driven off a cliff in my mind.

"Hey, you may need to give me some pointers if you cracked that code. At any rate, I'd love to have you all over at the lake house this Friday. Lynn is, ah, well, as you know, a very special, intelligent young woman whose company I've not had the pleasure of enjoying in its entirety. Let's just say she is of interest to me this summer, and it would be nice if July was a little more cooperative in aiding that to happen. We do all go way back."

He tapped me on the shoulder to encourage me up the stairs onto the pool deck. "Think about it. Be great to see you all there."

It was loud and massive out there. I squinted when the bright sun hit my face, half blind from being in that dark den of inequity, literally under the dragon's wing, I might add. I didn't know if I had been invited, insulted, threatened, or all the above.

Do people even talk that way? *What the fuck did he just say to me?!*

All I knew for certain was the entire Pure Pines High School would have jumped through their skin for the invite I had just received and by Spencer, their god himself. I'll bet not one of them knew at what cost.

I scanned the crowded pool area. There were four guard stands. Two were across from each other in the shallow area, and two were seated stands by the diving boards in the deep. Spencer was still standing next to me as if he was showing off his kingdom to me.

This was insane. Where was July? If I had any balls, I'd pick her up and carry her out of this messed-up summer hell. This was worse than the football locker room at Pure Pines. Although I must admit, I felt massive relief that July clearly had no use for Spencer. He couldn't snow her. *But how had he snowed Lynn? Was she interested in him?*

I tried remembering the few times my best friend mentioned Spencer but with little luck. As a dude, I'm afraid I missed some of those subtle signs. She had mentioned him quite a bit, though, as if she had spent time with him, I was unaware of.

God, this was such a reckless Reagan thing, not Lynn. *How could Lynn want anything to do with that jerk?* I would have to ask Reagan about this. I'm not sure what troubled me more about the situation. The fact that July gave him the cold shoulder, led me to believe he was worse than I knew. Otherwise, she would never stand in the way of Lynn's crush. There was also the moment he practically threatened me with her. I may be reading into it, but he threw enough out there about July to make the hair on my neck stand up. I didn't want him near her or Lynn.

In my search for July, I saw that the guard across from us was a tiny young blonde. She smiled flirtatiously from across the shallow end at Spencer. An older female guard who appeared to care less nudged her from the guard stand, and they moved to switch places.

I continued to squint past the diving boards until I landed diagonally in front of me on the very tall college basketball dude I was just introduced to. He was talking to a brunette seated on the guard stand. The rapid thud in my chest warned me it was her, even though all I could see past his shoulders blocking my view was the back of her hair.

What was this guy doing still standing there? Why hadn't he released her off of her stand yet? Did he tell her I was here?

A guard whistle blew, and everyone got quiet, looking for the emergency. I saw the two girl guards on the other side of the pool shaking their heads and laughing. I looked back toward the tall guy and saw him wrestling with July. They were laughing, and he was... *Wait*. I couldn't see very well from where I was standing, but it looked like he grabbed her guard shirt hanging on the stand and put it on.

All the kids were cracking up, watching the tall guard pace back and forth with her red innertube, wearing her shirt that looked like a tight tummy top on him. He posed like a girl and strutted while the crowd roared. I saw July's head tilt back in laughter. *What the heck was happening here?*

Two more whistles blew from across the pool, and one of the guards pointed to her own shorts. The tall guy, Court, grabbed July by the waist and began wrestling her shorts off. She was still sitting on the high lifeguard stand, facing the opposite direction of me, so I could barely see what was happening. Court was so tall he covered her. He could reach her in the high stand from standing with his bare feet on the concrete. He slid July's shorts off with her kicking, screaming, and laughing. Then he attempted to put them on for the rest of his little show. When he couldn't pull them up, he twirled them on his finger as if contemplating his next stunt.

"We've got a lively bunch, here. It beats the heat." Spencer, the sociopath, whispered in my ear while laughing with them all.

Okay, so this wasn't as bad as I thought. This Court guy must be the class clown per se, and they were just giving her a hard time because she's got a visitor. Just then, Court shot her shorts across the deep end.

Twenty little kids came running and dove in to get them as they floated in the middle of the pool. He put a foot on the front of the guard stand and reached up to grab her by the waist. *Wait a minute. Get your hands off her. The clown was no longer funny to me.*

The girl's voice from the front rang behind me as she came up the steps, yelling for Spencer.

"Spencer! Cleta's on line one for you! She needs the noon head-count and wants to know what guards are scheduled for tonight's Wagner party." As she moved to hand him the cordless phone, she looked around at all the chaos, just in time to see July push Court into the pool from the guard stand with her foot.

He sank backward into the pool, wearing her guard shirt as all the pool patrons cheered. "Spence! You know you aren't supposed to have those two beside each other on rotation. Cleta begged me to hold you to that!"

Those two? A sick feeling was unleashed in the pit of my stomach, and I heard her laughter. *Look at her. Look at them looking at her.* I wasn't even standing where I could see her all the way, yet I had never seen her smile that big.

"Relax. It's going to hit a hundred today, they're just having a little fun. Plus I think this puts Court up one." Spencer announced proudly as he moved to give Court a hand out of the deep end.

"I wouldn't bet on it." The cashier girl pointed to the guard room window. The small room she had knocked on moments before had a large window on the outside facing the pool. Two more whistle tweets blew from the window, and I saw July look over her shoulder toward them. Almost simultaneously, as Spencer reached a hand down to offer Court help out of the pool, July swung down the side of her guard stand that did not have the ladder and began running, limping on what looked like her hurt foot toward the diving boards.

I saw a flash of her red guard bikini from the top of the stairs. I'd never seen her run so fast. The whistleblower from the guard room window tossed her a rolled-up ball of material, and July caught it like a beach ball while running past.

"You wouldn't dare!"

Court's voice rang from the side of the pool where he had not successfully gotten out yet. Girls cheered from the guard room window. I stepped up to walk further out onto the pool deck and toward where July had just ran from to see where she was going.

Court pulled himself up from the side in one swoop and pushed Spencer out of his way. I didn't realize how close I had gotten to those two until Court dripped on me. I was too busy searching for July, along with the rest of the patrons, staring from the pool and all across the deck.

Two whistles blew from the high dive ladder. Less than thirty yards away from me and almost twenty feet above me, the object of my affection was standing in his button-down dress shirt, slowly walking the plank of the high dive and putting on her own show.

"JULY!"

Something stung me deeply when Court yelled her name loud and intently. He stepped forward, and Spencer flicked his hand up to stop him. "Uh-uh, my friend, turn about fair play."

Ugh. I didn't like that either, Spencer taking up for her.

"Besides, I want to see where this is going!" Spencer's eyes were dancing up at July on the high dive as if this were entertainment specifically laid out for him.

I, for one, had enough. July hadn't even noticed I was standing there. *Weren't these people supposed to be making sure little kids don't drown?!*

"That's my good shirt!" Court screamed from Spencer, holding him back. "Come on, July! You know I'm going out tonight. I just had that ironed!"

Excuse me, how did she know he was going out tonight. Who was this Court guy already?

"I'm sorry, I can't hear you from up here..." July mocked from the middle of the board. "It's a really great shirt though; so nice and pressed so neatly." She yelled from where she stood.

The light grey button-down had faint vertical stripes going down it from the collar to the hem, and the tail covered July's swim bottoms in the back and nearly went down to her knees in the front. *Man, that dude was tall.* The sleeves draped well past her wrists down to her fingertips as she walked to the end of the board, swallowed by the shirt. I noticed a large white square of a gauze bandage on the top of her foot, and she seemed to favor it, almost not bearing weight on it as she tip-toed closer to the end of the board.

I looked around me. EVERYONE'S eyes were on her. I don't even think the cashier girl gave Spencer the phone; if she did, he hadn't answered his boss yet. Everybody was watching *her.*

She was hot. I couldn't deny it. Everyone saw it. She looked naked underneath Court's shirt, even though I knew she wasn't. However, that imagery did not help my state of confusion. *Again, I had never seen her smile or flirt like that. That's what it was, she was flirting with him! What the hell!*

"Don't you dare jump! Don't do it!" Court shook his head pleadingly while he watched her as enamored as the rest of the pool was.

"Don't jump in this?" July shook her head, toying with him, and unbuttoned the top buttons as if she were going to take it off. "You don't want it to get wet or you don't want me to jump? Because I promise I'm not going to jump." July unbuttoned one more button dangerously close to what I could only imagine was her cleavage in that red guard suit. Court stepped forward and tilted his head at her, bypassing Spencer, me, and the cashier. He wasn't sure what she was going to do.

Before anyone could move or Court could beg or run to the board, I watched her dive pristinely off the end of the high dive, wearing his button-down. She said she wasn't going to jump. As her hands broke through the water and her body followed in an impressive straight line, my heart sank into my chest. *Was I too late?*

I would be damned if I could stand there through another show. Especially one of his retaliations that I could only imagine would be far worse than the shirt she semi-ruined.

Thank god another guard came out to start their rotation, and Spencer motioned for everybody to get back to work. Little kids began to line up for the diving board, and things felt like they were returning to normal. I stepped up toward the deep end, seeing her swimming underwater toward the side. She looked like a fish or a mermaid or something. She was really good at this.

Court stepped in front of my view and grabbed her arm as she came up to the side. At first, it scared me how fast he pulled her out of the water, but then I realized she was so small compared to him, and with his height, it was nothing to pull her up. It wasn't like he yanked her arm out of socket... no, he just swooped her up like fucking Hercules. I stepped back as he dripped all over me while he walked her past me. "Sorry, man."

Even at that, she hadn't noticed me yet. I watched Court pull her towards him a little too close and unbutton every one of those fucking buttons. *Oh, come on!* She held her arms out like a stubborn child, and he ripped the shirt off her. She stood firm and cut her eyes at him. Enjoying the win.

He pulled a sopping wet tee shirt out of his guard shorts' pocket and slapped her damp guard shirt in her hand. "By the way, you have a visitor." Court stepped aside to reveal me behind him.

Her dark brown eyes fell on mine as she stood there, dripping in front of me in the least amount of clothing I had ever seen her wear. Court walked off shouting, "That's one." He hoped the effect would be a match point as he left her in front of an unexpected visitor. After all, he had no idea who I was, so I suppose depending on how well we knew each other, this could have been a win or had the effect of embarrassment he hoped for, only... *Uh oh. Oh no. It wasn't that...*

Oh, brother.

That match point was for me. July wasn't standing there like a drowned rabbit, hunching over, embarrassed to be half naked and soaked in her scant two-piece guard suit. No shorts or shirt to cover her at all... Nope. She was standing in front of me like a boy's dream, dripping from head to toe in a shiny red swimsuit like a God Damn Bay Watch character!

If she was honest about it, which that Court fucker knew, the adrenaline pumping through her veins this very second that made her glorious chest rise and fall as it dripped in front of me was from wondering what *he* was going to do to her next to get her back!

It wasn't because she was surprised to see *me*.

"What are you doing here?" Hearing her voice surprised me after the incredibly long stare she used to catch her breath. *Case in point.*

"What are you doing here?!" I tried to make it come out like a joke and less father-like or jealous boyfriend, but I couldn't help myself. "I came here to check on you-- on your foot, and here you are running around like—"

"Like what?!" Her face changed, and her voice changed because I was so upset. *Dang it!* That is not how I intended this to go. However, it was how he did. I could almost feel that Court guy watching us from the guard window. July rang her shirt out, then peeled the wet material over her head to cover herself a little.

"Oh, a lot that helps." *Whoops.* Said that one out loud.

"What?!"

"Nothing." I rolled my eyes. Her white tank top of a wet guard shirt was shellacked to her body, accentuating every curve of her chest. I kept thinking about what Lane said. JESUS! I had to get out of there. At that moment, a tiny shadow appeared on the deck between us. July and I looked down at the kid looking up at her, grinning from ear to ear.

"Miss July! I got your shorts for you!" He reached up to proudly hand her the dripping red shorts. He'd been the lucky one to retrieve them. July knelt in front of him. There it was again, that beaming smile that made her eyes dance. Thank god it wasn't just that Court guy who did that to her. She had come into her own. She was happy, and kind, and fun.

Why didn't I get to see this side of her?! Maybe I had never given her a chance to be happy with me.

I watched the little tyke smile up at us both as he walked away like he'd just gotten a golden ticket. Then, something happened to me. Survival of the fittest took over. "Do you have a break now?"

She nodded.

I grabbed her hand as if I was meant to hold it and led her past the pool deck, the guard room window of prying eyes, and down the steps I had been led up. She didn't say a word, and she didn't pull her hand away either.

I think she was stunned. As we walked through everything toward the car, my thumb grazed the part of her hand I held, and gently, very affectionately, I knew I felt hers graze mine back. It felt warm and right and so strange that the simple act of holding hands was a sensation I had so little experience of with her. It hit me deep in my gut just how much I had missed out on with her.

Something even stranger happened when we exited the pool's front entrance: When we stepped outside, her hand dropped from mine. I looked back at her strangely, and she stopped where she was standing. I glanced down at her bare feet, realizing I'd dragged her out here with her bandaged foot, but somehow, I knew that wasn't it.

She looked radiant, standing in the sun, looking up at me. The strands of her wet hair that had already begun to dry showcased a slight red hue that I wasn't used to with her natural darker brown hair. Her eyes shined lighter when the sunlight hit them next to her all-over tan. Looking at her reminded me of the sketch that guy drew that had her eyes and hair too light. The drawing still existed folded in my glove compartment as a private possession of mine. I think I kept it because it was too much of a likeness to throw away, and I fully intended to give it to her one day, but I never found the opportunity.

"Will you come to my car?" I asked her as gently as I could. It was an honest request. I should demand nothing of her. She paused in thought for a moment, then followed me. Even after the dip in the water, she had the slight smell of *her* mixed with sunscreen or something papaya-like and amber-scented. She smelt like a Sunday at the beach, and I wanted to savor her.

She looked down at her dripping-wet attire when we got to my car. I could tell she was about to try to spare my vintage interior. I didn't want to be spared in any way. I just wanted *her*.

"Just get in. Get in. I don't care." She rolled her eyes at me and walked up to the fence that separated the pool from the parking lot, still catering to that left foot. She blew a whistle at one of the blonde rookie guards and told them to bring her a towel off one of the guards' stands.

I liked watching her demand things. I'm not even sure it was her towel she made them bring her. I couldn't help but smile inside as I knew how fun that was for her. I walked around to her side and opened the passenger door for her. She put the towel down cautiously on my seat and got in. It was all I could do not to find some way to touch her at that moment.

Looking down at her sliding into my car, I wanted more. It might be odd of me to say, but I missed it. I longed for something I had pushed away for so long, and there it was. And it couldn't have felt better. What had I done to her? This feeling, this serene feeling, I knew I didn't deserve it, and I hoped it was finally here to stay... not the calm before the storm.

"HEAD OVER FEET"

Alanis Morissette

H is car door shut us in together, and he started the ignition to turn the air on. We sat for a long moment in what felt like chasing the calm. We just... hung out for a few minutes, listening to each other breathe.

He looked over at me and stared for an extended beat. "How's your foot?"

I smiled and looked down at it. "It's probably fine."

"Let me see it."

Something was demanding in his voice. A desire to comply came over me.

And then, as if we had always been this way, as if I had sat in his car a million times, I turned toward him in my seat and gently placed my leg across his lap. A corner of his mouth drifted up uncontrollably as he surveyed what had been put in his care. He leaned in and began to lift one side of the bandage carefully. "I assume you have plenty more of these in there." I smiled and nodded for him to continue. He peeled the gauze patch off and grimaced. "It's a pretty big gash."

"Not as big as the one on your knee." It came out of me softly and childlike.

"No." He smiled in agreement, almost flattered. "Not as big as the one on my knee." He left my leg in his lap and rested a hand on my knee, occasionally tracing it with his fingertips. We stayed in that collective moment that felt euphoric after what we had been through or not been through together.

How could the simple act of being together as if we were allowed to be, or as if we *were* together, feel just as good as the other thing we had done? It was the strangest thing. One I hadn't realized I missed or needed.

He tilted his head in thought. "Still, do you think you should have been running around, climbing all over the pool deck, and diving off boards on a foot you potentially fractured?"

"*Thought* I may have fractured, but the swelling went down." We were both still smiling even though the speed of our voices and the tone of our conversation were working their way back to normal. We had to. My break would be over soon.

That, and I knew he was getting to the very tall pink elephant currently on the last leg of his rotation.

"I bumped into Spencer, and your friend, or arch enemy, Court."

"Yes, I know. I can't say anything about Spencer that's not obvious, but I can tell you that what you witnessed is just par for the course for lifeguards. Our boss, Cleta is working dispatch today, and when—"

"The cat's a way, the mice will play?"

"You got it, especially with lifeguards. This city pool is notorious for guard pranks. Years ago, someone dipped all the cotton balls from our first aid cabinet in pickle juice from the concession stand and stuck them to another guard's car. The acid ate some of the paint off in the heat.

"No... don't tell me!"

"Yup. So, it's been toned down a lot, and just so you know, we may ask the first years to perform simple tasks and pawn the worst schedule off to them, but there is a hard rule of no hazing rookie guards. The pranks are reserved for the pros, and...

"Let me guess, you're—"

"Extremely good at this. Like, what you saw was not me and a guy named Court, it was the two pros. I had his shirt pulled out of his locker and reserved for that moment before he ever got the idea of embarrassing me in front of you. I just happened to have his locker combo unbeknown to him. I learned from the best my rookie year, and twelve years of swim team growing up, watching all the guards before that. If that explains what you saw a little better."

He smiled, looking down at my leg and then at me. His blue eyes sparkled at me, and I couldn't help but match his smile.

"Not that ah, you owe me an explanation, but I do understand that one and like it much better than what I came up with on my own. That is, not knowing who I was dealing with here in terms of the City Pool's Queen of Pranks. Lane may have left that part out over his explanation of summers here."

Hmm. Had he talked to Lane about me? "Well, Lane is also on vacation this week. So."

"I see." He kept grinning, and so did I. It was contagious and provoked by a mood that seemed to encompass us both. I wasn't sure how we got here, what it meant, or whether it was okay. If I had my wits about me as opposed to being completely taken off guard by how kind and sweet he was, I probably would have asked what the hell we were doing. But I had never experienced this side of him.

I trembled a little as he dropped his fingertips to the back of my knee, tracing the tender, ticklish part slowly and torturously. An unsteady breath slipped out of me when he looked up at me. His wide grin let me know it did not go unnoticed.

He looked away from me and moved his mouth to prepare to speak. I think it almost scared me. I had no idea what he was going to say, and I felt the moment too fragile for us to ruin it with our first real talk.

I put my hand on the door handle to prepare to leave. It was hard to do somehow, but whatever part of my right mind was still functioning tried to lay the groundwork for me to exit his vehicle and not be late back on rotation.

A deep breath snuck up on me, and I exhaled before he opened his mouth.

"I have to go."

I opened the car door to step out when I felt a strong pull on my remaining arm. I hadn't looked back at him entirely before his lips pressed firmly on mine. My mouth opened slightly, just to draw in a breath, and his tongue entered to find mine.

It was insane how quickly direct contact with him in that way could make me lose my mind to the point where I was breathless. Everything in my body was heightened and on edge for more. The weight of the passenger door I had opened closed as my hand left the handle to run my fingers through Adrian's thick, dark hair.

His breathing changed, too, and his tongue pressed deeper into mine. He kissed me harder, with a desire that ignored any intention of stopping soon. I kissed him back just as deeply, and for what felt like minutes, I marveled at the insanity of what continued to ignite between us. His smell, the way his mouth tasted in mine, and his unrelenting desire for me. It was still so crazy, even after what we did. You would think some of the mystery had worn off, but it must have had the opposite effect... it was unfinished. And the way he held the back of my neck and head in his hand, gently but firmly pressing me into his, I could tell he wanted more.

It was hard not to. This experience in his car led me to believe that we had not only unwittingly relied on interruptions in the past but also that it had been far more necessary than we knew to have something force our restraint.

"I have to go," I whispered into his mouth, my lips curving into a smile on his. His wet, swollen lips paused on top of mine. He left them there for a moment, and we breathed in each other. Then he dragged his teeth across my bottom lip as if he wanted to bite it but instead refrained. Thank God for that. I was shaking already, and it took everything I had to push out of the car and stand up.

I grabbed the rookie guard's towel on the seat and wrapped it around my waist as I slammed his door shut. I didn't even know if I could look back at him or wave; I was so out of it. I just walked forward, limping a bit as the pain from my foot reminded me of what had started this impromptu day. As I approached the steps to the pool house entrance, I felt a sinking feeling of loss.

I paused on the second step and looked back to where I had just come from.

He was still there. Adrian was watching me go in. His blue eyes hit mine, engaging a thousand butterflies that replaced the sinking feeling in the pit of my stomach. He was looking at me as if to confirm that this had, in fact, just happened, and he wasn't going anywhere.

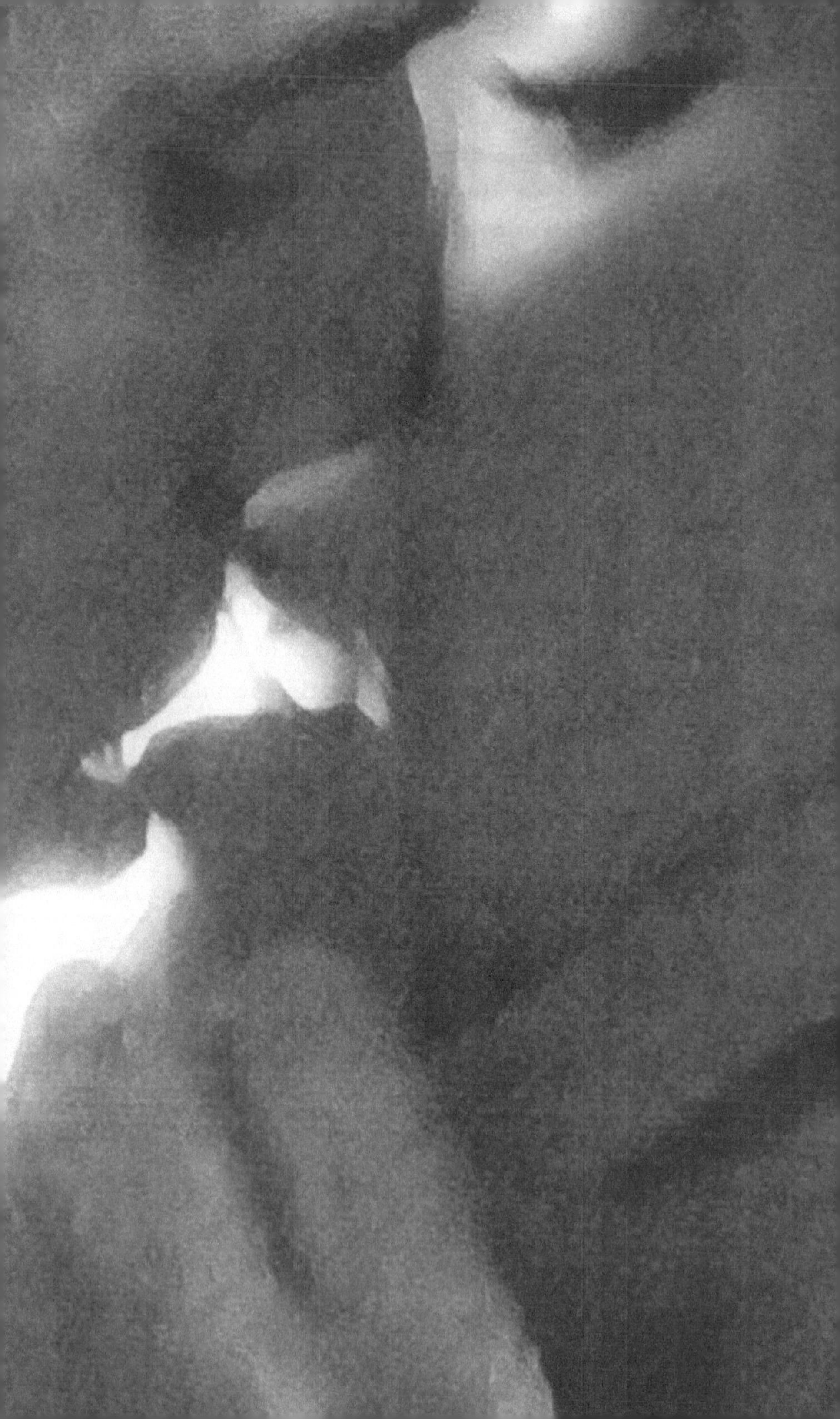

Gin Blossoms

The next time July and I spoke, it was over Spencer's Lakehouse party she had not invited me to. The issue was that he had invited me and asked me to bring Lynn. I should have known July was on the up and up, and there was always more to the story. I just wish she would have told me. I had no right to accost her over it.

It was a night or two before the infamous party. It wasn't that it would be a big one. It was more that it involved both Prairie and Pure Pines' finest, and a range of high school and college-age kids intermingling. It wasn't during the school year, and it wasn't under the protection of the city pool.

I hadn't expected many Pure Pines people, but I should have gathered as much with it being held at Spencer's Lake House. I guess I just thought of it as more of a guard party. Maybe this was July's thing, and she didn't want anyone else there.

All week leading up to it, I had heard Lynn and Reagan talk about going, yet nothing from July, and no official invite from them either. At that point, I wasn't sure what was assumed about the two of us from their end or ours.

July had worked eight to twelve-hour shifts the days after I surprised her at the pool, and I had slowly started working a few hours at the Country Club to see if my knee could take it. So far, so good. I still hadn't called July, but I knew we were good. It had only been three days or so.

Still, this party thing was driving me nuts. I heard an engine and radio blaring up Lynn's driveway. I looked out my window to see the top open on Lynn's jeep, my two best friends' hair, and July's blowing through the open air. They were all three singing Luniz and Michael Marshall's "I Got 5 On It" so loud I could barely hear the music.

I was glad to see they were having a good time, but I was pissed July hadn't invited me. Why I was behaving like a spoiled child, I couldn't decipher, nor could I seem to put a lid on it.

Surely, she didn't think I wasn't calling, or this was the same situation as before. I thought we covered that in the car that day.

I gave them time to settle in, then headed over to knock at Lynn's. Lynn's dad answered the door. He looked like he was just taking a nap. "Adrain! Thank God. Get in here and set these girls straight. I haven't had a moments peace since they arrived!" He patted me on the back and welcomed me inside, then yawned on his way down toward the opposite end of the house.

I walked into the living room to see the girls hanging out and arguing over which CD to play next. They had a few shopping bags around them: one from Hastings, our music haven in the town half an hour away, where the mall was. A few other clothing bags surrounded them, and I averted my eyes from the alarmingly recognizable pink Victoria's Secret bag that sat equidistant between Reagan and July.

"Where have you been?!" Reagan saw me first.

I saw July and Lynn look up at me, joining Reagan's inquiry. It was at that point, staring down at the three of them together, looking up at me, that I realized we hadn't quite talked about or worked this scenario out yet. Imagine that. I went from not wanting to say anything to our friends and not knowing if she would, to marching right over here like her boyfriend, as if it was my right to speak to July when I wanted.

"I was around. I just saw you all pull up."

"Good! I'm glad you're here to settle the score." Lynn went right for it. "Could you please tell July we're all going to the Lake House Party and she's just being a prude! Spencer said he invited you already, so why would we all not go?"

That's what I was wondering.

"Lynn, I just don't think it's a good idea. Look what happened at the last party with someone practically roofying the masses! You know Kane's going to pop up with all the Prairie elite and that's no good for Reagan."

"How about you both just leave Kane to me." Reagan was obviously offended at having her affairs factored into the equation.

"You just don't want us to go because you think it's a special party for all your lifeguard buddies." That level of immaturity sounded strange, coming out of Lynn's mouth.

"That's not fair, and you know it. I told you I wouldn't go, and we could do something else with our rare night off together. I just think it's not great to drive all the way out to secluded Lake Cherokee with people who are way out of our league. Knowing Spencer, there's going to be a bunch of people from all ends we didn't count on being there, and I—

"No. I know Spencer, and I'm not worried about it." Lynn actually seemed mad at July.

"July, I'm not picking sides, but we have the invites without you." Reagan sounded more like the voice of reason this time.

I stared at July, wondering why she was so against this party. *Was it me?* Did she not want me there with her guard friends? I was looking at an entirely different July.

I didn't really care about the party. Spencer made it grimy and uncomfortable with his unclear comments about Lynn and July. Thinking back on when I bumped into him at the pool, I didn't want July and Lynn to go without me. That's where my main concern was coming from.

July's eyes met mine. She looked upset.

"Come outside with me?" I asked her as I nodded to the door for us to escape. No one said anything as July got up to follow me out until...

"Should we remind you, it was *you* that was so hellbent on going somewhere and bitching that we hadn't been out in a while... it was the one day you pulled your head out of the depression of being in a funk over him, and remembered you had friends!"

"Lynn!" Reagan shouted.

"Oh, I guess I went too far stating the obvious? Well, she's going too far on this party." Lynn was a level of anger I hadn't seen in a while, and I had never seen it directed at July. She and Reagan went head-to-head like that sometimes, but Lynn was usually more protective of July.

I didn't care that her dig included me, and basically called us out. I saw July's eyes well up and I put my hand on her lower back to lead her out before she said anything she would regret. It was too late. I had to remember she was still the July I was in debate with. July took a step or two toward the front door with me, then she paused and looked back over her shoulder.

"Careful Lynn, or I'll think you're just upset you lost your designated driver." July stepped past me to leave, and slammed the door behind her.

I caught it and closed it quietly so we wouldn't wake Mr. Stokes again, although I'm not sure anyone could have slept through that shouting match. July stormed out into the front yard and seemed perplexed, as if she didn't know where to go. I walked her to the side of the yard that Lynn's house shared with mine, leading her toward my pool deck for privacy.

"What do you need?" July was trying to hold back tears as she asked.

"*What do I need?* July, just tell me what's going on. How can I help?"

"I would love to go to the party... for us all to go. But I would rather not go than have Lynn around Spencer."

"I don't understand. What's Lynn got to do with Spencer?"

"He's not good, Adrian. I'm afraid I can't tell you why, but I just don't want Lynn around him. I've tried every way I know to divert her attention from him. Only now, I think she's hurt because she has it in her head that I don't think she should be with him for alternate reasons. Which would never be the case."

"Wait... be with him?! Lynn is into Spencer?! How and when?"

"Don't ask me. I guess you and I aren't the only ones with a secret." She looked away from me.

And there it was. The first time, we had acknowledged it between us.

It made me sad she called us a secret, but it also made my heart skip wildly that she referred to us as having something together. Hearing it from her mouth felt good, as if she no longer denied it.

I immediately remembered the awkward conversation where Lynn talked about Spencer under the guise of him working at the pool with July this summer. And then *Spencer's, "She's a real special girl..."* comment.

Maybe that wasn't meant in a creepy womanizer way. Maybe he was putting it out there and letting *me*, her best friend, know he was into her.

"But why wouldn't she come right out and tell us?" I immediately felt stupid for saying that.

July just looked at me. She'd all but already said it. I knew her look was referring to the fact that we never told them about us, so why would Lynn share.

"Okay, then why wouldn't you tell me?"

"How often do you and I have personal conversations?!" July's eyes were on fire. She was right. This was our first one other than the recent pool visit. I deserved that. I stepped closer to her, pulling her into me.

"We have personal conversations now."

I hugged her tightly, and my face brushed her soft cheek as I brought hers to my shoulder. Although she was upset, and had every right to be since I guess our moment in my car was left unresolved... I only felt the emotional distance from her. Her body collapsed into my arms as I cradled her, and I could feel her heart pounding against mine. It was funny to hold her so close and familiar when I knew she was still upset. I don't think our bodies cared.

I originally moved my face to look at her with the intent of getting a read on what she was thinking. To see if she wanted to talk it out more. *I was trying.* However, the close proximity of our embrace... fuck, every time I touched her, hearts pounding, that smell of roses, hot candy, and something sophisticated trapping me where I stood. It wasn't just me. My face slid past hers and all I did was run my hand up her forearm replacing the hug. A trail of goose bumps rose below my fingertips across her skin.

"July." I whispered her name into her ear as I took a half step to press our bodies closer. I didn't even get to look into her eyes before my lips were tracing above hers. If I had looked at her, it would have been over for me. Her brown eyes searching mine were just as arousing as anything I longed to see or touch on her body. She let out an uneven breath into me. Now I had the goose bumps.

I was still worried about Lynn and our reservations over Spencer, but it was only the second time I had felt whole since my knee. The first was when I took her hand in front of everyone at the pool and then here, holding her outside my house... I didn't want to force a kiss and exchange our first real conversation with the physical that always won us over, but I had to kiss her. Maybe I was making up for lost time. Maybe I just couldn't get enough.

My hand was on her neck, then her cheek, pressing her lips to mine before I could complete my thoughts. She automatically opened for me, and our tongues met as they had days ago at the pool, only deeper, and somewhat needier than before. I think it surprised us both.

"I have to go back in."

It was the first time she ever pulled away from me. "I have to let Lynn know it's not her. It's about him." July's cheeks were flushed. Was it from me or worry over Lynn? I took a step back to create distance between us, and honor what was going through her head.

"What does Reagan say?" I wondered if she had any insight.

"From what I can tell Lynn hasn't said much to Reagan past what she hasn't said to you or me about him. I don't know why it would be a secret, but again, that's rich for me to say. I just don't want Lynn getting hurt by someone she trusts for reasons beyond my understanding, and I know there is more to Spencer than meets the eye."

I could sense July was truly concerned about Lynn, which made me want her even more.

"Look, what if we all go to the party and watch out for Lynn, unless... I mean if you don't want me to go..."

"What?" She looked shocked.

"ADRIAN!" My stepmother's voice rang from the garage door. "I need you home, I can't find your dad!" I looked at July with a funny smile.

"That's an odd thing to say. Did she lose him?" I joked as best I could under the circumstances. July gave me a half smile back and looked over into our drive.

"Isn't that your dad's car?"

"Yeah, weird. I've gotta' go." I looked down at her one more time, taking in the smell of her hair, the way the soft skin of her face felt on the tip of my nose... warm, it felt warm. I think I learned in that instance just how extremely difficult she was to walk away from. I stepped away from her, leaving her standing in the side of the yard, and I immediately regretted it.

I was slightly baffled, and certainly distracted by what could possibly be going on with my dad. But sill, with so much left unsaid between us... Well, I could only hope I had finally made enough effort to show her I was in. I had a sinking feeling as I took the initial steps toward our driveway, and I hated leaving things undetermined. I hated leaving *her.*

"Adrian..." July's voice was certain and determined when I heard it call out to me.

I pivoted on the spot to look back on her demand.

"I want you to come-- I want you there. With me." She blurted out what was weighing on her mind and I could not have been more relieved or grateful.

"Will you go to the party with me? I'm asking you to."

She looked so serious and concerned with her eyes locked on mine, awaiting my reaction. I had only given her a little and she was giving me her all back. In a moment that all her attention was pulled to our mutual best friend, she gave back to me so I wouldn't feel neglected. How did she know I needed that from her?

I starred back at her, much longer than I should have, and then I couldn't help it. I had no control when it came to her. I felt the corners of my mouth rise into an embarrassingly large smile I could not contain. She had me hooked, and any doubt I had felt was left to my own ignorance and jealousy. She dissipated it in seconds. It was all I could do not to run back to her and take her right there in the grass she stood.

July

"HIGH AND DRY"

Radiohead

"You swear she's not mentioned Spencer to you?" I was interrogating Reagan for the third time that evening.

"I swear. I wasn't even suspicious or onto her in any way. Which either means I'm a shitty friend or—"

"I'm overreacting." I said it for her.

"Careful there. She may think it's a black and white thing if you keep objecting."

"Reagan! How dare you even suggest that? And yes, that's my biggest fucking fear. Since I can't tell her the real truth, she'll dream up the worst of me. I hope you're joking about that even being a remote possibility."

"Well, what is the truth behind your hatred toward Spencer? Did he do something at the pool?" Reagan expected a candid answer.

He hadn't done anything or acted in any way beyond his regular entitled Pure Pines demeanor. He hadn't been that bad to work with, either. I just knew what I saw that day, and I couldn't let Lynn be deceived by a monster.

Lynn had plenty of clout of her own. Elite guys from surrounding schools were begging to take her out, and she was going to waste her time with that piece of shit? He was well into college. What was he even doing back this year?

"God, Reagan, since when did we all start keeping secrets. I mean real ones that could hurt each other. Look at you. Your pager's been going off all night. I know you're making plans with Kane, and what about his bitchy girlfriend? She's no saint Reagan. The stunts we heard she pulled last year—"

"You don't know anything about it or what I've got going on with Kane."

"Is he coming tonight? At least give me that much."

"Yes."

My heart sank for her, and I shook my head. But I shook it off; I had to. I already had enough beef with Lynn, and then there was my ambiguous now semi-private relationship that my friends had been kind enough not to interrogate me about.

"You know what we need?" A genuine smile took over the tension in my face and spread broadly across my cheeks.

'I'm just impressed you thought of it first." Reagan pulled a bottle of vodka and two shot glasses from her vanity drawer.

"You can drink because your boyfriend agreed to be the DD!"

"Stop it. You know he's not my boyfriend. That's your friend." That smile remained on my face at hearing my best friend refer to Adrian as my boyfriend, even if it was a tacky joke. Reagan poured two shots and clanked my glass.

"I saw you guys, you know. I went to get something out of the kitchen, and I could see you from Lynn's kitchen window. I almost called her over to watch, but I figured you were in enough trouble with her." She poured us another shot I did not intend on and passed it to me. "You know he's really smitten. I mean, you're not going to get rid of him that easily, if you wanted to. I don't pretend to know how you feel about him or what you want, because you sure as shit haven't told me. You've been hellbent on suffering through this one alone. But I can tell you, I know Adrian. And he's not like that with anybody else. He wasn't with Natalie. I've never seen him touch or look at anybody like he does you."

"You got all that from creeping out a window one time?"

"July, Lynn and I have watched you two this entire year. It's absolutely exhausting. You are both so ridiculous we've just stopped caring. I've never seen two people who haven't even slept together torture themselves so much."

"And just how do you know we haven't?"

"Because I know you! Here, wear this, not that." Reagan threw a dark green shirt at me. It was a sleeveless tailored button down with a collar, and she threw me the shorts that matched it from her dresser drawer.

"I can't get into those."

"Yes, you can. Hurry, Lynn will be her in ten minutes." I looked down at the colorful denim, but printed shorts. They were a darker shade of the jade green top with tiny purple flowers printed on them. They were snug but super cute, and the top was a great color. Striking almost. It was summer sexy, with the collar giving off an Audrey Hepburn vibe.

It was disgusting the wardrobe Reagan had at her disposal via she and her mom's great taste and her dad's credit cards. After years of politely resisting, I got tired of fighting her. If I shut up, got dressed, and asked no questions, it usually achieved a head turning look I would have never had at my disposal otherwise.

"You look good."

"Thank you for this, I'll be careful in it."

"Please don't."

A honk outside announced Lynn, and we ran outside to hop in.

"Are we waiting for Adrian to follow or..." Reagan asked as she shot a look toward Adrian's while climbing up to the front seat of the jeep.

"No. He's not coming." Lynn landed that plane a little colder than necessary.

My heart sank to the bottom of my stomach. I felt mortified and let down. Then I saw Lynn's eyes find me in the rearview mirror.

"Relax, he's meeting us there later. He had to take care of something at home. Something with his dad. "Sorry, July. I had to. The idea you would make us miss this party when we all three look this good!" She winked at me in the mirror and turned the music up. She was blasting NIN's "Closer." *How appropriate for this party was all I could think.*

However, past all the sarcasm, I was grateful she had forgiven me.

The problem was it put the cart before the horse, as so many things surrounding our little group seemed to do lately. How could she have forgiven me when she didn't even know the truth of why I wanted her to stay away from Spencer?

Then, Adrian. The thought of how fickle our situation was. The power it had to destroy me. Was I sure I wanted that? To be with someone who's track record of disappointing me super exceeded the one day at the pool and yesterday's conversation in his yard... in his arms?

My stomach flipped, just remembering how it felt to be held by him, and then again, when I recalled his blue eyes darting toward mine, requesting I walk outside with him in front of the two people that meant a great deal to us both.

I looked out the window, entranced, remembering how he had looked at me the day before. His arms and hands were strong and something I always wanted around me. The way he smelled sent something through my veins that was primal. Pheromone-like in a way I would never be able to grasp. How could I be so physically and emotionally invested in someone who had so little investment in me?

However, what was invested was palpable and visceral. Something that would not release me.

Even uncertain about where we stood, I worried about him. What was this about his dad? This was the second time he was mentioned as an issue. I couldn't help but be concerned. Adrian was super close to his dad. They did everything together. I hoped all was okay, but I had a funny feeling something was off.

The drive down was beautiful. The East Texas sun sat purple in the sky, following us above the water as we neared Lake Cherokee. People used to say more people were believers here in the Piney Woods of Texas, not because of all the churches, but because they had proof in the sunsets. And they were brilliant masterpieces, always in some exceptional version of a color you hadn't seen in a while.

There were a few cars when we pulled up, but nothing like the Tomlin Twin party. I saw Court's red truck but no blue Mustang yet.

I noticed Lynn and Reagan's surge of anticipation on our arrival, and I should have been excited, too. If it weren't clouded by Spencer, it would have been the first time I got to mix these two worlds together.

Of course, if I thought deeper about it, Spencer was why the worlds of Prairie lifeguards, their high school in- crowd, and their Jr. College basketball players were mixing with several hand-picked Pure Pines elite. Lane and I certainly wouldn't have warranted that kind of gathering. I wondered if he would be in there.

I prepared myself to loosen up and make sure Lynn and Reagan had a good time while I kept an eye out for them both. *Damn it, Reagan, why did Kane have to be a factor?* I envisioned enough trouble watching out for Lynn with Spencer. Now. I would have to peek around corners to be sure Reagan was safe. Maybe that's what Adrian was for. He said he'd be here to help, and I knew he would be. He would never let Lynn down.

The vibe was much more subdued and cool, than you would expect a college party to be. The decor of the stunning lake house was part of that. Lean the wrong way, and you might break a vase taller and more expensive than you. There was a massive great room with high wood beam ceilings and large slate tiles that met a circular cut-out in the middle complete with a white shag rug and an indoor suspended fire pit hanging above it.

All of that, plus massive windows looking out to the lake for the most spectacular panoramic view.

There was a pool table in a room further back that felt a little more casual. Although there were very few cars outside, there were more people inside chatting with a drink in their hand than I thought there would be.

We made our way to the pool table room, and I was immediately swooped up by Court. He sat his pool stick down and picked me up by the waist, then sat me on the pool table, interrupting the game. He leaned in close to my face.

"I just want to say this once loud and clear while everyone is sober-ish and listening. We are in a truce. This is a party; your friends are here…" He looked back at Reagan and Lynn, who stood with their mouths open. "And, again, we are in a truce. No pranks, no jokes, no bodily harm, mental anguish or embarrassment. Deal?"

I looked back at my two besties, who had no idea what to think, and then leaned into Court's face, about a centimeter from it. "Well, Court, if I'd just known how much this party meant to you, as well as how much... embarrassment and mental anguish my winning pranks had caused you, I would have refrained for your health and well-being a long time ago."

"Woo-hoo!" The group of guards watching cued and whistled.

I smiled factiously and extended my hand to shake. He tilted his head to the side and moved his hand away.

"You said these lovely ladies were your friends, right?" He picked me back up and dropped me on the floor on his way over to Reagan and Lynn. I was laughing so hard I almost cried.

"*No!* Truce, truce, truce!" I screamed, climbing on his back to get him away from my friends.

"That's what I thought." Everyone who knew us clapped, and he introduced himself to Reagan and Lynn, thanking them for being good sports.

"That's one." I shouted over my shoulder as we headed toward what looked like a kitchen behind the pool room.

"*Oh, damn,*" Lynn said out of nowhere. Reagan and I looked in the direction she was looking, and we saw Devin standing there next to most of our varsity cheerleaders. They were eyeing Court like they wanted to eat him and apparently had seen the entire display.

I glanced away when I felt Devin's eyes on me. I figured I'd say hello to the others when they were out from under her wing. As I looked back toward the pool table to divert my eyes from her, I saw Court staring back at me. I couldn't help but wonder how much that little horseplay witnessed would cost me with Devin. *Damn it*. However, the thought occurred to me that in that moment, we weren't in Pure Pines anymore... and I wasn't sure if that was a good thing or something potentially far worse.

July
"HIGH AND DRY" PART 2

Radiohead

Reagan had just begun helping herself to a cocktail when Spencer turned the corner to greet Lynn.

"Thank you for coming." He approached her and hugged her tightly, then kissed her on the cheek. Charm oozing off his biceps and smile. We had barely made it to the kitchen for a drink, as in I didn't have one yet, and he had already found us.

Lynn's dimples were showing, and her eyes were dancing up at him.

"Reagan." Spencer nodded her way, then he looked over at me. "That one hates me. I don't know why. I try so hard to get in her good graces." He put on a show for Lynn while looking at me and speaking loud enough to make his point comedic. "She practically runs the pool, not me. Has free and total reign as your best friend, and she doesn't even thank me with your presence. That's all I ever asked her for."

I rolled my eyes and took the drink Reagan poured me. I tried not to stare when I saw Lynn whisper something in Spencer's ear. I also tried not to throw up.

A drink later, Reagan was nowhere to be found. I walked back over to Lynn, who was holding hands with Spencer and facing him while they flirted.

"Hey."

"Are you having fun July?" Spencer turned his attention to engage me in their conversation.

"Have you guys seen Reagan?"

"She's in the office having a conversation with Kane who just arrived a bit ago with..." Spencer nodded toward a group of girls from Prairie at the door. Great. One of them was the girlfriend. Lynn grabbed at my arm to pull my focus back to she and Spencer.

"Hey, Spencer said you don't have to worry about Devin anymore. Not here at the party or ever." Lynn was confident in her delivery. I looked over at Spencer, skeptical. *Who made this guy the fucking Godfather?*

"Trust me. She's more afraid of you now than you should ever be of her." Spencer put his hand on my shoulder protectively. What an act! I knew, 'least said best' where Devin was concerned, so I didn't look a gift horse in the mouth.

"Do you mind if I talk to her?" Spencer asked Lynn sincerely. I was so confused. Talk to who?

"Do you want me to come with?" Lynn was asking in front of me as if I wasn't standing right there.

"No, I've got this one. July? Do you mind stepping over here with me?"

What the fuck was going on?! Was I in the Twilight Zone? Where was Adrian when I needed him? Or "Hey Court... no more Truce, just come throw me in the lake and you're the winner!" I'd rather that than this. Anything but this.

Was he about to take me to the back of his lake house castle and brainwash me into a drug trafficking ring? *What was happening?*

I looked back at Lynn, silently pleading, and followed him to a secluded bay window off the central kitchen.

"Look, I know what you thought you saw at the twin's party that night. I wasn't sure what or how much you saw or thought you saw until I realized how upset you were with me. Then, with Lynn, when she and I began to spend more time together this summer. I never wanted to conceal that from you, and I didn't want to have to ask her to, but you just wouldn't yield. I wouldn't have either. You're a good friend, July, and you weren't wrong about the awful thing you thought you saw."

"What is this? You want forgiveness?" I was so confused by his audacity.

"No, I'm afraid even you can't give me that. I just wanted you to know the truth about Lynn and me. Unfortunately, I can't explain as well as I would like to, as it is not my secret to tell, and it implicates someone I regretfully promised I would not reveal. Under the circumstances, I do believe you saw this person and can draw your own conclusion by default. I can only say to you that what you thought you saw and what you assumed happened, did. Just not with me."

My face softened, and I listened to him earnestly for the first time.

"I had a buddy that was going to be down for the weekend, a well-known-in Pure Pines buddy. He asked me to drive down and hang out and promised a great time, plus we could pop by the Tomlin party for old time's sake. The good time he had in mind is not something I am or ever will be into."

Spencer paused and looked at me to make sure I heard that part. "He sensed I would disapprove, so when we dropped by the party, he kept his little roofie plan to himself and a few other guys he passed them out to, who he thought would have the night of their life. After not seeing him for a while, I was about ready to leave without him until he found me. His eyes were crazy. He was a sweaty mess. He took me to the twin's parents' room, and I saw what I'm glad you didn't have to...

Presley's little sister passed out, and she was completely naked. It didn't look good. I grabbed her clothes off the floor, thinking I would help her get dressed, but then I heard light breathing and a slight gurgle in her throat. She was unconscious, and she was going to choke on her own vomit. I poured cold water on her face from the sink, slapped some clothes on her as best I could to give her some immediate dignity, and put my fingers down her throat to get her to throw up. The truth is, I wasn't sure what I was doing, but I was horrified. Imagine what you thought, but I was sitting right next to my best friend, the monster who did this trying to save the girl.

Someone else had barged in before you. Luckily, it was one of our guys. I demanded they get her sister, and that's where what you saw ended."

I was stunned, silent.

"He never told me exactly what happened, but I do know one of the reasons he came and got me was he realized she was a virgin, and I think all that did was register to him that he might be in more trouble should something happen to her. I wanted to kill him. Later, he put his hand on my shoulder to thank me and I punched him so hard he flew. Still, it doesn't make me a hero in the least. I got him to promise to turn himself in or whatever you do in these cases, and he lied and told me he had spoken to her and her parents, and they came to an agreement."

"I'm so sorry, Spencer."

"Yeah, well, I knew you must be feeling the way I did if you couldn't help that girl, and when I realized you thought it was me who did it, I wasn't in a hurry to let myself off the hook. Again, it's not my secret to tell, and I guess I felt I deserved your judgment for not doing anything more about it."

As I searched the sincerity in Spencer's eyes, I realized the saddest part was, I don't think he could have done anything about it. He would have just ended up in trouble himself for it. There is no way a Childress would have gone down, and even though Spencer never divulged that part, we both know that his Pure Pines "buddy" was his best friend I saw looking pathetic on the side of the jacuzzi, none other than Trent Childress.

Spencer cleared his throat and continued.

"The Lynn of it… well, I couldn't say much because it was so new. I wasn't sure how she felt about me. You do know her older sister, Mel was in my class, right?"

"Yeah, I remember."

"Mel and I were kind of friends the way Adrian and Lynn are, back in the day. A few nights after the party before I went back to UT, I stopped by to see if I couldn't find her or happen to catch her home. She'd spent the weekend at school, but Lynn came out and talked to me. We went for a drive, and I told her the whole story. I don't know why I broke my promise to tell her, but I needed to. She's been a friend to me this whole time, and I came back this summer, partly to check on the situation my former buddy did not resolve, and partly for Lynn, because…"

"She's beautiful, and smarter than you and compassionate, and the best thing that's happened to you this year." I said it for him.

"Does it show on my face?" His eyebrow raised, and he looked down at the floor and laughed.

"I'm sorry I had the wrong guy."

"Don't be. The worst part is, for Presley's little sister's sake—"

"Robyn." I corrected him.

"I wish I could say that you should've walked in on them sooner before anything happened to Robyn, but the truth is, with me not there and it being him, it could have been way worse for you. Not even the unthinkable, but you would have been in the position of knowing what I know, and he may have threatened you."

"Has he threatened you?"

"Not yet, but he senses I'm down here working for the summer to hold him to his promise. So, it could get worse before it gets better." I shook my head in dismay of the hateful, diseased place that raised us, and I reached up and hugged him. He bear-hugged me back and whispered Thank you in my ear. When we broke away, I punched him hard in his massive bicep.

"Ouch! What was that for?!"

"Now I have to eat humble pie with Lynn!" I smiled and laughed as he walked back toward Lynn. I knew she and I would need to talk, but then she winked at me as he walked over and threw his arms around her. *Good. We were good for now.*

I grabbed a drink and moved toward the other room when I noticed Kane's girlfriend had separated from her little entourage and seemed to be looking for Kane.

I walked around in the opposite direction of her, hoping I would find the office. I did, and Reagan was engaged in far more than a conversation with Kane. At least, that's what I heard through the locked door. *So there was that.* Thank God they had the sense to lock the door.

I downed the last bit of my drink and headed toward the kitchen. I didn't know what was wrong. I was happy. Happy things worked out for Lynn, and Spencer wasn't bad after all, but I had still gotten the wrong guy.

Or, what if I hadn't? Everything Spencer said made sense, but I still felt unsettled about him. Maybe it was because I had been so wrong and couldn't trust my gut.

Robyn endured what would shape the rest of her life alone, and with no resolve. The remote happy ending was a small high that could not override the sinking feeling in my stomach.

And then there was Reagan. She was purposefully careless with her actions and had so many secrets between all of us. I hated that.

Speaking of secrets, mine still hadn't shown up. I guessed he wasn't going to.

I headed back to the kitchen to grab another drink. For the first time in my life, I felt like I needed one. I never really drank or desired to, but that night felt like a runaway train going nowhere. I figured I'd grab another to be sociable and try and find some of my guard friends hanging out. I would let someone else worry about our DD who didn't show up.

I was relieved to find the kitchen empty of people. There was a pan of Jello shots one of the guards had contributed. I slurped one down. Then, I took my time to consider what libation I wanted to fill my red solo cup with next.

After a long pour of the clear Russian spirit I started the night with, I added a splash of soda and raised the glass to myself. As I brought it down the hatch, I felt a firm hand grip my wrist.

I flipped around, my brow furrowed, to see none other than Court standing in front of me.

"I think maybe you're cut off. How much have you had tonight?"

"I thought we called a truce." I said that a little dryer than intended.

"We did."

"Then "F" off and hand me back my cup."

"Woah, that's a big negative on the cup return. What's wrong with you?"

"*What's. Wrong. With. Me?* Hmmm. Do you know? Cause it would be great if someone else knew. I give up." I left him with my cup and grabbed another Jello shot on my way out of the kitchen.

"Where are you going?"

"Does it matter? Out. Away. I'm walking away." No sooner did I turn the corner than I was hoisted up and carried by the six-foot-three-well-meaning coworker giant.

"Stop bouncing me up and down you psycho. We called a truce." My head fell to his chest, and I could smell his cologne. I started laughing.

"What's so funny?"

"I've never seen you in a shirt before. Can you put me down now please?"

"Can you tell me where you are headed?"

"Oh God, Court, not to a car with keys to put in an ignition. What are you Smokey the fucking Bear? Or whatever." *Okay, I may have, in fact, been tipsy, as that reference was totally lost on me as well.* "I may be a walking after-school special, but I'm not a bad one. I don't even have a car here to drive under the influence, and if you're worried, I'll go skinny dipping in the lake and drown; well, I can't promise anything."

"Alright. Upsy daisy." Court placed me on the pool table again. I squinted toward the great room to see the few people meandering inside were headed outside. Most everyone had taken the party to the dock by the lake.

I looked around, sitting on the pool table. "Why am I here again?"

"You're drunk."

"Let's go with buzzed."

"Three sheets."

"One and a half."

"Fine." Court settled. He leaned in toward me, his hands on the pool table beside my hips and his face studying mine closely.

"Court Townsend, are you trying to smell my breath? Are you giving me a breath-o-later' test?"

His eyes widened at me in surprise, and his mischievous smile rose. "First of all, it's a breathalyzer." He stood tall and stepped forward between my dangling legs. "Second, if I was giving you one, you'd know." He gingerly pulled a piece of hair out of my face and placed it behind my ear.

I may have been buzzed, but the way he was looking at me told me it was more than a joke. More than our usual banter. His face was so close I could feel his warmth next to me. I could have misgauged the moment in my inebriated state, but I knew he was attracted to me.

"I'm sure your girlfriend would know too."

"I'm sure you're right, which is why I refrained from that, but you're still not walking out of here by yourself. You can walk that way to your friends, or I can take you out there to them or..."

"Or what? Stay in here with you Court? Is it my lucky day? What's your deal?"

"My deal is I had a buddy my first year of college who walked away from a party only— what was that—one and a half sheets to the wind? Let's just say he never came back the same. I'd hate for that to happen to you, just because somebody got under your skin tonight."

"Under my skin? Interesting choice of words. Well, I'm real sorry about your friend, and I'm real happy for your girlfriend as it turns out she's got a darn good Samaritan on her hands." I pushed him away and slid off the pool table. I started walking toward the front door. Court followed close behind me until he grabbed me and pinned me to the wall in the entry way. He bent down to my level. "Stop it." He insisted.

"Why?"

"You know why." He brought his face closer to mine again.

"Why?"

"Because you make me crazy." Court locked eyes with mine and watched for my reaction. I said nothing in response. He had greenish-brownish eyes, which were sincere, but I could tell he'd also had a drink or two too many.

He was innocuous in that regard, as I always felt safe with him. Safe, comfortable, and I could say anything I wanted. I didn't mean to be glib, but after the night I'd had, I don't think I had room for more shocking news.

It was funny if you thought about how private Adrian and I were, yet we were both single. Court and I had a natural flirtation with our displays that was fun and oddly public. But I think that was because we had the safety net of him being involved in a serious long-distance relationship with a girl back home.

Court and I were seldom alone together at work. However, those few one-on-one moments in the guard room or parties we ended up working together were always full of a certain unexplored energy.

I was comfortable with it and even welcomed it that summer because it distracted me from losing my mind over Adrian… wanting or needing more time with him. Wondering what he thought or if he wanted me at all.

Court would never act on our attraction, nor would I. I told myself it was because of his girlfriend, and he was loyal to a fault. Loyal, yes, but also mischievous. Court was full of life and the kind of trustworthy you wanted to get into trouble with. He made me laugh. He challenged my outgoing, playful side to come out and dance and kept me from being an introvert all summer

The real reason he toed the fine line was most likely my age. I wasn't quite eighteen yet, and I knew the twenty-one-year-old knew that. I also felt he was conscious of my innocence. Apart from my private lessons with Adrian, I was still very naïve about the opposite sex and sex in general. Part of me assumed that's what kept him at bay, but another part of me knew full well that was what fueled his attraction to me. That guy wanted to corrupt me every way to Sunday and have me for breakfast the morning after.

Little did he know Adrian had beat him to it, maybe not entirely, but enough to keep me from barking up anyone else's tree. I was curious, sure, and with Court... in more ways than I'd ever been with anyone other than Adrian.

But I was also loyal to a fault. My heart was on my sleeve as if it had Adrian's name monogrammed on it. I think Court sensed that, too, even though he never asked or brought it up. I don't think he wanted the answer.

I also didn't have a response for him because I knew it was the alcohol talking or possibly some rouse to keep me from going outside by myself tipsy. However, I think it challenged him slightly that I didn't take him seriously enough to have a reaction.

"July, if I didn't have a girlfriend—if I wasn't –"

"You'd what?" I yelled in his face. He looked angry at me for pushing the issue, and then his face changed to something between fear and wanting as he leaned in even closer. I couldn't be one hundred percent certain, but I'm pretty sure his lips were aiming for mine. I pushed him away and headed out the front.

I opened the front door with Court following behind me just in time to see a blue Mustang pull up and park. Adrian turned off the ignition and stepped out of the car.

"Nope," I said to Adrian and did an about-face that turned me smackdab into Court's chest. He caught me and whispered down into my hair.

"This is the one under your skin, huh? Why is he so late?"

"Exactly!" I spun around and away from Court, facing Adrian.

"July." Adrian stood in front of me and said my name.

"What?" I shot back at him as if I was angry he ever knew my name. "The party's out there if you're interested, I was just leaving."

"Stop it July!" Court's voice rang from behind me. *Oh, now I had two bosses.*

"What's going on?" Adrian looked to Court.

The answer came from me. "Let's see. Lynn is totally in love with Spencer and he... her, and it's absolutely fine because it turns out he's not so horrible and I was totally wrong. Just literally keeping my best friend from happiness for sport. Reagan is either still upstairs fucking Kane while his girlfriend searches for him somewhere out there through the party, or she has found them by now and is beating Reagan's ass. Court here is Smokey the Bandit and was worried I had one too many much and was headed out to watch me drive a fictitious car, but that's okay... He has a girlfriend, and he would never..." I rolled my head back to Court's direction. "And don't worry Court, Adrian here doesn't have a girlfriend at the moment, but he would never..." I looked back and forth between the two of them. "Does that pretty much cover it?"

Neither responded. "Oh yeah, and Devin's out there too; maybe she's got an idea to set you up with someone else, or maybe she's waiting for us to join the party so she can trip me into the lake in front of all my friends!" I took a sideways step off the sidewalk and stumbled. I saw Court take a half step toward me, but Adrian had already scooped me up bridal style. My neck and hair dangled down as limp as my legs did as he carried me to his car. I didn't say a word as Adrian buckled the seat belt around me, and I saw his jaw clench again.

He walked up to Court, and I heard him dryly ask him to watch me. Then Adrian disappeared toward the deck where everyone was partying.

Court took a few steps closer down the sidewalk but kept his distance. When he looked my way, I gave him an over-exaggerated wave. Not long after that, Adrian was at the driver's side. He looked back at Court for a moment, and Court stared him down. This time, they didn't nod at each other.

"Aren't we going back for Reagan and Lynn?" I finally asked.

Adrian did not respond.

"I'll ask again…"

"They're fine. Lynn only had one, and if she feels like she can't drive, they plan to crash at the lake house. She's going to call and let me know either way.

"Great, then take me back and I'll stay with them."

"You're not staying there. You're drunk and I'm taking you home."

We drove in silence a little longer. My hand lay loosely by my leg, and Adrian grazed it by accident as he switched gears. A jolt of electricity rang through us both, and I made a point to move out of his way.

"Why are you drunk?" he asked.

"Why weren't you here?"

Neither of us answered the question.

"Why was Court waiting with you?" This time, he demanded.

"Where's Natalie? I always thought she was such a pretty little blonde." I turned my body away from him to lean against the window.

"I hate you," I whispered as my eyes drifted to sleep.

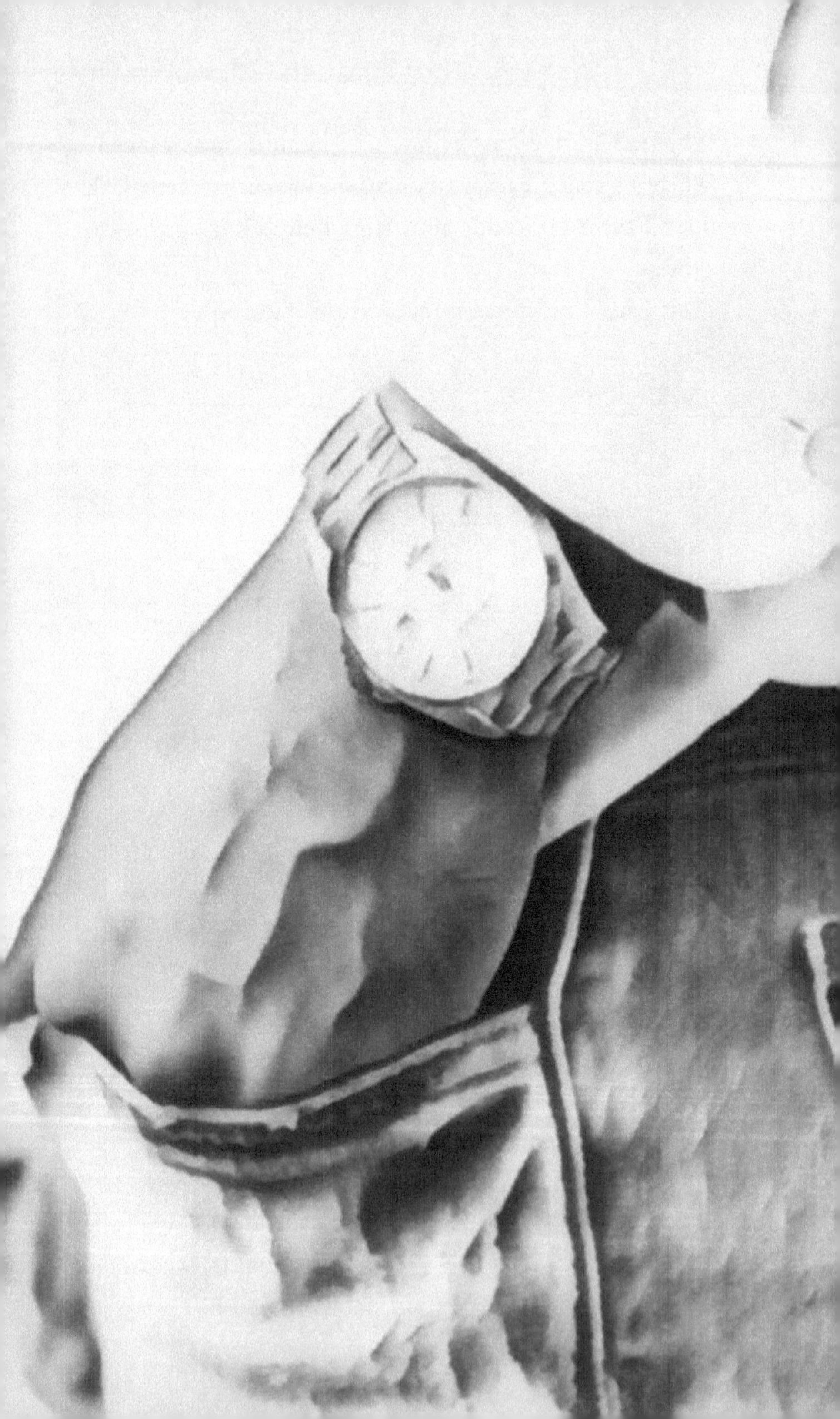

Pearl Jam

W eeks flew by, and I wasn't in a place where I could think past what was going on with my dad, much less what wasn't going on with July and I— I hadn't told anyone how severe the situation had become with my father, because I'm not quite sure I understood it myself.

My stepmom was having trouble with it, understandably, but without Dad's valid input, I had no one.

I put July out of my head. I put that night away. It was too much. She never even knew why I was late, and with everything she listed going on that night at the party, how could I blame her for getting tanked? She probably thought I wouldn't show, even though I had a solid reason for being late. I simply wasn't ready to talk about my dad. I couldn't make it real for anyone else when it was not yet real for me.

I knew July was hurting, and I knew I could potentially hurt her again with my silence. It was fight or flight, and I had to fly and fight for my dad. There wasn't room for my feelings for anyone else. I knew this logically, yet night after night, in the late hours of my evening... I would weigh out the situation and our actions. I don't think I'd watched football replays as much as I replayed, well, *us*.

I hadn't asked, but Lynn told me about the Spencer re-solve. She didn't say who it was at the Tomlin party nor who Spencer's "buddy" was, but it wasn't hard to guess. I weighed that pressure into July's situation. The idea that she held that in for so long while I was flaunting Natalie in front of her, and how Devin had fueled that situation to start something with July. It was a lot for someone to go through, and there were so many other things I didn't yet know she was facing.

Then, I factored in mine. My knee, my dad, and everything I lost that Spring semester.

Only, fuck if she wasn't the only thing that made it better! I ran to her in a crisis in the office that day, and she was the only one I wanted to see after that when things turned upside down with coach. I didn't know it at the time, and still, it seems ludicrous our trajectories crossed paths that day. Even more so that I unknowingly relied on it.

My best friend was standing there. Reagan, another friend for life was standing in arms reach, and I latched on to the only one I wanted to stand by me in the moment. It was automatic. As uncertain as my behavior had been toward July, I never question the certainty of how much I wanted her. I questioned the why often, usually to talk myself out of pursuing her, but I never questioned whether it was real or not.

That night of the lake house had been replayed the most in my mind. She never gets drunk. She was a mean, angry little cuss, but she was adorable and even sloppy drunk... she was beautiful. There was no denying that. I shouldn't have asked why Court followed her out. Wasn't it obvious? Who wouldn't want to?

I had looked over several times as she slept peacefully in the passenger side of my car. As angry as I was at her for— nothing, really— our circumstances... I couldn't help but imagine her sleeping next to me or wondering about her outfit. That shirt I'd never seen her wear. The vibrant green was so demanding with her dark hair. It made her eyes deeper. If she hadn't been tipsy, I wanted to pop the buttons off it and watch it fall to the floor. I wanted to hold her so badly, but I was angry, and just defeated. Defeated by the situation with my dad, and defeated by the fact that I could never get her right. The one time I did was a day I knew I was slowly losing her to someone else.

Maybe I was too late. She said she hated me. How could I blame her?

It had been a very long day, and my stepmom was handling something with a specialist for my dad. I went to Lynn's for support, encouragement, a laugh or two... anything before I collapsed.

I didn't plan on divulging anything about my situation with my dad, but she knew me all too well. One familiar chuckle between the two of us, and my eyes teared up and laid the ground work to give me a way.

"Hey, hey. What's going on? Just talk to me Adrian." Lynn's concern went from taking great care, to fear, and demanding I tell her what was wrong.

I tried to take a deep breath, but I don't think I had a steady one left in me. I looked up at the ceiling and pressed my lips, waiting for words or breath to come. Lynn rubbed the back of my shoulder, and made an instant plan.

"Adrian. Liston to me. You are alright, and it's going to be alright. There is nothing out there that we can't figure out or work together to fix. I'm going to go get us some provisions. You're going to catch your breath, and we are going to figure it out. We always do."

She left me in her room with the door cracked and she went to grab us something to drink. I don't think she had ever seen me this upset. She'd certainly never seen me with tears in my eyes. I think she was giving me time to find my dignity. I put my head in my hands contemplating how to tell her. I wasn't sure what I would be capable of saying about my dad upon her return. Then I heard the doorbell ring. Lynn's mother, Ruth, answered it.

"I've got it, Lynn." I heard her mother call out to the kitchen as she approached the door. When the door opened, I heard crying from a voice I recognized that in a turn about fair play... I don't think I'd ever heard cry before that moment.

"Oh, come in here, baby. What's the matter? What's happened?" I couldn't see, but it sounded like Ruth was consoling July. "Come on in and tell us all about it. Lynn's just there in the kitchen."

"Oh, Mrs. Stokes!" July cried again. I couldn't stand listening to her cry, not knowing what was wrong. I wanted to bust out of the room and help her, but I knew I had already been privy to something I wasn't meant to hear.

"What's wrong, July, what's happened?" Lynn's voice moved from the kitchen toward July. "Did you come straight from work?"

"I'm so sorry. This is ridiculous. I just didn't know it would feel like this."

"What's happened?"

"It's so stupid, really. It was our last day at the pool for most of the college guys that have to head back and –"

"Court." Lynn filled in the blank.

"Mrs. Stokes, he's not even..."

"Go ahead, July, tell us what happened."

"Okay, he pulled me to the side and made this big production out of having feelings for me. I guess is what he was trying to say. He has a long term girlfriend, and he's leaving to go back to school, so it was absolutely a moot point. I don't understand why this feels this way." July began crying again.

"This Court, a lifeguard fella? Wait. Honey... are you saying that although there was nothing that would be done about it, a young man let you know how much you meant to him?" Lynn's mother's voice was sweet as she tried to unravel the dilemma. "Sweetheart, that's a wonderful thing. Maybe that's why you're upset because you'll miss him."

"It's not him. He's not the one I want. I must sound ridiculous. He doesn't give me—" July tried to laugh through her tears. "Butterflies, I guess. At least he doesn't give me the most."

If I wasn't fuming and about to come unglued with my anger at that Court Bastard, I would have almost found this conversation amusing, if not endearing. July pandering to Mrs. Stokes, trying to make her understand, and Mrs. Stokes attempting to calm her down the way only *she* could. She was a brilliant, wonderful mother that way. Lynn was a lot like her.

"So there's another one who does give you these butterflies? My, my, Lynn, have you girls kept me out of the loop! But how do you know, July? Have you kissed this Court fella?"

"No. And I know because the other one gives them to me just by walking into the same room."

"I see. Now I know what's going on here. You're not mourning the one who left with nothing you can do about the situation. You're mourning, the one who's still here that you can't do anything about."

"I don't understand. And why does it hurt so bad, when it was the wrong one who said it?" July was still crying. I had never known her to be this overwhelmed.

"That's just it. This is a broken heart, baby. That's what it feels like. You didn't realize you had one until someone else tried to claim it. That's what's going on here, I promise. It feels good when someone tells you how much they care for you. I think it hurts so bad all of the sudden because you are realizing you don't have that from the other one... the one you want. Surely, I get to know who this other young man is. Don't I?"

"Momma." Lynn tried to say it quietly to get her attention.

"Lynn, you girls used to tell me everything. July is clearly upset, maybe it would help if I knew just who this was that caused all those butterflies just from walking into a room..."

"*Momma!*" Lynn spoke loud enough this time that Mrs. Stokes and July looked up to find me in the hallway.

July's face was red and humble when she looked up from her mascara stained guard shirt and saw me standing there.

I was just as humiliated standing there as she was at the reveal of me.

Mrs. Stokes looked confused at first, and I could tell Lynn was so taken aback by July's confession she had never heard, that she'd almost forgotten I was back in her room until she saw me.

I looked right at July and tried to be as straightforward as possible.

"It is him. I waited, and I lost you. You're crying because he told you how he felt, something I never did." I turned away from them and walked out the front door.

"Adrian!" Lynn called after me. "These damned white people!"

"Lynn!" Her mother's reprimand was the last thing I heard past the door that had just shut behind me. The protective part of me was glad to hear Lynn making light of the situation or at least cracking a joke for July's sake, but I couldn't look back. Although I was on my way home to handle it differently, I feared I too now shared the same affliction as July... A broken heart.

"I'LL STAND BY YOU"

Pretenders

I hadn't really slept or eaten in a week.

Summer was coming to a close. Somehow, the summer that promised to be one of the greatest of our lives had fallen short of expectations and mirrored the worst parts of our junior year. I hadn't seen anybody or talked to them since I left Lynn's that day. I just went to my last scheduled shifts at the pool and came home.

I didn't care what was going on with Reagan or Lynn.

I no longer worried about Robyn and whether Spencer could make good on anything as planned. She was someone who had people who wanted to help her but didn't want to take it. I couldn't seem to help myself or people who wanted my help, much less her. I gave up.

I didn't care why Devin was suddenly at the guard party. It didn't matter if what Spencer had said or done to her to show off in front of Lynn would make it worse for me at some other point. I just. Didn't. Care.

I even saw my best childhood friend, Anna George, playing out back with her entire family that day. It was after their family reunion picnic that happened every summer, and I had a standing invitation. The year before, I was working and bummed that I missed it. This year, I saw all the cars parked outside Anna's house. I just peeked through the window at all the people playing out back, missing that time when things weren't so complicated. Then I closed the curtain and went back to my bedroom.

I didn't care anymore, and I hoped that meant a better focus on grades or whatever the hell this place wanted from me so I could run, not walk away from it.

I never had a cool bone in my body. If someone had asked me if I thought I tried too hard, or not hard enough… I don't think I would have known the difference.

As to the name I was done saying, the thought I was done thinking… It was as expected. I had not in fact heard a word from him since he walked out that day. Mom had been home for a good three week stretch with no travel interruptions, and I had adjusted to that change of scenery and pace. I got used to staying in my bedroom consecutively, and having breakfast for dinner, a favorite thing of mom's when it was just the two of us.

At one point I remember mom going through the caller ID on our kitchen phone, checking her missed calls from all the time she had been away. I was grabbing a Diet Dr. Pepper from the fridge when I heard her call out a few random last names she wasn't familiar with. For a split second between the beeps of her deleting miscellaneous numbers, I caught myself looking over my shoulder toward the phone.

It was as if a surge of energy or a charge ran through me. An once of hope at the reminder that I had been at my grandparents several nights in a row while mom was away. *Maybe he had called!* I laughed cynically at myself before I embarrassed myself further by asking my mom to hold off on deleting. I knew he hadn't called. He never had before, and at this point with what we had never becoming official... now officially over. Of course he hadn't called. I walked out of the kitchen that night without giving it a second thought.

It was a little after seven one evening, barely starting to get dark, when I laid down, fully clothed, on top of my made bed at my mom's house. She was in the living room catching up on all the shows she'd missed during her travels. We had gotten used to being home together and spending time with each other, so she hadn't thought much of me taking my personal space. I had been working so much, I think she just assumed I was worn out when I escaped to my bedroom leaving her to the living room tv remote.

I lay with my arms above my head in a relaxed state. It's funny how relaxed you can get when you don't care. I started wondering what this place really was. My grandparents' town they were proud of and thrived in no matter how hard it was or how many hits they took. I thought about how much better they were than me. As people.

I thought about the friends I'd left behind before we walked the halls of the high school and the ones who had left me. It was hard to determine if most of us were incredibly lucky, regardless of how Pure Pines measured success, or if... we'd done a long, awful dance and it was time to pay the fiddler.

I didn't know about life and how it was measured past the Piney Woods Curtain that shielded Pure Pines from the rest of the world. But I did know that nobody deserved anything. Not good or bad. That is the one truth I could rationalize for myself.

Robyn didn't deserve anything bad to happen to her at that party, and none of the in-crowd or elite groups that made up Pure Pines High School or Prairie High deserved automatic popularity and status above anyone else. Even if the world was set up that way, where one could "deserve" something... there would still be no guarantee. I liked the idea of moving on, knowing nothing was owed to, or deserved by anyone. It might have been the one thing I understood at seventeen that would take me past the tall pines that both sheltered and haunted me.

I watched as the last bit of sun went down outside my curtain. I bet myself that if I bothered to get up and look, what remained of the sunset would have been worth the effort to see. Instead, I closed my eyes to shut the world out and took a shallow, uncertain breath.

"JULY. Lynn's on the phone." My mother called out to me from our living room.

Mom must have answered right away, as I didn't hear it ring. If I had, it would have given me time to prepare an excuse not to come to the phone. I got up and walked into the living room, reaching across my mother for the phone I would use to tell Lynn I didn't feel well.

"July! Are you there?!" Lynn was hysterical. "July! You have to come. *Now*. You'll park in my drive and walk over when you can, but you have to. Please!!!" Lynn was sobbing. "Oh, July it's so bad. It's horrible. There are cop cars here, and they are taking Michael away. Oh, my God, July!"

Michael was Adrian's dad.

I was frozen. Lynn sounded like someone in front of a burning building. I couldn't move or speak, much less ask her what happened.

"Are you there?" Lynn tried to confirm through her crying.

"Yes." I finally managed something audible.

"July, he won't talk to me. He won't come out without his dad. We are watching from the window, and I can't take it any more. I know Adrian can't take it. His dad is... July they think it's Alzheimer's, a rare early-onset case. It's what's been wrong these last few months. It's what's been showing up as crazy erratic behavior, and by the looks of things tonight, it's almost like Michael got this bad before he could even understand or be told he had it." She burst into tears again. She must have heard me take a deep breath.

There was a pause.

"July! You HAVE to come. It has to be you. Adrian went and got him tonight. Michael was lost in town where his shop is. He's was disoriented and he didn't know anybody for a second. He swung at and fought people. Oh, July, just get here, please!"

A single hot tear ran down the side of my face uncontrollably. I wiped it immediately away.

My mother would not let me take her car if she knew I was upset. I hung up the phone and slipped on some shoes calmly and methodically. My heart was so heavy in my chest I could hear the palpitations echo through my ears as I paced my walk across the living room to retrieve the car keys. "Mom, I'm going to run to the store with Lynn."

"It's just after seven. It's closed."

"Yeah, she missed it already, so we have to head up to Prairie real quick." My mom heard her keys rustle when I pulled them off the in-table.

"Then why doesn't she just come pick you up on her way?"

"Come on, mom. Lynn drives me everywhere, all the time. Maybe it's my turn to drive. May I please take your car?"

"Go ahead. But you call me from her house when you get there and when you two get back from the store." I was out the door before I could respond.

And this is where it all flooded back on the inside. Every fear and emotion ever felt with him. My hand turned the ignition, and I pulled out steadily and focused on the road ahead. My stomach felt like a million leafless tree branches were scraping the inner walls of it.

Outside, I remained calm and stoic, but inside, I felt like someone threw me across the room. I didn't know how to help, and I didn't care if I was the last person he wanted to see— I was going to him. I don't think anything could have kept me from it.

The complete horror in Lynn's voice and the devastation for her best friend was enough alone for me to go, if not just for her. But when I thought about that day his stepmom couldn't find his dad, and then the party... *He was late because he was probably driving somewhere to find him.*

I swallowed a gulp to keep from crying. I forced myself to find enough strength to walk into a sandstorm where everyone was getting buried alive, and I was the worst-case scenario of anyone who could save them.

Why did he do this alone? It took me the rest of the drive to fully consider... if Adrian's dad was his person, what was left in that house in his absence? A stepmom and step-siblings. Adrian was alone without his father.

I couldn't imagine how lost he felt, not to mention terrified for his dad. I pulled into Lynn's driveway and quickly killed the lights. I didn't want to add to the spectacle.

My God. I had never seen such a situation at a house. It was like driving past a wreck on the interstate, only I was standing right in front of it. My heart sank to my feet, and I didn't know what I had to offer or how I would approach this. I felt smaller than I'd ever felt in life. I parked as far up Lynn's driveway as I could, and stepped out quietly, walking in through her garage.

Lynn, her mother, and one of her older sisters were at the kitchen window watching. They were all in tears. Lynn heard me walking toward them from the side door and rushed to me. Her face was swollen from crying. She threw her arms around me, and just cried on my shoulder for the longest.

When she released me, she pulled me over to the window with them to explain.

"Daddy's over there with Beverly and the boys. They are all home. They had to contain Michael in cuffs three times now, and if they can't get him settled down, they are going to have to bring him in. Not to book him, but so he won't harm himself until he understands, or gets his mind back. He doesn't know where he is right now. It just happened so fast.

"How could it happen? To someone so young?"

"Momma said it's rare, but it can happen in the forties or fifties, and that's what they call early-onset. It's much worse, they say, because the brain destroys neurons, and the memory deteriorates much faster when they are younger." It seemed to calm Lynn down a little to explain to me what her mom had explained to her. That was Ruth Stokes' ability to make you feel like everything was going to be alright... only she looked just as upset as we were in the moment. I knew that wasn't a good sign.

There was a bit of commotion outside, and the cop cars moved away to let the ambulance pull out and away from the driveway. It drove out without any sirens.

"He's not in there," Lynn confirmed. "Michael's not in the ambulance."

Ruth took a deep breath and tapped her hand over her chest. "That's good. That means they didn't need to take him in to admit him."

Lynn hugged her mother, grateful for her hopeful assessment. Then she turned to explain more to me.

"Adrian's been with his dad all night. He's the one who found him and brought him home. Oh, July, we watched him running after him outside to catch him so the cops wouldn't tackle him down a second time. Then it got settled, and he went back inside with him. If they'd had to take him in the ambulance, Adrian would have gone with him. He hasn't left his father's side. Beverly's so upset and hysterical, and I don't even know what the other boys are doing. Dad tried to get them to come over here."

"Wait, it looks like they're leaving now." Lynn's sister announced from the window. One by one, the remaining cop cars from a town or two over pulled out of the drive, leaving a dark, seemingly empty house.

We watched as Lynn's dad walked toward us from Adrian's house. He walked in and immediately hugged his own wife and daughters. He was visibly shaken by the traumatic ordeal.

"They finally got him somewhere comfortable where the paramedics could sedate him. He's going to be out the rest of the night if not half of tomorrow. Thank God for Beverly and those kids. His arms and wrists are all bruised up from being man handled. It was tough to watch, but everyone there was as gentle as they could have been." Lynn's father gave detailed information, and I was so glad he had been there to help. He looked exhausted himself.

"And Adrian?" Lynn asked her dad.

"Oh, honey, that boy's in bad shape. He's gone through hell these last few weeks. And tonight's probably aged him three years. You talk about having to be the man of the house. I don't think he's had a chance to come up for air yet. We can all be grateful to know he'll at least get some rest tonight with his father out. He'll sleep the rest of this episode off. I imagine they'll have to go in for more testing as soon as he's awake and aware. This one really hit him bad."

That part was the hardest to hear. It confirmed that Adrian had been going through these enough times for Lynn's parents to know these were episodes of dementia. Episodes, plural, where Michael couldn't remember who he was or where he was, or couldn't recognize the people around him. *How painful for Adrian.* Lynn's dad led his wife out of the kitchen, and they all seemed to disperse while Lynn and I remained glued to the window.

We saw Adrian's bedroom light come on as if it meant go time for me. Meanwhile, neither of us knew how I would get to him, or even if I could when I did. We looked at each other and stepped away from the window. I hugged Lynn, and she nodded at me to go on over.

I slipped out the kitchen door her father had just come home through. It was completely dark out now. Almost pitch black compared to the well lit spectacle the red and blue lights made, and it was oddly quiet. I don't think I heard a cricket or cicada one over my single footsteps as I walked through the side yard that joined Adrian's pool deck. I had no plan. I couldn't knock and disturb them, much less throw rocks at his window. I didn't know if he would see me out there, but something told me it was the place to wait.

I walked toward where we stood earlier that summer when he held me close and listened to my concerns over Lynn. That seemed so trivial and adolescent at this juncture. There was a small bench by the start of the deck, and I sat on it facing the back of the house, determined I would see him if he stepped outside for some air. That's all I had to bank on to keep from disturbing his family at all costs. I looked up at the night sky full of stars, then slowly brought my head back down to reality.

Just as I had hoped, the back porch light came on, and the patio door from the house opened in front of me.

The house was quiet. It felt almost empty. Strangely so after all the chaos that had ensued only minutes before. Those minutes felt like an eternity. They could only be described as unbearable. Everyone in the house had dispersed to bed once we got it all settled. It's like they disappeared. I needed some air. I took my shirt off and tossed it on my bed so I could breathe. I felt claustrophobic and unjustly liberated at the same time.

I walked through the house, securing every door and double-checking that all was locked up, just in case. I flipped the backyard light on and opened the patio door to step out for some air. I don't know if I held out hope for a breeze or the security of the empty night as opposed to the emptiness I felt inside that full house.

No sooner than stepping out and feeling the summer heat on my bare chest did the porch light reveal that the night was not empty. There she was. She stood up from the bench she had been waiting on. She was in the exact spot I had left her that day, the first time my stepmom had called me in to look for my dad.

She didn't move. She just let her eyes meet mine. It hurt to see her, but it was excruciating not to be next to her. I ran as fast as I could to her, and her arms were immediately around me. I don't think I can recall ever crying past being a kid or the day I started to in front of Lynn, but I was instantly sobbing onto July's shoulder. Physical tears of mine began soaking the collar of her blouse.

"He didn't even know how to get home! He didn't know where he was! He didn't even know *me*!!!" I sobbed so hard I was shaking, and I held her so close I was afraid I had squeezed her too tight at one point.

She didn't break. She didn't waver, and she never asked to come up for air from me. She just anchored herself, the palms of her small hands pressed firmly on the skin of my back, holding me in return. She let me sob uncontrollably like a child.

"July."

I whispered her name, turning my wet lips toward her ear and staining her cheek with my tears.

"July."

I repeated it as if it were mine to say over and over. A slight sound came from deep within her. An almost inaudible moan of relief or satisfaction. I pulled her body up to mine, cradling the side of her face into my neck as she rose to the tip of her toes to reach me. We stood there, breathing together, into each other for the longest moment.

Then I separated us. I wiped my face with my hand and looked back at her. I reached for her hand, and she gave it to me. I walked us to the drive and pulled my keys from my pocket. I opened the passenger side of my Mustang for her, and in what felt like record speed, we were down the driveway, flying through the streets. I switched gears to go faster, and she didn't seem to mind. She just rode beside me, letting me get it all out as we tore down the open road.

I had no way of knowing what was next with my dad. It was inconceivable to think about anything with me that didn't involve him. There was already talk of us having to move. My grandfather was coming down to lay down the law, not knowing the full extent of what was happening. I actually felt terrible for the ruthless man to that end. All I knew was that I couldn't think about any of that anymore tonight.

I just wanted to be out on the road with her.

I could smell her in my car the way I did the first time she rode with me, and it got to me just as it had before, and just as it did anytime I stood too close to her. She showed up for me tonight like she was mine. She couldn't have known how much that would mean to me. It was brave. This wasn't the first time she had impressed me with her bravery.

I looked down at the speedometer for the first time since we hit the road and allowed my car to do what it was made to do. I was going too fast. I slowed into the next deep curve on the two-lane highway we flew down, but I knew it may have been too fast for her. I looked over at July to see if she was okay. She looked spectacular just sitting in my passenger seat. She was so beautiful I didn't cut my eyes off her and back to the road as quick as I should have.

I felt her hand reach out and squeeze my bicep tightly. "ADRI-AN!" She screamed, looking toward the front of the car.

I turned and immediately hit the brakes. We stopped abruptly, my arm across her body, protecting her from the dash. Just as soon as we stopped, a deer walked out from the side of the road, almost slowly, as if time were suspended. Another one followed as the first one went through the bright beam of my headlights.

The first one turned and looked back at me, its eyes shimmering in the car lights the way it had the first time and in my dreams. There were two this time, watching us as we watched them pass. Just like the one I'd seen that time before, maybe it was even the same doe, these two didn't know to be afraid of us. It was majestic.

At that moment, I didn't care what was happening to me or us, and I didn't care if she wanted that damn lifeguard instead of me... I pulled her face to mine, and my lips were on hers. Her mouth opened for mine immediately, and she kissed me passionately back. I slid my car into park as I pushed my tongue through her lips to find hers. It was as if we were racing towards each other, and I wanted to consume her.

Her lips were soft even though she was kissing me back harder than she ever had before. She smelled and tasted delicious, and I wasn't going to be able to get over what that did to me. I craved it. Ignoring that I was parked in the middle of the road, we must have bypassed heavy breathing and gone straight to panting. I just know we hadn't stopped kissing, and after I leaned in, pulling her as close to me as the car would allow, I didn't want to. She ran her fingers through my hair while our lips stayed connected, and all I wanted was to feel the sensation of her touch all over.

Something ignited when we came together and were in each other's arms like this... undeniably, it was an experience like none I'd ever known. There was so much between us that hadn't been said. So much we had neglected, but I couldn't deny the immediacy I felt when she was right next to me, or how she responded to my touch. I had to believe we had made some sort of an investment in each other, both physically and emotionally. I knew I had.

Up until this situation with my dad, I had always known the biggest obstacle between July and me was not being able to handle how much I wanted her.

I did not realize that I would never be prepared for how much I *needed* her after that night. I had no right to ask anything of her. It would have been selfish to even suggest. I didn't know what the next day would look like in my life much less the next couple of months. Not to mention senior year, locking down college. All of that was still suppose to happen, or would it not with my dad? That's how much I didn't know, but I had to ask her. I had to know from her.

I pulled back from the embrace I held her in. I released her completely, and I watched her face drop away from mine. It was almost painful to look at her. She seemed in fight or flight mode herself, not knowing what I was going to say. I hated not touching her when we were this close, even for a few seconds.

"July-- I need to..." I hesitated when she turned to the passenger side window to look away from me. I can't imagine what she thought I was going to say, but I understood. My voice came out hoarse. I felt how strained my throat was from the longest day of my life as I swallowed and committed to the words. "Are you with me?"

She instantly turned back to me with eyes widened and a rush of color to her cheeks. I couldn't read her expression before she was pressed against me, burying her face into my neck. I felt her hot tears roll down my skin, and then I heard her say what I wasn't likely to forget.

"Do you have to ask?"

Epilogue

FALL, 2000

*An Excerpt from So F*cking Special: 1998*
*Book 2 of The So F*cking Special Series*

I sat in only my second course of the day, trying desperately to focus. It had been the longest week of my life with a new professor, an extended reading list, interning at non equity auditions I stupidly still attempted to make. This wasn't Jr. College anymore. I was about to fall asleep in my chair when I heard a sound coming from my purse I had never heard before. I pulled my Nokia out, thinking I may have set an alarm on my phone by accident. I fumbled to figure out what the alert was while a few eyes near me shot annoyed glances my way.

I had gotten the sound turned off when I noticed a written message across the screen.

SMS_TEXT MESSAGING 775 248-9002

Hey...

I had no idea what it was much less who it was from. I waited until class was released, and turned to a girl gathering her books next to me to ask if she knew what it was.

"Oh, yeah. So it looks like someone sent you a text message. I guess you don't have their number saved so it's showing up with their entire number across the top. That will go away once you find out who it is and save their number in your phone. You can put their name or whatever."

"Oh."

"Let me see it again. Yup, I don't have one like yours, but yours sucks. You're going to have to hit your number keys for letters multiple times to get to the letter you want in order to type a word."

"Is that bad?"

"No, it's just a bitch and takes longer to write a message, which is supper frustrating when your pissed and fighting with someone. It usually comes out as gibberish in that case." She handed me my phone back and I stared at the message wondering who it could be from as I thanked her.

"Don't worry, they say we're going to be able to send pictures soon, and let's hope they are worth a thousand words!" She smiled back at me as she walked briskly out into campus. I headed out of the classroom and slumped into a chair in the hallway to attempt my first text message to God knows who.

It took me forever to type each key multiple times to form each word. Then I looked at the finished product before hitting send, and felt like I was in a Sy fy thriller or horror movie.

SMS_TEXT MESSAGING

Who is this?

The sound was still turned off from when I silenced it in class, but I watched as a little email looking envelope for an icon popped across the screen with three dots indicating I press the home key to open it.

SMS_TEXT MESSAGING 775 248 9002

It's me.

At that moment, I had no one in my life that could be identified through that sentiment alone, yet I knew exactly who it was.

SMS_TEXT MESSAGING 775 248 9002

I got your number from Lynn. I hope that's okay.

SMS_TEXT MESSAGING

I guess there's not much I can do about it now.

I raced through the settings to determine how to save his name to the number.

ADRIAN:

How are you?

I rolled my eyes as I read the last one. Were we seriously making small talk via messaging from two thousand miles away? Two people who had never spoken on the phone or even emailed. We had email for the last three years, why didn't that strike his fancy? It was a hell of a lot easier than typing one key three times to get each letter of a word out. *What did he want?*

ADRIAN:

NYC, huh? You made it to the Big Apple.

ME:

That's what my address says.

ADRIAN:

SMART ASS.

There was a long pause, and I had no idea what to write or if I should. Maybe he was just sending a salutation on his new toy, like how you nod and tell someone "Happy Holidays." Maybe he was just letting me know that after all these years, he finally got my number. I looked down before I got antsy enough to put my phone back in my purse and head to my next class late. And then I saw the notification envelope again...

ADRIAN:

July...

And that was it. An hour and a half went by in my Art in non-Western Civ class, and nothing more. Again, maybe I was supposed to respond to that. Although I didn't know it at the time, I had bigger fish to fry than what to say back to Adrian via typing on the tiny screen of our own version of a portable chat room. Technology was wild.

I wasn't prepared for the fact that the little SMS_TEXT MES-SAGE-ING envelope popping up on my phone would not only make me late to class more than that day but open up a whole new level of Adrian occupying my thoughts on the regular. Something two thousand miles had failed to stifle.

This book could not have been made possible without the support, skills, and guidance of authors Kassy Paris and PJ Jones, the friends and staff of Air Sign Pictures, the faith of publishers RupertBossier, one mother, and a current significant other, multiple best friends, great loves, and a small East Texas town with a burger joint and a football field.

COMING SOON

FROM AUTHOR RAYE MURPHY...

COMPLETE SO F*CKING SPECIAL SERIES PICKED UP FOR PUBLICATION.

SO F*CKING SPECIAL: 1998

SO F*CKING SPECIAL: 2002

www.ingramcontent.com/pod-product-compliance
Lightning Source LLC
Chambersburg PA
CBHW061854310726
48972CB00004B/1024